BABY LOVE

BABY LOVE

JACQUELINE WILSON

Illustrated by *Rachael Dean*

PENGUIN BOOKS

PENGUIN BOOKS

UK | USA | Canada | Ireland | Australia
India | New Zealand | South Africa

Penguin Books is part of the Penguin Random House group of companies
whose addresses can be found at global.penguinrandomhouse.com.

www.penguin.co.uk
www.puffin.co.uk
www.ladybird.co.uk

Penguin
Random House
UK

First published 2022

001

Text copyright © Jacqueline Wilson, 2022
Illustrations copyright © Rachael Dean, 2022
'A Note on Adoption' text by Adoption UK
'A Note on Sexual Consent' text by School of Sexuality Education

The moral right of the author and illustrator has been asserted

Typeset in 12.5/20pt Baskerville MT Pro by Jouve (UK), Milton Keynes
Printed and bound in Great Britain by Clays Ltd, Elcograf S.p.A.

The authorized representative in the EEA is Penguin Random House Ireland,
Morrison Chambers, 32 Nassau Street, Dublin D02 YH68

A CIP catalogue record for this book is available from the British Library

Hardback ISBN: 978–0–241–56710–4
International paperback ISBN: 978–0–241–56711–1

All correspondence to:
Penguin Books, Penguin Random House Children's
One Embassy Gardens, 8 Viaduct Gardens, London SW11 7BW

For Kelly, with many thanks

This book is set in 1960 and contains sensitive content that reflects the attitudes of the time. It includes scenes of a sexual nature that are not suitable for younger readers. For more information please see the notes at the end of the book.

1960

I was in all the newspapers when I was fourteen. I wasn't named, but Mum and Dad could never forgive me. I've still got the clippings, though I can't bear to read them.

1960 seems so long ago, like another world altogether. People talk about the Swinging Sixties, all the mad fashion and great pop music, but it wasn't like that then, not for ordinary girls like me anyway.

The Beatles formed a band that year, but no one had heard of them yet. It was all Elvis and Cliff. I couldn't listen to either because we didn't have a record player. My parents were saving up for a radiogram, though a washing machine was first on their wish list. It was going to take them a very long time before they had enough to buy either. They didn't believe in hire purchase.

We did have a television. Mum never missed a panel game

called *What's My Line?* She was in awe of the panellists because they always wore evening dress and had posh accents. They were the Upper Crust. I suppose we were the Soggy Bottoms.

We couldn't afford a proper house so we lived in a prefab with a corrugated iron roof, but my mum kept it pin neat and my dad clipped our privet hedge every week, sometimes twice. *We* were considered posh down our road.

Then I ruined everything. I wasn't ordinary any more. I was notorious.

1959

I had an older sister and an older brother, but they both died shortly after they were born so I grew up as an only child. I didn't know about them while I was growing up. Mum and Dad never once mentioned them. I sometimes said I wished I had a little sister or brother to play with. They just shook their heads at me and said being an only child was much more special. I never dreamt I'd had two potential siblings.

I only found out last summer. Mum had just started her job at Wallis the dress shop, and Dad was busy driving day-trippers to Brighton and Eastbourne and Worthing, so I was left to amuse myself during the holidays.

I didn't mind in the slightest being home by myself. I read a great deal and wrote some very bad poetry. If I felt lonely I chatted to Miss Wong, a very glamorous Chinese girl in a painting hanging on our wall. Mum felt it was posh to have pictures on the wall and Dad said Miss Wong was a real good-looker.

One day I decided to have a good ferret through the Cubby Hole. As we lived in a prefab we didn't have an attic, but we had a very big walk-in cupboard where Mum stored old things.

There was a trunk full of her clothes, including her wedding dress. I tried it on though it wasn't very pretty and the white silk had yellowed. It wasn't proper silk, because you couldn't buy that during the war when she got married. Apparently my grandma had made it out of parachute silk.

I took the dress off, tried on an uninspiring purple evening dress instead, and wound a drooping fox tippet round my neck, but the bad-tempered little animal face unnerved me, and I thrust all the clothes back in the trunk.

There was a big box right at the back that had once held a dozen Christmas crackers. That surprised me, because we never bothered having crackers with our festive roast chicken as there were just the three of us. Perhaps my parents were more sociable in the past. I lifted the lid and then stared in surprise. There were knitted baby clothes: two sets of matinee jackets and bonnets and booties with tiny satin ribbons, one in pale pink, the other powder blue. They both looked brand new. There were more baby things too – a little china mug with rabbits, a tiny teddy bear, a bottle with a rubber teat, a tin of Johnson's baby powder, even a jar of zinc cream to prevent nappy rash. I opened it and saw the cream had never been used.

I thought they must be *my* baby things, but I couldn't work out why they'd been kept untouched in the cracker box. I put everything back carefully apart from the pale pink bootees. I still had my big baby doll Rosebud, though of course I didn't play with her now. She had a full set of her own clothes but her feet were bare. The pink bootees fitted her perfectly.

I forgot all about exploring the Cubby Hole until Monday, Mum's day off when she did her weekly spring clean. She took my doll and my Whimsie china ornaments off the windowsill to give them a good dusting and discovered Rosebud's new shoes.

'Where did you get these bootees, Laura?' she demanded, holding Rosebud upside down and brandishing her newly shod feet at me.

My heart started thudding. I knew I wasn't really allowed to go rooting through the Cubby Hole.

'Oh, I just found them,' I said vaguely.

'I know where too! You found them in the cracker box, didn't you!' Mum said. She was actually shaking.

I shook my head and pointlessly denied it.

'Yes you did! You found them in the *cracker box*!' Mum said, her voice rising.

There was a programme on children's television called *Crackerjack*. I thought it very silly, especially when the audience had to shout out 'Crackerjack!' when someone won a prize. Mum sounded as if she was taking part in the show so I couldn't help grinning, and Mum slapped my face.

It was the first time she'd hit me and I burst into tears of shock. Mum did too. She sat on the end of my bed, sobbing, clutching Rosebud to her chest.

'Mum? Mum, don't cry,' I said. 'I'm sorry. I didn't mean to upset you so.'

'I know,' said Mum, struggling to gain control of herself. She rubbed her eyes and blinked at my face. 'Oh dear, your cheek's gone all red. I didn't really hurt you, did I? But you shouldn't have gone poking in that cracker box. It's private.'

'Are they my baby things?' I asked.

'No. If you must know I knitted these little booties for your sister when she was newly born,' Mum said in a rush. 'But she'd come too soon. She passed before I could even bring her home from hospital, poor little soul,' Mum said, tears trickling down her face.

I wasn't entirely certain what Mum meant. The word *passed* confused me. I imagined maternity nurses passing this tiny stranger sister all around the ward as if they were playing pass the parcel.

'It took me a long time to get over the shock. But then I started expecting again, and I went full-term with your brother. He was a big bonnie baby, eight pounds four ounces, but there was something wrong with his insides. He had an operation but it didn't work. I never got a chance to dress him in his little blue outfit and take him home either. My boy!' Mum rocked backwards and forwards on the bed, weeping for him too.

I felt so sorry for her, but very embarrassed by her outburst.

'What was he called?' I asked, simply for something to say.

'William, after your dad,' said Mum. 'Though we planned to call him Billy to save confusion.' Her voice broke.

'Baby Billy,' I said, trying to imagine having a big brother. And a big sister too. We might have been a very different family then.

'What was my sister called?'

'Laura,' said Mum.

This was a shock. Laura was *my* name.

'Laura?' I repeated.

'Well, I've always liked the name,' Mum said defensively.

'Did you dress me in the pink booties and the little woollen coat and bonnet?' I asked.

'No!' Mum sounded shocked. 'They were knitted for *her.*'

'So what colour outfit did you make for me?'

'I didn't. I thought it would be bad luck. I didn't get anything prepared. I was stuck when it was time to take you home from the hospital. Your father wasn't demobbed yet, so I had to give a neighbour some money to go shopping for baby clothes. She bought you a white set of woollies from Woolworths,' said Mum.

'Woollies from Woolworths,' I said. It sounded comical – and strange. I loved Woolworths and had grown up spending my pocket money there, treating myself to two ounces of lemonade powder in a tiny paper bag and a little pink rubber doll the size of my thumb. But Mum always looked down on Woolworths, especially their clothes.

'I chose all your other baby clothes from Bentalls,' Mum said. 'You had some lovely little dresses, pink and white, and there was one pale yellow frock with a chicken embroidered on the front – you looked a treat in that.'

'I've seen the chicken dress,' I said. It was in the photograph album.

I went to the bureau in the living room and found it. It was near the front, after Mum and Dad's wedding photo, with my Aunt Susannah a very glamorous bridesmaid. I was sitting on Mum's lap, and looked rather like a chick myself, with my fair hair in a little quiff. Mum rather spoiled that photo though, because she was frowning, her lips tightly pressed together.

'Why do you look so miserable?' I asked.

'Oh, I daresay you'd been playing up,' said Mum.

'Was I a naughty baby then?' I asked, surprised. I always tried to be very good now – or did my best not to be found out if I did something bad.

Mum sighed. 'No, you were actually quite a dear little thing, but I was so anxious, you see. I thought I was jinxed and that I'd lose all my babies. I kept waiting for something bad to happen to you.'

I remembered my first day at school. Lots of the new Infants were crying, but I didn't. Mum was the one in tears, forever telling me to listen to the teacher and avoid all the rough children in the playground and steer clear of the Jungle Gym because I'd fall off and bang my head.

Mum was still looking at me.

'Nothing bad is going to happen now,' I said. 'I'm practically grown up.'

'Don't tempt fate!' said Mum.

She fussed anxiously every time I got a cold, and she took a whole week off work at Easter this year when I had flu. It was high fever can't-get-out-of-bed flu, so Mum phoned Dr Bertram, our family doctor. He listened to my chest and said I might have a touch of pneumonia. Mum panicked then and kept me in bed long after I was better. She didn't even let me go back to school when the new term started.

'We need to build you up a bit first,' she said. She gave me liver or mince or steamed plaice, all of which I hated. It was a relief when I went back to school, even though the school dinners were awful too – fatty stew and lumpy mashed potatoes and soggy cabbage. I'd missed a fortnight's lessons and had fallen behind, so our form teacher Miss Wiltshire suggested I take someone else's workbooks home for several days to copy from them.

'Ask Nina Bertram if you can borrow her books, dear,' she said.

Nina Bertram was very much a teacher's pet. She was generally very popular, though a few girls hated her, but that was probably because they were jealous. She wasn't exactly pretty. Her face was a bit too long, and her skin was sallow, but she had long glossy black hair past her shoulders and startling blue eyes. She looked as if she could see inside you and read your thoughts.

She spoke in a posh voice, but when there were no teachers around she could tell the filthiest stories. I was on her dinner table and couldn't believe some of the tales she told. All the other girls shrieked with laughter and got into trouble with the dinner ladies, while Nina sat there demurely, everyone's favourite. She had a mottled green Parker pen, and a real gold St Christopher necklace (it was the only jewellery we were allowed to wear at school, apart from a wristwatch). Nina's watch was Swiss and was rumoured to have cost a fortune.

Nina lived in one of the big houses on Riverside Drive. Her father was a doctor (the one who had listened to my chest) and her *mother* was a doctor too, though she worked in a skin clinic. They were both called Dr Bertram, which sounded funny.

All the teachers at our school expected Nina to go into medicine too because she was so good at all the sciences, but she said she thought that idea boring. Nina wanted to be an actress. We were both in the Drama club at school, and had parts in *Romeo and Juliet*. Ours was a girls' school, but boys from their grammar down the road were invited to take part. Max Russell, the boy playing Romeo, was a sixth former, tall and sporty and handsome. Practically every girl in our school had a crush on him. Inevitably, Nina was chosen to play Juliet.

She was so good that the local paper wrote a whole column about her because they were so impressed. Nina made you believe she really *was* Juliet. I watched her cry real tears at rehearsals but then moments later she'd be larking around with Max Russell and the other boys.

I didn't have a proper part. I was just Female Courtier. I learned the whole of Juliet's lines. I wasn't the understudy, I just wanted to play Juliet in private. I acted it out scene by scene in the bathroom, watching myself in the mirror. I tried so hard but I knew I wasn't a patch on Nina.

I couldn't help being in awe of her. We were in the same class, we went to the same Drama club, we ate at the same table every day – and yet we'd barely spoken all that time. It took me all day to pluck up courage to talk to her. I waited till the bell rang for the end of lessons, and then sidled up to her as she was packing her bag. It was a regulation school satchel, but inevitably superior – made of conker-brown shiny leather and lined with tartan.

'Nina?' I said tentatively.

She looked up, tossing her hair out of her face. She raised one arched eyebrow.

'Sorry to bother you, but Miss Wiltshire wants me to borrow your workbooks so I can catch up on all the lessons I missed,' I said.

'Oh, what a bore,' she said.

I didn't know if she meant it was a bore for her or a bore for me. I just stood there, feeling a fool.

'OK, OK,' she said, thrusting her science and biology workbooks at me. 'Here, have these for a start. Can you read my handwriting?'

It was a silly question. She used black ink, not blue like the rest of us, and her Parker pen helped her write in a clear round script, without a single blotch or crossing-out.

'No, it's so messy. Can't read a word,' I said.

She blinked at me in surprise, taking me seriously for a second. Then she laughed, looking at me with more interest. 'Well, you'd better put your new specs on,' she said.

I'd started to get headaches last year. Mum panicked and took me to the doctor – Nina's father again – and he said it was probably just my age, but I should have my eyes tested by an optician all the same. Mum made another appointment and the optician said I was a little short-sighted and prescribed glasses. She didn't want me to wear the pink National Health sort – she paid for proper grown-up spectacles with upswept frames. I absolutely hated them. I'd worn them at school for several days but saw some of the girls nudging each other and sniggering. I only wore them at home now when Mum was around. I didn't think Nina had even noticed I *had* glasses.

'No, I'll manage without,' I said.

'They don't look too bad,' Nina said surprisingly. 'Actually, *I'm* supposed to wear glasses too, and mine look awful. Catch me wearing them at school!'

I was amazed. I wondered if any of Nina's friends knew she had glasses. She was treating me as if *I* was a friend.

I borrowed her workbooks for a week, copying and making notes. I got a bit lost looking at her maths because she hadn't put all her working-out down on the page. I suppose I should have asked Mrs Henshaw, the maths teacher, to explain, but I asked Nina instead.

'Oh yeah, this new stuff is such a bore. I got my brother Daniel to explain it and I sort of understood, but it was quicker just to get him to give me the answers. Look, tell you what, come round to mine for tea tonight and we'll work them out together,' she said casually.

'Yeah, fine,' I said, matching her tone – but my heart was thumping. Would I be back in time for Mum coming home from Wallis Modes? She'd go bananas if I wasn't there and think I'd been run over or kidnapped. But it couldn't be helped. *Nina Bertram was asking me to tea!*

It was a wonderful tea. I thought it might be a *cup* of tea with a Penguin biscuit, but it was a fantastic spread: thick pink ham cut off the bone with a salad of cos lettuce hearts and runner beans and grated carrot, and new potatoes in salad cream, and chunks of beetroot and tomatoes cut into flowers. We never had that kind of ham at home; we had Spam, with limp lettuce and a tomato each. We filled up with thinly sliced bread and butter, and a slice of Mum's sponge. She prided herself on the lightness of her home-made sponges, but she skimped on the jam filling, so it wasn't very interesting. At the Bertram house we had bread on a board and put as much butter as we wanted on our slice, plus raspberry jam, and then had a choice of chocolate cake or trifle. Nina's brothers had both. I rather wanted both too, but Nina just toyed with a small portion of cake, licking the cream between the rich dark layers like a little cat, so I said no thank you when Dr Bertram (female) offered me trifle.

Mum always said she didn't have time to fix elaborate teas

now she was working, but Nina's mother worked till four at the skin clinic and then rustled up the tea effortlessly, looking utterly relaxed. She had long black hair and a long pale face just like Nina's, and those beautiful blue eyes. She wore very dark red lipstick which made her look stunning, but it left red marks on her teacup and the end of her Du Maurier cigarette. She smoked a lot while we ate, but Dr Bertram (male) tucked in heartily.

'I like a good high tea before my evening surgery. It gives me a second wind,' he explained to me.

I was surprised at the general chit-chat at the table. Mum talked to me at teatime, but it was generally an inquisition about school. Dad was usually out till half seven or so after driving all the day-trippers back to the coach depot, so he didn't have tea with us. He rarely contributed to the conversation even on his days off. He said he liked a bit of peace after he'd been required to act the fool and lead the singing of *Ten Green Bottles* on the journey back from the coast.

The two Dr Bertrams nattered away to themselves, to the two boys, Daniel and Richard, to Nina and to me. I loved listening to everyone talking, surprised that Nina and Daniel and Richard could chime in, even contradict their parents, but never get told off for cheek. I seemed to be expected to have an opinion on all kinds of things too, which was unnerving.

Mrs Dr Bertram asked me about our teachers and the way

our lessons were taught. Mr Dr Bertram asked about my health and was I glad to be back at school? I said I was much better now, thank you, and agreed that it was good to be back in the old routine. My conversation with the adult Bertrams was limp and lacklustre, but it was fun nattering to Nina's little brother Richard about my favourite animals. He asked me what I'd choose if I were allowed a pet. I suggested a small crocodile to keep in my dad's lily pond, which made him snort with laughter. Daniel called his brother Little Richard, after some pop star – and then asked me about my own taste in music.

I was lost here. I didn't know much about pop music. The girls at school liked Cliff Richard but I sensed Daniel might not be impressed. I remembered hearing someone at Drama club saying Cliff was just a copycat Elvis.

'Elvis?' I suggested tentatively.

'Yeah!' said Daniel, and he ruffled his hair into a quiff and adopted a sexy leer.

'Jesus, Dan, you look ridiculous!' said Nina – but I thought he looked cool.

He was seventeen, nearly eighteen. I'd never even spoken to any boy that age before, let alone a striking one like Daniel. I was so flattered that he approved of my taste that I felt myself blushing. I bent my head, feeling a perfect fool.

I worried that I wouldn't understand when he showed me how to do the new maths problems after tea, but luckily I caught on quickly. He was good at teaching, calm and patient, going over things again to make sure Nina and I really understood.

'Yeah, yeah,' said Nina, who hadn't been listening properly. 'Come on then, Laura, let's go up to my bedroom. I'll show you my records.'

I saw the time on her Swiss watch.

'Oh God, I think I'd better go home. My mum will be worried,' I muttered.

'Well, phone her then,' said Nina.

'Yes, do,' said Daniel. 'Then I'll play you some Elvis.'

I kept protesting but they took me out into the hall, Nina pulling me by one arm, Daniel the other. It was such a heady feeling that I got the courage to dial home on the smart cream telephone on the hall table.

'Nina! Oh my Lord, where *are* you, what's *happened*? I've been frantic!' Mum said hysterically on the other end of the line.

I pressed the receiver right against my ear, hoping Nina and Daniel couldn't hear. I waved the back of my hand and they retreated to the stairs.

'It's OK, Mum,' I said. 'I'm at Nina's. Nina Bertram in my class.'

'The doctor's daughter? Oh, Laura, did you feel faint? Did someone from school drive you round to Dr Bertram's? I *knew* you were going back too early!' Mum gabbled.

'Mum! Nina asked me round to tea,' I said. I rolled my eyes at Nina and Daniel and they smiled sympathetically.

'Parents!' Nina mouthed, although she had no idea what it was like to have a mum like mine.

'She asked you round to *tea*?' said Mum, as if she'd suggested I go to the moon with her.

'Yes. And now her brother's helping me catch up with my maths,' I said.

Daniel mimed patting himself on the back.

'You don't need any help! You're practically top of the class,' said Mum indignantly, but she sounded proud all the same. 'So, shall I come round to collect you now?'

'No!' I said quickly. 'No, don't be daft, Mum. Nina's house is only ten minutes away.'

It really was, but it was in a totally different world of big houses with rolling lawns and two shiny cars parked outside.

'Or Dad could fetch you when he comes home?' Mum suggested.

'*No*, Mum, I'll be fine,' I said, shaking my head and sighing for the benefit of my audience.

'Well, make sure you don't outstay your welcome. And thank

Dr Bertram for having you. And be careful going home, do you promise?' Mum pleaded.

'Yes, yes, bye,' I said, and put the phone down quickly while she was still talking.

'Sorry about that,' I said to Nina and Daniel. 'My mum's a bit . . .' I pretended to screw my finger into my temple.

I felt guilty pretending that my mum was screwy, but she *was*. I couldn't imagine Mrs Dr Bertram getting in such a terrible fuss. But then Nina going to tea with someone was clearly not a big deal. She had loads of friends. I hadn't been asked to tea with anyone since primary school, and that was with a soppy little girl called Mary-Jane who just wanted to play Mothers and Fathers.

I felt I was playing a much more grown-up game with Nina and Daniel as we listened to records on her Dansette player. I sat in the only chair, Nina lounged on her slippery pink silk eiderdown, and Daniel sprawled on the floor, tapping his foot and singing along to the words. Little Richard came up too, clamouring to come in and be one of the big ones.

Nina sighed, but let him join us. 'Though we're not playing your records, chum,' she warned.

'Not even "How much is that Doggy in the Window?"' said Richard. He put his hands up like paws, pretending to beg. 'Woof, woof!' he said, trying to look cute.

He did look very sweet actually, his black hair cut in a bob like Christopher Robin, and his school shirt hanging loose like a smock.

I wished with all my heart that my own sister and brother hadn't died. But now I had this new ready-made family. I'd somehow become Nina's friend.

I found out the next day that Nina had fallen out with Patsy, her former best friend. They had had a terrible row about Max Russell, who had played Romeo. Patsy had met up with him at some party over Easter and said he'd kissed her when she went home. To me it sounded like an ordinary goodbye kiss, not the real passionate sort. It wasn't as if Max was now Patsy's boyfriend. He hadn't ever been Nina's boyfriend in real life, just onstage – but when Patsy blurted it all out, showing off, Nina felt she'd been betrayed. Patsy was Nina's worst enemy now.

It all seemed like a fuss about nothing, but I knew better than to say that to Nina.

'Oh, Nina, that's awful!' I said, acting the soul of sympathy.

I despised myself for not being honest, but I couldn't help it. I wanted her to stay *my* friend now. I wanted to be friends with her whole family, especially Daniel.

My own family were very impressed that I'd become friends with Dr Bertram's daughter. Mum hadn't even been cross with me when I came home that first time I'd been invited to tea. She wanted to know all about the Bertrams and their house and their furniture. She asked if they had a radiogram and a refrigerator and a washing machine. She even wanted to be told every item I'd eaten at tea.

'Good Lord, what must it all have cost!' she said. 'I think they must have been putting on an elaborate spread just because they had you there as a visitor!'

'No, I think they always have a tea like that. And Nina's parents have supper together later on when he's finished his evening surgery. With wine,' I said. I'd seen Mrs Dr Bertram preparing it and sipping a glass of red wine when I went home at last.

'Wine!' said Mum. She was teetotal herself, apart from a thimbleful of Harvey's Bristol Cream sherry at Christmas.

Dad had a bottle of beer occasionally when he came home from a particularly long and tiring trip, but Mum always wrinkled her nose and said it smelled disgusting. I thought it did too, but I felt sorry for Dad having to drive for such long hours while entertaining people. Still, he came home with a plateful of tips every day, mostly silver. Once some old lady gave him a five-pound note, which was almost as much as his weekly wage from the coach company. When I was little I'd seen all this cash and thought my dad was very wealthy – but now I realized we were poor.

'Poor but honest,' Mum said fiercely.

We weren't actually always honest either. Mum wore a white cardigan on sunny days that had been left behind on a coach trip, and she read copies of *Woman's Own* that had been kicked under a seat. Dad gave me forgotten fruit gums or Spangles, and now I was older and such a keen reader he handed over any paperback going begging. We never went short of umbrellas either.

I wondered if Dr Bertram collected up leftover umbrellas from his surgery. I couldn't imagine it.

I worried that my friendship with Nina would fizzle out when I'd finished copying all her work, but she seemed to take it for granted that we carried on going home together, and more often than not I had tea at the Bertrams.

'They seem to have taken a real fancy to you, Laura,' said Mum. 'But it's a bit worrying. I don't want Mrs Bertram to think you're cadging their food all the time.'

'She's *Doctor* Bertram, and she doesn't seem to mind a bit,' I said – but I was starting to worry too.

Nina started hinting that she wanted to come to tea with me for a change. I made excuses for a while, saying that Mum had to stay late at the dress shop doing alterations, so wouldn't be there.

'So?' said Nina. 'Even better. We could have your house to ourselves and play records and dance and have some fun.'

'I don't have a record player,' I muttered apologetically.

'Then we'll sing,' said Nina.

'But what about tea if Mum's not there?' I asked.

'We'll make our own with any old thing from the fridge,' said Nina.

We didn't have a fridge. We kept our food in the kitchen cupboard, and there wasn't very much of it. The only thing I ever made for myself was a jam sandwich. Mum didn't like me using the cooker in case I burned myself or left the gas on and fell down unconscious.

I tried to think up some plausible excuse. We were studying *Jane Eyre* at school and I wondered if I could invent a mad/ dangerous relative who lived in the attic, only we didn't have one, and they would have to be very small and wizened to fit in the Cubby Hole. Then I realized Nina was nudging me sideways, stopping me turning down her avenue.

'What are you doing?'

'We're going to yours,' she said.

'*Now?*'

'But I haven't asked Mum yet,' I said, my heart thumping.

'Do you have to?' Nina asked curiously. 'Anyway, if she's out working she won't know, will she? Come on. I'm dying to see where you live.'

Oh God, oh God, oh God. This was it. She must have guessed I didn't live in a big posh house like hers – but she didn't know it was a lowly prefab. I'd heard her being scathing about Patsy, mocking her for living in a house with fake pillars and a box tree fashioned into the shape of a peacock. What on earth would she say about our prefab with its corrugated iron roof and our privet hedge and our lily pond? I was in such a panic my eyes filled with tears behind my hateful fancy glasses. I prayed Nina wouldn't notice.

'What's up?' she said at once.

'Oh, I've just got something in my eye,' I said, blinking. 'And – and I've got a bit of a headache actually. Do you mind if you don't come back to mine today? I think I just need to go and have a lie-down.'

'No you don't,' said Nina. 'You need me to help the headache go away. I know exactly how. Dad showed me.'

'You can't make headaches go away,' I said.

'Yes I can. Or if I can't, I've got two aspirins in my satchel because it's my period,' said Nina. 'Bloody bore. Ha!'

'Ssh!' I said, going red, because there were some boys from Brackford going home on the other side of the road. Brackford was a Secondary Modern and some of the boys were very rough. 'If they hear you going on about that sort of thing they'll laugh and yell and call you names,' I warned her.

I was embarrassed too. Mum and I never once had a proper discussion about periods or how babies were born. We weren't that sort of family. She'd just put a bulky packet of sanitary towels and an ugly webbing belt in my underwear drawer last year and muttered that I might be needing them soon. I was used to it now, but would *never* talk about my time of the month in public!

'Then I'll laugh and yell and call them much worse names,' said Nina cheerfully. 'Which is your house then? Are we nearly there?'

'Down this street, along the little shopping parade and round the corner,' I said.

'Lucky you, living near some shops,' said Nina.

You wait, I thought. But I had a flash of inspiration when we went past the parade. Mum always gave me a shilling to keep in my shoulder purse for emergencies. This definitely counted as one of them. I paused at the little bakery on the corner.

'What's your favourite cake, Nina?' I asked, as we peered through the window.

'Mm, I don't know,' said Nina, licking her lips. 'They all look pretty yummy. I love shop-bought cakes and yet we hardly ever have them. Oh, look at those cream doughnuts! They look fantastic!'

'They're *my* favourites!' I said. 'Hang on!'

I hurried into the shop and asked Mrs Bun for two cream doughnuts.

'Two! You greedy girl, Laura!' said Mrs Bun, laughing as she slid them into a paper bag.

'They're not both for me. One's for my friend,' I said, nodding proudly at Nina in the doorway. 'They're a treat for our tea.'

'Oh, you're having a friend for tea, are you, dear? That's nice. Here!' She slipped two mini sausage rolls into another bag. 'Have these on me.'

'Did she really give you them for nothing?' said Nina, when I came out the bakery.

'Oh, I've known Mrs Bun since I was little. She's lovely,' I said.

'*Mrs Bun!*' Nina screamed. 'Like in the Happy Family cards? She's really called Mrs Bun the Baker's Wife?'

'Well, she's actually called Mrs Bunkle, but everyone calls her Mrs Bun,' I said.

'And you get to have lovely things like cream doughnuts every day?' said Nina, sounding genuinely impressed.

'Not every day,' I said. Hardly ever, in fact. Mum made her dull sponge and fairy cakes with a dab of icing most of the time, and we only had bakery cakes for treats. When Dad got promoted to being the Happy Days chief coach driver we had doughnuts and cream horns and jam tarts in every colour, and toasted him with a bottle of Tizer.

That really was a Happy Day. Dad was given a proper uniform and a pay rise – there was even mention of transferring Dad to the chauffeuring branch of the company in the future. That meant a smart suit and tie at all times, and driving the rich: company directors, cinema stars, sporting heroes. And we'd be rich too, what with those wages and five-pound tips an everyday occurrence. We wouldn't just have our own radiogram and refrigerator and washing machine. We'd have a whole new house, a three-bedroomed semi on a nice tree-lined road, maybe even somewhere detached.

Mum had such high hopes. But Dad stayed a coach driver and we stayed put in the prefab and it didn't look as if we'd ever move out of Paradise Road. I don't know who gets to name streets, but they must have had a sense of humour naming ours.

'*This* road?' said Nina, when I reluctantly steered us round the corner. 'Oh my God, you live in Shanty Town!'

I felt myself blushing to the roots of my hair.

Nina couldn't help seeing my distress. 'I'm so sorry, that was so tactless! Please don't get upset, Laura. I didn't mean it in a horrid way. But isn't that what everyone calls it?' she said.

'I suppose,' I muttered. 'But it's not like it's the official name. Like some people might call Riverside Drive Posh-nob Palace.'

'*Do* they?' Nina asked.

'Well, *I* do,' I said. 'Because your house *is* like a palace compared to ours. It's this one. Number five. Lily Cottage.'

Nina stared over our trim hedge at the lily pond, with a plaster gnome sitting fishing in the water.

'Don't you dare laugh,' I said fiercely.

'I'm not laughing!' Nina protested, though her eyes were very bright. 'I love your house! It's so sweet, like a little doll's house. And you really do have a lily pond!'

'With a gnome instead of a pet crocodile,' I said, fumbling in my shoulder purse for the door key.

I let her inside and she walked round wonderingly.

'It's all so neat!' she declared. 'It doesn't look as if anyone lives here! There's not even a dent in the cushions.'

'Mum thumps them into place every morning. She sighs whenever Dad or I sit in a chair,' I said. 'And she has a fit of the vapours if we use the settee because the cushions don't fit properly and it takes her ages to pummel them into place.' This was all true enough, but I was making Mum into a caricature. It was easier that way.

I went on burbling about the chair backs and the lace doilies and the green chenille cloth draping the table, pretending Mum measured them into place with a tape measure. I said each ornament had an exact position on the shelf. I held my breath when Nina picked up the Royal Doulton crinoline lady, because she was Mum's favourite and had cost a fortune. Nina put her back carefully enough, but facing the wrong way. I twisted her round quickly when she wasn't looking.

She was peering up at our Miss Wong painting. It was hard to read her expression.

'She's Chinese,' I said.

'Yes. I've seen those paintings before,' said Nina. 'Where's your bedroom then, Laura? Or do you sleep in a cupboard?'

There was a little beat. I saw she'd realized it was all right for me to joke, but I minded if *she* mocked everything too.

'Sorry! So, you do have a bedroom, don't you?' she said, a little flustered.

I had a mind to open the door to the Cubby Hole, just to disconcert her, but I could see it wouldn't really be funny. I opened the door to my bedroom instead.

'Oh, it's lovely,' she said.

I wasn't sure if she meant it or not. It was still a very little-girly bedroom, pink and frilly, with little satin ribbons tying up the curtains. Nina wandered over to my bedside table and picked up the latest paperback left on the coach. I'd only just started it last night, and it seemed a bit boring so far.

'Oh my God, it's *Peyton Place*! Are you allowed to read it?' Nina shrieked.

'Of course,' I said. 'My parents have been letting me read adult novels for ages. I mean, we're a bit old for Enid Blyton, aren't we?'

Nina rolled her eyes and started flicking through the book. 'OK, sarky – but this is a *really* adult book. I've heard all about it. Here!' She started reading aloud, giggling.

I listened, astonished.

'Are they . . . doing it?' I asked.

'Yep! I thought you said you'd read it?'

'Well, I haven't got that far,' I said. I went over to her and read a further passage.

'She's wearing a *halter*?' I said, puzzled. 'Isn't that a thing you put on a *horse*?' I had such a weird image in my head. I wrinkled my nose and shuddered.

'It's not that sort of halter, silly! It's a top that ties at the back of your neck. It shows off your midriff. I think I might get one for the summer, actually,' said Nina, smoothing down her baggy school shirt to show off her small waist.

'Me too,' I said, though my figure was small everywhere and I knew Mum would never allow it anyway. My summer tops had been Aertex shirts up till now.

Nina was busy flipping forward. 'Oh my God, listen to *this* bit!'

I didn't really want to listen. It all sounded pretty horrible. And I was a bit scared that Mum or Dad might suddenly come

31

bursting in and hear her, though I knew neither was expected home for ages yet.

'Look, you can borrow the book if you want,' I said. 'Let's have our tea now.'

'OK. Where did you get *Peyton Place*? You didn't just go into W.H. Smith's and *buy* it with your pocket money, did you?' Nina asked.

'No, of course not. My dad gave it to me,' I said, without properly thinking.

'Your *dad* bought it for you?' said Nina, amazed.

'No, he didn't buy it. He – he got it from work,' I said. 'Don't look like that – he didn't realize it was so filthy, else he'd never have given it to me in a million years.'

'What sort of work does your dad do?' Nina asked.

I was really stuck now. I knew Dad should really hand in forgotten items to Lost Property at Happy Days. Well, he always kept anything for a week or so, in case anyone phoned up and enquired. *Then* he took things home. It wasn't stealing if no one wanted them any more.

'He works for this company – he's quite high up now,' I said vaguely. 'Come on, I want my cream doughnut!'

I pulled her into the kitchen. She stuffed the book in her satchel while I put the kettle on for a cup of tea and laid a doughnut and a sausage roll on our best plates, from Mum's wedding present

32

set. I used two cups and saucers from it too, though we generally had our drinks in stripy mugs.

I put the tablecloth over the green chenille, just in case we spilled anything. I tried to do it all properly, even remembering to put the milk in a little jug. The tea was pale yellow when I poured it. Perhaps I should have let it draw more. Nina seemed more concerned with the milk.

'It's got little bits in it!' she said.

'It's just where the cream's got separated,' I said. 'It's still OK.'

Nina sniffed it suspiciously. 'I don't think so! Don't you keep your milk in your fridge?'

'We haven't got one,' I said.

Nina put her cup down, her tea untouched.

I thought quickly. 'Tell you what – we could have Lucozade instead,' I suggested.

Mum always kept a bottle at the back of the cupboard because I was prone to bilious attacks, and it was the only thing I could keep down.

'OK, let's have Lucozade then,' said Nina, though she looked surprised.

I suppose it was a very odd tea – sausage roll, cream doughnut, and Lucozade. I was tempting another bilious attack later on. Nina seemed happy enough though, almost effusive, to make up for her fussiness over the milk.

Then we did our homework together, with children's television on in the background. We snorted at it in a superior fashion. I worried when it suddenly started to rain, because it always made such a row on our roof. Nina peered upwards, astonished.

'Sorry about the noise,' I said quickly. 'You get used to it.'

'Crumbs, what's it like when it starts hailing?' said Nina, but she seemed to find it fun. I relaxed then and was almost enjoying myself, but I badly wanted Nina to go before Mum got home.

I didn't know what to do. I couldn't just *ask* her to go because it sounded so rude. Besides, I often stayed really late at Nina's house because I was having such a good time. The six o'clock news started on the television. Wallis Modes shut at five thirty, but sometimes it was twenty to six before they'd got rid of the last customer. Then there was the cashing-up and a quick check along the dress racks, with the shop shut and locked by quarter to. It generally took Mum half an hour to walk home from the town. She'd be in at quarter past six, maybe twenty past if she was tired.

I was just steeling myself to suggest to Nina that she'd better get going when I heard the key in the front door.

'Cooee! Are you all right, dear?' Mum called, as she struggled through the hallway with the food shopping she'd done in her lunch hour. 'I'm nice and early, aren't I? Mrs Bloom gave me a lift in her car when it started tipping down with rain.'

She came into the living room, a plastic rain hat slipping sideways on her head. She saw Nina and looked comically startled, her mouth gaping.

'Mum, this is my friend Nina,' I blurted out. 'Nina, this is my mum.'

'How do you do, Mrs Peterson,' said Nina, totally composed.

Mum swallowed. 'Hello, dear,' she said, taking her rain hat off hurriedly and fluffing her hair. 'I'm Nina's mother,' she added unnecessarily. 'So, are you Dr Bertram's daughter?'

'Yes, I am. The daughter of both Dr Bertrams,' said Nina, smiling.

'Yes, I hear you've all been lovely to my Laura,' said Mum. 'We're very grateful.' She was acting as if the Bertrams were the royal family and I was their newest maidservant. I went hot all over.

'Mum!' I said sharply.

'Don't use that tone to me, Laura!' Mum hissed. 'Right, Nina dear, I'll just get my coat off and then I'll get started on some tea for us.'

'We've had tea already,' I said.

'But I had nothing in!' said Mum.

'Don't worry, Mrs Peterson. We had a lovely treat tea – sausage rolls and cream doughnuts washed down with Lucozade,' said Nina.

I narrowed my eyes. I wasn't quite sure whether she was taking the mick. Perhaps she hadn't really enjoyed it? Would she go home and tell all her family about our bizarre meal? What would her mum think?

My mum clearly thought this dreadful. 'Oh, for goodness' sake, Laura, how could you offer Nina such a ridiculous meal? I'll rustle up something nutritious in two shakes of a lamb's tail, just you wait and see,' she said, whipping off her coat.

'It's very kind of you, but I'm truly full now. And I'd better be getting home anyway,' said Nina, rising to her feet.

'You have told your mother you're here, haven't you?' asked Mum. 'I'd hate for her to be worrying. You can use our telephone if you like.'

'No thanks – Mum never fusses,' said Nina, putting on her school blazer. The sleeves were rolled up and she had a ban-the-bomb badge pinned to the lapel. She managed to make even our dreadful school uniform look cool and stylish. She swung her satchel nonchalantly on her shoulder. 'Goodbye then, Mrs Peterson. Thank you for having me. Bye, Laura.'

She sauntered off in her non-regulation Dolcis pumps.

'Oh, Laura!' Mum said the second the front door closed. 'How could you ask Dr Bertram's daughter round here without a by-your-leave?'

'She's my *friend*. And I go round to her house heaps and heaps of times. I don't know why you're making such a fuss,' I said, though of course I did.

'You gave her shop-bought cakes and sausage rolls – and *Lucozade*!' Mum shrieked at me. 'Why in God's name didn't you at least give her a decent cup of tea?'

'I did, but she didn't like the milk. She thought it was going off – and it *is*,' I said.

'Oh!' Mum burst into tears and had to sit down at the table.

She was still weepy when Dad came home half an hour later. He couldn't really understand what all the fuss was about.

'Don't be so daft, woman!' he said. 'Come on, what about *my* tea? *I* haven't had no cakes and sausage rolls!'

He was trying to jolly her along, but she wouldn't be consoled, though she made him egg and chips. She offered me some too, but I told her I felt sick now.

'So now's the time to drink the ruddy Lucozade!' said Mum. 'Oh, dear Lord, what will that girl think of us? She'll tell her parents that's what we have for tea and they'll all look down on us. The sad folk from Shanty Town!'

'Stop that!' said Dad, hurt. 'I can't help it that this is all we can afford. I'm trying my best, Kathleen. I'm working my socks off as it is.'

'I know, I know. I'm sorry, William, I'm just so het up,' Mum said miserably. She glared at me. 'See what you've started?' she said.

I marched off to my bedroom, slamming my door. We didn't

say goodnight to each other. But in the morning Mum came to wake me with a cup of tea and then sat on the end of my bed.

'I've got a letter for you to give to Nina,' she said, thrusting a Basildon Bond envelope at me.

'What?' I sat up groggily. 'You've written to her? Oh God, you haven't apologized, have you?'

'No, of course not. Watch out, don't spill that tea,' Mum said.

'So what have you written?' I asked. The envelope was sealed.

'It's an invitation to tea next Monday,' said Mum. 'And I'll make a special effort. I was thinking, we might even have a small chicken on Sunday, and then we can give her a chicken salad for her tea. Now, no one could fault that, could they? Monday's my day off, so I'll have time to make one of my sponges – and fairy cakes too, I dare say. And we won't have any nonsense about the milk either, as I'll buy a fresh pint down the parade that morning.'

'Oh, Mum!' I didn't know whether to laugh or cry again. 'You don't have to do that.'

'I want to!' said Mum. 'I don't want to let you down. Now you give her that note, Laura. Don't go all dreamy on me and forget. Promise?'

'I promise,' I said.

When I got up I saw there were several half-written invitations in the wastepaper basket, and the dictionary was on the chenille cloth. I checked the finished version on my way to school. She'd forgotten to look up *sincerely* and spelled it 'sinserely' by mistake. It was an awful letter anyway, much too formal, and yet grovelling at the same time. I tore it up into little shreds and stuffed it in someone's dustbin.

I realized I still had to invite Nina round though, so on our way to her house after school that day I linked arms with her.

'Hey, my mum wants you to come round for a proper tea at ours on Monday. Is that OK?'

'Sure,' said Nina. 'I'll borrow another of your paperbacks. *Peyton Place* is amazing!'

She didn't seem particularly bothered. I dreaded it all over again. When I left for school on Monday morning Mum had her hair in curlers and pinny on, and was charging round the house with the carpet sweeper, looking frantic. But when we came home that afternoon the house was immaculate, and so was Mum. She'd sprayed her hair into a helmet, outlined her eyes, applied pearly lipstick, and wore the navy and cream Wallis shift dress she'd bought for Dad's work do.

She'd made the same effort over tea. It was the chicken salad, with hot rolls and butter, and a fruit surprise – tinned mandarins in orange jelly. She'd poured the evaporated milk into a little jug. There was the usual sponge, but with lavish buttercream, and the promised fairy cakes, some with silver balls, some with hundreds and thousands sprinkled on the icing. We even had a plate of

Penguin biscuits laid out in a red, green and blue pattern on the ribbon plate that usually hung on a hook in the living room.

'It's like a party!' said Nina, and Mum glowed.

There was very little party atmosphere though. Mum asked a few questions about school, using her posh telephone voice, and we answered in a desultory manner. Then Mum asked if Nina was a keen reader like me and wondered if she had a favourite book. I held my breath, wondering if she was going to mention *Peyton Place*, but Nina said she liked Pamela Brown's books about a children's theatre. She said she wanted to be an actress herself.

'Don't you want to be a doctor like your parents? Acting's all very well, but it's not really a proper career, is it, dear?' Mum said.

'Oh, Mum, Nina's brilliant at acting! She was fantastic as Juliet! Don't you remember, they even wrote about her in the paper?' I protested.

'Yes, I know, but it's still a bit of a waste of her education. Farleigh Grammar is such a marvellous school. Our Laura got a scholarship, did you know?' said Mum.

'*Mum!*' I said, practically dying.

Dad came home early. He disappeared to change out of his uniform the moment he came through the door, clearly on Mum's orders. He came into the living room in a clean shirt and a tie and his grey trousers, but he'd put his comfy old slippers on. Mum frowned at them but didn't like to say anything in front of Nina.

'Hello, hello, hello!' said Dad. 'So we have a special guest, eh? I'm Laura's dad, as if you haven't guessed. And I'm pretty certain you're Nina?' He spoke in his hearty *Happy Days* manner. He cracked corny chicken jokes as he ate his own salad. I expected him to launch into *Ten Green Bottles* by the time he started on the fairy cakes.

Surprisingly, Nina seemed to find him genuinely funny and giggled away. She blinked in surprise when he insisted on walking her home.

'Can't have a pretty little thing like you wandering about by herself,' he said.

I cringed, but Nina seemed delighted.

'That's really kind of you, Mr Peterson,' she said, and when she was fetching her blazer and satchel she told me she thought he was a right laugh.

I accompanied her home too. Dad even stayed in a jolly mood on our walk back.

'She seems a lovely girl, your Nina,' he said.

'She is,' I said, though I wondered what he would think if he heard her own jokes.

'I'm glad you've got such a good friend,' said Dad.

'So am I,' I said, and I felt such a sudden fizz of happiness that I did a little dance along the pavement.

Even though the tea party at my house was a partial success it was much easier for everyone if we slid back to the old routine. I went to Nina's two or three times a week. Her mother joked that she felt she had two daughters now. I worried that this was a hint that I was coming round too often, but she seemed fond of me. I thought she was wonderful. I couldn't believe she was actually about Mum's age. When she was working at the skin clinic she pinned her hair up and wore a white overall, but at home she let her hair hang loose past her shoulders, and she wore tight black trousers and black ballet shoes, often with a man's big blue striped shirt with the sleeves rolled up.

I don't think it belonged to her husband. Dr Bertram dressed quite formally even on his days off. He always wore a tie, even on really hot days, and it was hard to imagine him in shorts and sandals. I wasn't quite sure what I thought of him. Maybe I'd have felt more comfortable with him if he hadn't been my doctor as well as my best friend's dad. I always dreaded being left alone in the Bertram living room with him. I never knew what to say. I think he felt the same way with me, because he generally consulted some of his medical notes or read a newspaper instead of trying to make conversation.

I sometimes felt a little awkward with Daniel too, but that was because I liked him so much. He teased a bit, but all boys did that. And he wasn't really a boy any more anyway. He was much taller than me, and quite broad-shouldered too. He didn't have the usual short back and sides haircut that made male necks look so red and raw. His hair was longer and flopped over his forehead. His father was forever telling him to get a decent haircut, but Daniel just laughed.

He wasn't always at home. He had heaps of friends and was often out with them. I wondered if any of these friends were girls. I didn't like to ask Nina if Daniel had a girlfriend. She'd guess *I* liked him and tease me unmercifully. Or she might go off me herself. She could get quite jealous at times. She still wasn't speaking to Patsy.

I had the easiest relationship with Little Richard. He could be a bit irritating, using daft expressions like *Suffering codfish!* or *Crikey O'Riley!* or *Mouldering Mousies!*, and his jokes were even worse than Dad's, but he could be fun too. Sometimes Nina would get in a bit

43

of a mood and I couldn't get her to snap out of it, but Little Richard could always make her laugh, no matter what. He'd pretend to be a little puppy whimpering, or a laughing hyena, or a hen trying to lay an egg. 'Don't be so ridiculous, Richard,' Nina would say, but she'd always snort with laughter.

I think he had a little crush on me because he was always showing me his latest Meccano creation or his dinosaur drawings, and he'd offer me a liquorice bootlace or a gobstopper when he'd spent his pocket money in the sweetshop. Thank goodness Nina didn't mind my getting close to her *little* brother.

But Nina herself was of course the whole reason I was there. I was scared she might go off me at first, but we got closer and closer that whole summer term. Nina gave me a blue and silver fountain pen for my fourteenth birthday. It wasn't quite as special as hers, but I treasured it. We managed to swap desks too with another girl so that we could sit next to each other in class. We wandered round the playground with linked arms. We huddled close reading magazines together. We made up silly dilemmas to send to the *Woman's Own* problem page and sent several, but they never got published. We used false names of course. I was Lulu Paradise and Nina was Narissa Bibliothèque. We sometimes pretended to be these exotic girls. Lulu was incredibly fair with an hourglass figure and was the muse for a famous artist. Narissa was half French and looked like Brigitte Bardot. She had a whole string of boyfriends and described their love life in extreme detail.

'Nina, you haven't *really* done that, have you?' I asked her.

'Some of it,' said Nina. 'Don't look so shocked!'

'What if your mum and dad found out?' I said.

'As if they would!' said Nina. 'Anyway, I'm not Nina now, I'm Narissa. So what about you, Lulu? How far have you gone with a boy? Don't you do naughty things with your artist?'

'He can look at me, obviously, so he can paint me, but he can't touch,' I said, flicking away his imaginary hands.

'You don't know what you're missing,' Narissa said, in her cod French accent.

I wasn't sure either Lulu or I wanted to find out. I'd read *Peyton Place* now and I didn't like the sound of sex at all. Nina's harping on about it was the one thing I didn't like about her. But other than that I adored her. She was like my missing sister.

I decided I would wait until I got married. Maybe, just maybe, Daniel and I would get closer as the years went by, and we'd fall in love. If we ever became man and wife then Nina would be a real sister, and Little Richard my cute young brother. It was a fantasy that made me feel dizzy, but it *could* just happen.

I couldn't wait for the summer holidays, when I could go round to Nina's house and stay all day long. We didn't go away anywhere ourselves. The summer was Dad's busiest time, driving people to the seaside day after day, so he couldn't take any time off for his own holiday.

Of course I knew the Bertrams would have a proper summer holiday away somewhere. Nina had mentioned that they went to France and stayed in some weird-sounding place called a *gîte*.

'It's just a house,' she said. 'It's near a river though, and we go swimming, and see friends we've known for ages, and generally have a barbecue in the evenings, all of us. The parents sometimes get drunk – it's a hoot.'

'*Drunk?*' I said. It was impossible imagining either Dr Bertram stumbling around, singing in a slurred way, and being sick, like the old tramp that hung around the coach station most days.

'Well, not *drunk* drunk, just merry. *You* know. Daniel drank far too much wine last year and had to stay in bed the next morning because he had such a hangover,' said Nina. 'Pathetic! I had nearly as much as he did and I was right as rain.'

I hoped Nina wouldn't want to drink wine when she was with me. I'd never had so much as a sip but I knew our Christmas sherry tasted disgusting, like syrupy cough medicine.

'So how long are you going to be staying at this gîte place? A week?' I asked.

'A fortnight,' said Nina, surprised.

'A whole fortnight!' I echoed.

46

'We'd stay longer if my parents didn't have to work,' she said.

'Still, it means we still have a whole month when we can hang out,' I said.

'Yes, of course,' said Nina. 'Well, I'll probably have to stay with my granny for a few days. We always do. And then I sometimes see my cousins in Scotland. But we'll still have heaps of time together.'

Nina was away here and there for nearly a whole month. It seemed endless. I couldn't settle to anything. I didn't want to read or write. Talking to Miss Wong seemed pathetic now. It was wonderful weather, and everyone kept saying that 1959 was a record year for sun, but I felt so lonely I couldn't appreciate it. The prefab became unbearably hot and stuffy. I tried lying on the grass at the back but I started to feel sick and dizzy after ten minutes or so. I even went paddling in the lily pond at the front, and accidentally tore one of the heads off the flowers, which made Dad furious. Once I ran a cold bath and lay in it, naked, trying to cool down, but I kept banging my head on the taps.

'For goodness' sake, Laura, will you stop moping,' Mum nagged.

She made me go shopping with her on her day off, but that was incredibly boring. I made the mistake of telling her this, and she burst into tears. I got another telling-off from Dad for upsetting my mother.

I had one postcard from Nina, posted from France. There was a photo of some seaside on the front, and a very sparse message on the back: *Bonjour! Love Nina xxx*

47

'She's got lovely handwriting,' said Mum. 'Is that where she's staying then?'

'Search me,' I said.

I had no message at all when she was staying with her grandmother, and then another postcard from Scotland, a silly one of a man dancing in a kilt. There was another three-word message. *Back this weekend xxx*

I woke early on Saturday and waited in all day for a phone call. Perhaps she simply meant she was *travelling* back, which would probably take all day. I sat tensely all evening. I even checked the phone for the dialling tone to make sure it was still working. Sunday was worse. I couldn't wait any more. I walked round to the Bertram house that afternoon. Mr Bertram and Little Richard were busy cleaning the car in the driveway. Little Richard was washing it clean with a hose.

'Oh whoopee, it's Laura!' he shouted, turning to me. I had to dodge quickly to stop being soaked.

'Watch that damn hose, Richard!' Dr Bertram shouted.

'I'm giving Laura a wash!' Little Richard said gleefully, but he turned the hose away from me.

'Boys!' said Dr Bertram. 'Hello, Laura. Are you enjoying the holidays?

'Yes, thank you,' I said automatically. 'Is Nina indoors, Dr Bertram?'

'I'm afraid not. She's gone to some barbecue with Daniel and some of their friends,' he said, wiping the car dry.

Some of their friends? Wasn't *I* one of their friends? Why hadn't Nina got in touch with me?

'Right. Sorry to have bothered you,' I mumbled.

'Oh dear, did you come round specially to see her?' said Dr Bertram, squeezing out his cloth.

'No! I was just passing. I'm going to see . . .' I couldn't think for the life of me who I could pretend to be visiting, but it didn't matter. Dr Bertram wasn't really listening, and Little Richard was busy watering the grass now, which had burned brown in the constant sun.

I gave them both a casual wave and then bolted down the road. I had to keep up the pretence I was going somewhere. I ended up in the park. It was small and uninviting, especially now when the flowers were all wilting. I sat on an iron bench by the duck pond. It was so hot it burned the back of my legs.

Mum had taken me to feed the ducks here when I was little, but it had never been much fun. She was so scared I'd throw myself into the pond along with the bread that she clutched the back of my dress, showing my knickers. She wasn't at all keen on the ducks getting out of the water and quacking eagerly round our ankles.

'Mind those birds don't peck you, Laura!' she always cried, as if they were angry swans.

They were swimming around listlessly now. Perhaps the heat had got to them too, or maybe they were simply full of bread. I heard some young people messing about over on the tennis courts. One of the girls had glossy black hair and my heart thumped, but it wasn't Nina, just some stranger laughing her head off.

I thought of the real Nina, clearly long back from her various holidays, but not bothering to get in touch with me. I shut my eyes quickly, but I couldn't stop a tear spurting down my cheek. I wiped it away fiercely.

'I don't care,' I muttered. 'I don't want her to be my friend now. She just messes people about. She's selfish and thoughtless and doesn't care about anyone but herself. I really don't like her any more. Good riddance!'

I stayed in bed the next morning. I'd told Mum truthfully enough that I felt rotten and just wanted to sleep in. Mum fussed terribly, even taking my temperature. She had originally planned to take me out shopping as it was her day off, but her manager wanted her to come into work to unpack new stock.

'But I can't help her out now. I'll have to stay home to make sure you're all right,' said Mum.

'I'll be fine. It's just stomach cramps,' I lied. She gave me a cup of tea and two aspirins and told me I had to phone her at work if I felt any worse.

The phone went half an hour after she'd gone. I thought she was just checking up on me. But it wasn't Mum at all. It was Nina.

'Hey, you,' she said. 'Coming round?'

She said it as if we'd seen each other yesterday. I swallowed. I could barely speak.

'OK,' I said. 'Now?'

'Yep. Bring your swimming cossie. See you later, alligator.'

'In a while, crocodile.' We were quoting a silly song.

'No now, silly cow,' said Nina, improvising.

'Toodle-oo, silly moo,' I said back, and we hung up, laughing.

I flew into the bathroom, shoved on some clothes, ferreted in the back of my cupboard for my old swimming costume, chewed on a Shredded Wheat, washed it down with several swigs from the milk bottle, and then rushed out the door. Of course I still liked Nina. I loved her. She was my best friend in all the world and who cared that she hadn't got in touch the very second she got back home?

We flung our arms round each other when I arrived at her house. Then I gave myself hiccups and made ridiculous noises all the way through Nina's account of her French holiday and how she'd actually gone out with a boy called Pierre.

'A real date?' I asked.

'Yes, he came calling for me, and we walked all the way into town, and then we had crêpes – you know, a bit like our pancakes but much better, more sophisticated – and he insisted on paying.

Then we walked back in the moonlight hand in hand. It was heavenly,' said Nina, sighing.

'Did he – *hic!* – kiss you?'

'Yes!'

'On the lips?'

'Yes he did!' said Nina triumphantly.

'What did it – *hic!* – feel like?'

'Wonderful! I mean, I've been kissed by boys before of course, but Pierre is simply incredible. He's such a sophisticated kisser,' said Nina, hugging herself.

'"Sophisticated" seems your new – *hic!* – favourite word,' I said.

'What do you mean?' said Nina.

'Well, you keep using it,' I said.

'Twice! And don't worry, I won't ever use it about you, not if you belch like a bullfrog every five seconds,' said Nina. 'Honestly!'

'I can't help it,' I said. 'So, did you see him again?'

'Well, no, because we went home the next day. But we're going to meet up again as soon as possible. He might even come and stay with us over Christmas, him and his family. He's Daniel's friend too, and our fathers go fishing together,' said Nina.

'Oh,' I said. I felt a little crestfallen. Wasn't I going to be part of Nina's Christmas?

'Then the week with Granny was OK – she's ever so sweet, but to be truthful it was a bit boring too. She took us to the zoo, which was still quite fun, I suppose, and then she took us to Battersea fun fair, and that was great, but the rest of the time we just mucked about at her house and played Monopoly. Little Richard still likes board games, but Daniel and I find them *so* boring,' said Nina.

I'd only played Monopoly once, *with* Nina and Daniel and Little Richard, and I'd found it an amazingly entertaining game. I'd jumped my tiny rocking horse token round the board, while we all laughed and joked and groaned and protested at each other's progress. I'd hoped that we might play this magical game again and again.

We only had one board game at home, and that was Snakes and Ladders. My Aunt Susannah had sent it to me for Christmas. I could hardly remember her. She was Mum's younger sister and she'd fallen out with her long ago, when I was very little. I just had this dim memory of a funny lady in colourful clothes who smelled deliciously of musky perfume when she gave me a cuddle. From what I could remember she seemed the exact opposite of Mum. I never found out why they quarrelled. Mum wouldn't say, just murmured mysteriously, 'She's no better than she ought to be,' which didn't even make sense. Apparently she wasn't even really called Susannah, she was just plain Susan. 'That's just typical of her,' Mum sniffed. I decided that Susannah was a much more dashing alternative. I wished Mum would make it up with her. She would have nothing to do with her. She didn't even send her a Christmas card. I don't think Aunt Susannah sent her one either, but she always remembered to send me a Christmas present and a birthday one too. They were my most special presents. She sent little notes with them, with 'Love from Aunt Susannah' and a whole row of kisses and hearts. Snakes and Ladders was an ordinary board game, but Aunt Susannah sent snakes in the parcel too. Not real ones of course, but three glorious velvet snakes. Perhaps she'd made them herself, because I'd never seen anything like them in the toy shops. There was a green father snake, with a twirly moustache and a winking eye, a purple mother snake with silver sequins sewed down her long back, and a bright pink little girl snake with a pink net ballet skirt and one tiny satin ballet shoe tied on the end of her tail. I adored my snake family and played with them endlessly. When I eventually grew tired of pretend games I kept them slithering across my windowsill, but one day I left my window open and they got rained on. They weren't totally spoiled, but Mum chucked them out in the rubbish and she shouted at me when I tried to rescue them. We played the board game only once, Mum and Dad and me, sitting at the table after Sunday lunch. It wasn't really much fun. Mum sighed impatiently every now and then and Dad kept yawning. We didn't play it ever again.

Now it looked as if I wouldn't be playing Monopoly either. Nina continued her monologue about her holiday adventures, saying her Scottish trip had been OK, but there had been an awful lot of midges.

'Look, I'm still all over bites,' she said, sweeping her hair up and showing me her back and shoulders. They were a beautiful golden colour now, and I couldn't see a single bite for the life of me.

'You're brown all over,' I said enviously.

'And you're chalk white!' said Nina. 'What have you been doing all summer, shutting yourself up in a cupboard?'

'Yes, I squeezed up on a shelf with the jam and the marmalade and the HP Sauce. It was a terrible squash but at least I had something to eat,' I said.

'What?' said Nina, shaking her head. 'You're mad, you!'

'I know,' I said. 'I was pining for company. Yours!'

'Well, I'm here now, you daft thing. Did you remember your cossie? Let's go to the Lido,' she said.

'The Lido?' I echoed stupidly.

It was four or five miles away, off the main road. I'd seen postcards of it in the local newsagents. It was a big square white building with an enormous bright turquoise pool. I'd actually asked Mum if we could go there several times, but she said places like that were germ traps, and it would get too crowded anyway. She took me to the local indoor Coronation Baths instead, for swimming lessons. It was a gloomy cavern which smelled so strongly of chlorine it made your head spin. I learned to swim quite quickly and rather enjoyed swimming there, though my eyes were crimson for ages after each lesson. I'd have been happy to carry on, but as soon as I'd learned to do a neat breaststroke Mum didn't see the point of my going any more. 'You won't drown now, even if you fall in a river,' she'd said.

'Won't it take us ages to walk all the way to the Lido?' I asked Nina.

Both the Dr Bertrams were at work and couldn't give us a lift in a car. Daniel was disappointingly out with some friends, and Little Richard had gone to the skin clinic with his mother and was doubtless charming all the blotchy patients in the waiting room.

'We'll get the trolleybus. It stops right outside,' said Nina.

I hated going on the electric trolley because it jerked so as it drove along, making me feel sick. I hoped my emergency money would cover the fare there and back – but presumably you had to pay an entrance fee at the Lido?

'What's up *now*?' said Nina impatiently. 'Don't you want to go?' She sounded as if she might ask someone else if I didn't show more enthusiasm.

'Of course I do,' I said. I hesitated. 'I'm not sure I can afford it, that's all.'

'Oh, sorry!' said Nina, immediately contrite. 'It's on me, of course. I've got heaps of cash.' She threw her bulging purse up in the air and caught it again one-handed. 'And I'll buy us some sandwiches and stuff from the Lido cafe for lunch. We'll stay there all day, OK? We'd better take a book with us too.'

She was in the middle of reading a family saga called *Jalna* and was in love with the hero Renny Whiteoak. She said I could borrow any of her other books, but I chose one of the Dr Bertram books from the main bookshelf, *Madame Bovary*, because it was a Penguin classic and looked impressive.

The trolleybus ride was a particularly jerky one, and after five minutes or so that awful nausea spread through me and I could barely respond to Nina.

'What's the matter with you, Laura? You've gone all sweaty! It's not *that* hot,' she said.

'I feel sick,' I mumbled.

'Oh, for God's sake. You're as bad as Little Richard in the car. He threw up twice on the way to the ferry. The smell!' said Nina.

'Stop it! I think I'd better get off the trolley,' I said.

'But we've only just got on!'

'*I'm* going to throw up!' I said.

'No you're not!' Nina said fiercely, and she pinched my arm hard. 'You are *not*, do you hear me?'

She was so commanding that I managed to last the entire journey. When I stumbled off the bus I made for the gutter, but Nina still had hold of me.

'You're not doing it here either, making a spectacle of both of us. Just lean against the wall and breathe deeply. You'll feel better in a minute,' she said.

It took several minutes, but it started to clear, and after a bit I said shakily, 'I think I might be all right now.'

'There!' Nina said triumphantly.

'Maybe you really should be a doctor like your mum and dad if you can cure people just like that,' I said, hanging on her arm.

'Maybe I should be a hypnotist! That would be much better. Imagine being able to make people do exactly what I want!'

'Yes, well, you can do that all right,' I said. 'You can be Madame Nina, notorious for her dark powers, and have a novelty act onstage.'

'And you can be Miss Laura, my assistant and sidekick,' said Nina.

'No! I want to be . . . I want to do . . . I don't *know* what I want to do, but it will be something wonderful and different and exciting!' I said, feeling the colour coming back to my face. 'Something that will make me famous and be in all the newspapers!'

I must have said it too loudly, because a bunch of four boys with rolled-up towels under their arms turned round and laughed at me.

'Idiots,' I said loftily, but Nina smirked and tossed her hair over her shoulder, though the boys were particularly gawky and only about eleven years old. They all looked impressed but wary and ran off.

'Come on, Laura,' said Nina, and she linked arms with me as we walked up the road to the Lido.

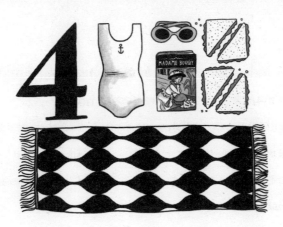

A large queue had already formed and it took twenty minutes before we were inside. We were each given a big metal contraption to store our clothes in. There was another queue for the wooden changing rooms by the side of the huge pool, so we squeezed in together when one became free at last.

I felt shy of stripping off in front of Nina but it was so dark inside we could barely see. We kept bumping into each other and getting the giggles.

'So was it a good barbecue?' I said casually.

'What? Here, can you do up my bikini top? It's so fiddly,' said Nina.

'You're wearing a bikini?' I said. I only had a childish blue costume with a white anchor on the front. I'd had it two years and it was getting too small for me.

'It's got little hearts on it. Mum bought it for me in France. Which barbecue are you talking about?'

'The one you went to this weekend,' I said. *The one you went to instead of seeing me!*

'Oh, that one!' said Nina. 'Yes, it was great. Daniel's friends are such a laugh. Especially Jimmy.'

'Ah!' I said.

'He's always been fun, but now he's getting really good-looking. They were all drinking beer and getting a bit squiffy and playing daft games and then Jimmy started dancing with me, whirling me round and round the garden, and then we just had this moment when we looked into each other's eyes. It was magic!' said Nina. 'Come on, hurry up, it's so stuffy in here.'

'Did he kiss you?' I asked.

'No, but I think he wanted to. *I* certainly wanted him to!' said Nina, making silly kissing noises in the dark.

'But I thought you were in love with Pierre!' I said.

'Well, yes. But I won't be seeing him for ages, will I? So it would be great if I got off with Jimmy just for now,' said Nina. 'Come on!' She started to open the door.

'Wait a minute!' I said hurriedly. I needed to pull my costume up a bit at the top and yank it down a bit at the bottom. I was suddenly so worried about emerging into the sunshine in my childish costume, with nearly all my skinny white body on show to everyone.

Nina sighed theatrically. 'Ready now?' She pulled the door open wide, not pausing for me to answer. She looked incredible in her bright bikini. She was brown all over too, but when she reached up to hand in her clothes at the window of the locker room I saw her armpits were smooth and white.

I hadn't thought of shaving off the hair under my own arms. I'd have to keep them pinned to my sides all day. Nina must have shaved her legs too, because I'd seen the dark hair on her legs when we had PE. They were now bare and smoothly tanned.

I still only had a light down on my own legs, but I wasn't sure they passed muster. This was a whole new tiresome world of grooming. It was so much easier being a child. Well, I still *looked* like a child beside Nina. She gave me a quick glance up and down but didn't comment.

'Grab your towel and book – and have you got sunglasses? Oh well, never mind. Come on, hand in your stuff and let's find a good spot to sit. Not down the kiddie end, and not too near the diving boards either or we'll get splashed. Halfway is probably best, on the left to catch the sun,' she said.

I pulled the elasticated locker token onto my wrist. I didn't wear any other jewellery. Nina still wore her famously expensive watch and she had the gold St Christopher medal on a long slim chain that stopped just short of her cleavage. She also had a gold chain round her ankle! I'd seen a woman in the town with an ankle chain and admired it, but Mum had given me a little shake and whispered that women who wore those type of chains were extremely common and most likely prostitutes.

I couldn't stop staring at Nina's ankle chain.

'Do you like it? It's great, isn't it? Nearly all the girls were wearing them in France,' she said, lifting her leg and rotating her slim ankle so that the chain glinted in the sunlight.

I nodded silently. Mum must have got it wrong. Nina was posh, not common, and she might be boy-mad but she certainly wasn't a prostitute. She bossily conducted us to the perfect spot on the long decks around the pool, put down her towel and then arranged herself carefully, sitting with her head slightly tilted back, one leg pointed, the other raised, as if she were posing for a film magazine.

I hunched up beside her, feeling terribly self-conscious. Lots of sunbathers were staring at us, especially the boys. Even some of the fathers were having a good peer.

'They're all *looking*!' I muttered.

Nina put on her sunglasses. 'Take no notice. You haven't got any suntan lotion, have you? You're going to go bright red if you're not careful. You're so *white*.'

'Well, I'll look like a raspberry ripple ice cream, and they're delicious,' I said, and made her laugh.

'I've missed you, Laura,' she said.

'I've missed you too,' I replied.

We sat there and I gradually relaxed. It was only mid-morning but the decks were filling up already and the shallow end of the pool was a whirlpool of shouting, splashing children. A few dedicated swimmers hurtled up and down the swimming lane, never pausing, and boys larked around near the deep end, pushing each other in.

'Look at those boys over there!' said Nina. 'No, not the idiots. The two on the diving platform.'

They were even browner than she was, one dark with longish hair and one fair with a crew cut. They were both lean, their stomachs flat, but they had broad shoulders. They didn't really look like boys any more. They were standing casually chatting, seemingly unaware that half the girls on the poolside were staring up at them.

'The fair one keeps on looking at me,' said Nina, giggling.

'Really?' I didn't see how she could tell if he was looking at her or any of the other girls nearby. Or me, for that matter.

Nina gave him a little wave all the same. 'Go on then, dive!' she shouted, and she mimed a dive with one hand.

He must have been looking at her after all because he shrugged and then left his dark friend and climbed up to the three-metre board. He paused a moment, and then went on up to the five-metre board at the top.

'Do you think he knows how to dive?' I asked. 'It can be ever so dangerous diving from the top.'

'Don't be so daft, it's only water,' said Nina. She raised her voice. 'We're watching!'

'Oh God, what if he does a belly flop?' I asked.

But he walked lightly and confidently along the board, went to the very edge to stand on his toes, then soared outwards into the air in a perfect swallow dive. He entered the water with scarcely a ripple. When he surfaced Nina clapped. He grinned and waved at her and then climbed the steps back to join his friend, glinting with drops of water.

Nina nodded at me triumphantly. 'There now!' she said.

'Nina, will you stop it! He's much too old for you. He looks at least eighteen,' I said.

'So?' said Nina. 'And he's got a friend. *You* can have him.'

'I don't *want* him!' I couldn't tell if she was joking or if she was really serious. What was the matter with her? She seemed to have gone crazy this summer.

The two boys stayed by the diving platform for ages. The fair one occasionally did further perfect dives from the five-metre board. The dark one preferred the springboard. He ran along to the end, jumped up and down violently, and then took off like a rocket. It was quite impressive but nowhere near as breathtaking.

'Blondie's much better,' said Nina smugly, though she clapped the dark one too.

'They're both total show-offs,' I said sourly.

'Stop being so stuffy,' said Nina, and she tapped the end of my nose.

When they both grew tired of diving they swam to the side of the pool and eased themselves out. They grabbed their towels and came sauntering along the decks.

'Oh my God, they're coming towards us!' I said.

'Of course they are,' said Nina.

'It's all your fault, making eyes at them! What are we going to say, what are we going to do?' I gabbled in a panic.

'Just act naturally,' said Nina out of the side of her mouth, though she had bent her head sideways and was half smiling in a totally *un*natural manner.

They weren't coming to see us at all. They walked straight past and went to join a little group of older girls, who were all at least fifth-formers, maybe even older. They greeted the boys with hoots and giggles.

'Idiots!' Nina snapped.

'They weren't looking at us at all!' I said.

'Yes they were. You probably put them off, acting like a frightened rabbit,' said Nina. 'Honestly, Laura, you can be so childish at times. And you *look* like a little kid too in that old swimming costume.'

I had to blink hard not to burst into tears. I couldn't think of a funny quip that might stop her being so mean. I turned my back on her and opened *Madame Bovary*. At first I was so upset that I couldn't take a word in, but after ten minutes or so I settled into the story. I wasn't very interested in this boy Charles Bovary, so I skipped a lot until he'd grown up and taken a wife, Emma. She was fascinating.

Nina read her own book for a while but grew bored. She sighed heavily.

'You should wear your glasses,' she said. 'You're really squinting.'

I took no notice.

'Laura! Stop sulking!' She picked up someone else's toffee wrapper and flicked it onto my book. I brushed it away without looking at her.

'All right, *be* like that,' she said, and flipped over onto her tummy. She lay for a while, browning her golden back, and then she suddenly stood up, grabbed her bag, and marched off.

I stared after her. Was she going to join the group of girls with the two diving boys? Was she simply going home without me? I thought of calling her name, running after her – but that was exactly what she wanted. I wasn't going to pander to her this time.

I'd simply stay here at the Lido, sunning myself and reading my book. I'd even have a swim. I didn't have any money for lunch, but I wasn't that hungry anyway. I'd show her she couldn't treat me like that.

I read on, but I couldn't help glancing up every now and then. It was a relief to see she was waiting in a queue outside the Ladies room, standing with one hand on her hip. Then I saw her going into the cafe a few minutes later. Well, good luck to her. I read on.

After fifteen minutes or so a shadow fell over my page.

'Sorry I've been so long,' said Nina. 'I had to wait ages! I've bought us both lunch. But shall we have a little swim first?'

It wasn't a proper apology, but it was nearly one. She had said sorry, after all.

'Yes, that would be great,' I said.

It was a joy to discover that I was a better swimmer than Nina. She floated on her back, her hair spread out now like a black halo. She looked eerily serene floating there, a water nymph in her element, but then someone doing backstroke bumped into her and dunked her under the water and she bobbed up red in the face and spluttering furiously.

'What an idiot! The water's all gone up my nose. I absolutely hate that feeling. Come on, let's get out now,' she said.

I wanted to stay in, but decided it wasn't worth an argument. We went over to our special spot and towelled ourselves. Nina had brought another towel with her, so she still had a dry one to sit on.

'Look, I'll spread it out so that you can share it,' she said. 'You're ever such a good swimmer, Laura.' She delved into her bag. She'd bought two sandwiches, one egg and cress and one cheese and pickle, two packs of crisps, a red and a green Penguin biscuit, and two bottles of orange juice.

'There! Good picnic?' she asked proudly.

'*Great* picnic. So is half for me?'

'Yep. Let's divide the sandwiches so we get half egg, half cheese. And *you* get to choose which colour Penguin you want,' said Nina, larking about as if we were five-year-olds. Though actually, it did matter. I knew perfectly well that all the Penguins tasted the same beneath their bright foil wrappers, but green were still my favourites. When we'd eaten the biscuits we twirled the foil round our fingers and twisted it at the bottom to turn them into pretend wine glasses and then toasted each other.

I saw out of the corner of my eye that the two divers were still lounging on the deck with the girls. The fair one had his arm round one of them already. I was so glad they hadn't come over to us. I hoped Nina didn't mind too much. I couldn't work out whether she could see them from where she was sitting. She certainly didn't seem to be taking any notice of them.

We chatted for a while and then lay back for a proper sunbathe.

It felt good to feel the sun all over me. My swimming costume was nearly dry already. I hoped I was getting a tan. Maybe by the time we went home I'd be almost as brown as Nina. After a while I turned over onto my tummy and tried to tan my back.

It was getting almost too hot now. I raised my head and for a few seconds couldn't see anything, just a white glare. I blinked, panicking, and the colours slowly slid back, the turquoise water, the white Lido, the reds and greens and yellows of everyone's swimming costumes and towels, Nina's blue-black hair glinting in the sunshine, the white of her bikini, the brown of her skin.

'Am I starting to get a little bit brown?' I asked hopefully.

'Er . . . let me see. Mm. No! More like red. You're starting to fry, Laura. You'd better go and cool down in the pool,' she said.

'You come too.'

'No, I'm too comfortable. I've just got to a really good bit in my book,' she said. 'Oh, I wish people in stories were real. I'd give anything to meet Renny. Men are so much more interesting than silly boys. I can't wait till I'm old enough for proper affairs,' she said dreamily.

I dived into the pool and swam about in the deliciously cold water, wondering whether I'd *ever* feel ready for affairs. I forgot to look where I was going and swam further into the deep end than I realized. Suddenly something hit me with such force that I was thrust down under the water, almost to the bottom of the pool. I curled into a ball, so dazed it was hard to remember which way was up, but then I pointed my arms and kicked simply by instinct.

I rose to the surface and gasped in air. Then something seized me and I shouted, convinced I was being attacked.

'*Ça va? Vous êtes OK? Pardon. Je m'excuse.*'

It was the dark-haired diver, treading water, his black hair plastered to his forehead. I couldn't understand a word he was saying, but he looked tremendously sorry.

'What happened?' I gasped, coughing.

He mimed diving with one hand and then took hold of me by the shoulders. I wondered what he was going to do now, but he was simply steering me to the side of the pool.

'It's OK, I can swim by myself!' I said indignantly.

He kept hold of me, calling me a *petite fille*.

It was French for *little girl*. He thought *I* was a little girl, which was insulting, but it seemed ridiculous to keep arguing so I let him pull me out of the pool. I sat on the side, still coughing up water. I was terrified it might look as if I were vomiting.

'I'm not being sick!' I gasped.

'*L'hôpital?*' he asked anxiously.

'No, I'm fine now, really,' I said, standing up shakily. 'Thank you.'

I started walking towards Nina, who was deep in her book,

not knowing I'd nearly drowned. But he followed, insisting on taking my arm by the elbow, trying to help me.

'I'm all *right*,' I said, but I couldn't shake him off.

I got to Nina at last. We were both streaming with water, and a drop landed on her book.

'Hey, watch out!' she said, looking up crossly. She stared at the dark boy hanging onto me. 'What's going on?'

'It's nothing. He was diving and he landed on me and now he's scared he's hurt me,' I said.

'I should think so too! Great clumsy lout! Push off!' said Nina, flapping her hand at him.

He looked crestfallen and I couldn't help feeling sorry for him. 'It wasn't his fault. I was swimming right by the diving boards, like an idiot,' I said. 'And now I've given him a horrible shock.'

'He should have watched where he was diving, all the same. You apologize to my friend,' said Nina fiercely.

He shook his head blankly and gave a despairing shrug.

'Is he a bit thick?' Nina asked me.

'No! He's French, that's all,' I said.

'We are both French,' someone said. He spoke perfect English, but with a delightful accent. It was the handsome diver with the blond crew cut. 'My friend might be very clumsy but he is not thick. He's a brilliant science student but not gifted at languages.'

71

'But you are!' said Nina, and she sat up straight and gave him a dazzling smile.

'Thank you, *mademoiselle*,' he said. He turned to me. 'Are you truly all right, *ma petite*?'

'*Oui!*' I said, irritated by his change of tone. They were still treating me like a little girl. '*Très bien, merci.*'

'Oh, a little linguist!' said the fair one. '*Comment tu t'appelles, mademoiselle?*'

'*Elle s'appelle Lulu,*' Nina said quickly. '*Et moi, je m'appelle Narissa.*'

I towelled myself vigorously, alarmed. What kind of game was she playing now?

'*Ah, bonjour Narissa, bonjour Lulu. Je suis Yves, et mon ami ici s'appelle Léon,*' he said. 'May we join you?'

'*Bien sûr,*' said Nina, smiling. Her accent was much better than mine, probably because of her holidays at the gîte.

I peered round to see what had happened to the girls they'd been sitting with before. They weren't there any more. They'd obviously gone home. So now these two boys were making friends with us! Nina was actively encouraging them, patting the space next to her. Yves sat right beside her, almost touching her. I stayed standing up, towelling. Léon stood awkwardly beside me, still dripping.

'*Va chercher ta serviette et tes affaires, petit con,*' Yves said to him quickly. He smiled at Nina. 'We are students on an exchange visit. We love England. We love English girls.'

'*Vraiment!*' said Nina, showing off now. 'So, you're actually students at university?' Even she seemed a little alarmed that they might be nineteen or twenty.

'No, we go to school, in the sixth form. We are seventeen,' said Yves. He flashed his hands several times until he'd shown her seventeen fingers. He wore a garnet signet ring on his little finger. 'How old are you, Narissa?'

'Oh, I'm sixteen,' Nina lied smoothly.

'Really!' said Yves. He looked at me. 'You can't be sixteen too, Lulu?'

'Yes, she is. She just looks very young for her age,' said Nina. 'But she's very mature. Look, she reads adult stuff.' She showed him my borrowed book.

'*Madame Bovary!*' said Yves. He looked impressed. 'But it's a French book!'

'I'm reading it in translation,' I mumbled.

'It is a very sophisticated book for a little girl,' said Yves, grinning.

'She's not a little girl, I keep telling you,' said Nina. She felt in her bag and brought out a brush and a lipstick. 'Sit the other side of me, Lulu.'

I wanted to walk off, but I sat down meekly and let her brush my damp tousled hair and smear bright-red lipstick on my mouth. I knew I probably looked a clown, but Yves smiled and said, '*Très belle.*'

'*Et moi?*' said Nina, turning her own mouth into a scarlet cupid's bow.

'*Très très belle*,' said Yves. He leaned towards her and for one alarming second I thought he was going to kiss her there and then. Maybe Nina did too, because her mouth was pouting invitingly.

But Léon came hurrying up, clutching towels and duffel bags. He was drier now, and he'd tried to smooth his hair back, though it kept flopping forward. He sat the other side of me. I wriggled nearer Nina, trying not to make it too obvious. He saw *Madame Bovary* and raised his eyebrows.

'Yours?' he said, looking very surprised. '*Vous êtes intellectuelle!*' I hoped it was because he thought me very young, not very thick.

'They are both *sixteen*,' Yves muttered to his friend. I didn't like the way he put the emphasis on our age.

Maybe Nina didn't either, because she said, '*Mais nous sommes les jeunes filles très sages.*'

'We've heard that English girls like to have a little fun,' said Yves.

I wasn't quite sure what he meant by 'fun', but I hated the way he said that too.

'Nina, it's getting a bit late,' I said.

'*Narissa!*' Nina hissed.

'I think we ought to go home now,' I said.

'What? Don't be daft, Lulu. We're having a lovely time,' she said.

She might be enjoying herself, but I certainly wasn't. Nina and Yves were chatting away, sometimes in French, sometimes in English. She was telling him all the things she liked about France. She even told him she had a French boyfriend, but said they weren't going steady.

'So you are fancy-free?' Yves asked.

'Yep, that's me,' said Nina, smiling.

'And your friend Lulu?'

I scowled at her.

'Oh, she is too. She's never had a boyfriend yet,' said Nina.

How could she say that, even if it was true!

'She just likes to read about romance?' said Yves.

It was true, but it was kind of insulting the way he said it.

I turned my back on both of them – but that meant I was staring at Léon. He looked almost as uncomfortable as me, but he did his best to smile.

'You OK?' he asked.

I don't think he was really concerned, he was just trying to think of something to say.

'Yes, I am. Honestly,' I said.

He was looking at my skin, maybe checking it for bruising.

You have pretty skin pale,' Léon said earnestly.

I was embarrassed that I was so white when they were all so tanned. Did he really think it was pretty? I couldn't help feeling a little thrilled.

'And good swimmer,' he said, miming the action with his arms.

'And you're a good diver,' I said, feeling I had to return the compliment.

'*Pas comme mon ami Yves*,' said Léon.

I warmed to him a little more. I knew what it was like to be the second-choice friend.

'Much faster. More dashing,' I said.

I'm not sure he understood, but he looked pleased.

Then we were silent, both trying to think of another topic of conversation. Nina and Yves seemed to be having no problem at all. They were nattering away as if they'd known each other years. Yves reached out and put his hand lightly on Nina's shoulder. She didn't make any attempt to shrug it off.

'Your friend says you like science,' I said desperately to Léon.

'*Oui.* I go to the Sorbonne next year,' he said.

It meant nothing to me but I nodded wisely.

'You like science?' he asked.

'Sort of,' I said. 'Experiments,' I added vaguely.

He started going on about his own scientific studies, but I couldn't understand a word he was saying. He saw I was looking blank.

76

'*Je m'excuse*. You prefer the literature?' he said humbly.

'Yes, I do,' I said.

'You want *écrire, quand vous êtes* . . . woman?' he asked. He waggled his fingers in the air, miming typing this time. I hoped he was asking me if I wanted to be a writer, not a typist.

'*Peut-être*,' I said. 'Or maybe an actress?' I didn't really mean it seriously. I was just desperately trying to make conversation. Unfortunately Nina heard me.

'Are you telling him you want to be an *actress*, Lulu?' she said incredulously. 'That's what *I* want to do.'

'Well, I can be too, can't I?' I said.

Nina shrugged. 'I suppose,' she said.

'You will be a beautiful actress, Narissa. Brigitte Bardot! Marilyn Monroe!' said Yves.

'I want to be a proper stage actress,' said Nina. 'I was Juliet in a recent performance of *Romeo and Juliet*. I was nervous, but I think it went OK. Thank goodness I got a great write-up in the newspaper, but they might just have been being kind.' She made it sound as if it had been a proper public performance, not just a school play. 'Of course Lulu had a part too, didn't you? She was very good actually.'

She was acting *now*, pretending to be modest.

'What part did you play, Lulu?' Yves asked. He still sounded patronizing.

'Oh, nothing special. Just one of Juliet's noblewomen,' I said, as if I didn't care.

That was the part I seemed to be playing now, only I didn't feel at all noble.

'Still, I'm sure you were a big success,' Yves said, catching Nina's eye.

I saw they were both struggling not to laugh. I blushed painfully. 'I need to go now,' I said, standing up. 'I'm getting sunburned. Nina – Narissa – are you coming?'

'Can't you just go and sit in the shade somewhere? I'm sure Léon will go with you,' said Nina.

'No, I'm going home,' I said. I looked at her, waiting.

'Bye then,' said Nina.

I couldn't believe she could be so mean. But I wasn't going to plead with her, even though I wasn't sure I had enough money for the trolley fare home. I'd just have to walk. I marched off, not saying goodbye to any of them. I hoped Nina might come running after me, but she didn't.

I got my things and took my time changing in the dark cubicle. I might have cried a little, but I wiped my eyes fiercely before coming out into the sunshine again. Léon was standing self-consciously nearby. He'd changed too, into a striped T-shirt, blue jeans and white tennis shoes. He actually looked quite good in them. He was smiling at me tentatively.

'You want I walk you home?' he asked.

'Oh! No, thank you! I mean, it's very kind of you, but it's a long walk,' I stammered.

'Then we walk *together*,' he said, pointing at himself and then me.

So I nodded, because it would seem so rude to refuse again.

We set off. For the first five minutes we said nothing at all. I couldn't think of a thing to say and he couldn't seem to either. What was the point anyway, when we couldn't speak each other's language properly? We kept clearing our throats, about to attempt a pleasantry, but thinking better of it. We glanced at each other, grinning foolishly whenever our eyes met.

'Nice houses. You live this road?' Léon said at last.

'No. I live ages away. But you don't have to come all the way with me. We can say goodbye here,' I said. I offered him my hand to shake but he misunderstood and held onto it.

'I come. I like you, Lulu. You pretty girl,' he said.

No one had ever called me pretty before. Mum was very sparse with her compliments because she said she didn't want me to get above myself. If I asked her if I looked all right, she'd just give a little sideways nod and say, 'You'll do.' Dad didn't even go as far as that. He never made a fuss of Mum either. He just wasn't that sort of man.

Certainly no boys had ever singled me out and admired me. No girls either. They used to play a cruel rating game in our class, giving everyone marks out of ten. I got five. It wasn't the worst score. Poor Elspeth only got one.

I knew Léon probably didn't *really* think I was pretty. He was just saying it because it was one of the few English words he knew. But it was sweet of him all the same.

'Thank you!' I mumbled, tucking my chin down shyly.

'Yes. Very pretty. Pretty hair. Pretty eyes. Pretty dress,' he insisted.

He was sounding like a vocabulary lesson now. And my hair was a mess because I hadn't brought a brush and my eyes were red from swimming in chlorinated water and my dress was last year's and limp with too much washing. But I still loved him saying it. I wondered about telling him he was handsome. Was *beau* the right word? Could you say that to a boy or would he consider me fast? Perhaps he thought me the wrong sort of girl already because I was letting him hold my hand.

I wished he'd let it go. I was hot with embarrassment and scared it might be starting to get sweaty. It was awkward walking along together because he was tall and took big strides in his tennis shoes and I was small for my age and wearing childish flip-flops. He seemed worried about it and flashed his hands in the air – five, five, five and then one finger, enquiring if I was really sixteen.

'*Oui,*' I said, because I didn't want him to think Nina and I had been lying all along.

Then he pointed to *Madame Bovary*. '*Un vrai roman!* Yves say English girls act grown up.'

I shrugged uncertainly. He was looking unsure too.

'He say they kiss the boys,' he said.

My heart started thumping. 'Some do,' I said.

'*Et vous? Vous embrassez les garçons?*' he persisted, holding my hand tight.

I swallowed. '*Non!*'

He looked terribly disappointed. 'Because *je suis un âne?*'

I remembered a list of animals in my French textbook. 'Did you just say you're a *donkey?*' I asked.

'*Oui*. My friend Yves say I am awkward,' he said dolefully, and he let go my hand.

I understood and sympathized. 'Your friend Yves is like my friend Nina – I mean, Narissa,' I said. 'But you're not a donkey. You are good-looking.'

'*Vraiment?* Then we go home *et vous m'embrassez?*' he said eagerly.

'*Non!*' I couldn't have him going all the way home with me. I could tell by his clothes he was quite a posh boy. He might be shocked if he saw where I lived. And what if any of our neighbours saw me taking a boy into our prefab? They might tell Mum! She would go berserk! '*Ma mère est très très méchante!*' I didn't mean Mum was wicked, but I couldn't think of the French word for *strict*.

'Ah!' said Léon, catching on. '*Nous allons nous promener dans un jardin?*'

He wanted us to go for a walk in my garden? I imagined us trudging round and round Dad's lily pond until we were dizzy. Then it dawned on me.

'A park?'

'*Oui!* You know a park?' he asked.

'I do,' I said.

'*On y va,*' he said, taking my hand again.

'Well. We *could* go there – but just for a walk?' I said.

He nodded happily. I wasn't sure if he understood or not. I wasn't sure what I meant either. I didn't want to be thought of as a girl who would deliberately go into a park to be kissed. I didn't even *want* to be kissed, did I? But it would be something to tell Nina. I was sick of her treating *me* like a donkey.

So I took him to the park. It wasn't as if anything terrible could happen there. It was such a bland, boring park, with the kiddy swings and the ducks and the regimented flower beds. It was crowded with sunbathers lying flat on their backs as if felled, and children crying for ice cream.

'You want ice, Lulu?' Léon asked.

He bought us both a strawberry ice lolly. We had to eat them quickly because of the sun. Red juice dribbled down my arm before I was finished. Léon reached out and gently touched my mouth.

'Coty lipstick!' he said.

I giggled and he laughed too, pleased he'd managed a little joke. We walked on, hand in sticky hand, scuffling along the gravel path and then walking across the clipped green grass of the cricket pitch.

'English cricket!' said Léon. He let go of my hand and mimed being a cricketer. I smiled obediently. It was a bit like being kind to Little Richard when he told his interminable corny jokes.

Léon pointed. '*Alors, le petit bâtiment, là?*'

I didn't catch what he said but looked where he was pointing.

'That's the changing hut for the people that play cricket,' I said.

'They no play today?'

'No, it's generally just on Sundays. And it's incredibly boring. I wouldn't bother watching if I were you,' I said.

He wasn't listening. 'We go hut,' he said.

'But there's nothing there,' I said doubtfully. 'And it's probably locked anyway.'

But he insisted we walk over to it. There was a padlock on the door but someone had already broken it. Léon pushed the door

84

open cautiously. There were several empty bottles of beer scattered on the floor. One bottle had spilled.

'Tramps,' I said, wrinkling my nose at the smell of stale beer.

'Bad tramps,' said Léon. '*Cette petite maison est pour vous et moi.*'

'Our house?' I said. 'So what's happened to our furniture?'

Léon stepped around the beer puddle and pointed into the gloom. 'Sofa,' he said, indicating the torn leather on the changing room bench. 'And many cupboard,' he continued, patting the clothes lockers.

I quite liked this game. 'It's a bit gloomy in our house. Shall I open the shutters?' I went to the window.

'No! It bedtime. *Bonne nuit, petite Lulu!*' Léon whispered.

I knew where this was going now. I took a deep breath, wondering what being kissed was going to feel like. I was worried it might be slobbery and disgusting. But Léon was very gentle, stroking my cheek first, and then very lightly kissing me on the lips. It wasn't horrible at all. In fact I liked it. I liked him. He was sweet and funny and he seemed to like me quite a lot.

We leaned against the wall and he kissed me more, pulling me really close. I thought I wouldn't know what to do, which way to turn my head, but it seemed so easy and natural now it was happening. It felt so good, so very good. Nina hadn't told me it would feel so lovely.

'*Ma petite Lulu*,' Léon whispered, lifting my hair and kissing the nape of my neck.

He was trembling, which made me like him even more. It clearly meant just as much to him too.

'*Voulez-vous coucher avec moi?*' he murmured.

I didn't know what *coucher* meant. It wasn't a verb we'd been taught at school. Perhaps it meant *cuddle*? I didn't know how to respond. He started pulling at my clothes. I wasn't so sure now about what he was doing.

'Léon?' I said doubtfully, but he was so absorbed I wasn't sure he had heard me. It was starting to hurt now. 'Léon, don't!'

He gave a great sigh and then collapsed against me. I waited to see what he was going to do next.

'Léon, are you all right?' I asked, worried now.

'*Oui, oui. Et vous?*' he muttered.

'Well. I suppose. Don't do that again, though,' I said, adjusting my clothes.

I wasn't sure exactly what had happened. It was all over so quickly. We couldn't have actually *done it*, could we, the huge forbidden thing that Nina was always talking about? Had Léon actually been *inside* me? Surely it couldn't count if it was just for two seconds?

I heard children calling to each other outside, playing some kind of game.

'Quick, hide!' one shouted.

'Someone might come in! We have to go!' I hissed urgently.

Léon seemed just as anxious as me. We both made for the door and rushed out into the blinding sunshine. Thank goodness the children were running in the opposite direction. I peered round, scared that someone might still be watching and guess what we had been doing. I felt hot shame all over me now. What if anyone ever found out?

I looked at Léon, who looked as hot and sweaty and furtive as I felt. I couldn't bear it.

'I have to go now,' I said, and started running.

'Lulu!' he called after me.

'My name's not Lulu,' I said, running faster.

I kept looking over my shoulder, scared he might pursue me, but he just stood there looking bewildered. I felt bad that he was in the middle of a strange park and he probably didn't have a clue how to get back to the Lido, but I couldn't help it.

I ran and ran and ran though I had to stop every now and then to gasp for breath. It seemed to take hours. When I reached the shopping parade I slowed down at last, trying to walk as if I didn't have a care in the world. Mrs Bun waved at me from behind her window and I made my arm wave back, grinning at her in a sickly manner.

Our neighbour Mrs Smithson was lumbering down her path as I turned in our gate.

'Hello, young Laura,' she said, wincing as she took each step. Her bare legs were swollen and purple and she'd had to cut holes in her sandals to accommodate her bunions. 'This weather doesn't half give me gyp,' she said. She was looking at me. 'You look a bit hot and bothered too!'

'Yes, I wish it would cool down,' I gabbled, struggling to find my door key, desperate to get indoors.

'What have you been up to then?' she asked.

I knew she meant it in a general way, and probably wasn't even very interested, but my heart started thumping inside the tight bodice of my dress.

'Just swimming,' I said, and managed to find the key at last.

'Up at the Lido? Oh, I used to have a grand time there when I was your age,' she said.

I murmured something vague and got inside my own door at last. It was stiflingly hot inside the house – Mum always shut the windows tight for security though we had nothing to interest any burglar. It smelled stuffy too, of lavender floor polish and the sickly air freshener Mum put in the toilet.

I hurried to the bathroom and ran myself a bath. The immersion heater wasn't on but I didn't care. I wanted the water to be as cold as possible. It was a shock getting in, and far worse when I lay down with the icy water lapping round my ears, but I lay there as long as I could, my heart pounding. Then I sat up and soaped myself, scrubbing hard. I was shivering so much when I clambered out that it was hard work towelling myself dry.

I washed out my knickers and swimming cossie, then went into my bedroom and put on clean underwear and another old frock and a cardigan too. It was still stiflingly hot in the house but I couldn't stop shivering. I made myself a cup of tea and gulped it down immediately, scalding my throat. I helped myself to a custard cream from the tin, and then another and another, munching fast until I had a sickly goo of biscuit coating my teeth, but I couldn't stop until the packet was finished.

It was still a good two hours before Mum was due home. I didn't know what to do with myself. I tried to read a few pages of *Madame Bovary* but I couldn't concentrate. I did some colouring instead, sitting on the chair and leaning hard against the edge of the table until my chest hurt. I had a special historical colouring book with people in intricate costumes. The hardest section was the Elizabethan one, because the women wore elaborate crinolines studded with hundreds of jewels and I could never get my crayons sharp enough to tackle them. But I tried desperately hard now, feeling that if I could only colour in a whole page without going over the lines once then somehow the whole memory of today would be erased.

I was still colouring when Mum came home looking tired out, dark circles under her eyes.

'Oh my Lord, this heat!' she said, flopping down onto the sofa. 'Good heavens, Laura, why are you wearing your winter cardi? Are you still feeling rotten, pet?'

'I just felt a bit shivery, that's all,' I mumbled, studding a crinoline with tiny rubies.

Mum heaved herself up again and felt my forehead.

'Yet you're burning! I think you might have a temperature now! What have you been doing?'

'Nothing! Well, I went to the Lido with Nina actually, but I came home early,' I said, selecting an orangey-red for the Elizabethan lady's hair. She looked regal, as if she might be the queen herself.

'You shouldn't go somewhere like that Lido by yourself!' said Mum, fetching the thermometer from the big chocolate box in the sideboard where she kept our medical supplies: the Elastoplast and aspirin and the Kwells and the Ex-Lax and the Fisherman's Friends.

'I wasn't by myself – I *said*, I was with Nina,' I insisted, but Mum thrust the thermometer into my mouth so I couldn't talk any more.

'Let's have a look at your face,' said Mum, pushing my hair back. 'It's bright red! I think you've got sunstroke. No wonder, if you've been lounging around at that Lido. You didn't go in swimming, did you? Not with those stomach cramps you had this morning.' She sounded suspicious now.

'Of course I did,' I mumbled. 'You know I get the cramps before, well, my monthly begins. And swimming helps . . .'

'Don't try and talk or you'll get a mouthful of mercury, you numpty!' Mum fussed. 'I don't like you swimming there, not in the holidays when it gets crowded. I don't think the water's chlorinated enough. You get little kids going to the toilet in the water! And those diving boards are a dreadful hazard. There'll be a terrible accident one day! Don't you dare go there again!'

There had already been a terrible accident. A strange French boy had jumped on top of me and walked me back to the park and we'd done terribly embarrassing things together in the cricket changing rooms and now I was so worried I wanted to die.

'All right, I won't go back there,' I said.

'That's right!' Mum said, looking surprised that I wasn't putting up more of a fight. 'So what have you been up to now?' She peered over my shoulder. 'Oh, you've done that very nicely! Quite the little artist, aren't you?'

I started putting my crayons back in their box, neatly in shade order.

'It's all right, you can carry on with your colouring if you want. I don't have to set the table just yet,' said Mum.

'I've finished for now. I'll lay the table for you, Mum. You look a bit tired. I'll make you a cup of tea,' I offered.

'You're a good girl, Laura,' said Mum, as I'd hoped. I so wanted to be Mummy's little good girl now, instead of the bad girl who flirted with strange boys and let them fumble with her in the dark.

'Perhaps you'd like to invite Nina round here tomorrow so you could do some colouring together? I could put on a good tea for you?' Mum offered.

As if Nina would want to do something as childish as colouring! I didn't want Nina round here. It was all her fault I'd ended up with Léon. She'd been horrible to me. I was a fool to let her treat me like that just because I was so desperate to keep her as my friend. I didn't really want her as a friend now. I decided I didn't care less if I never saw her again.

Even so, I waited for her to ring the next morning as soon as Mum and Dad were out at work. The phone stayed silent. I kept going to look at it, several times lifting the receiver from its cradle to make sure there was still a dialling tone. I'd given up and got all my crayons out again when it rang, making me jump. A slash of orangey-red jerked across my Elizabethan lady's face, as if she'd just been slashed with a knife and was bleeding to death.

I sighed and went to answer the phone.

'Where *are* you?' said Nina.

'Where do you think I am?' I said impatiently.

'Why haven't you come round? I've been waiting and waiting,' said Nina.

'I'm busy,' I said.

'What? Don't be so daft. Listen, we're planning a picnic up Blackwood Hill,' she said.

'You and Yves?' I said.

'Are you crazy? He was such a poser. No, me and Daniel and Little Richard. Jimmy was going to come but he can't make it. We thought *you'd* want to come. Still, if you don't want to . . .'

'I do. I'll just finish something and then I'll be round in half an hour, say?' I said.

'See you then. If we haven't left already,' said Nina and put the phone down.

I knew she was just winding me up now but I was out of the prefab in five minutes, leaving my crayons all over the table. I was wearing a pink and white check long-sleeved shirt and my blue jeans, clothes that covered up as much of me as possible. My hair was a bit of a mess still from swimming yesterday so I'd hurriedly tied it up in a ponytail. I peered at my reflection in the shop windows along the parade. I looked reassuringly myself again.

I'd quickly manipulated a florin out of my piggy bank, expertly wiggling it out with a knife. I went into the baker's shop and bought four jam and cream doughnuts.

'Oh my! You'll be sick if you try and eat them all yourself!' said Mrs Bun.

'No, I'm going on a picnic with my friends,' I said proudly.

'Well, have a lovely time, dear,' she said.

I so hoped I would. I knew Nina was only joking when she said they might go without me if I wasn't at their house quickly enough. Or was she? I couldn't trust her any more. I couldn't even trust myself.

I scurried along, trying hard not to let the doughnuts jiggle around too much in their paper bag. The door to Nina's house was open when I got there. Little Richard was sitting on the doorstep. He jumped up and charged towards me.

'She's here!' he yelled. 'Now we can go on the picnic!' He threw his arms round me. 'I do *like* you, Laura!'

I was so touched I nearly burst into tears.

'I like you too, Little Richard,' I said, hugging him back. The doughnuts shifted in their bag. 'Whoops! We're getting the cakes all squished,' I said, gently wriggling out of our embrace.

'Cakes? What sort of cakes?' Little Richard asked, his eyes gleaming.

'Doughnuts. The long kind with cream. Nina likes them. Do you like them too?' I asked anxiously.

'I totally adore them,' said Little Richard.

'So do I!' Daniel was in the doorway. He looked even browner in his white T-shirt and khaki shorts. 'Hey, Laura. Have you had a good summer so far?'

'Great,' I said, and it *was* great now. Even Nina acted pleased to see me.

'Are there cakes in that bag?' She had a peep. 'I hoped you'd bring some! Mum's made us some bread pudding, which is OK, but a bit boring. No jam, no cream, no sugary bits!'

'And we've got egg and tomato sandwiches and cheese rolls and apples and Twiglets and orange juice!' said Little Richard. 'And I'm helping Daniel carry the picnic, aren't I, Dan?'

'If you're very good, you can carry all of it if you like,' said Daniel, winking at me.

Little Richard took him seriously and looked anxious. 'I'm not sure I'm quite strong enough to carry *all* of it,' he said.

'Then I'll carry you *and* the picnic,' said Daniel, lifting him up onto his shoulders and galloping down the hall with him. Little Richard clung to his hair, squealing with delight.

'Brothers!' said Nina, rolling her eyes. 'So, how did you get on with that Léon bloke? I saw you go off with him when you came out the changing hut. He looked a bit gormless if you ask me, but maybe that was because he couldn't speak English.'

I swallowed, not sure what to say.

'Come on! Did he get the trolley with you? You did have enough money on you, didn't you? I felt a bit bad about that,' said Nina. This was clearly meant as an apology.

'We walked,' I said.

'What, hand in hand?' Nina teased.

'Some of the time,' I mumbled.

'Really! Hey, did he *kiss* you?' she demanded.

'Did Yves kiss you?' I asked quickly.

'Maybe,' said Nina. Then she sighed. 'No, if you must know, he went and started diving again, showing off, and then this girl went up on the diving boards too. Peroxide blonde with a great figure and a very tight swimming costume. She couldn't dive for toffee, practically belly flopped – it was just a pathetic ploy to get Yves interested in her.'

'And was he? Interested?' I asked.

'Well, he went off with her, didn't he, so I was left all on my tod. Charming!'

'Oh, poor Nina!' I said.

'I wasn't really that into him anyway. Anyway . . . Léon? Tell me all about it!' said Nina.

I glanced at Daniel and Little Richard, who were still larking around, probably in earshot. Nina looked too and pulled me into the kitchen. The picnic was set out on the table, wrapped in separate tinfoil parcels. She started packing them in two duffel bags, presumably the big one for Daniel and the small one for Little Richard.

'We won't let him carry the doughnuts. He'll fish one out and eat it before we even get to the forest,' she said. She put her head close to mine. '*Did* Léon kiss you?'

I screwed up my face. 'Yes.'

'And did you like it?'

'No. Well, I suppose at first I did,' I said honestly.

'It can't have been a real film-star kiss in broad daylight out on the street,' said Nina.

'Well, we weren't. We went in the cricket changing hut in the park,' I said, feeling my cheeks burning.

'What? *Laura!* I never thought you of all people would neck with a strange boy in a hut!' Nina gasped.

'Shut up! The boys might hear!' I said, panicking.

'It was just kissing, wasn't it? You didn't go any further? You didn't get to number three or four, did you?' Nina whispered.

The girls at school all had an elaborate numerical system to show what they'd done with a boy. It saved the embarrassment of spelling it out. Up until yesterday I hadn't even got to number one.

A few of the girls had gone as far as seven or eight. No one had got to ten, the last forbidden number, not even Nina.

'Laura, please. Tell me! I'm your best friend, aren't I?' said Nina.

'Yes, but I don't want to talk about it,' I mumbled.

I *couldn't* talk about it, because I wasn't sure how far I *had* gone. Could *I* have got to number ten without actually realizing it? I could spell things out to Nina and she might know, but I wasn't a total fool. She wasn't the sort of girl you could trust with a terrible secret. She would swear on her life she wouldn't tell anyone, but I remembered some of the secrets she'd confided about Patsy and some of her other friends. She wouldn't be able to resist it. She'd spread it all round the school the first week we went back.

I took a deep breath. 'He tried to go a bit further, but I wouldn't let him. I didn't even like him that much,' I said. At least the second sentence was true.

'Oh well. Never mind. At least you've had your first proper kiss,' said Nina.

I wished I hadn't. Thinking about it now made me feel queasy. I found I was wiping my lips hard on the back of my hand, as if I wanted to scrub them clean. I shut my eyes.

I'm not going to think about it any more. It didn't even happen. It was just a silly dream. I walked home from the Lido by myself.

'Laura?'

I opened my eyes.

'What's the matter?' Nina looked concerned.

'Nothing.'

'Your face was all screwed up like you were in pain.'

'Oh. It was just a tummy cramp. You know, it's the first day of my period today,' I lied.

'Poor you. Would you sooner stay at home then?' Nina asked.

'No, it's fine. Don't say anything to the boys!' I said.

'As if!' said Nina. She gave me an unexpected hug. 'But whisper to me if it's really bad and we'll go home together, OK?'

'Sure,' I said, hugging her back.

The four of us set off for Blackwood Hill, Daniel and Little Richard bearing their duffel bags manfully. It was already very hot, the sun so bright we had to squint, though Nina had sunglasses. She looked glamorous and mysterious in them, much older than me. But Daniel wasn't remotely in awe of her. When she started going on about her romance in France he yawned noisily.

'Do pipe down about that twit Pierre. I can't stand him,' he said.

'Yeah, because he just happened to beat you at tennis three times in a row!' said Nina.

'Only because he sees some special tennis coach. Can *you* play tennis, Laura?' Daniel asked.

I shook my head. 'I'm not really into sporty things,' I said. There *was* tennis at school, but all the girls who chose it seemed to know how to play already, so I'd always picked rounders instead.

'Actually, tennis can be quite good fun. I could teach you a bit if you like,' Daniel offered. 'You could come to our club.'

I was thrilled, but alarmed. I knew the Bertrams were all members of Lakeside Tennis Club. It was very posh and alarmingly expensive to join. I didn't have any white clothes or tennis shoes or my own racquet so I didn't see how I could possibly play.

'You could come as our guest and borrow Nina's racquet and some of her tennis gear,' said Daniel, as if he could read my mind.

'Well. Maybe,' I said.

'Great,' said Daniel, as if it was all decided.

I glanced anxiously at Nina, wondering if she'd mind. 'Is that OK?' I asked her.

She shrugged. 'Sure. If you want.'

I did want! I felt a surge of pure joy. This was what I liked most of all, being with all the Bertrams and feeling part of their family.

We stopped for a rest before we tackled the long steep chalk path up to the top of Blackwood Hill. We all had a few gulps of orange juice but saved the rest for when we got to the top. Nina wouldn't let Little Richard take even one bite of doughnut. Little Richard stuck his tongue out at her, behind her back.

'Nina's no fun any more,' he said. 'I wish *you* were my sister, Laura.'

'I wish I was too,' I murmured.

I was boiling hot myself when we got to the top, and worried I might have damp marks under my arms, but it was still glorious to be out of the wood and up at the summit, looking out for miles and miles.

'Here at last!' said Daniel. 'Nosh time now.'

'Hurray, hurray! Can I eat my doughnut first?' Little Richard said, jumping up and down with sudden energy.

Nina was delving in the big duffel bag and spreading out the food. Little Richard grabbed the smaller bag and extracted the doughnuts joyfully. Daniel looked at me and gave my hand a squeeze.

'Thanks for cheering him along, Laura. You're so good with him,' he said.

'It's OK. I like him,' I said. *I like you too, Daniel*, I thought. *I like you so much.*

I wondered what Nina would think if she saw we were effectively holding hands. It was so different being with Daniel to being with Léon. *No, I wasn't going to think about him ever again. He didn't exist.*

'Come on, let's have some grub,' said Daniel.

The picnic was splendid, but the doughnuts were voted the best part.

'Manna from heaven,' said Daniel, munching enthusiastically.

'Yummy scrumptious delicious,' said Little Richard, running his tongue up and down the cream.

'Perfect,' said Nina, delicately licking sugar off her fingers.

I gazed out over the fields and cottages to the misty blue hills. I felt so light with happiness I felt I could leap off the ground and fly up into the cloudless sky. The sun was very hot and I felt my face burning. Nina had lain down to sunbathe, stretched right out with her skirt fanning the grass and her toes carefully pointed – but after five minutes she sat up again.

'I'm getting fried to death,' she said. 'Let's find some shade.'

We went back into the woods and Daniel supervised Little Richard while he climbed an ancient oak tree and scrambled inside the hollow trunk.

'I love this old tree,' said Little Richard. 'Is it really old, Daniel? From before I was born and Mum and Dad were born and Granny and Grandpa and—'

'Shut up! Yes, oak trees are very old,' said Nina. She hitched herself onto a low branch and sat swinging her legs. 'The oldest trees ever.'

'Not as old as yew trees. They're the oldest trees of all,' said Daniel. 'Let's get you out, Little Richard, and we'll go and find some. That's why this is called Blackwood Hill.'

'Are yews black then?' I asked.

'No, they're green, but they're deadly poisonous, so they're called the death-tree,' said Daniel.

'Really? You know so much, Daniel,' I said.

'For God's sake, stop gushing, Laura,' said Nina. 'Daniel

knows zilch. He just mugs things up in books. I can't see why on earth you've got such a crush on him.'

'I haven't!' I said, feeling a fool.

'Oh, please do have!' said Daniel. 'Stop being a cow, Nina. Of course I read a lot of books. That's where all information comes from.'

'Are yews really deadly poisonous?' Little Richard asked, awed. 'Let's go and find them!'

'Right,' said Daniel, reaching into the hollow and pulling Little Richard out.

'So you can lick them like you licked your doughnut and then we'll watch you screaming in agony with the poison,' said Nina.

'You're such a tender big sister,' said Daniel. Little Richard was looking disconcerted. Daniel ruffled his hair. 'She's just teasing,' he said.

'I wouldn't lick *trees*,' said Little Richard.

'Of course not. You're not a baby,' said Daniel.

I wanted to say I thought he was a wonderful older brother, but I knew it would make Nina groan.

'Come on then,' she said impatiently. 'Where are all these poisonous trees?'

We found a circle of them deeper into the wood, their branches spreading as if they were reaching out to each other. Their trunks were gnarled and knotted, contorted over the centuries, yet there were young shoots spurting here and there.

'Each tree looks like it's got dozens of little ones too,' I said.

'It regenerates. It can do it all by itself. That's why they last so long. People reckon they can live a thousand years or more,' said Daniel.

We looked at them with awe, even Nina. She held out her slim brown arms.

'Imagine all the little Ninas bursting out of my own skin,' she said.

'Terrifying to think there could be any more of you,' said Daniel. 'One's more than enough, eh, Laura?'

I laughed uncertainly. I knew it wouldn't be wise to gang up on Nina, but it was a heady feeling having Daniel on my side.

I wandered round the outside of the yews, and then squeezed into their inner circle.

'What is it called, that thing witches do? You know, when they walk round seven times anti-clockwise to make a spell. Widdy something?'

'They *widdle*? Charming!' said Nina, and Little Richard shook with laughter.

'Widdershuns,' said Daniel. 'That's what it's called. Do you want to give it a go? Come on, you lot.' He stepped inside the circle too, gesturing to Little Richard.

'The branches might touch us,' he said, shaking his head.

'That won't hurt us,' said Daniel. 'Look.' He put his arms as far as he could round one of the trunks.

'Don't!' Little Richard cried, and ran to him, trying to pull his hands away.

'It's OK, little buddy, truly. People make things out of yew wood. Just don't *eat* any of the tree. Come on, we'll make a spell. Shall we make warts grow on the end of Nina's nose? Or turn her into a witch?' Daniel wondered.

'She's a witch already,' I muttered.

Nina looked strangely pleased. 'Of course I'm a witch,' she said, stepping into the inner circle too. 'Beware! *My* magic spell will be ultra-powerful.'

She led the way, skipping gracefully as if she were doing a dance. We followed her, counting when we'd completed each circle. It began to get a bit tedious after three circles.

'I'm a bit bored now,' said Little Richard. 'I don't think I want to do this any more. And I don't really know *how* to make a wish.'

'Eye of newt and toe of frog,' said Nina. 'Boiled up with all sorts of other manky bits of creatures in a cauldron. That's the way *I* make my secret spells.'

'Seriously?' asked Little Richard. 'You have to cut up little animals?'

'No, that's just in *Macbeth*,' I said. We'd been taken to the Old Vic on a school trip last year and sat on the punishingly hard benches up in the gods. I hadn't been Nina's friend then. She'd been larking around with Patsy and her other friends. I'd sat on the end of a bench by myself.

'Just wish for something,' I said.

'Like what?'

'Well, you could wish you had the power to conjure doughnuts out of thin air whenever you get peckish,' I suggested.

'Oh, that would be a brilliant spell!' said Little Richard. 'Will it really come true?'

'Definitely,' said Nina, snorting.

'Don't get your hopes up, pal,' said Daniel. 'Still, I don't think my spell is going to work either.'

'What's that going to be?' I asked.

'Not telling,' said Daniel.

'I can guess,' said Nina.

I wondered if his wish could have anything to do with me.

'You're fussing about next year and whether you can get into Cambridge,' said Nina.

'So?' said Daniel, blushing. She was obviously right.

'You're moving to Cambridge?' I said, devastated. 'What, all of you?'

'Not us, dummy. Daniel wants to go to King's, like Dad,' said Nina.

It still didn't make much sense.

'King's is one of the colleges at Cambridge University. And I'm not sure I'll make it, even if all three witches in *Macbeth* cast spells on the A-level examining board,' said Daniel. 'And I've got to take a special Entrance and Scholarship exam at Christmas.'

'Do you want to go to Cambridge too, Nina?' I asked.

She shrugged. 'I'd like to act in Footlights – but I think I'd sooner go to RADA.'

They both seemed to be talking in code.

'Don't be so *dim*, Laura,' said Nina, yawning. 'Footlights is an acting club at Cambridge, but I want to go to the Royal Academy of Dramatic Art.'

'How do you know about all this?' I asked, as we carried on circling. Little Richard was skipping ahead now, spurred on by thoughts of magic doughnuts.

Nina shrugged. 'I don't know. Mum and Dad, I suppose. When we talk about our futures.'

I supposed Mum had talked about my future when I'd passed the eleven-plus. She hoped I'd be able to do a secretarial course and get an office job. *I* didn't hope that at all.

'So what will your spell be then, Nina? Which future will you choose?' I asked her.

'I'm not going to waste a spell on my future. Why would I need to anyway?' she said.

She was speaking the truth. She was top of our class and she was brilliant at acting. She didn't need any magic spell.

'Don't be so unbelievably arrogant, Nina,' said Daniel, giving her a shove.

'So what *are* you going to wish for?' I asked.

Nina smiled. 'Aha! That would be telling,' she said, though she probably simply couldn't make up her mind. She loved being mysterious.

'What about you, Laura?' said Daniel.

'I'm not telling either,' I said, though I knew.

When we'd finished the seventh circle at last, we all closed our eyes and wished silently. Little Richard shut his eyes and blew his cheeks out with effort to make his doughnut spell come true. Nina simply stood still, gazing up to the top of the tallest yew. Daniel rolled his eyes, pretending not to take it seriously now, but I saw his lips moving. I kept mine shut and my eyes open but my whole being was wishing, *Please let me be part of the Bertram family for ever!*

The ancient magic of the yews seemed to seep into me. I felt their sap running in my veins like blood. It was as if the spell was truly working. When we came out of the wood into the bright sunlight again, I felt as if I'd been reborn.

*

109

I still felt so very happy that evening over supper. It was spam fritters and chips. Mum was generally too tired to cook anything elaborate when she got home from work.

'Whatever's got into you tonight, Laura?' Mum asked. 'Why do you keep on grinning?'

'I don't know. I'm just happy. We had such fun today,' I said.

'Yet you seemed so down only yesterday. We couldn't get a word out of you,' said Mum.

'Well, I was just feeling a bit fed up, that's all,' I mumbled.

'We can't keep up with you nowadays. You're so moody! You never used to be like this,' Mum said.

'For goodness' sake, Mother, don't nag the child because she's happy!' said Dad, covering his chips with brown sauce.

'I wish you'd stop calling me "Mother". I'm not *your* mother! And do you have to shake half a bottle of sauce on those chips? It's so common,' said Mum.

'Why are you so put out, eh? Just because our Laura's had a lovely day up at Blackwood Hill!' Dad asked, deliberately giving his chips another dollop.

'Don't be silly! Though I can't understand why she liked it so much. We walked all the way up there once and it was a bit of a disappointment. There's nothing there, not even a refreshment hut, so we couldn't give the kiddie an ice cream, and there were no facilities! I remember I had a tummy ache all the way home,' said Mum.

'Well, you should have peed behind a bush like everyone else,' said Dad.

I laughed, though I knew it would irritate Mum more.

'William! Language!' said Mum. 'I just don't see why Laura suddenly thinks it's the most marvellous place in the world, when she sulked last time because she had to go without a choc ice.'

'I was only a little girl then,' I protested.

'And you're still a little girl now, even though you think you're all grown up. I'm not happy about you roaming around with those young Bertrams all the time. Why on earth didn't Mrs Bertram go to keep an eye on you?' Mum asked.

'She's *Doctor* Bertram and she works at this clinic, you know she does,' I said. 'We don't need looking after. Daniel's seventeen, for God's sake!'

'Don't blaspheme!' said Mum.

'As if you care! We don't ever go to church,' I said. 'I don't see why you're making such a fuss about everything. I thought you *liked* me being friends with Nina.'

'She seems a nice enough girl, though she's a bit of a madam. But I don't see why you want to see her every wretched day. *And* her entire family,' said Mum. She stood up and went to the kitchen to make our Instant Whip for pudding, though she had barely touched her main course.

'What's up with her?' I said to Dad. 'She always fussed about having to leave me on my own in the holidays and yet now I've got friends to go round with she's fussing even more. I can't win. She's gone barmy!'

'Now now, don't talk about your mother like that. I shouldn't have been so tactless, winding her up like that. She's going through a bit of a funny time. It's because of her age. We have to make allowances for her,' said Dad.

It seemed like I'd been making allowances for Mum all my life.

'Nina's mum must be around the same age and yet *she* doesn't make a huge song and dance about everything,' I muttered.

'Hey, hey, none of that! Can't you see that's half the trouble? She thinks you'd sooner have this Mrs Bertram, Doctor, whatever, as your mother. She worries you want to be one of them,' said Dad.

I was shocked that Dad of all people had worked it out. Dad never seemed to take much notice of Mum or me. He ate his meals, read his paper, watched the television, dozed in his armchair. He might ask us if we'd had a good day, but didn't really properly listen if we said yes or no. He never seemed to give me a second thought, and yet now he knew exactly what was going on inside my head.

'That's not true,' I lied.

'Of course it is. And it's only natural. But it upsets her all the same. She's worried you'll start looking down on us,' said Dad.

'That's nonsense!' I insisted, but perhaps he was right about that too.

'Anyway. Cut your mother a bit of slack. Don't go on and on about your lovely times with the Bertram family,' said Dad.

'All right. I won't,' I said, as Mum came in with the pudding.

'Oh yum yum, strawberry, my favourite!' I said.

Mum gave me a sharp look. 'Are you being sarky?' she said.

'No! I love Instant Whip,' I said, which was true enough. I offered to do the washing-up just so I could have a good scrape round the blue plastic serving bowl.

I didn't say another word about the Bertrams for the rest of the evening. I sat watching Arthur Askey on the television with Mum and Dad and I laughed when they did, but I wasn't really taking anything in. I was going over the magic day in my head. We still had a week and a half of summer holiday left.

I hoped we might go to Blackwood Hill again the next day, or at least have another picnic. I phoned Nina up the next morning, after I'd winkled more coins out of my piggy bank.

'Shall I bring some more doughnuts?' I asked eagerly.

'What?' she said, as if it was the most outlandish suggestion. 'Why?'

'Well, because everyone likes them,' I said. I swallowed. We clearly weren't going on another picnic. 'I wanted Little Richard to think his spell was working.'

'Oh. Yeah. Right. Well, Little Richard isn't around today. It's his friend's birthday and they're going on some kind of outing,' said Nina, yawning. 'What time is it? You got me out of bed, you know.'

'Sorry! So are we going on an outing too?'

'I haven't really thought what we're doing yet,' said Nina.

I didn't know if she was meaning her and me, her and Daniel and me – or just Daniel and her. I knew she was just playing games with me. I shouldn't let her get away with it. I took a deep breath.

'OK then. Bye,' I said, and put the phone down quickly.

I hoped she'd ring me back immediately. But she didn't. I waited, agonized, until half an hour had gone by.

'All right then, see if I care,' I said to the silent phone.

I picked up *Madame Bovary*. I was halfway through now, because I hadn't been able to sleep properly for two nights. I knew what happened at the end. I hadn't been able to resist peeping. I was horrified. All the books I'd read so far had happy endings. Poor Emma Bovary's ending was the worst ever.

In spite of my hurt feelings I found myself getting so absorbed in the book that I jumped when the phone rang. My heart started thumping. *Don't be such an idiot – it'll just be a wrong number*, I told myself. But it was Nina.

'Hi you,' she said. 'Right, it's all settled. We're going to see *The Nun's Story* at the Granada.'

I hated the way she calmly carried on our interrupted conversation. Why did she want to go to the pictures on such a sunny day? Why not another picnic? Why not a game of tennis for that matter? Daniel had suggested I come to their tennis club. He'd never want to go and see a woman's film about a nun, not in a million years.

But I actually wanted to go and see it. I'd read about it in Mum's *Picturegoer*. It was meant to be very moving and dramatic, and Audrey Hepburn was beautiful, even in a nun's veil and habit. And I wanted to see Nina too, though I despised myself for going along with her little games.

'So, shall I meet you outside the Granada this afternoon?' I asked.

'Well, you *could*. But don't you want to have lunch together first? There's the Black and White Milk Bar opposite. It's a bit of a dive but they do nice chips,' said Nina. 'See you there half twelve?'

She rang off without waiting to see if I'd say yes. I very much wanted to go to the Black and White. A '*bit of a dive*'! Mum had taken me there for a treat once, though she was horrified that they charged five shillings and sixpence for a plate of sausage, beans and chips. They *were* very good chips though, crisp and golden and very fluffy inside.

I had to tackle my piggy bank again, scraping its insides until there was just one solitary coin left so at least it could still rattle. Then I changed clothes. I'd been wearing my shorts and a V-necked T-shirt and white socks and plimsolls, a suitable outfit for another trek, but they made me look childish. I thought *The Nun's Story* was probably an X-rated film. I'd need to look sixteen.

My stomach lurched, remembering Léon and the Lido, but I thumped my head fiercely, trying to knock all thoughts of that day into oblivion. I caught sight of myself in my bedroom mirror. I looked like a crazy person. A crazy much-too-young person.

I took my shorts off and put on a flared cotton skirt. I rolled each sock up and stuffed them carefully into my bra cup so it looked as if I had a proper chest. I didn't have any unladdered nylons so I went bare-legged, putting on my one and only pair of grown-up shoes, though the heels were barely an inch high and very stubby.

Then I thought about make-up. I had a pale pink lipstick that hardly showed, nothing else. Mum said I was too young for full make-up. Perhaps she thought she was too young herself, because she hardly ever wore any. I went into her bedroom and peered in the drawer of her dressing table. She had some loose powder with a giant powder puff, a Christmas gift from Aunt Susannah, but only used once. I tried applying the powder on my own face but had to brush most of it off because I looked as if I'd tipped a flour bag over my head.

I opened a little floral bag and discovered a rouge compact and some blue eyeshadow. I applied a little of each, but my face looked like a china doll now, so I rubbed most of that away too. There was also a small tin of mascara with a brush. It was very dried up, so I had to use a bit of spit, and then carefully applied it to my eyelashes, being careful not to smudge. That seemed more effective.

I peered at my face critically, practising expressions. I tried to look knowing, like Nina, but couldn't manage to make my eyebrows tilt in the right way. I attempted a flirty sideways glance, fluttering my newly defined eyelashes, but I could see I looked ridiculous. I gave a sigh, brushed my hair hard until it crackled, and then read some more *Madame Bovary*, glancing at my watch every five minutes until it was at last time to set off for the town.

My shoes were biting my feet by the time I got to the Black and White Milk Bar, and I was walking with a limp. I knew I was getting a blister on either foot. I crouched down to examine the little red weals and nearly toppled over when Nina pounced on me.

'What on earth are you doing?' Nina said.

'Nothing! Just getting a stone out of my shoe,' I said, feeling silly.

I looked enviously at Nina's soft footwear, those French canvas shoes with soles made of rope. She looked marvellous in a navy shirtwaister belted tightly, showing off her curves. She didn't need to use any socks as padding. I prayed mine would stay tightly tucked inside my bra. I'd die if one worked its way up and started poking through my V-neck.

'Hey there, Laura!' Daniel looked incredible, in a glowing white T-shirt and fawn khakis. He wore espadrilles too, fawn to match his trousers.

'Hey, Daniel,' I mumbled, trying to sound cool.

Nina was staring at me. 'Why are you wearing all that make-up when we're only going to the cinema?' she demanded.

I blushed like a fool, making my rouge totally redundant.

'I always wear make-up,' I said.

'No you don't! It looks a bit weird,' said Nina.

'No, it doesn't. I think you look great, Laura,' said Daniel.

I knew he was only being kind, but I was thrilled. I smiled at him, hoping I hadn't got lipstick on my teeth.

'Will you two stop gurning at each other?' said Nina. 'Let's go and eat. I didn't bother with breakfast and I'm starving.'

I spent ages reading the laminated menu when we were sitting down in a booth, but decided on sausage, beans and chips again. Daniel chose that too.

Nina barely glanced at the menu. 'I'll have a cherryade and a Knickerbocker Glory, please,' she said to the waitress.

I stared at her. Were we having puddings too? And what a pudding! I'd seen pictures of Knickerbocker Glories – glamorous film stars were often photographed tucking into a towering glass of ice cream, generally licking the cherry on the top. But weren't they desperately expensive? I knew exactly how many coins I had in my purse and they weren't enough. I still had to pay to get into the cinema. I'd have to pretend I wasn't hungry and see if the waitress would let me just have a glass of water with my meal.

'What about your main course, miss?' the waitress asked Nina. She looked only a couple of years older than us, if that. She was wearing a frumpy black frock with a white apron, and a tiny white cap on her head like a frilly Alice band. I wondered what she felt about wearing that waitress uniform and calling girls like Nina 'miss'.

'No main course, thank you,' said Nina. 'I'll steal their chips if I fancy something savoury.'

The waitress shrugged her shoulders and walked off. She was wearing black shoes a little too big for her, so they slipped every time she took a step. I thought her feet must be hurting as much as mine. I surreptitiously slipped both my shoes off under the table. The relief was incredible.

'Don't think you're having any of *my* chips,' Daniel told Nina.

'Or mine,' I said.

'Well, you two aren't getting any ice cream, even if you beg,' said Nina.

I felt like begging when she was served. It was even bigger than I'd imagined, the fluted glass reaching right up to Nina's chin. There seemed to be three types of ice cream, vanilla, strawberry and chocolate, with slices of peach, and an enormous whirl of cream with the cherry on top.

'Yum!' said Nina complacently, picking up her long spoon and tucking in.

The sausages, beans and chips were OK, but ordinary. I couldn't help watching Nina eat. She was enjoying herself, licking her lips, even rolling her eyes.

Daniel laughed at her. 'Stop acting like an idiot, Nina.'

She stuck out her pink tongue. 'You're just envious, wishing you'd thought of ordering one,' she said.

'Not me,' said Daniel cheerily.

'Yes you are. And Laura's positively drooling,' said Nina.

Daniel looked at me. 'Would you like one too, Laura?'

'Oh, no thank you. I'm not hungry enough for pudding. I mean, dessert.' I wasn't sure which was the right word.

'Tell you what, let's share one, you and me,' said Daniel. 'It's my treat. I went car-washing up and down our road on Sunday and earned a fortune. Go on, say yes.'

He ordered another Knickerbocker Glory and two spoons, while Nina had a frothy coffee, a little put out. It was so strange sharing with Daniel, taking it in turns. I took tiny spoonfuls at first, but he told me off.

'Tuck in properly! And you can have the glacé cherry – I don't like them,' he said.

He manoeuvred most of the cream to my side of the glass too. I ate and ate and ate. I was truly full now, but the sweet soft ice creams easily slipped down my throat.

'This is utter bliss,' I said.

'It's a big ice cream, that's all,' said Nina. 'Come on, you two greedy guts, we'll miss the start of the programme.'

It was agony slipping my feet back into my shoes. They seemed to have risen like dough in the hot cafe. I wondered if I was going to have to go to the cinema barefoot with my shoes in my hand, but at last I managed to cram them on my feet. It was torture walking across the road, but I strode out determinedly, feeling like the little mermaid in the fairy story. It was worth the pain to be with Daniel – and Nina too, of course.

He insisted on paying for the cinema tickets as well as our meal. Nina took it for granted, but I was fervently grateful.

'I told you, I'm really flush at the moment. Don't worry, Laura.'

I hoped I might get to sit in the middle, but I ended up beside Nina, at the end of a row. It was a disappointment, but I decided it was maybe just as well, as I was starting to feel a little sick from all the ice cream. At least I'd be able to make a dash for the Ladies room if necessary without disturbing anyone.

I felt unpleasantly queasy throughout the black and white film, a silly detective story, and not much better during the Pathé

News, but when *The Nun's Story* began I became so absorbed in the film I forgot all about my lurching tummy. Audrey Hepburn was so beautiful – even *more* beautiful in her nun's habit, her little elfin face so pure, her eyes enormous and long-lashed. She led such an extraordinary life in the convent. It was so hard and harsh, worse than the strictest school ever, and yet it was somehow glorious too. My heart started thumping. I suddenly desperately wanted to be a nun too.

I felt it would be marvellous to embrace Jesus and live in a House of God. I wanted to lead a simple life with no messy problems. I wouldn't have to worry about wearing the right clothes and making friends and kissing boys. I'd wear the same traditional outfit every day and I'd be friends with all the sister nuns. There wouldn't be any boys, especially not French ones who fumbled with me in the dark.

I supposed I would be sad to say goodbye to Mum and Dad, but we seemed to get on each other's nerves nowadays. I would miss Nina, but when I was a nun I'd shun her as a bad influence. I would miss Daniel too, especially now he seemed to like me, but perhaps we could spend one beautiful day alone together before I went into the convent. When we parted he might kiss me gently on the lips and tell me no other girl would mean so much to him. Then we would wave a sorrowful goodbye and it would be bitter-sweet and splendid.

I was so caught up in this dual romance, with Audrey on the screen and with Daniel in my head, that I cried a little, and had to mop my eyes quickly when the lights went up at the end of the film. I was worried that Nina would mock, but she seemed surprisingly moved herself.

'That was so wonderful,' she said, stretching. 'Do you know, I rather think I'd like to be a nun myself.'

I frowned at her. This was *my* fantasy! Now if I said anything about wanting to be a nun she'd just think I was copying her.

Daniel laughed. 'You're a scream, Nina! You, a nun! You'd be thrown out of the convent the first week for corrupting all the others.'

'No I wouldn't. I'd learn all my prayers and chants and what-have-you quick as a wink, and I'd sing so beautifully in chapel that Mother Superior would fall in love with me and promote me to head nun within weeks,' said Nina, punching him.

'I thought pride is meant to be a sin,' I said. 'Not to mention personal vanity.'

I got punched too, right in my solar plexus. When we went home – the Bertrams' home, not mine – Daniel suddenly burst into the living room wearing a white tea towel on his head.

'*I* want to be a nun too!' he declared. 'Don't you think I'd make a beautiful Sister Daniella?'

We were having so much fun that I actually dared say, 'See you both tomorrow?' when I left.

'Of course,' said Daniel.

'No you're not,' said Nina.

I thought she was just playing silly games again, but Daniel thumped his head with the palm of his hand.

'Sorry, Laura, I forgot. Dad's got a couple of days off, and we're playing golf,' he said.

'Oh. Well. Never mind,' I said lamely. I couldn't hide my disappointment.

Nina frowned when I looked at her. 'And I'm tied up too, not that you seem interested,' she said sharply. 'Though I daresay Little Richard might want to play with you if you bribe him with doughnuts.'

'Don't be such a cow, Nina,' said Daniel. He smiled at me apologetically. 'How about Saturday? We'll go to the tennis club, OK?'

'Yes, that would be great,' I said. 'Bye then. Bye, Nina.'

She didn't bother replying. I pretended not to notice. I walked back to Shanty Town with the word *Saturday* spinning round and round in my head like a broken record.

Mum was already back from work, making a shepherd's pie in the kitchen. The prefab was thick with the meaty smell of it. Our whole home was as hot as the oven.

'Shepherd's pie when it's eighty degrees outside?' I said, blowing out my lips dramatically.

'It's your father's favourite. He likes a hot meal when he gets home. You know he has to make do with sandwiches for lunch,' Mum said reproachfully. She got up early every morning and made them for him: one round of corned beef, one round of fish paste, packed in an Oxo tin, their strong flavours mingling, plus a thermos of almost black tea.

'Well, I don't want any, thanks. I had a big lunch out,' I said without thinking.

'What do you mean? The Bertrams took you out for lunch?'

Mum said, opening a tin of peas clumsily and catching her finger on the jagged top.

'It was just Daniel and Nina and me,' I said.

'So where did you go?'

I shrugged elaborately. 'Just a cafe,' I said.

'Which one?' Mum demanded, sucking her finger.

'For goodness' sake, does it matter?' I said.

'Don't take that tone with me! And of course it matters! I'm not having you hanging out in some unhygienic greasy spoon, picking up germs,' said Mum.

'Well, you're being unhygienic bleeding all over the peas!' I said. 'And it was the Black and White Milk Bar, if you must know.'

'You went *there*?' said Mum. 'What, just for one of those frothy coffees? They're a total waste of money if you ask me. And where's the sustenance in that? You should have had a proper meal!'

'I did!' I said, and carried on recklessly. 'I had sausage, beans and chips *and* a Knickerbocker Glory.'

'You never!' said Mum.

'Well, half of one. I shared it with Daniel,' I said.

'You never!' Mum repeated, literally at a loss for further words.

'So what?' I said boldly.

Mum's words came back in a torrent. 'How on earth could you afford to eat yourself silly at the Black and White? They paid for you, didn't they, those Bertrams! How can you shame me like that? They'll think your own family can't afford to feed you. And you mustn't ever share food from the same dish, especially in a restaurant. It's far too intimate, even if you're courting. Which you're absolutely not, even though you're standing there like the cat's got the cream. You're still a little girl for all your showing off. You're waiting till you leave school before you start on boyfriends – and there's no point setting your cap at someone like that Daniel Bertram. He might want to play around with you and get your hopes up, but that sort would never want a girl like you.'

'He's taking me to his tennis club on Saturday,' I blurted out defiantly.

'Oh no he's not!' said Mum.

'Yes he *is*,' I insisted.

'You can't play tennis,' said Mum.

'Daniel's giving me a lesson,' I said. 'I've got my white Aertex blouse and my shorts so I'll be properly kitted out too. And Nina or Daniel will lend me one of their old racquets. It's all sorted.'

'Well you'll jolly well have to unsort it, because you won't even be here,' said Mum, running her bleeding finger under the tap. 'You're going on holiday, so there!'

'Don't be daft, Mum! On *holiday*? What are you on about now?' I said, sighing.

'Don't you *dare* talk to me in that stuck-up manner!' said Mum, and she seized hold of me by the shoulders and shook me hard.

I was stunned. I jerked away from her, brushing at my blouse. 'You've made me all wet! And there's a smear of blood, look!' I said shakily.

'Well, I'm the one who'll have to soak it in cold water, not you. You never dream of giving me a hand with the washing even though I'm out at work and you're just mooning about with the blooming Bertrams. Anyway, we're going on holiday on Saturday. It's all fixed.'

'But how can we? We can't afford it – and you and Dad have got to work,' I said.

'There's been a last-minute cancellation on the Coast and Castles trip around Wales, so two seats are empty. Dad's boss says we can have them for nothing, you and me. They're not best pleased at Wallis Modes that I haven't given them proper notice, but I haven't taken any leave all the time I've been working there. And your dad and I thought it would be a lovely treat for you to have a proper holiday,' said Mum.

She had tears in her eyes. She dabbed them with the hankie up her sleeve, and then wrapped it round her finger. The cold tap was still running, water spattering into the sink. I turned it off, my hand shaking.

'I'm not going,' I said.

'Don't be so silly. Of course you're going!' said Mum.

'I'm not.'

'Oh yes you are!'

We were beginning to sound like a pantomime. I'd have burst out laughing, only I was near tears too. How could they do this to me? And making out it would be a lovely treat for me! A coach trip with my mum and dad and most likely twenty old-age pensioners! They just wanted to stop me having a wonderful time with the Bertrams. I wouldn't be able to play tennis with Daniel after he'd promised he'd take me to the club on Saturday. There would be no more chances of trips to the Granada or picnics on Blackwood Hill in the last week before school started.

'I'm *not* going and you can't make me!' I shouted. Then I ran to my room, threw myself on the bed and sobbed.

I was small and thin but I was still too big to be picked up bodily and stuffed into the coach on Saturday morning. I wasn't a little girl any more, no matter what Mum said. They really couldn't make me do anything any more. I just had to stand firm and show them.

But of course I couldn't.

Dad came home from work and sat on the end of my bed. 'What's all this then, Laura? Mother's desperately upset. Come and say sorry and then we'll all have tea,' he said gruffly.

'I'm not sorry,' I mumbled into my pillow.

'Well, you jolly well should be! We've arranged this little trip as a lovely surprise and this is the thanks we get!' said Dad. 'Now stop this nonsense and come in the kitchen. Mother's dishing up. We don't want to upset her any more by letting it get cold. It's shepherd's pie!'

'I don't want any wretched shepherd's pie,' I said. 'And I don't want to go on a coach trip to Wales, thank you very much!'

'I'd have got a thick ear if I'd talked back to my parents like that,' said Dad. 'You deserve a good slap, you ungrateful little baggage.'

I stayed in my room while Mum and Dad presumably had their shepherd's pie supper. I didn't care. The smell of it was making me feel sick.

I thought Mum might come with a plate of bread and butter and a glass of milk later on. She always acted as if I'd die of starvation if I missed a single meal. But she stayed away. I decided I didn't care, but I was thirsty after all that crying, and starting to get really hungry now. I got undressed properly and climbed into bed, but I was too het up to go to sleep. I distracted myself with *Madame Bovary*. I felt as despairing as she was, but when I read the last few horrific chapters I resolved that if I ever wanted to kill myself I would never choose arsenic.

My light was still on when Mum and Dad went to bed, but they didn't come in to say goodnight to me. Dad sometimes didn't bother, but Mum came to tuck the sheet and blanket round my neck and give me a pat on the shoulder every single night. I didn't *want* her to come in, I might even have yelled at her to go away, but it felt very strange even so.

I couldn't get to sleep for a long time after I'd put the light off. Then I nodded off and had a weird dream. I was in the dark somewhere, maybe even that awful cricket hut, but it was *Daniel* who was kissing me, and this time it was beautiful. I woke up, my heart thudding.

Then I heard someone moving around furtively in the kitchen. It was still pitch dark. I peered at my *Lady and the Tramp* alarm clock. It was half past three. I slid out of bed and pattered towards the kitchen, wondering what on earth was going on. Could we have burglars? Should I yell for Dad?

I pushed the kitchen door open. Mum was standing there in her nightie, a chiffon scarf round her curlers. She was drinking a glass of water and jumped so violently that half of it spilled down her front.

'Oh, for heaven's sake, Laura, you gave me such a fright!' she gasped, dabbing at her chest with a tea towel.

'You gave *me* a fright! I thought you were a burglar,' I said.

'As if we've got anything worth burgling,' said Mum bitterly. She rubbed at her eyes. 'I'm going to make a cup of tea. Do you want one?'

'All right,' I said. She looked terrible, her eyes red, with purple smudges underneath. 'You sit down, I'll make it,' I offered.

She looked surprised but sat down at the kitchen table obediently. I *did* help out in the house. I might not help with the washing, mostly because Mum said I was useless at scrubbing Dad's collars and didn't wring the clothes out properly, but I took my turn with the ironing, sometimes. And the carpet sweeper. Not often, but none of the other girls at school seemed to have to do any housework. Nina certainly didn't, but then the Bertrams sent their washing to the laundry and had a cleaner come once a week.

'Well, put the kettle on then!' said Mum.

I did as I was told and made a pot of tea. I put it on the table to brew, found two cups and saucers, and fetched the milk from the larder. There didn't seem much point pouring it into a jug.

'Fetch the biscuit tin too. You must be starving hungry, going without your supper like that,' said Mum.

There were bourbon biscuits in the tin, my favourite. I nibbled the top half of one until I got to the chocolate cream and started licking it.

'Do you have to eat it like that?' said Mum, sighing, but it sounded as if she were telling me off out of habit, not because she really cared.

'Sorry,' I mumbled. I meant to sound ambivalent. She could take it that I was just apologizing for my table manners.

Mum poured the tea and then reached out and patted my hand. 'I'm sorry too,' she said.

We said nothing more for a few minutes, just sipping tea.

'I couldn't sleep,' Mum said unnecessarily.

'I took ages to get to sleep myself,' I said. I noticed Mum had Elastoplast wadded all round her finger. 'Did you cut it deeply?'

'Oh, it's nothing. Fingers always bleed a lot when you cut them,' said Mum. She wiggled it. 'See, it's fine.'

'Remember when you knitted me finger puppets when I was little,' I said. 'Red Riding Hood and the Wicked Wolf. I loved playing with them. What happened to them?'

'I don't know. I probably threw them out when you lost interest in them,' said Mum.

'That's a shame. I really liked them,' I said.

'Yes, but you're not little any more, are you? As you keep pointing out,' said Mum.

'Oh, Mum. Do you wish I still *was* little?' I asked.

'Well, you never talked back to me then. You were a dear little thing, no trouble at all. But now, since you palled up with that Nina . . .' Mum's voice tailed away.

'Do you wish I hadn't then?'

'It's no use wishing this, wishing that. You've changed so, Laura. *You* wish you were one of those blooming Bertrams,' said Mum.

'No I don't,' I said, blushing.

'Your dad and I knew it was hard for you when they were off on their grand holiday abroad and you were stuck at home. We

133

thought you'd love the chance of an unexpected holiday yourself, especially as it's the Welsh castles tour. You're so keen on castles!'

'Oh, Mum, that was just when I did my castle project in standard four at primary school!' I said. I wasn't remotely interested in old castles now, but Mum looked so sad and worn out I couldn't tell her that. 'Still, I suppose castles are OK,' I said.

'And there's the coast part. Wales has got some lovely beaches – and we're having a wonderful heatwave this summer. It will do us all good to lie back and do a bit of sunbathing,' said Mum.

I imagined sitting in a deckchair between Mum and Dad with scores of old people burning their knobbly knees bright red and felt more depressed than ever, but I forced a weak smile on my face.

'I'd like to get a suntan,' I said. 'Nina's as brown as a berry. And Daniel and Little Richard.'

'He's not that little, is he?' said Mum. 'Laura, this Daniel – you've not really got a crush on him, have you?'

'Oh, Mum, of course not,' I lied. 'He's just my friend.'

'Well, as long as that's all it is. I'm sorry you'll miss going to play tennis but there'll be other opportunities if you're really that keen. And I daresay we'll be able to kit you out with a proper pair of white plimsolls so you don't let us down at this posh tennis club,' said Mum, draining her cup of tea.

'Maybe,' I said.

Mum yawned. 'We'd better try to get some sleep or we'll be exhausted in the morning. Up those little stairs to Bedfordshire, eh?' She used to say that to me when I was little, and I was always baffled because we didn't *have* any stairs.

'Night, Mum,' I said.

'Night, pet,' she said. She didn't give me a hug goodnight but she pouted her lips and made a little kissing sound. I did the same, a little embarrassed, and went to bed. I felt relieved that Mum and I were friends again, though I still wished with all my heart that she and Dad hadn't fixed up this wretched 'holiday'. I thought of missing the chance of having one more precious week with Nina. With all the Bertrams. And Daniel. And Daniel. And Daniel.

The details of my dream were already fading. I tried putting my arms around myself under my bedclothes but it didn't feel the same at all. I imagined it, straining to hear Daniel's voice whispering to me in the dark as he held me close. I fell asleep and didn't wake up until Mum came into my room with a breakfast tray, as if I was an invalid.

'It's twenty past eight, Laura, so I'm off to work. I thought I'd let you sleep in as you were up in the night,' she said, putting the tray of tea and cornflakes by the side of my bed.

She'd been up in the night too, longer than me, but she was washed and neatly dressed in her black shop frock with a freshly powdered face, though the dark rings under her eyes still showed.

'Do you feel OK, Mum?' I asked, reaching for my cup of tea.

'Of course I do,' she said, a little huffily. Her eyes went to my dressing-table mirror, and she fluffed up her hair and pinched her pale cheeks. 'There! Right, I'll be back usual time. You be a good girl. Don't get up to any mischief.'

She waited until she was at my bedroom door, and then she said as casually as she could, 'Will you be seeing the Bertrams today? Nina and Daniel and the little one?'

'Richard. Little Richard, like the singer,' I said.

Mum looked blank. She'd heard of Cliff and Elvis but the rest of rock and roll had passed her by.

'Maybe. I don't know. Not Daniel, though. He's playing golf with his father,' I said.

'Golf, eh?' said Mum. She pulled a mocking face. 'What, in a tweed cap and plus fours?'

'Of course not,' I said, irritated, though I thought people playing golf looked a bit ridiculous too.

'Oh well. Anyway, I've left half a crown on the kitchen table, just in case you go out for lunch. You must pay your way. I'm not having them think we can't afford to feed you,' said Mum.

I knew she *couldn't* really afford it, and would have to skimp on her housekeeping money, but I didn't argue with her.

I ate my breakfast hurriedly and got ready to go out. Nina didn't phone. She was playing this game with me again. I made

136

myself wait until nearly eleven o'clock so that she couldn't possibly say I'd woken her up, and then I rang. No one replied. I tried again, on the hour, and then every hour after that.

Nina was either ignoring me deliberately or she was out. Without me. I wondered about going out for lunch by myself. I could afford a plate of chips and a milkshake at the Black and White Milk Bar. Yes, I'd go there, and maybe I'd chat to the waitress, and then I'd go off round the town, window shopping. I'd have a lovely time and prove to Nina once and for all that she couldn't mess me around.

I didn't go. I went out, but only down to the bakery, where I bought a Bath bun and a cream doughnut. I ate them quickly back at home. I couldn't help wondering whether the phone had rung while I was out. I dialled the Bertram house one more time, but there was still no answer.

I tried reading to distract myself, but all my own books seemed so simple and childish after *Madame Bovary*. I drew for ten minutes, trying to do a sketch of Daniel, but it didn't look anything like him and I tore it up. I started colouring a page of my Tudor colouring book, but the intricacies of those jewelled farthingales made my eyes blur and I kept going over the lines.

If only I had my own brother and sister, Billy and the first Laura. *We'd* go to the cinema and for walks up Blackwood Hill and swim at the Lido. No, I didn't want to think about the Lido ever again. Just thinking of that brilliant turquoise water made my stomach lurch. And I could never ever go back to the park because of the changing hut.

I actually smacked myself, the palm of my hand on my temple, because I'd been such a fool, and I started crying. I lay on my bed and had another weep, and then fell asleep. I didn't wake up until I heard Mum's footsteps walking up our path, back from work already.

I leaped up, rubbing my eyes, and running my fingers through my hair. 'Hello, Mum,' I said, as brightly as I could.

'Hello, dear. Have you had a good day?' she said, putting the kettle on. 'I see the money's gone. So you went out for lunch with Nina and her brothers then?'

'Yes,' I lied. I couldn't tell her the truth. It would make me look so stupid. I had a lot of change left over from the buns, but if I gave it to her she'd tell me off for not paying my way.

'And where did you go, eh?' Mum asked.

'Oh, round the town for a bit,' I said vaguely. 'And we played Monopoly back at their house.'

'That's nice,' said Mum, trying to sound enthusiastic. 'Well, I'm glad you had a lovely time. You know, as it's the last day you'll be seeing them for a while.'

'No it's not. There's tomorrow!' I said.

'Don't be silly, Laura. We've got to get ready for the holiday.

I've made an appointment at Etienne's to get my hair shampooed and set, and they'll fit you in for a haircut too. Then we've got a bit of clothes shopping to do. I need a new white cardigan – my old one's starting to go a bit yellowy – and you could do with a new swimsuit. I thought we'd go and buy you some white plimsolls too. They'll look nice and fresh on holiday and then you can wear them when you have these tennis lessons.'

'But the holidays will be over then!' I said.

'Well, whenever,' Mum said vaguely. 'Do you want a cuppa too? Then I'll get the supper on while you sort out your clothes for the holiday. I'll put anything that looks a bit grubby into soak after supper. Oh, it's exciting, isn't it! Going on holiday!'

I wondered if Mum was really thrilled or if she was acting for my benefit. I had the cup of tea with her, and even had a biscuit, though I was still full of buns. Then I shut the kitchen door on her and crept into the hall. I dialled the Bertrams' number for what seemed like the twentieth time – and someone answered. Mrs Bertram.

'Oh! Hello, Mrs Bertram. It's Laura here.'

'Sorry? Who's that?'

My heart started thudding. Didn't she really know who I was? But I'd kept my voice so low I was practically whispering, not wanting Mum to hear.

'It's *Laura*! Nina's friend,' I hissed.

'Ah, Laura, yes of course,' she said. 'I'll call Nina to the phone.'

But it was Little Richard who came to the phone first.

'Hello, Laura! Guess what, my team won at football and I scored three goals. Not one, not two, *three*! I'm going to be in the big boys' team now. They're all teasing me and calling me Little Stanley Matthews! Wait till Dad and Daniel hear! I bet *they've* never scored three goals in one match,' he said breathlessly, and then started on a detailed commentary of the match.

'Well done. That's brilliant,' I said, when I could eventually get a word in. 'So, is Daniel still out then?'

'Yes, playing boring old golf! I wish they'd jolly well hurry up and come home because I simply have to tell them my thrilling news,' said Little Richard. 'You're impressed, aren't you, Laura?'

'You bet I am,' I said. Someone else was talking to him in the background. 'So, is Nina there then?'

'Yes, she keeps nudging me, telling me to pass the phone over. But *we're* having a conversation, aren't we, Laura?' said Little Richard.

'Yes, we are. A lovely one. But I think I'd better have a word with Nina now, if that's OK?' I said.

'Right you are then,' said Little Richard.

'I gather he's been burbling on to you about his big triumph at kiddy football,' said Nina.

'He sounds very happy,' I said.

'He's absolutely fizzing with excitement,' said Nina, yawning.

'So, what have you been doing today? I'm pretty sure you weren't playing football,' I said, trying to be funny.

There was a little pause.

'Oh, I've just been mooching about,' Nina said casually.

'What, by yourself?' I asked.

'No, Patsy came round, if you must know. She wanted to show me her new puppy. It's totally adorable. We took it for a walk,' said Nina.

'But I thought you and Patsy were deadly enemies now!' I said.

'We've known each other since we were little tots. She gets on my nerves sometimes, but she's OK really,' said Nina.

'Oh.' I couldn't think of anything else to say.

'Don't sound so devastated!' said Nina. 'It's not like she's my best friend any more.'

There was a pause again. She was hoping I'd ask if *I* was still her best friend. I pressed my lips together, not wanting to beg her.

'Don't be like that,' said Nina. '*You're* still my best friend.'

She was playing such mean games with me. It was ridiculous too, as if we were in Infants, having a cry-baby argument one minute, and then wandering around arm in arm the next.

'So, what shall we do tomorrow? Shall we go to the Lido again, just you and me?' she said.

'No!'

'It's OK, we don't have to say anything to those French posers if we see them there,' said Nina.

'I never want to see them again!' I said.

'Well, just come round to my house and we'll hang out. Maybe do some baking? I can make a great banana cake. And a sponge. We could even find a doughnut recipe and try making our own – wouldn't that be fantastic?' she suggested.

'I'd love to, I really would, but I can't. That's the reason I'm ringing. I've got to do boring shopping with my mum tomorrow because we're going on holiday on Saturday,' I said.

'No you're not! You're just winding me up! You're not going anywhere on holiday,' said Nina. 'What's this, are you playing hard to get?' She sounded more amused than annoyed.

'I *am* going on holiday, truly. Mum and Dad just sprang it on me. I don't *want* to go,' I said, whispering now, just in case Mum could hear me from the kitchen.

'Where are they taking you then? To the seaside? Don't forget to take your bucket and spade,' said Nina, teasing now.

'We'll be at the coast some of the time. And in the country. All over Wales,' I said, sighing.

'Touring? But you haven't got a car!' said Nina.

'I know. We're going on a coach trip,' I said.

'A *coach* trip?' said Nina. Then the penny dropped. 'Oh my God, you're going on one of your dad's coach trips!'

'I know. Don't laugh,' I said.

'I'm not,' said Nina, but I could hear her snorting a little. 'Well, that's lovely for you.'

'Shut up. It will be awful. And it lasts a whole week. I won't get back till school starts,' I said miserably.

'Well, that's a bit rubbish,' said Nina. 'What am *I* going to do?'

'I'm so sorry, Nina. And can you tell Daniel I'm sorry too. I won't be able to play tennis on Saturday,' I said.

'You can't play tennis,' said Nina, an edge to her voice now.

'Yes, I know that, but Daniel said he'd teach me, remember?'

'Oh well, never mind,' said Nina dismissively. 'OK. Have a nice time. See you at school.'

'Nina, it's not my fault,' I started saying, but she'd put the phone down on me.

We set off really early on Saturday morning, carrying suitcases. Dad just had a light sports bag that he slung over his shoulder. He'd be wearing his uniform every day, so he only had to take clean shirts and underwear and pyjamas, with one open-necked casual shirt and a pair of flannels for an off-duty evening. He was also hauling along Mum's big case. She'd packed most of her wardrobe, even putting in her bulky mackintosh though it had hardly rained all summer long.

I had my holiday clothes in a big shopping bag and I'd stuffed my school satchel with a couple of my old Noel Streatfeilds and a lost property paperback of *Young Bess*, because I liked the idea of a Virgin Queen. I resolved to keep to myself as much as possible, reading all the time so I didn't have to make conversation. When my eyes got tired, maybe I could go off for long solitary walks in new white plimsolls. I insisted on wearing them without socks so I wouldn't look too childish, and I already had two red marks on my heels.

When we got to the Happy Holidays coach park all the other drivers were hanging about, having mugs of tea and buns and cigarettes. They greeted Dad warmly, larking around, telling him he wouldn't be able to get up to any hanky-panky with his missus and kiddie on board. Mum bristled a bit, but she could tell they didn't mean it seriously. They were very polite to her, offering her tea in a proper cup and saucer. They made a fuss of me too, calling me Tuppence and gently pulling my ponytail.

Dad seemed so different with them, laughing and joking. He had a cigarette too, though he didn't usually smoke – Mum didn't like the smell and said it lingered in the house. But at eight o'clock Dad straightened his cap and brushed his shoulders, ready for action. We all queued for the one lavatory – the men let Mum and me go first. I didn't really need to go but Mum insisted.

'It'll be several hours before the first stop. You need to go now!' she hissed.

'But isn't there a toilet at the back of the holiday coaches?' I asked.

'Yes, but you mustn't use it unless it's an emergency. They're horrible chemical things and you don't want to make the coach smell,' said Mum. 'We'll be sitting right at the back too. We can't bag the good front seats with the views because all the other passengers will think it's favouritism.'

'Oh God,' I murmured.

'Now then. Don't blaspheme. And take that look off your face. I'm not having you showing me up,' said Mum. 'We're going to have a lovely holiday, just you wait and see.'

I tried to believe her while we waited for the first passengers to start rolling up. I knew the majority would be elderly couples, but I hoped there might be a few families with children so I didn't stick out so horribly. Maybe a girl around my age? A small boy as funny as Little Richard? An older boy as kind and interesting as Daniel?

Then they started to arrive, loaded with cases, handing them over to Dad to stow in the luggage compartment at the side of the coach. They were all in their fifties or sixties. A few were really ancient, with walking sticks, and Dad had to give them a helping hand up into the coach. He was endlessly cheery with everyone, welcoming them with seemingly spontaneous patter, but after a while I could chant his little spiel backwards.

They mostly laughed along with him, glad he was so friendly, but two schoolmarm ladies were quite fierce with him and got tetchy when he wouldn't let them drag their cases up into the coach so they could keep an eye on them. They were put out that two other couples had already bagged the front seats and said we should start a rota so that everyone had a turn.

I kept my head down, reading *Young Bess*, not wanting to say hello to any of them, though Mum was nodding and smiling cravenly.

'Hello, dear,' said one of the schoolmarms, managing to make the word *dear* sound like an insult. 'That looks a good book.'

'She's a great reader, my Laura,' said Mum.

'What is it?' said the other old girl. 'A detective story?'

'It's a history book,' said Mum proudly.

'Hardly serious history!' said the first schoolmarm, peering at the title.

'Still, it's good if it gives her an interest in the Elizabethans,' said the other.

When they'd stopped paying us attention Mum dug me in the ribs. 'What were they on about?' she whispered. 'Isn't it suitable?'

'Of course it is,' I said.

'Well, I don't know, do I?' said Mum.

She read a lot herself, but mostly Mills and Boon romances.

I tried to read when the coach set off at last, twenty minutes late because a couple came scurrying up long after the allotted time, red in the face and perspiring, blurting out tales of missed buses.

'There's always one!' said the schoolmarm, and her companion tutted again.

Mum tutted too, because Dad was always complaining about the late-comers, hating his carefully planned schedule being disrupted.

I found *Young Bess* a surprisingly easy read and riveting right from the start. I wished I had the knack of flirting with eager courtiers but keeping them at arm's length. But I soon started to feel travel-sick, even though the story was engrossing, and after ten minutes I felt so awful I had to close the book and lean back with my eyes closed. Oh God, was I going to feel like this the entire holiday?

When we got to the first rest stop I could barely stagger off the coach. Dad helped everyone down the steps. He looked at my white sweaty face.

'Oh dear, feeling sick, buttercup?' he said in his professional cheery manner. He reached in his pocket and brought out a little packet of pills. 'Take a couple of these and you'll feel much better.'

'You can't give her drugs, William!' said Mum, horrified.

'They're just Kwells, travel-sickness pills. They work a treat. The driver's little friends. I don't want any puking on my coach!' said Dad.

I swallowed the pills with a cup of tea in the cafe. I'd have swallowed anything just to stop feeling so dreadful. And in ten minutes I felt normal again, and even fancied a currant slice with a second cup. Mum herded me to the toilets afterwards and started chatting to some of the other ladies. They talked about the luck of having such lovely weather, and how the itinerary seemed very promising.

'And the coach driver seems a lovely fellow, so helpful!' said one woman, and the others all nodded and agreed.

Mum glowed – and I felt proud of Dad too. But it was totally cringe-making when we drove across the border into Wales and Dad started warbling Welsh songs, 'Men of Harlech', even Shirley Bassey's 'Kiss Me, Honey Honey, Kiss Me' – but the whole coachful joined in, even the two schoolmarms.

'He's got them in the palm of his hand,' said Mum. 'He's a right card, your dad.'

I wondered if we were going to keep quiet all holiday that we were related to the 'right card', but we sat at his table that evening at dinner in our hotel.

'Isn't it grand?' said Mum. 'And we're staying here for nothing!'

I thought the thick white tablecloths and the potted plants in the corners of the dining room were grand too, but the food wasn't very nice: watery Brown Windsor soup, beef and carrots and lumpy mashed potato, with tinned fruit and custard for pudding. We had better meals for school dinners, but I knew Mum and Dad would be upset if I pointed this out.

When the meal was finished some of the coach party made a beeline for the bar next door. Mum and Dad were teetotal at home, apart from Christmas and the odd beer for Dad now and then. He looked apologetically at Mum. 'They'll expect me to go. It's part of the job, being the life and soul of the party,' he said. He lowered his voice. 'The more they like me the higher the tip at the end,' he murmured.

'Well, I don't like the idea of you going off drinking, especially with all these women on their own,' said Mum semi-seriously. Did she really think the two schoolmarms and the other grannies in their short-sleeved frocks showing off their flabby white arms would start flirting with Dad the minute her back was turned?

'Why don't you go with Dad?' I said quickly. 'I'll go up to the room and read. I'll be fine. I'd *like* that,' I said.

So Mum gave me the room key and I went up by myself. Mum and I had a double room at the front, with a glimpse of the distant mountains. Dad had a small single room right up in the attics. I wished they'd let me sleep up there, but it was the rules that the driver had this faraway room which no one knew about.

'It still doesn't seem right that you just have a little cupboard of a room when you're working so hard all day,' said Mum.

'It stops them forever knocking on my door because their water wasn't hot enough for their bath or wanting a blow-by-blow account of tomorrow's itinerary,' said Dad. He tapped his head. 'There's method in my madness.'

So I was stuck having to share a double bed with Mum. Still, I reckoned I had an hour or so with *Young Bess* by myself, so I got washed and undressed quickly, leaped into bed (the mattress sagged in the middle, but then so did mine at home) and started reading. The story got better and better and I kept looking at the time, hoping Mum wouldn't come back too soon. It got later, past my usual bedtime, and then later still. I was so tired now that my eyes kept blurring and my head nodded.

What on earth had happened to Mum? Could she still be in the bar? But she hated bars, saying the smell of drink and cigarettes turned her stomach. Had she and Dad gone for a walk? Mum had worn her high heels down to dinner – she surely couldn't walk for more than five minutes wearing them. Anyway it was dark outside and they didn't have a torch.

Perhaps she'd tripped in the dark? Or had Dad suddenly collapsed after using up all that energy being the life and soul of the party? I couldn't help getting worried, though I saw the funny side of it. I was like the parent, fretting because my children were late coming home.

Then at last, at quarter to eleven, I heard a tentative knock on my door. I shot out of bed and ran to see if it was some hotel staff person come to break the news that my parents had been in a terrible accident – but it was Mum herself, her hand raised to tap again. We both jumped.

'Mum! Why are you knocking?'

'I wasn't sure if this was the right door! I couldn't remember the exact number. I was terrified of walking in on a complete stranger!' Mum giggled. She walked in, swaying slightly, and then threw herself on the bed, letting out her breath in a huge whoosh. 'My goodness, what a day!' she said, kicking off her shoes. 'This is the life, eh, Laura?'

I stared at her. She was acting so oddly, seemingly unaware that it was so late. Could Mum possibly be a little bit drunk? It was so unlikely that I started giggling too, joining Mum on the bed.

'Have you been down in that bar all this time?' I asked.

'Well, I had to keep your dad company, didn't I?' Mum said. 'But I'm so tired now.' She nestled into her pillow. 'Don't think I'll bother with my rollers just this once,' she murmured. 'Night night, dear.'

'Mum! You can't go to sleep in your frock! Come on, I'll unzip you,' I said. 'You've had too much to drink, haven't you?'

'No, I haven't, you cheeky baggage!' said Mum, laughing merrily. 'You know I always stick to bitter lemon. Though someone bought me a port and lemon when they treated your dad to a beer. It would have been rude to refuse it, you see. And then it was our turn to treat the other couple – you've got to stand your round, and I suppose I had another little port, but I wasn't really *drinking* as such,' she protested.

She stood up to take her frock off and staggered a little. 'Whoops! I've gone a bit dizzy!' She clutched hold of me. 'Any port in a storm! Hey, I've made a joke! Any *port* in a storm – do you get it?'

'Oh, Mum! You're *really* drunk!' I said.

'I'm not, am I?' she said. 'Oh dear! And in front of my own daughter!' She looked suddenly anguished.

'Don't worry, Mum. It's funny. I *like* you like this,' I said, helping her undress. She was so much warmer and softer and sillier drunk, and I loved the way she was holding onto me.

'My little Laura!' she said, breathing port fumes into my face. 'I really think I need to go to sleep now.'

She climbed back on the bed without bothering to wash her make-up off, cream her face or do her hair. She didn't even bother with her nightie, staying in her nylon petticoat. She was asleep in seconds. And snoring too.

It was so astonishing that I couldn't stop giggling, but after a few minutes it started to get annoying. I hoped Mum hadn't made a complete fool of herself down in the bar. I wondered if Dad was in a similar state up in his attic, but I expect the 'life and soul of the party' was more used to drink. I was wide awake now and wanted to read some more of *Young Bess*, but when I switched my bedside lamp on again Mum told me to put out that light this instant. 'You'll wake people up!' she had the nerve to murmur.

I lay on the very edge of the bed and tried to imagine I was a future queen with all the boys flocking round me. It was unlikely to happen in real life. Daniel was so kind to me, but it was probably because I was Nina's friend. The only boy who had showed any interest in me was Léon, and I'm sure that was only because his friend had bagged Nina. Anyway, I wasn't going to think about him ever again. Thank goodness he had only been here on holiday so there wouldn't be any chance of bumping into him again.

Mum was up and washed and dressed by the time I woke up. She was even wearing make-up, a smudge of rouge on each cheek and a dark red lipstick, perhaps because she looked so pale.

'Come on, up you get, Laura. The breakfast gong will go in ten minutes,' she said.

'How do you feel, Mum?' I asked.

'Perfectly all right,' she said calmly.

'Didn't you have too much to drink last night?' I said.

'Don't be so silly!' said Mum. 'You know I don't drink. I had a bitter lemon just to be sociable, that's all.'

However, Dad looked at her anxiously when we went down to breakfast, though he didn't say anything. I saw her surreptitiously swallowing two aspirins when she had her cup of tea. She gave me two Kwells too.

'I don't really want them, Mum,' I protested. 'They make me feel so sleepy. I'm sure I'll be OK today.'

'Take them!' Mum repeated.

I was glad she'd insisted, because we went on a very narrow windy road up in the mountains. We were in our place on the left-hand side of the coach, and I had the window seat. When I looked out it seemed we were teetering right on the very edge. I couldn't help catching my breath. Some of the other passengers squealed.

'Soppy dates!' said Mum, though she was even paler now, her rouge standing out like the cheeks on a Dutch doll. 'There's no real danger, and your dad's a really steady driver.'

However, when we rounded a really tight bend Mum gripped my hand, and hers was as sweaty as mine. When we parked at the viewing place at the top someone shouted, 'Three cheers for the driver!' and Dad stood up and gave a funny little bow. The passengers all knew that I was his daughter now. Mum had been telling everyone our life story while they were in the bar last night. Now one of the more smiley ladies grinned at me.

'I bet you're proud of your dad, poppet!' she said.

'Yes, I suppose so,' I said awkwardly.

'I think it's lovely that you and your mother go on holiday with him, all of you together!' she said.

I didn't think it lovely at all, but it would seem churlish if I disagreed. I just nodded and wandered off, pretending I wanted to have a proper look at the view.

'Funny little thing!' I heard the lady say to her husband. 'She's so shy!'

I felt my cheeks burn. I didn't *want* to be shy. Inside I could be as fierce and rude and imperious as Nina. But as I stared across the green valley to further blue mountains beyond I calmed down. The breeze soothed my cheeks. It had been hot for so long that it felt wonderful to be in such cool, clean air. I breathed it in deeply, trying to imprint the view on my mind, watching a bird soar and feeling my spirits soar with it.

'Don't get so close to the edge, Laura! For heaven's sake, come here, you silly girl!' said Mum, grabbing the back of my dress and probably showing my pink knickers off to the whole coach party.

She got on my nerves all day long, nagging me about this and that, sometimes shaking her head at one of the other women and going 'Kids today!' in a world-weary fashion. I was so fed up and bored that I fell asleep on the coach, my head resting uncomfortably on the hot glass window, though Mum tried to get me to turn round and put my head on her shoulder.

I slept so long that I couldn't fall asleep that night in the next hotel.

The days passed, each one blurring into another. Even the castles seemed indistinguishable to me. They even all started with the same letter: Conway, Caernarvon, Criccieth, Cardiff. The two schoolmarms (they really *were* teachers at the same grammar school) seemed really excited by them all. They took notes if we had a guided tour and even attempted sketches in black biro.

Mum had told them that I was at a grammar school too, and they thawed towards me.

'Why don't you take notes too, Laura? You could do a special castle project,' History schoolmarm said brightly.

'I've already done one, at primary school,' I said.

'She made a lovely castle. It was on display on Parents' Evening,' said Mum.

'I'm talking about a proper project, not messing about with cardboard and plasticine,' said the schoolmarm briskly.

'Or maybe you could find a novel set in medieval times,' said English schoolmarm. 'You like reading, don't you? Why not give Dorothy Dunnet a try? There's a brilliant second-hand bookshop where we have our afternoon stop. I'm sure you'd find some of her novels there.'

I nodded weakly in acknowledgement, resolving to stay on the coach when we had the afternoon stop so she couldn't boss me into buying books I didn't want – but actually the big bookshop was a total delight. Dad stayed chatting to another coach driver in the car park – he wasn't keen on bookshops – but Mum and I went there. It was in an old converted fire station, with thousands of books on two floors. Mum went to look at the Romance section while I wandered upstairs and looked along the literature shelves.

There was a woman sitting comfortably on the bare-board floor with her legs stretched out, absorbed in a book. She was wearing a man's blue linen shirt and tight trews. They were teenage clothes and her blonde hair was tied up in a ponytail, but she seemed older, maybe in her twenties.

I cast a shadow over her as I browsed. She raised her head and blinked at me.

'Oh, sorry! Am I in the way? Are you looking for anything in particular?' she said. 'We've got a big children's section downstairs.'

She obviously worked here. It seemed a very pleasant kind of job. Maybe I could work in a second-hand bookshop too if I didn't make it as an actress?

'Actually, I only read adult novels nowadays,' I said. 'I've just finished *Madame Bovary*. You know, by Flaubert.'

I was trying to show off, but I wasn't sure how to pronounce his French surname. I tried 'Flough-bertte'. Her face didn't move a muscle but I could tell from her eyes I wasn't saying it correctly.

'Or however you pronounce it,' I mumbled.

'Have you really read *Madame Bovary*?' she said.

'I think it's the greatest book ever, but very sad,' I said.

She nodded. 'Absolutely! Well, I think we've got some other books by Flo-bear, but I don't think they're anywhere near as gripping.'

'Oh well,' I said.

'Do you know something? I think you might like this,' she said, handing me the book she was reading.

'*Selected Short Stories* by Katherine Mansfield,' I read. 'Oh, I'm not sure I like short stories. By the time you get into one it's almost finished. It's too much effort.'

'I know exactly what you mean,' she said. 'But these are very easy to read, honestly. The characters are all so real, especially the children. Try it.'

I looked at the pencilled price inside the front cover. It seemed alarmingly expensive, more than a brand-new book.

'It's a first edition, though it's a bit scruffy, and of course it hasn't got a dust wrapper,' she said. 'Still, I think we could reduce it.' She took a stub of pencil with a rubber on top out of her trews pocket and rubbed out the price. She substituted one that was half the amount and looked up at me quizzically.

'Is it *your* bookshop then?' I asked.

'No. I just work here. I like books – and I like the countryside. You should try walking up into the mountains. There are wild ponies!' she said.

'I'm only here for the afternoon, worst luck,' I said.

'That's a shame. Well, what do you think? Have you got enough pocket money for the revised price?'

'Not really,' I said. 'And Mum will probably think it's still much too much.'

As I spoke I heard Mum in the distance. She was calling, 'Laura! Laura! Laura!' like an agitated bird.

'That's her,' I said, sighing.

Then Mum came rushing up, very pink-cheeked, clutching a doctor-and-nurse romance in one hand. 'Laura, for goodness' *sake*! I've been looking for you all over the shop. We've got to be back at the coach in five minutes and you know how embarrassing it will be for your dad if we're late,' she said. Then she looked at the woman still sitting on the floor and the colour drained from her face. 'Susan!' she breathed.

'Oh my God! Kathleen!' she said. Then she looked at me. 'So you're *Laura*! Hey, I'm your aunty!'

'You're Aunt Susannah!' I said, delighted. She was a wonderful surprise. I could see now she looked a little like Mum, but her style was so different. She seemed an entirely different generation. She could almost have been Mum's daughter.

'Susannah!' said Mum, spitting out the word contemptuously. 'She's plain Susan and always will be. What on earth are you doing here? Did you follow Laura deliberately?'

'Mum! Aunt Susannah *works* here!' I said. 'She didn't even know who I was. She was being lovely to me, talking to me about books.'

'Working here, in a dusty old bookshop in Wales?' Mum said incredulously. 'What happened to the posh office job then? And the posh Managing Director?'

'Oh, Kathleen, for God's sake,' said Aunt Susannah, shaking her head. 'You haven't changed, have you? Don't you want to make friends after all this time?'

'No, I don't! And you keep away from Laura. I don't want you to have anything to do with her,' said Mum.

'She's my niece!'

'And I'm her mother and I'm doing my best to bring her up decently. You've got a nerve expecting anything different, especially after what you did to our *own* mother,' Mum hissed.

'Oh God, not that again! You're acting like I murdered her!' said Aunt Susannah. 'It was a blood clot that gave her a stroke – not me!'

'Brought on by the shock,' said Mum. She seized hold of me by the arm. 'Come away, Laura. We've got to get back to the coach!'

'But I want to talk to Aunt Susannah!' I said. I turned to her. 'I don't know what Mum's on about, and I don't care anyway. *I* want to be friends!'

'I wish we could be,' said Aunt Susannah. 'It was lovely meeting you, Laura. It's so cool that you like reading. You're a girl after my own heart.'

'No she's not! And I think she just reads these difficult books to show off half the time,' said Mum. She gave my arm a big wrench, almost pulling me off my feet. 'Come *on!*'

I looked helplessly at Aunt Susannah. *I'm sorry!* I mouthed at her. She just smiled sadly and shrugged. People book-browsing further along the shelves were staring, wondering what was going on. Mum gave a little groan of embarrassment and hustled me down the stairs and out of the shop.

'Why did you have to make such a scene, Mum?' I protested breathlessly as she hurried me along, still keeping a firm grip. 'Aunt Susannah – Aunt Susan, whatever – she's *nice*. Why can't we be friends with her? What has she *done*?'

'Never you mind,' said Mum. 'And don't say anything to your dad either. That woman's poison, even though she's my own sister.'

'Well, at least she's not a thief like you,' I said, as we got to the car park.

'What do you mean?' Mum panted.

'You've not paid for that book!' I said, pointing to her paperback romance.

Mum stared at it in her hand. 'Oh, good Lord!' she gasped. 'I'll have to go back!'

But Dad was standing at the front of the coach, his hands on his hips, scowling in our direction. We were obviously late.

Mum panicked. She put the book on top of the little wall round the car park. 'Perhaps someone will take it back to the shop for me,' she said. She rushed over to the coach. 'I'm so sorry,

162

William. It wasn't our fault. There was a bit of a disturbance in that big bookshop. But we're only a few minutes late, aren't we?'

Dad tutted at us. 'Keeping us all waiting,' he muttered, though if we'd been any other passengers he'd have laughed it off.

I begged Mum to tell me why she was still so angry with Aunt Susannah but she told me sharply to be quiet.

Neither of us could get to sleep that night. After a while I heard Mum making soft snuffling sounds. I thought she was snoring at first. Then when she reared up on one elbow and blew her nose on her hankie I realized she was crying.

'Oh, Mum,' I said, reaching out across the double bed to her. 'Don't be so upset. Is it because of Aunt Susan?' I didn't dare add the 'annah' part because it enraged her so.

'No!' Mum said, though it obviously was.

'Look, I'm really sorry if you can't stand her because of something she's done. But she hasn't done something to *me*, has she? And she is my actual aunt. Why can't I still be friends with her?'

'Because,' said Mum.

'Because what?' I asked, though I knew what she would answer.

'Because I say so.'

When we got back to the prefab late on Saturday night, all three of us disgruntled and exhausted, there was a slim package lying on the hall floor, along with several bills. It was addressed to me. Mum flinched when she saw the handwriting, but I snatched it from her before she could stop me.

It was the Katherine Mansfield book, and a postcard with a picture of wild ponies on a rugged mountain.

Dear Laura, I read.

It was a joy to meet you. You've changed so much since I last saw you! I hope you enjoy these stories. I like 'The Doll's House' best. Your mum and I shared a doll's house when we were kids, but it didn't have a real little lamp.

I hope we can be friends one day.

Love

Susannah xx

I felt sick on the first day of term. As soon as I spooned my breakfast cornflakes down I had to rush to the toilet and spray them all up again. Mum was hovering outside anxiously.

'What's the matter? Did you bolt the cornflakes too quickly? Have you got a pain?' she gabbled.

'I'm fine now. Don't fuss, Mum. I was just a little bit sick,' I said weakly.

'But you're hardly ever sick! We had fish pie last night – I wonder if that cod could have been off?' Mum said worriedly, feeling my forehead. 'Dear oh dear, you're perspiring!'

'Well, of course she'll be a bit sweaty if she's just been sick,' Dad called from the kitchen. He only had a Teatime Mystery Tour today, and that didn't start until two o'clock.

'I'd better take her temperature,' said Mum, running to the first aid box in the kitchen cupboard.

'Mum, I'm all *right*!' I said, but she stoppered my mouth with the thermometer.

'She's just a bit anxious, that's all, what with school starting. And she'll be worrying whether Nina's going to be her friend or not. She blows hot and cold, that one,' said Dad.

I could feel my cheeks burning.

'There!' said Dad, nodding triumphantly. 'You let that Nina run rings round you, Laura.'

'No I don't!' I protested, but I couldn't talk properly with the thermometer still in my mouth.

'Don't try and talk! If you bite into that thermometer you'll break the glass and swallow the mercury and it's deadly poison!' Mum said dramatically. She took it out of my mouth and peered at it closely. 'It's normal,' she said, almost sounding disappointed.

I'd never felt less normal in my life. I really was worried that Nina wouldn't be friends any more, even though it wasn't *my* fault I'd gone on the wretched coach holiday.

I couldn't help being worried about something else too, though I kept telling myself it wasn't possible, and I wasn't going to think about it. I had to put it right out of my mind. If the fear crept back I sang a song inside my head, any silly song, 'How Much is that Doggie in the Window?' or 'There's a Tiny House by a Tiny

Stream', or 'The Yellow Rose of Texas', faster and faster, until the dog with the waggy tail ran to the tiny stream and the Texas lady came out of the tiny house in her yellow dress and patted the puppy.

'Laura? Oh Lord, she looks all dazed. You'd better go back to bed. I'll have to be at the shop by quarter to nine. William, you look after Laura this morning, and then I'll see if I can get someone to cover me for this afternoon,' Mum gabbled. 'If she's sick again you'd better call the doctor.'

'Mum, for goodness' sake, I'm *fine*,' I said determinedly.

I kept on saying it as I hurried to school, walking to the words as if I were marching. I heard scurrying footsteps behind me. I turned and saw one of the red-haired Flannagan children from the prefab up the road. It was hard to tell them apart because there were so many of them, all scruffy and needing a good wash and mostly up to mischief. But this girl's red curls were recently brushed and subdued with many kirby grips, and her clothes looked brand new, though much too big for her – her blazer arms went right down to her fingertips and her school skirt brushed the top of her socks. She was so small I'd have thought she was only about nine, and yet she was wearing Grammar school uniform, though the skirt looked home-made and she was wearing a white T-shirt instead of the regulation blouse. She had a striped school tie but she hadn't knotted it properly.

'Are you at the Grammar now?' I asked.

She nodded proudly. 'I got a scholarship,' she said.

Just like me. I'd thought I'd been given my scholarship because I was top at my primary school and had done well in my eleven-plus – but now I wondered if it was simply because *I* was a poor kid from the prefabs too.

'So did I,' I said. I hadn't looked as lost and pathetic as this little girl when I started, had I? Mum had bought me the full proper uniform and had sent me off looking immaculate, but neither of us knew how to manage the correct knotting of the tie, and Dad had already left for the coach station. I'd been told off by my new form teacher and some of the girls had laughed at me.

'Shall I do your tie for you?' I offered.

'Yes please, Laura,' she said.

'How do you know my name?' I asked her.

'Everyone knows you. You're the posh girl from the prefab with the lily pond,' she said.

It was startling to find that I was thought posh round here.

'Well, everyone will think you're posh now as you've started at the Grammar,' I said. 'There! Now, you have your tie hanging shorter this side, and you bring the other end round and up and push it through and – there! Did you see how I did it?'

'Not really,' she said. 'Couldn't you do it for me every morning?'

She seemed to take it for granted that we'd be walking together daily now. I didn't really mind too much. She was quite sweet. She said her name was Moira and she was the third Flannagan child, but she was the one who had to mind the little ones because the older two were boys.

'That's not fair,' I said.

'I know, but that's life,' she said, sighing.

She was the only Flannagan who liked school.

'The boys are the worst. They keep bunking off until they get expelled. Mum's given up on them. Dad doesn't bother either. He says he was just as bad when he was young. I'm trying hard with my little brothers, teaching them to read and that, but they're too fidgety and they won't sit still. Ants in their pants, the lot of them,' said Moira, folding her arms in the giant blazer and shaking her head like an old woman.

'Never mind. Perhaps your own children will like school and work hard,' I suggested.

She looked at me as if I were mad. 'I'm not having any children,' she said. 'I'm not getting married. I'm going to live on my own in a flat, even if it's very little, and I'll keep it ever so neat and ever so clean. You don't want to get married, do you, Laura?'

'No, not particularly,' I said, though an image flashed inside my head. Me in a long white dress and lace veil looking radiant, looking up at a man with thick black hair and blue eyes. *Bertram* eyes. Oh God, I was just like one of the characters in Mum's tacky romances.

'You're blushing,' said Moira.

'No, I'm not, I'm simply hot, that's all. Come on, you don't want to be late for school your first day, do you?' I said.

'Will you sit next to me?' she asked, trotting beside me. She was very light on her feet because she was wearing plimsolls – she would get into trouble for them as we were all supposed to wear Clarks shoes: T-bar sandals in the summer and terrible clod-hopping lace-ups in the winter.

'I can't sit next to you, silly,' I said. 'I'm starting in the fourth year now. You're a first year.'

'But I won't know anyone,' she said, looking stricken.

'You'll soon make friends,' I said, though I knew that probably wasn't going to happen.

'I want *you* to be my friend,' Moira insisted.

'Well, I can still be your friend even though we're not in the same class. I'll look out for you at dinner time if you like,' I said, and then added, 'though I might be with my own friend, Nina.'

I wished I hadn't said that. It was as if I was tempting fate. Maybe Nina would be ignoring me completely, back best friends with Patsy. Though she *had* phoned me yesterday afternoon, asking if I'd enjoyed my coach trip with all the old darlings.

She was already in the classroom, chatting to Patsy, both of them perched on the same desk, their brown legs dangling. But Nina jumped off when she saw me and greeted me warmly, actually throwing her arms round me though she wasn't usually physically demonstrative.

'Hey you! Ye gods, you look positively normal! I thought you'd be wearing baggy trousers and wide-fit sandals after your coach trip experience!' she said.

'What's that you're saying, dearie? Speak up, I swallowed my deaf aid by accident,' I said, doing a daft old-lady imitation.

Patsy looked blank but Nina laughed and started up her own monologue about losing her false teeth and how she'd had to gum her way through the nice pork chop she'd bought for supper in her string shopping bag. Patsy giggled hysterically now and I saw how it was going to be, both of us vying for Nina's attention.

Our new form teacher was Mrs Morris, who had curly hair, a big bust like the prow of a ship, and milk-bottle legs that she planted firmly apart. You couldn't chat too much when she was talking because she was very strict, but you could risk passing a quick note when she was writing on the blackboard. I scribbled a message to Nina and passed it along to her. She grinned and wrote back, lobbing her note quickly in my direction. Then Patsy wrote to Nina and she wrote back. There was a whole flurry of notes, but Patsy and I didn't write once to each other.

We went to the cloakrooms together at break time and shared our snacks. I had a thin slice of Mum's jam sponge in a cellophane bag, Nina had a packet of raisins, and Patsy had a Turkish Delight.

It was in two sections and I thought she'd give one to Nina and keep one for herself, but she gave me a bite from each first. It tasted overly sweet, sickly, like Patsy herself.

We ate lunch together in the canteen, Patsy and I sitting either side of Nina. We were like the Three Marys in the *Bunty* comic. I saw Moira standing in the middle of the room, clutching her tray and looking bewildered, not knowing where to sit. I felt a pang, but there was no room on our table, and first years never sat with fourth years anyway. I concentrated on my mashed potato, and when I looked up Moira had vanished, swallowed up by the crowd.

When we were outside in the playground Nina linked arms with Patsy and me, and we walked round together, awkwardly joined. Nina talked the most, telling Patsy all about the different boys she'd met this summer. She mentioned our day at the Lido and I started prickling all over. She was making out she and that Yves had had some kind of grand romance.

'What about you, Laura? Didn't you get off with anyone?' Patsy asked.

'No!' I said hastily.

'Yes, you did!' said Nina. 'She went off with Yves' friend Léon, bold as anything, and then went all coy about what happened next.'

'Really!' said Patsy, giggling. 'I didn't think you even liked boys, Laura! So did he kiss you?'

'*No!*'

'Then why are you blushing?' she said.

'I'm not. I'm just hot,' I said lamely, fanning myself in a ridiculous manner.

I caught a glimpse of Moira shifting from foot to foot on the edge of a clump of first years. No one seemed to be taking any notice of her. I waved to her to give her some encouragement.

'Who are you waving at?' Nina asked.

'Just one of the first years. She looks so sad,' I mumbled.

'Which one? Oh, *I* see, the little redhead in the giant blazer?' said Nina.

'What does she *look* like?' said Patsy. 'Where do they *find* some of these kids? I bet she's from Shanty Town. She's probably got nits. Or worse.'

I burned all over. Nina looked at me. 'Poor little kid,' she said quickly, trying to smooth things over.

'Yes. She *is* poor, so that's why she looks a bit odd. And she's little, but she can hardly help that. And so what if she's from Shanty Town?' I said crossly, and hurried away from them.

'Laura!' Nina called. I heard her muttering to Patsy, who gave an embarrassed shriek.

I went up to Moira. 'Hey, Moira! How are you getting on?' I asked.

She looked at me so thankfully I could have cried. 'OK,' she muttered, though she looked anything but. The other girls stared, surprised that a fourth year was bothering to talk to her.

'Come over here,' I said, tugging at Moira's arm. Her wrist was as thin as a Twiglet and looked as if it would snap if I pulled any harder.

She came obediently, giving me a radiant smile. 'I told them you was my friend but they thought I was fibbing,' she said, giving a skip.

'Well, they know better now,' I said, feeling bad because I probably wouldn't have come over to her if Patsy hadn't been such a cow.

Nina had obviously told her where I lived now, and Patsy would likely spread it all round the class to get back at me. *See if I care*, I thought, though I did care, desperately. I took Moira to the little alcove behind the bike sheds where I used to hang out before I made any friends.

'This is my special hiding place when I want a bit of peace and quiet,' I said. 'It can be yours too if you like.'

'Oh, *thanks*, Laura!' she said, as if I'd said she could share my mansion.

I leaned against the brick wall and she did too. She seemed a little fidgety, still shifting her feet. 'What's up?' I asked.

'I want the toilet!' she said. 'But when I tried to get back in the school after me dinner this old bossy-boots said I had to stay out and play. I'm desperate!'

'Ah. We're supposed to go before we have lunch. To wash our hands,' I said.

'But I don't need to wash my hands – they're still clean as clean, I just want to wee!' said Moira.

'I'll take you,' I said. 'Come on.'

She trotted beside me eagerly, like a little puppy. It was Mrs Morris on playground duty, standing near the girls' entrance. I was worried now. She seemed so strict.

'Excuse me, Mrs Morris,' I said timidly.

'Ah! Laura?' she said. I was impressed she knew my name already. You could tell if the teachers cared about you or not by the speed with which they learned your name. Some of them still got you muddled up with someone else by the end of term.

'This is Moira, she's a first year, and she didn't realize you had to go to the toilets as soon as the bell goes. Could I possibly take her inside now and show her where to go?' I asked, using my poshest voice. I was good at it now.

Mrs Morris sighed, but she stood aside to let us into the school.

'Thank you so much,' I said.

'Thanks, miss,' Moira chirped, giving a little hop.

I took her to the toilets. She was delighted with them. 'They're so clean and shiny!' she said.

I couldn't help wondering what her own toilet at home was

like. 'So, the lessons this morning were OK?' I asked her. 'How did you get on in maths?'

'It was OK. I quite like sums and these were different new ones. But French is a bit weird. I can learn them words but I can't say them the proper way yet,' said Moira.

'Neither can I,' I said.

'And I haven't got the right clothes for PE' she went on. 'I just used to tuck me skirt into me pants before, but the PE lady says I have to have proper shorts. And she turned her nose up at my plimsolls! I'm supposed to have a different sort, would you believe!'

'Oh dear. They're so fussy here. As if it matters! Will your mum be able to get you some?'

'Oh yeah. And the proper school blouse and a satchel and a fountain pen and a party frock and a fur-trimmed coat and my own bedroom,' said Moira. I must have been looking at her pityingly because she grinned and said, 'That was a *joke.*'

'I might have some old school shorts at home. And some other stuff. You can have them if you want,' I said.

She threw her arms round me, though her hands were still soaking wet. 'You're the best friend ever,' she said.

It was so much easier being Moira's friend than it was being Nina's. I wondered if she was going to gang up with Patsy and laugh at me now because I came from Shanty Town. But though

Nina could be horribly mean, she wasn't actually a snob. At the start of afternoon lessons *she* gave *me* a hug.

'Sorry about Patsy and her big gob. She's sorry too, though she's too embarrassed to tell you,' Nina said.

Patsy didn't look particularly sorry, but she screwed her finger into her temple to indicate she'd been stupid to say that stuff about Shanty Town. We were an uneasy trio still, and Patsy and I both had to grin and bear it.

We were both invited back to Nina's house after school. Moira was waiting patiently for me at the school gate – the first years were let out ten minutes before us. I felt a pang when I saw her face light up.

'Oh dear, here's your little friend,' said Nina.

I took a deep breath. 'Sorry, Moira, I'm going round to my friend Nina's house today. You know the way home, don't you? And I'll look out for you tomorrow morning,' I said.

'Yes, OK,' she said, not making any fuss, but she drooped horribly.

'You can come round to my house too, if you like,' said Nina.

I wasn't sure if she really meant it. But Moira shook her head anyway. 'No thanks, got to get back,' she said, and ran off, her dirty duffel bag thumping on the back of her huge blazer.

I should have gone after her. But I wasn't *really* her friend. I'd only got talking to her that very morning. Nina was my actual friend, and if I didn't re-establish my friendship with her I'd be left with no one. Moira would pal up with other first years soon enough. I reasoned like that inside my head all the way to the Bertrams' house until I'd almost convinced myself.

Mrs Bertram gave me a warm welcome, pressing a chocolate brownie on me, and asking me all about my holiday. She was just as nice to Patsy, of course. Little Richard greeted me with a great whoop and started chatting at great speed, telling me all about his new roller skates.

I went outside with him so he could skate along the pavement and back.

'Watch this! And this! Look, one-footed!' Little Richard yelled and immediately keeled over.

I hurried to pick him up.

'Oh goodness, Little Richard, look at your knees!' I exclaimed.

'It doesn't hurt a bit,' he insisted, as blood trickled down into his socks.

'Come inside and your mum will get you mopped up,' I said, holding onto him.

'Will you hold my hand if she puts that purple stuff on?' said Little Richard.

'Of course,' I promised.

I loved it that little kids like Richard and Moira really liked me. I seemed to have the knack of getting on with them. When I grew up maybe I *did* want to marry and have children. Then the bright sunlight dazzled my eyes and everything started going black. I started gabbling, 'How much is that doggie in the window? . . .'

'Laura? What's the matter?' Little Richard asked anxiously. 'What are you muttering?'

'Nothing! Come on, little pal, indoors. You're so brave. I'd be howling if I'd skinned both my knees,' I said quickly.

Mrs Bertram sighed when she saw the state of him. 'Again?' she said. 'Come and sit on the draining board and I'll get you mopped up, you silly boy.'

'It's probably my fault,' I said. 'I shouldn't have encouraged him.'

'Nonsense. He was determined to show off to you,' said Mrs Bertram, smiling at me.

I held Little Richard's hand while his mother dabbed gentian violet on his sore knee and then joined Nina and Patsy upstairs. I heard them whispering together, Patsy giggling in her irritating manner. Were they whispering about me? Then I heard Nina say, 'Shut up, she's my friend!' That made me feel a lot better. I crept further away and then walked up to her bedroom door again, stomping a little so they could hear me.

'Hi there,' I said, opening the door.

My heart sank when I saw they were both squashed up on Nina's dressing-table stool, experimenting with eye make-up.

'Hey, what do you think, Laura?' Nina said, batting thickly caked eyelashes at me.

'Oh, very glamorous,' I said insincerely.

'Here, I'll do yours,' she offered, waving a little wand brush at me.

I let her have a go, but I looked as if I had spiders attacking my eyes.

Then they started on hairstyles. Patsy's mother ran a hairdressing salon and Patsy helped out there on Saturdays. She knew how to do French pleats. She turned Nina's shiny black hair into a hard helmet, until the smell of hairspray made my eyes water and my mascara smudged. This was all so boring. I had much more fun with Little Richard.

I heard someone walking along the landing and the thump of a bag being dumped on the floor. I was pretty certain it was Daniel. I hoped he might put his head round the door to say hello, but he didn't come near us. I sat it out for a while and then yawned and stretched.

'It's getting quite late. Shall we just make a start on our homework?' I said.

They groaned at me. 'You little swot!' said Patsy.

I knew it was a pathetic suggestion on my part, but I couldn't help it. Patsy wasn't the slightest bit interested in doing well at school. She actually said, 'I'm not the brainy type,' as if it was something to be proud of. She was only at the Grammar because her parents paid for her. Nina was ultra-brainy, but she didn't need to work at it. We had double homework, plus a whole long list of French verbs to learn, but she could flash through it all in less than an hour.

I sighed. 'Well, I'd better be going anyway.'

'OK, swotty,' said Patsy.

'Stop that,' said Nina, digging her in the tummy with her hairbrush – but she didn't ask me to stay longer.

'Bye then. See you tomorrow,' I said.

I went out of Nina's bedroom feeling depressed. I walked towards the stairs. Daniel's door was ajar.

'Bye, Pat-a-cake,' he called.

Pat-a-cake! 'I'm not Patsy,' I said.

'Oh! Laura!' Daniel came to the door. He'd taken his school tie off and rolled up his shirt sleeves. His hair was all over the place and yet he still looked great. 'I smelled that awful hairspray so I automatically assumed you were Patsy. Hey, are you all right? You look as if you've been crying.'

I wiped my eyes with the back of my hand, probably smudging them even more.

'No, Nina's just been experimenting on me,' I said.

'Well, watch out! Anyway, how are you? Haven't seen you for a bit. You were away somewhere, weren't you?' he asked.

'Yes. Wales. That's why I couldn't come to your tennis club,' I said.

'Oh yes, I remember,' he said, though it looked as if he'd forgotten all about it. He paused. Then he said, 'Well, what about this Saturday then? Call round here at two o'clock?'

I nodded as casually as I could, but I danced up the street on the way home.

10

I worried about not having the right clothes, I worried that I was still so shy with Daniel, and I worried that it might take me a while to get the hang of the game. But I ran to the Bertrams' house joyfully at one thirty, wanting to be there in plenty of time.

I had to knock at their front door several times. I could see both Bertram cars so I knew they weren't out. Little Richard came to the door at last. He gave a cheerful cry when he saw me.

'Laura! Whoopee! I can do proper wheelies on my skates now,' he said excitedly. 'I'll show you in a bit. We're all in the garden just now.'

They were sitting on benches either side of a long table in their back garden, still having their lunch. It wasn't just the Bertram family. Patsy was there too, with her mother and father and an older sister, Lizzie. Patsy was pretty in a vacant doll-type way. Lizzie was dazzling, in a kittenish kind of way, like Brigitte Bardot. She was sitting next to Daniel.

'Hey, what are you doing here, Laura?' said Nina.

'This is a lovely surprise,' said Nina's mother, politely inserting the kind adjective in front of *surprise*.

Daniel hadn't told them about our tennis date! He was looking surprised too, as if he'd forgotten all about it!

'I'm sorry, I thought . . . but I must have got it wrong,' I mumbled, blushing. 'I'll go now.'

Nina was staring at my white sleeveless blouse and shorts. 'Hey, you've come to play tennis!' she said.

'Oh yes, tennis!' said Daniel, smacking his temple with the palm of his hand. 'I told you to come round, didn't I? Come and sit down for ten minutes, and then I'll take you up to the club. You'll lend Laura a racquet, won't you, Nina?'

'Sure,' said Nina. 'Budge up then, Patsy, make room for her.'

'There's plenty of salad left. And fruit tart. Help yourself, Laura,' said Dr Bertram (female), pouring me a glass of lemonade.

There was enough food to feed the whole street: big blue bowls of different salads, chicken and ham and egg mayonnaise, crunchy bread, and two different fruit tarts, raspberry and apple, with a jug of thick cream. I'd had half a Spam sandwich before I left home because I was too excited to eat.

'Thank you, but I'm absolutely full,' I lied.

'Isn't it wonderful that this heavenly weather is lasting,' said Patsy's mother. She looked rather like a film star too, but her face was harder, and she wore too much make-up, though it was expertly applied. 'Don't you just love lunching al fresco?'

She seemed to be talking to me. I presumed she was asking if I liked eating outdoors. I imagined Mum and Dad carting our table and chairs out the back door and the three of us sitting in the small square of back garden underneath the washing line, eating Spam and pickled beetroot. I gave her a wan smile.

'So, are you one of Patsy and Nina's friends, dear?' she persisted.

I wouldn't be Patsy's friend in a million years but I could hardly say so to her mother. I ducked my head and shrugged a little.

'She's very shy!' she whispered to Patsy, which made me want to grind my teeth. I hated sitting there, a total interloper, but I waited it out, telling myself that soon Daniel and I would be at the tennis club and it would all start to be just as I imagined.

But it didn't work out like that. They *all* came to play tennis: Nina and Patsy and Lizzie.

Nina quickly got changed and found me her old racquet. It looked brand new to me. Daniel got changed too. He looked marvellous in his tennis whites. Then we stopped at Patsy's house so that the sisters could change too. Their house was even grander than the Bertrams' but I didn't like it as much. It was too big, too shiny, with silly white pillars that didn't look real.

Nina and Daniel and I waited outside. They were gone a long time.

'Hurry up, girls!' said Daniel, looking at his watch. 'We won't get a court at this rate.'

'If there are five of us we'll need *two* courts,' said Nina pointedly. 'I don't see why Lizzie has to trail along too.'

I felt a flood of relief that she didn't like her much either.

'Oh, come on, she's good fun,' said Daniel.

He might just as well have poked me in the stomach with his own tennis racquet. 'Look, I can't even play yet. I could just go home,' I mumbled.

'Don't be daft, Laura! You're the reason we're going,' said Daniel, putting his arm round me. It was the first time he'd ever touched me – but it was just a kind gesture, almost paternal. 'I'm going to make you a great player, just you wait and see,' he said.

We could only get one of the courts, the furthest away from the club house. At least I didn't have too many spectators. Daniel showed me how to grip the racquet and how to do a forehand and backhand at the side of the court while Nina and Patsy and Lizzie had a few random rallies, taking it in turns to play. I tried a few practice strokes but they were mostly mis-hits.

'Don't worry, you'll get the hang of it in no time. Just relax a bit,' said Daniel. 'Let's have a proper game. I think you'll get into it then.'

He cleared the three girls off the court. They sat beside it, watching me. It made me ten times worse. It wasn't a proper game about winning points. The aim was for me simply to return the wretched ball over the net. Daniel lobbed the softest of balls directly at my racquet but I was so flustered I could rarely hit them back. I missed the ball altogether several times and swiped wildly at thin air. Patsy burst out laughing. Nina tried not to, but I could see her sniggering.

'Stop it, you two. It's not fair. We've all been playing for yonks,' said Lizzie, and Daniel flashed her a grateful look.

I struggled for another five minutes, clenching my teeth. I seemed to be getting worse if that were possible.

'I think you need a little rest. You've been working really hard,' said Daniel.

So I came off the court and sat down, and the four of them played a set, Daniel and Lizzie against Nina and Patsy. Daniel and Lizzie won, inevitably. I watched them, all four so fast and graceful. They made it look easy.

Daniel beckoned me up on the court again for me to have another practice, and for a few seconds I thought I could suddenly play properly. I actually hit the ball in the middle of the racquet and sent it smoothly back over the net. But then I missed the next ball and I stumbled when I was running backwards and ended up falling on my bottom. It hurt so much I had to fight not to burst into tears.

Daniel jumped across the net and ran to pick me up. 'Are you OK? Never mind! Happens to all of us,' he said, and his kindness made me want to cry even more. 'You haven't done too badly for a first time,' he added. 'Nina was absolutely hopeless for ages. But you'll get much better, I promise. We'll have to have another practice session some day.'

He didn't set an actual date. We both knew there wasn't going to be one.

I trailed back home. Mum and Dad were both at work so I was free to fling myself on the bed and cry, but somehow I was past tears now. I just lay there, burning with humiliation.

Things weren't the same after that awful tennis day. I was still supposedly Nina's friend, but not really her *best* friend now. Patsy was back in favour. We went around in a trio at school and sat at the same table at lunch and sometimes even strolled round the playground arm in arm but I didn't go home with Nina any more, and I didn't see her at the weekends. My pride made me pretend to Mum and Dad that I saw her all the time, and I even trailed round the town by myself one very long Saturday, having just one frothy coffee at the Black and White Milk Bar. The young waitress asked me where my friends were.

'Oh, I'm meeting them later on,' I said brightly, but I'm not sure she believed me.

I still had one proper friend left and that was Moira. I walked to school with her, I walked back from school with her too, and when I had any spare pocket money I bought us both cakes from Mrs Bun's. We went back to Lily Cottage to eat them, and then Moira stayed on for an hour or so before reluctantly sloping off home.

'It's so lovely here,' she said, whispering in awe as if she were going round a beautiful cathedral. 'It's so clean and tidy and quiet!'

She particularly liked my bedroom, with its pink eiderdown and furry rug, and the white neatly stacked bookshelf, old *Girl* comics and annuals on the biggest bottom shelf, hardbacks on the middle one, and paperbacks squeezed together at the top. She especially liked Rosebud, my baby doll.

I wondered if Moira was still young enough to play with dolls so I said she could take her down from the windowsill if she wanted. Moira picked her up reverently and sat rigidly on the edge of my bed, Rosebud in her arms. 'There now,' she said, rocking the doll gently. 'Good baby!'

She said it with a little grin at me to show she wasn't seriously playing, just going through the motions.

'I suppose you're probably fed up with babies because you've got so many little brothers and sisters,' I said.

'You've got it,' said Moira. 'This is the sort of baby I like. She don't cry, she don't throw up, she don't wet herself, and she's got pretty clothes.'

'Did you ever have a baby doll?' I asked her.

Moira looked at me with one eyebrow raised. 'I had some paper dolls once, cut out from a book, but my brothers tore them up for a laugh.' She laughed bitterly.

'Tell you what, you can have this doll if you like,' I said on impulse. Rosebud had always been my favourite doll and I'd thought I'd want to keep her for ever, but now she was starting to unnerve me, sitting staring at me every morning when I woke up.

'Are you joking?' Moira asked, astonished.

'No, truly, you have her,' I said. 'Her name's Rosebud but you can call her whatever you like.'

'I'll still call her that, it's really pretty,' said Moira. 'But can I keep her here, in your bedroom? To keep her safe?'

'It's OK, your brothers can't tear her up because she's plastic,' I said.

'Don't matter. They'll scribble all over her with biro and tear her clothes and pull her pants off so they can see her bottom,' Moira said wearily. 'Please let me keep her here, Laura!'

'OK. You can come and visit her every day,' I said.

'Promise? Apart from any time when your friend's here,' Moira said.

I nodded, touched that Moira was being so tactful, though we both knew Nina was very unlikely to come round now. Moira herself had actually made quite a few friends. The first years had started playing a new form of tag that was mostly dashing about and screaming. Moira always seemed in the thick of it, often thumped on the back and congratulated. At the end of school several kids pleaded with her to come home with them to do their homework together or watch television or simply have a laugh, but Moira always preferred to come home with me.

She sometimes stayed until Mum came home. Mum was quite nice to her and always gave her a sandwich or a big slice of cake because Moira looked half-starved and maybe really didn't get enough to eat.

'You have a plateful of that, dear,' Mum would say, smiling at her, but she was much sharper behind her back.

'Why on earth have you palled up with that poor mite?' she asked. 'I daresay she's a sweet little thing but she's a Flannagan, for goodness' sake. She says her pleases and thank yous, I'll grant her that, but her accent! She's so common, though I know she can't help it. And she doesn't look too clean to me. Don't you get too close to her, Laura, or you might catch something.'

'Oh, *Mum*,' I moaned. 'There's no pleasing you. You didn't

like me going round with Nina because the Bertrams are posh. And now you don't like me having Moira for a friend because she's not posh enough.'

'She's just not suitable, that's all. She's only a little girl. Why don't you get a nice friend your own age?' said Mum.

Nina and Patsy and all the so-called nice girls my own age chatted constantly about boys and how far you should go when you were with them, and I hated that sort of talk now. It was a great comfort to play dolls with Moira and read my old *Girl* comics and do colouring together. When Moira went home I studied hard, spending ages on my homework, filling my mind with maths and English language and history and science. I hated French though.

English literature was still my favourite subject. We'd started to read *Pride and Prejudice* which seemed a bit weird and stilted at first, but once I'd got used to the language I started to love it. I wished I lived back in Regency times when there were strict rules of decorum – though Lydia's behaviour was disconcerting. We were only set a couple of chapters at a time for homework but I read on right to the end of the book, needing to know what happened to Lydia. She didn't end up disgraced or dying. She married, even though she was only a year or so older than me, and presumably lived happily ever after.

My English teacher was very pleased with my *Pride and Prejudice* essays and gave me a higher mark than Nina now. I sometimes beat her at the other subjects too. Nina rolled her eyes and pretended not to care. She was heaps better than me at French though, and she was still team captain at netball. She always chose me first to be in her team, because I rarely missed a goal.

'How can she be quite good at netball when she's so hopeless at tennis,' Patsy said spitefully.

Nina and Patsy played tennis together every weekend while it was still warm enough. I gathered that Daniel and Lizzie played too. It sounded as if they were going out together now. There was no invitation for me to have any more tennis instruction from Daniel, but that was actually a relief. I'd made such a fool of myself that I didn't want to see him ever again, though at night I sometimes pretended he was my own Daniel and we were holding hands as we walked up Blackwood Hill.

We had an inter-schools netball tournament at the end of term and Nina and I were both in the junior team. The grammar school nearly always won these tournaments, simply because we had proper netball courts and a keen PE mistress who made us stay behind for practice twice a week. But this year the secondary modern the other side of town happened to have a junior team of big burly girls who pushed and shoved and snatched the ball, intimidating everyone, even the referee. It looked as if we might actually lose and bring shame on the school. I didn't really care. I didn't seem to share the same team spirit. I didn't join in the singing of the silly choruses and all the 'ra-ra-ra' nonsenses before and after each match. I played in a rather cowardly way in the tournament, scared of the girls competing with me. Some of them had been at my own primary school and now called me Snooty-pants and Posh-nob.

I veered away from them when they tried to barge into me. Someone desperately threw the ball towards me right at the end of the match when we were five goals each, and I flung it towards the goalpost automatically, barely taking aim. The ball wobbled at the rim for a second and then incredibly fell through the net. The whistle went for the end of the game. We'd won!

My team were all over me, cheering and slapping me on the back, hoisting me up and running round the court with me. Nina had actually scored three of the earlier goals, one more than me, but she was ignored now. The girls even tried to make me do a lap of honour in the dreaded communal showers. I nearly always lurked in the lavatory until everyone else had showered, and then got dressed under a big towel, hating anyone staring at me – but it was impossible now.

I blushed like an idiot and by the time I was towelling myself dry I was bright red all over. I glanced anxiously at Nina who was already dressed and brushing her hair.

'Such a fuss,' I murmured to her. 'And you played much better than I did.'

Nina shrugged as if she couldn't care less. 'But you got the winning goal. Well done, Tubs,' she said lightly.

I missed a beat. Then, '*Tubs?*'

'Hey, it was meant affectionately. Admiringly, in fact. Look at your boobies! They're getting bigger than mine. Shame about your little pot belly though. You've been eating too many cream doughnuts, girl,' she said.

I pulled my clothes on, desperate to hide my body. 'Don't you dare call me Tubs again!' I said.

'OK, OK. I promise I won't, little dumpling.'

'You're not funny,' I said, trying not to burst out crying.

'Hey, don't get upset! I was only joking,' said Nina, surprised.

'Yes, well, I'm sick of your so-called joking,' I said. 'You're just being spiteful because I got all the praise for that last goal. You can't stand it if anyone else gets any attention.'

'True enough,' said Nina, surprisingly.

'So why don't you just shove off and leave me to get dressed? Little friend Pat-a-cake will be hanging around outside somewhere to make a fuss of you,' I said, struggling into my underwear.

'Oooh, now who's being spiteful!' said Nina, getting up off the bench. 'I don't know why you're getting so fussed. I'd have thought you'd be thrilled to be getting a proper figure at last after being a stick insect all your life. You'll get all the boys wolf-whistling.'

'I don't want any stupid boys whistling at me, unlike some

people,' I snapped, thrusting my arms into my school blouse and doing up my buttons so hurriedly I managed to pull one right off.

'See, you're even busting out your blouse!' said Nina, laughing.

I shoved her furiously, but she caught me by the wrist.

'Hey, you! Don't let's fight,' she said. 'I'm sorry, sorry, sorry! You know me, I just can't help it. Let's be friends again, please!'

'I don't want to be friends any more,' I said.

Nina let my arm go. She shrugged. Her face darkened. 'OK,' she said calmly. 'But you'll regret it.'

I suppose I did regret it over Christmas. She didn't get in touch once. She didn't send me a present or even a card. I'd saved my pocket money and bought her a diary with a blue leather cover and its own little silver pencil, but I decided to keep it for myself. I'd even bought Patsy a small present, just a cheap biro. I kept that too.

I gave Moira a tiny baby doll from Woolworths. It was no bigger than my thumb, but it had a smiley face and a little outfit, a pink gingham dress with matching knickers.

'You can keep her in your pocket all the time so your brothers can't get at her,' I said.

'She's truly lovely!' said Moira, her pale face flushing. 'Can I call her Laura after you?'

'If you like,' I said, touched.

'I haven't got a present for you, though I wish I had, but I've made you a card,' said Moira, offering it.

She must have made it at school, using their thin card and crayons. It was a picture of two girls in uniform, one big, one small. They were looking up in the sky and there was Father Christmas overhead in his sleigh pulled by a little herd of reindeers. Father Christmas was throwing parcels at us, smiling broadly. It was all very carefully coloured in.

'Oh, Moira, it's fantastic!' I said, peering at every detail. 'It must have taken you ages.'

'I liked doing it. I didn't colour the pavement because it's meant to be snowy,' said Moira.

'I can see that. It's perfect. Thank you so much, Moira!'

We grinned at each other. I didn't dare ask her after the 25th if Father Christmas had paid her a visit. From the little I knew of Moira's home life it was likely he hadn't given it a thought.

Mum and Dad gave me books: new ones from W.H. Smith's – a story about a ballet dancer, another about three girls and their ponies, and the third was *Odhams Pictorial Children's Encyclopaedia*. They were very wholesome choices, and rather dull, though there was a picture of an island in the encyclopaedia that fascinated me. It was brightly coloured with yellow sand and green palm trees and a turquoise lagoon. I moved my finger across the sand and up and down a tree and made it dive into the water.

I hoped Aunt Susannah would send me a book too, maybe another selection of Katherine Mansfield's short stories. But the parcel from Wales was too big and flat and light for it to be reading matter.

Mum looked at it suspiciously. 'What's she sent you now?' she said.

I ripped the wrapping paper off and found two garments: a baggy black polo-necked sweater and tight black trews. I seized them with joy.

'*Black?*' said Mum. 'What's she thinking of? You're far too young to wear black! And these are awful – you'll look like a Beatnik!'

I desperately *wanted* to look like a Beatnik and have cool clothes and read strange books and dig jazz. Aunt Susannah was so clever!

'I'm not having you wearing awful clothes like that!' said Mum. 'I've a good mind to stick them straight in the bin.'

'You can't! They're mine,' I said, and I rushed to my bedroom to try them on. I pulled off my tartan pinafore and white frilly blouse. The black sweater looked marvellous.

'Cool cat!' I whispered to my reflection in the mirror.

I stepped into the trews. They clung to my legs in an amazing way, emphasizing the curves. But when I hitched them right up and tried to do up the zip I was stuck. They were far too small. I had grown far too big. I put my hand on my tummy and tried to pull them up higher – then I felt something squirmy inside me. A sort of *movement*!

I felt sick. I sang songs inside my head but I couldn't distract myself this time. I thought of the island in my new encyclopaedia, imagining I was there walking across the sand towards the beautiful blue lagoon, a light breeze cooling my hot face, but that didn't work either. I stayed in my bedroom, staring at myself in horror, the trews stuck on my hips, looking ridiculous.

I pulled them off again, took the sweater off too, and stuck them at the back of my wardrobe. Mum and Dad looked surprised when I came back into the living room in my pinafore.

'What did they look like then?' Dad asked.

'I looked a bit weird in them,' I said quickly.

Mum nodded smugly, and no one mentioned them again.

I couldn't sleep properly that night. Or the next or the next, on and on. When I did nod off eventually around two in the morning I had terrible dreams and would wake with a start, my heart thumping. My tummy felt so strange. I didn't dare touch it now.

'Are you all right, dear?' Mum asked. 'You're very pale and you've got huge dark circles under your eyes.'

'I'm fine, Mum,' I mumbled.

'You don't look fine to me,' she said. She lowered her voice because Dad was in the room. 'Are you having trouble going to the toilet?'

I blushed. Mum always fussed embarrassingly about constipation. I think I had to eat more squares of Ex-lax than Cadbury's chocolate during my childhood.

'No, I'm not having any trouble. Do shut up about it, Mum. I'm *fine*,' I insisted.

The Christmas holidays seemed to go on for ever. It wasn't too bad when Moira came round to Lily Cottage, but she couldn't come often now. Her mother had another baby the day after Boxing Day and so Moira had to stay home and look after the younger children.

I went round to their prefab once. It was even worse than I'd imagined: mess everywhere, kids squabbling and fighting and crying. Moira's mother was sprawled on the sofa in their living room, still in her nightie and dressing gown. She started breast-feeding the new baby right in front of me. I felt terribly embarrassed, but nobody else turned a hair. I tried to organize the children, suggesting different games, but they didn't engage with me like Little Richard. They just stared at me as if I was crazy and carried on creating havoc. One little boy wearing only a jumper and socks called me a very rude name. Moira gave him a shove.

'Don't you talk to my friend like that, Mr Cheeky Bum,' she said.

'Why isn't he wearing any trousers?' I asked her.

'Because he just wets them,' said Moira.

'He's a little devil,' said Mrs Flannagan. 'Playing up because he's jealous of his new little sister. Here, dear, she's had her little snack. Would you like to hold her for a bit?'

She held the baby out to me. I recoiled in horror. 'No, it's OK, thank you,' I said quickly.

'It's all right, you won't hurt her,' she said, misunderstanding. 'Babies are tough little things.'

I had to take the baby in my arms. It was the first time I'd ever held one. People always exclaimed over babies, cooing and smiling. I didn't know what to do. I thought this baby was horrible, her face red and screwed up, a drop of milk still drooling out of her mouth.

'She's cute, isn't she?' said Moira.

I nodded politely, though I thought her utterly hideous. Her face went even redder and she made a little grunting noise. Then there was a terrible smell. I very nearly dropped her.

'Oh-oh!' said Moira. 'I'd better change her.'

She took her from me, to my intense relief. I hoped she'd take her out the room, but she changed her on the living-room floor. I held my breath, trying not to heave. Moira was lovely with her little sister, expertly wiping her clean, chatting to her all the while. When the baby was in a fresh new nappy fastened with a big safety pin, Moira held her out to me again.

'Do you want another cuddle?' she said.

'I'd better not. I've got to get back,' I gabbled, backing away.

I ran home, feeling worse than ever.

'You'll never guess what we're calling the new baby,' said

Moira, when she came calling for me the first day back at school. 'Laura, after you! I suggested it, and Mum thinks it's a lovely idea.'

'That's . . . lovely,' I repeated lamely. 'You're ever so good with babies, Moira.'

'Well, I ought to be, I've had to look after enough of them. I like them best when they're very little, before they can crawl about and make mischief.' She gave me a shrewd look. 'You don't like babies much, do you?'

'They're OK,' I said awkwardly.

'You just have to get used to them,' said Moira. She looked at me. 'What's the matter?'

'Nothing! Absolutely nothing. Come on, let's hurry, we don't want to be late first day back at school, do we?' I said, walking as fast as I could.

'No, of course not,' said Moira, scurrying along beside me cheerfully.

We got to school in plenty of time, early in fact, but I couldn't face going into the classroom straight away. I went to the toilets and hid inside the end cubicle. I wondered how many times I'd gone to this same lavatory over the last few months, praying as I sat down, peering for any hopeful sign. But at my age, weren't things sometimes not all that . . . regular? I sat there, while girls came in and out, using the cubicles, washing their hands, styling their hair in front of the mirror, chattering all the time about their holidays.

I heard Nina's voice, talking to Patsy, and I sat with clenched fists, huddling down as if she could see through the metal door. I wondered if they might be talking about me, maybe making fun of me, but they were talking about a New Year's Eve party they'd both been to. It sounded as if Nina had enjoyed it the most because the boy they both liked had kissed her first as midnight struck.

Then the bell rang and they all hurried off. I waited thirty seconds or so, till I judged the toilets were empty, and then I ran out and got to the classroom just after Mrs Morris.

'I haven't sat down yet, so I suppose you're not officially late, Laura,' she said, looking at me. 'Oh dear, you still look half asleep.'

I was horribly wide awake in spite of my troubled nights, but not in the right mind to apply myself at school. I was told off twice that morning for daydreaming, and I knew when I handed in my maths I'd probably made a lot of silly mistakes. For once I didn't care.

I saw Nina peering at me several times. When the bell rang for lunchtime she leaned over. 'Are you all right?' she said.

'Of course,' I muttered, surprised she was talking to me.

It would normally have been a huge relief, because we'd had no contact since that netball tournament, but now it didn't seem to matter much. I went back to the toilets, not able to face the crowded canteen. I decided to stay there in the end cubicle until the start of afternoon school. I'd brought a book with me, but for once I couldn't get lost in reading. The words wriggled up and down the page, not making any sense, until I shut the book in despair.

I leaned my head against the wall, tears dribbling down my cheeks. I think I might have nodded off for a little while, because the next I knew Nina was calling my name. I swallowed and kept still.

'Laura? Laura, I know you're in there!' Nina said. I heard her walking past the washbasins and then thumping on the door. 'Please, Laura!'

'Oh, for goodness' sake, Nina!' said Patsy. 'It might be someone else altogether in there. Come *on*!'

'Don't tell me what to do,' Nina snapped. She knocked at the door again. 'Laura? It *is* you in there, isn't it? Have I got to go on tapping like a woodpecker till you deign to come out?'

'Oh, for God's sake,' I said, and I pulled the chain and stalked out, trying to hold my head up high. 'What's the matter with you? Aren't I even allowed to go to the loo in peace?'

I started washing my hands, trying to act as if I didn't have a care in the world.

Nina wasn't fooled. 'Laura?' she said softly. 'You've been crying! What is it?'

'Look, I thought we weren't even friends with her any more,' said Patsy.

'*You* might not be,' said Nina.

'She just wants you to fuss round her. She's pathetic,' said Patsy.

'No, you are,' said Nina.

'We're not even supposed to be in school after lunch. We'll get into trouble,' Patsy whined.

'You go then,' said Nina.

Patsy flounced out.

'At last,' said Nina. She came right up beside me. 'I *am* still your friend, Laura. I've really missed you. Is that what's bugging you?'

I shook my head.

'So what *is* it?' Nina asked, putting her arm round me. 'It can't be that terrible.'

'It is,' I said, and I burst out crying. 'I think . . . I'm going to have a baby!'

Nina stared at me. 'What?'

'A baby!' I sobbed.

Nina peered round, checking we still had the toilets to ourselves. 'Don't be daft, Laura, how could you possibly be pregnant?' she said. 'You haven't ever done it with anyone!'

'I have,' I said. 'Well, I must have done, mustn't I? I wasn't really sure if it happened or not.'

'What's *up* with you? Of course you'd *know*.'

'Have you done it then?' I asked, wiping my cheeks with the back of my hand.

'Hey, you're a bit snotty too,' said Nina, going to get me a little wad of toilet paper. She gently wiped my nose for me. 'There you go. No, I haven't done it! Several boys have wanted to, but I wouldn't let them. I'm not daft.'

'Well, I was,' I said, sobbing.

'Don't start crying all over again. Now calm down. Laura, I'm one hundred per cent certain *you* can't have done it. You haven't got a boyfriend! You haven't even kissed anyone.'

'It was that French boy. The one we met at the Lido,' I whispered.

'What, the dim one who couldn't talk?' Nina asked.

'He could talk! He just couldn't speak English, that's all. The way we can't speak French,' I said.

'But you didn't sleep with him!' Nina protested.

'Well, not sleep, but we did do it. I think,' I said.

Nina rolled her eyes. 'No you didn't! I was there, idiot!'

'He walked me most of the way home,' I said.

'So he kissed you goodbye? Laura, don't be so daft – you can't have a baby just by kissing. Was it French kissing, you know, with tongues?' Nina asked.

'Yes, but then he started pressing up against me,' I admitted.

'I told you. We walked through the park and went into that cricket hut place. And – well, that's where it happened,' I said, sniffing.

'Where what happened?'

'Well, I wasn't exactly sure what he was doing, and it was so embarrassing. I liked the kissing, and I kept thinking I'd tell him not to do anything more and then eventually I did push him away, but it had sort of happened already. It was just so . . . nothing. Not a bit like I imagined. The total opposite of romantic. He didn't even say he loved me,' I said.

'Well, you couldn't really expect him to, could you? I mean, you'd only just met him. Oh, Laura, how could you be such an idiot?' said Nina.

'Don't! Look, you and Patsy go on and on about boys and kissing and all of that. I thought that was just what I was doing, until it was too late. And now I'm going to have his baby!' I wailed.

'You can't be. Not if it was your first time and it was all over so quickly. You're just imagining it because you've got a bit tubby just lately. Sorry, sorry, I'm not being mean, I'm just being truthful,' she said, squeezing my arm.

There'd only *been* one time. There was another small squeezing inside me. 'Feel,' I said, and I took her hand and placed it on my stomach.

She felt the rounded part and then snatched it away quickly. 'What's that?' she said fearfully.

208

'It's the baby. It's started moving about a bit. Kicking. It's been doing that for a while now. I kept trying to convince myself it was just tummy ache, wind, whatever – but I can't pretend any more. It's a real baby and I can't bear it. I don't even like babies, I think they're horrible. And when Mum and Dad find out they'll kill me,' I sobbed. 'They'll die of shame.'

'Stop crying! So how far gone are you? We met up with those French guys towards the end of August, right? That makes it nearly five months. You idiot, why didn't you tell me sooner? I might have been able to help you then,' she said.

'What do you mean?'

'You know – get rid of it. If that's what you want,' Nina said.

'That's exactly what I want! So what do I have to do?' I asked desperately.

'Well, Lizzie told Patsy and me about this girl in the sixth form who thought she was pregnant so she threw herself down the stairs,' said Nina.

'What, to kill herself?' I said.

'No, to shake the baby up and make it come out.'

'But I haven't *got* any stairs. I live in a prefab, remember?' I said.

'Oh Lord,' said Nina, and she burst out laughing. 'Sorry, I'm not laughing at you, honestly, it's just the shock of it all!'

'I know,' I said, and in spite of everything I giggled feebly too. 'I suppose I could try the school stairs, but imagine if it started happening in front of everyone!'

'I suppose it's just as well. Lizzie said that girl broke her wrist, and she wasn't even sure it had actually worked,' said Nina. She suddenly exclaimed: 'Hey, you could try taking those weird little pills, Nurse Brown's Remedy for Lady Troubles!'

I vaguely remembered seeing a little advert for them on the back page of Mum's magazines.

'I always thought they were for periods, if you had bad pains,' I said.

'Yes, but someone told me that it was also to bring on your period if it was late,' said Nina.

'Who told you? Lizzie again?' I took a deep breath. 'Nina, do you think Daniel and Lizzie are, you know, doing it?'

'What? No! They're just friends. I'm not sure Daniel's even that keen on her any more,' said Nina.

In spite of everything I felt a little thrill. But then the horror of my situation overwhelmed me again.

'What am I going to *do*?' I asked.

'Well, you could *try* old Nurse Brown and her lady remedies. Maybe it's not too late?'

'Do you think it will hurt?' I said.

Nina pulled a face. 'I think so. You'd better take them in

the evening and then it'll happen overnight so your mum won't find out.'

'Where do you get them, at Boots the chemist? What if they realize what they're for? Oh God, I can't do it!' I said.

'Leave it to me,' said Nina. 'I'll get them for you.'

'Really? You won't tell Patsy, will you?'

'No, absolutely not,' said Nina. 'Promise. Trust me!'

I knew I couldn't really trust Nina at all, but she seemed like the only hope I had. Now I'd actually admitted it I couldn't stop thinking about it, no matter how I tried to distract myself.

It was a relief when I went home from school with Moira, because she chatted non-stop. When we got to Lily Cottage I helped her with her homework, and then we read a *Girl* comic together. But then Moira took her little baby doll out of her pocket and started playing around with her, making her kick her tiny plastic legs and wail like a kitten. I told her sharply she had to go home so I could get on with my own homework.

I thought I could still hear the wailing after she'd gone home. I looked at Rosebud and then seized her, shoved her on top of my shoes in my wardrobe, and shut the door on her.

When I was in bed at night I put my hands on my rounded stomach. 'Please go away!' I whispered. 'You're not real, not yet. I don't want you. You're nothing to do with me. Just disappear!'

*

Nina dragged me to a far corner of the playground the next morning and furtively handed me a little white paper bag. I peeped inside and saw a small round cardboard box with a picture of an old-fashioned nurse on the top.

'You got them!' I gasped.

'I said I would, didn't I?' Nina said triumphantly. 'I went after school.'

'With Patsy?'

'No, I told her I was meeting up with my mum.'

'You didn't meet up with her, did you?' I asked, horrified.

'Of course not, you berk! I didn't go to Boots, I went to that weird chemist type place down Market Alley – you know, the one with the hilarious model of a man wearing that truss thing,' said Nina, giggling. 'There was an even weirder real man inside in a white coat like he was a doctor. I asked him for the pills and he gave them to me, just like that. Well, he did ask why I wanted them.'

'He didn't!'

'I said they weren't for me, they were for my mother because she was having trouble with her periods, and he just nodded and sold them to me,' said Nina.

'How much do I owe you?'

'Oh, don't be daft. Have them as a gift! Take one after your supper and then all your troubles will be over by the morning. Hopefully. Well, it's worth a try, eh?' she said.

212

'You're a fantastic friend, Nina. Thank you so much!' I said, and I gave her a hug.

We were very close all day. Patsy hardly got a look-in.

'Good luck!' Nina whispered at the end of afternoon school.

I popped a pill in my mouth with the cup of tea Mum made after we'd eaten our liver and bacon. I thought I'd been discreet but Mum frowned at me.

'What's that you're taking?'

'Oh, just an aspirin. I've got a bit of a headache,' I said quickly.

'I'm sure you're sickening for something,' said Mum, feeling my forehead.

'It's just a headache, that's all,' I said. 'But perhaps I'll go to bed early.'

I said it in case the pill started working quickly.

Nothing seemed to be happening when I went to bed at eight. I lay awake, bracing myself for some pain. My tummy stayed soft and swollen without a single cramp. When I got up in the morning there wasn't a sign of any blood.

'Did it work?' Nina asked, as soon as she saw me at school.

I shook my head hopelessly.

'You did actually take one?' she said.

'*Yes!*' I hissed.

'Well, maybe you should have taken a few more. They're very little pills, after all. Try again tonight,' said Nina, refusing to give up.

So I swallowed four at teatime, gulping them down so quickly that I practically choked. I started to feel a little uneasy after a while, but still nothing happened, though there seemed to be a stirring in my stomach. I took another couple of pills in a last desperate attempt when I went to bed, but then almost immediately I had to get up to rush to the toilet. I had the most terrible diarrhoea that went on and on. There were bad knife pains in my stomach now, but no bleeding still, even when my bowels eventually calmed down.

I staggered out of the toilet to find Mum waiting outside, wringing her hands.

'Oh, Laura, what's the matter? You've been in there ages, and I heard you groaning!' she said.

'I've just got a bit of a tummy upset, that's all,' I snapped.

'Is it something you've eaten at school? It can't be from your supper – it was just steamed plaice and mash, and that couldn't possibly make you ill!' Mum declared.

'*I* don't know. Anyway, it's over now. Please don't keep fussing,' I said, and trudged back to bed.

But it wasn't over. I had to keep getting up to go again, and now I started to get really scared. I shouldn't have taken so many of the wretched pills. I'd clearly poisoned myself. What if I'd done myself some serious harm? What if I was *dying*?

I felt dreadful now. It was a hot night and I was sweating, and yet shivering too. What should I do? Mum was in bed asleep now with Dad. Ought I to wake them up? But what should I say? I couldn't tell them I'd taken the pills. They'd be horrified, especially if they found out why.

I lay there in the dark, crying, hauling myself up several times for further trips to the bathroom.

Mum woke up again and knocked on the bathroom door this time. 'Laura? Laura, are you all right? Please let me in!'

'Mum, for God's sake, I'm going to the toilet! Go *away*!' I hissed.

She was waiting for me when I came out at last. 'How many times have you been?' she asked anxiously.

'*Mum!* Don't be so gross,' I said.

'You're clearly ill. You must have some awful bug. I'm going to call the doctor!' she said.

'You can't do that! It's four in the morning. He'll think you're crazy. Anyway, I think I'm better now. Honestly,' I lied.

'Really? Well, come and wake me if you have to go again. Promise me!' she demanded.

'I promise,' I said. I didn't actually have to deceive her, because that was the last time. My insides stopped churning. I lay on my back, exhausted and feeling weak. I kept feeling my tummy and then recoiling. It was still in there.

Mum woke me up late with a cup of weak tea and a slice of toast cut into fingers, as if I was a toddler.

'I don't really feel like breakfast, Mum,' I protested. I checked the time on my alarm. 'I'd better get up. I'm going to be really late for school as it is.'

'You have to get something inside you. Just drink the tea if you really can't face any toast. You need the fluids. Have you stopped needing to go?' she asked.

'Yes.'

'You're sure?'

'Mum, for goodness' sake, *yes*!'

'Well, that's just as well. We don't want to risk any accidents! Now, Moira came knocking for you a few minutes ago, but I told her you were poorly. And I've phoned the shop and pretended *I* was the one with tummy troubles, so I've got the day off to look after you,' said Mum.

'You didn't need to do that! I'm fine now. I don't need looking after,' I protested.

'Well, we'll see about that. I phoned and we've got the first appointment with Dr Bertram this morning,' said Mum.

'What? I don't need to see a doctor!' I said, appalled.

'Oh yes you do. You've not been yourself for months, looking so pale and tired all the time. I hoped the Christmas break might perk you up, but now you're worse, if anything,' said Mum. 'I should have taken you to the doctor's ages ago.'

'I'm *fine*, I keep telling you. It was just something I ate, or a bug, whatever. It's OK now. I'm not going to see Dr Bertram!'

'I told you, we have an appointment,' said Mum.

'Well, you'll have to phone again and say we don't need it because I'm better now.'

'I can't possibly mess them about like that! You're going, and that's that. I want him to examine you thoroughly. We need to get to the bottom of this!' Mum insisted.

The thought of Dr Bertram of all people examining me made me feel so limp with horror my cup tilted and I spilled some of my tea on the eiderdown.

'See! You're weak as a kitten. And it's a devil of a job to get stains out of satin,' said Mum, dabbing at the eiderdown furiously. 'I'll make you another cup. You go and give yourself a proper wash. And put clean underwear on, just in case.'

'Mum, I'm not going!' I said, through clenched teeth.

Mum stopped dabbing and put her face close to mine. 'Oh yes you are, Laura! And if you utterly refuse I'll change the appointment to a home visit after surgery today,' she said.

She seemed in deadly earnest. I didn't know what to do. I couldn't stand the thought of going to the surgery – but it would be even worse if Dr Bertram came here to the prefab, prodding at my chest with his stethoscope in my own bedroom.

I thought wildly about getting dressed and running out into the street, and staying out all day – but Mum was so weirdly panicky she'd probably phone the police and report me as a runaway. And I'd have to come back some time. I couldn't run away for ever.

I decided I'd go to the surgery and tell Dr Bertram that it was an ordinary tummy upset. I'd say I wasn't ill at all; I was just working a bit too hard, worrying about not doing so well at school – which was true enough. I'd been so distracted lately that I'd been nowhere near the top in the end of term exams.

'All right, I'll go,' I mumbled.

'That's a good girl,' said Mum. She had tears in her eyes. 'I don't want to bully you, dear. I'm just so worried about you, that's all.'

I put my school uniform on, because the tunic was the loosest garment I possessed, and the gabardine had been bought too big for me so it would last several years. Dad was in the kitchen having a second cup of tea because he was just booked to do an afternoon trip to a stately home. He nodded at me.

'I hear you had a disturbed night,' he said.

'It was just a tummy upset. Mum's mad making me go to the doctor's. Can't you stop her, Dad?' I asked hopefully.

'No, better get you checked, pet,' said Dad. 'You haven't been looking a hundred per cent, not for a while. Can't have our little girl poorly!'

218

He was being so nice to me I nearly cried. What would he say if he knew the truth? What would Mum say? They mustn't mustn't *mustn't* know. Not yet. Not ever.

I walked to the surgery with Mum, dragging my feet, feeling sick now. Mum kept giving me worried little glances.

'You're so pale, Laura! You used to have such roses in your cheeks when you were a little girl,' she said.

'Yes, well, I've grown up now,' I mumbled.

Mum reached out and took hold of my hand, taking me by surprise. 'Don't worry, dear. I'm sure Dr Bertram will make you right again,' she said, though her forehead was creased with worry.

We got to the surgery ten minutes early in spite of my slow pace. Dr Bertram's Rover was in its own special parking bay, but the receptionist made us wait until the clock struck nine. Then she called 'Laura Peterson' on the loudspeaker, though we were sitting within easy earshot.

I stood up – and Mum did too.

'Mum?'

'I'm coming in with you,' she said determinedly.

Dr Bertram looked surprised to see the two of us. 'Laura! And Mrs Peterson?'

'I don't trust Laura to tell you properly what's wrong with her. She'll just shrug and say she's fine. You know what teenage girls are like, Dr Bertram. I daresay your Nina's the same,' said Mum.

Dr Bertram gave a tight little smile and fetched another chair from a corner. 'Do sit down. Now, Laura, what's troubling you?'

Mum got started before I could even open my mouth. 'She's been off colour for months, Doctor. Bit pale and pasty, with these dark circles under her eyes. That's not like our Laura. I've been so worried. I think she might have some kind of blockage inside her,' she said. 'And then last night she was violently ill, all night. Not sickness, the other.'

I sat staring at the wall, willing myself a thousand miles away.

'Well, that doesn't sound like a blockage to me,' said Dr Bertram briskly. 'How do you feel in yourself, Laura?'

'Fine,' I said.

'See!' said Mum. 'You see what she's like.'

'I think you're probably worrying unnecessarily, Mrs Peterson. Laura looks fine to me.' Dr Bertram stood up from his desk and pressed under my eye. 'Mm, perhaps she's a little anaemic, but that's nothing to worry about. Do you have heavy periods, Laura?'

I shrugged, blushing.

Mum was blushing too, but she whispered, 'I don't think she's had her monthlies for a while. She wouldn't tell me, but I've noticed she's not been using her pads.'

'Really? Is that right, Laura?' Dr Bertram asked.

I pressed my lips together and said nothing.

'She's shy. She doesn't like to talk about things like that,' said Mum.

Dr Bertram was looking at me intently. 'Perhaps I'd better give Laura a little examination, just to make sure there's nothing untoward going on,' he said. He opened a curtain behind him, where there was a narrow examination table, its deep red plastic covered with white paper like a tablecloth. 'Just pop your clothes off and lie down,' he told me.

'I – I don't want to,' I stammered.

He sighed impatiently. 'Come along, Laura. I've known you since you were a baby. There's no need to be shy. I simply want to help you,' said Dr Bertram.

'Laura! Do as you're told, you silly girl,' said Mum.

'Please hurry up, Laura. I'll have other patients waiting in the surgery by now,' the doctor said briskly.

I went behind the curtains, closed them tightly, took off my gabardine, pulled my tunic over my head and undid the buttons on my blouse, my hands trembling. Then I clambered clumsily onto the examination table in my underwear. I lay there, shaking.

I heard Dr Bertram murmuring to Mum, and then the snap snap as he eased on his plastic gloves. I put my hands over my face.

'Are you ready now, Laura?' he called.

I gave a terrified squeak. He came behind the curtains to me.

'There now. I'm not going to hurt you!' he said, in his poshest professional voice.

I peeped through my fingers. He was looking at my chest. My breasts flattened a little when I lay on my back, but they were still bigger and more embarrassing than usual. He gently pulled the cups of my bra aside, exposing the nipples. He looked slightly alarmed. He replaced the bra and then indicated my knickers.

'Just ease them down for me,' he murmured.

I did as I was told, blushing deeply.

He stared at my rounded tummy. He felt it carefully, prodding a little here and there. His eyebrows went up.

'Laura, Laura, Laura,' he said quietly, as if he couldn't believe it. 'I'd better make sure. Pop these right off,' he said, pointing to my knickers.

It was unbelievably embarrassing and humiliating, especially when he felt inside me. Then he nodded, removing his gloves and tossing them in the waste bin. He looked as if he wanted to toss me in the bin too.

He put his face close to mine. 'Did you know you're going to have a baby?' he whispered, his minty breath wafting up my nostrils.

'No! Well, maybe. But I didn't think it was possible,' I whispered back, barely able to get the words out.

'I wouldn't have thought it possible, a girl your age,' said Dr Bertram. 'How *could* you?'

'Dr Bertram? Laura?' Mum called anxiously from the other side of the curtain.

'I didn't mean to,' I whispered, starting to cry. 'It was just once, honestly, and it wasn't really my fault.'

Dr Bertram bent so close that I thought for a mad moment he was going to kiss me. 'Who did this to you?' he murmured urgently.

I shook my head, crying.

'You must tell me! It – it wasn't Daniel, was it?'

I stared up at him. *Daniel!* He couldn't be serious. I saw there were beads of sweat on his forehead. He really seemed to believe it. My heart started thumping. If only it were true! It would be wonderful, in spite of the shame. Daniel was so lovely. He would stand by me. He might even marry me in a couple of years. And eventually we would live together with our baby, and I'd be part of the family, one of the Bertrams at last.

I could say it was Daniel and make Dr Bertram believe me. Daniel would deny it, but people might still feel it *could* have been him. All I had to do was nod. I wanted to. I wanted to so much.

No, what was I thinking? How could I possibly drag poor Daniel into this mess?

'It wasn't him,' I muttered.

Dr Bertram didn't look convinced. Maybe he thought I was trying to protect him.

'Of course it wasn't Daniel,' I said more forcibly. 'I wish it was him, but he'd never do that. He's like a big brother to me,' I said.

Dr Bertram winced, obviously hating that idea, but he breathed out deeply. Then he gave me the most terrifying look of disgust. 'Put your clothes on and get up,' he said curtly. He joined Mum and said in an icy-cold voice, 'Did you not realize your daughter is pregnant?'

Mum gasped. 'No she's not!' she said. In spite of all her respect for people in the medical profession, people in *any* profession, she added, 'How dare you! My daughter's a good girl!'

'Well, she's hardly the Virgin Mary,' said Dr Bertram. 'And I would say she's at least four or five months pregnant. I can arrange a test, but I see little point. You must face the facts, Mrs Peterson.'

'But she can't be! She's far too young,' said Mum, looking at me wildly.

'Yes, she certainly is. I've had young unwed women weeping in my surgery with a baby on the way, but never anyone as young as this! Fourteen!' Dr Bertram's lips puckered. I thought for a moment he was going to spit at me.

'Is it really true, Laura?' Mum said shakily.

I made myself nod.

'Why didn't you *tell* me?' she whispered.

'I couldn't,' I said.

Mum turned to Dr Bertram again. 'Couldn't you help us? As you said, she's only a little girl. She can't go through with this! It'll ruin her life. Couldn't you . . . couldn't you do a little operation on her, before it's too late?'

He looked genuinely appalled. 'If you're suggesting what I think you are, then you're insulting me royally, Mrs Peterson. As if I'd ever perform an illegal operation! And certainly not at this stage, halfway through her pregnancy.'

'I know – it's a horrible idea, but I'm desperate! Can't you show her some compassion? Laura's Nina's best friend, for goodness' sake!' Mum said.

'Laura's not a suitable friend now. I'm not going to let Nina have any more to do with her. She's a bad influence,' said Dr Bertram.

'But they're at school together!'

'Laura will have to leave the school. She can't possibly keep going in her condition. What would it look like, a pregnant girl in Grammar school uniform?' He was rapidly writing something on a notepad. Then he tore off the page and handed it to Mum. 'This is the telephone number of Mrs Jeffries, a social worker.'

'We don't need anyone from the social!' said Mum, horrified. I knew what she was thinking. Only families like Moira's had social workers. Mum tried to push the piece of paper back to him.

'I should keep it if I were you. Laura will need a lot of help. It will be difficult finding a mother and baby home that will take in a girl so young. I can't do any more for you. Please go now,' he said.

I stared at him, wondering how I could ever have wished he were *my* father. I could understand why he was so cold with me, but I hated the way he was treating Mum. Her face was puckered up now in her efforts not to cry. She folded the piece of paper into a little square and posted it into her handbag and then she stood up.

'Come along, Laura,' she said, and she marched out of the room, her head held high. She was dressed up for the visit, wearing her heels, and she skidded slightly on the highly polished floor. I followed her, avoiding Dr Bertram's eye.

It had been even more terrible than I'd feared, but at least it was over now. And Mum had been amazing. She had stuck up for me. She had literally begged him to help me.

I turned to her when we were out in the street. 'Thanks, Mum,' I said softly.

But now we were on our own she looked at me almost as if she hated me.

'How could you do this to me, Laura?' she said. 'I can hardly take it in. You were such a dear little girl. I've always been so proud of you. And now you've ruined my life. People will blame me. I'll never be able to hold my head up high again. And neither will you. You're spoiled goods now, and no one will ever want you.'

Mum barely talked to me all day. I decided I might as well go to school, seeing as I was already wearing my uniform, but she stopped me.

'You're not setting foot outside this house,' she said fiercely.

'Oh, Mum, don't be like that,' I said humbly, putting my hand on her arm.

'Don't touch me!' she said, as if I was contaminated.

It was all so melodramatic. I had to fight not to burst out laughing because it seemed so ridiculous. I was still me, Laura, yet Mum was treating me like a stranger. She had a long cry in her bedroom. I hoped when she came out at last she might feel a bit better so we could have a proper talk together, but she still shunned me. She started doing the housework, viciously scrubbing the kitchen floor, her face red with effort. She looked as if she wanted to give me a good scrubbing too.

I offered to help, but she just shook her head scornfully and carried on cleaning all afternoon, her eyes sorrowful, her lips pressed together, looking like a martyr. She kept glancing at the clock, waiting for Dad to get home.

When he came through the door at last he was whistling cheerfully, an old cowboy tune – 'Home, Home on the Range'. He stopped abruptly, staring at us.

'What? What's happened? Oh Lord, what did the doctor say? Our Laura isn't seriously ill, is she?' he asked.

'No,' said Mum. 'You'll never guess what.'

'*What?*' said Dad, exasperated.

'She's only gone and got herself *pregnant*,' said Mum, and she started crying again.

Then it was even more terrible, because Dad cried too. He slumped in his armchair, his hands over his face, his shoulders shaking. I'd never ever seen him cry before. Mum made him a cup of tea, but he managed to spill most of it down himself. He swore, using a really bad word, but Mum barely flinched. Then Dad looked at me.

'Is it Nina's brother? Did he do this to you?' he asked.

'No!'

'Then who in Christ's name was it?'

'It wasn't anybody,' I said desperately.

'Don't be ridiculous,' Mum snapped.

'I mean, it wasn't anyone I really know,' I tried to explain.

'You mean you was . . . interfered with?' Dad asked, almost hopefully.

I thought of awkward Léon mumbling in French while touching me in the dark of that awful hut that smelled of sweat and linseed oil. I could never make them understand. I didn't understand it myself.

'I wasn't attacked or anything,' I whispered. 'It was this French boy I met at the Lido,' I said. 'He couldn't speak much English. I didn't really even like him very much. I don't know why I let him. I didn't really know what was happening, honestly. I'm sorry. I'm really really sorry. Please don't look at me like that!'

'You had sex with a *stranger*?' Dad said. 'What are you, a brazen little hussy?'

I'd never even heard the phrase before but I knew what he meant. It was as if he'd slapped me, spat at me. My own dad.

He spent a pointless hour interrogating me, unable to believe I knew so little about Léon that I didn't know his surname or where he'd been staying here or where he lived in France.

'I'm still going to make sure he pays for this!' said Dad, slapping his own thigh.

'You can't go to France and look for any random teenager,' said Mum. She looked at me, her eyes red-rimmed now. 'You went with a boy and you didn't even know his surname! What are you going to put on the baby's birth certificate? *Unknown*?'

'I don't know! I haven't even thought about any of this. I wasn't even sure I was really having a baby. I don't *want* a baby!' I said.

'To think I went through so much to have you!' said Mum, rocking slowly on her chair. 'We had to wait for years. And then, when I'd almost given up, you were third-time lucky. I nearly died having you, did you know that? Forty-eight hours in labour, and I was so weak at the end they had to drag you out with forceps.'

'Don't!' I said, wincing.

'You wait till you see what it's like!' Mum shouted, little beads of spit gathering in the corners of her mouth.

'*Please* don't!' I protested. Then, 'Does it really hurt a lot?'

'It's the worst pain ever,' said Mum.

'Stop it, you're frightening me!' I said.

'You'll know soon enough,' said Mum.

'Will you be there?' I whispered, because Mum was always there when I was ill.

'You won't be having it here!' Mum said. 'For God's sake, what are you thinking of? You'll have to go away now, before you start showing properly.'

'Go away?' I said, imagining myself begging in the streets and having the baby in some dank alleyway all by myself.

Mum took a deep breath. She opened her handbag and took out the tightly folded piece of paper. 'I suppose we'll have to get in touch with this social worker person. Dear God, the shame of it! She'll have to find us one of these mother and baby homes. Preferably far away, where no one knows us. Don't look at me like that, Laura. It's your own fault. You can come back home after you've had the baby. We'll make something up, pretend you've been ill,' said Mum.

'But people will know when I come back here with a baby!' I said.

Mum and Dad were staring at me as if I'd said something stupid.

'I can still come back here, can't I?' I stammered.

'You can, of course you can. What do you think we are? You're our daughter, in spite of everything. But you can't come back with a baby! You'll have it adopted,' said Mum firmly.

I was shocked. It was illogical, I knew. I didn't want this baby. I'd tried my hardest to get rid of it with those awful pills. And yet it seemed so dreadful to think of giving it away to somebody else.

'It'll be *my* daughter,' I said. 'Or my son.' It was the first time I'd actually thought about it like that. Up till now I'd looked at the thing in my stomach as some terrible unwanted growth that I couldn't think about because it made me so scared. I hadn't even imagined what it looked like. But now it suddenly became a very small person curled up inside me. It was still frightening – but it was mine.

'Can't I keep it?' I whispered.

'Don't be ridiculous! How could you ever look after a baby? You can't even look after yourself. And what would you do about your schooling? You can't just pop your baby in your satchel and take it out to feed it at lunchtime!' said Mum.

'But – couldn't you . . .?'

'I can't take on your child, Laura! People would guess it wasn't mine. We'd be pointed at in the streets and shamed as a family. We might be poor but we've always kept ourselves decent. We live at Lily Cottage, the nicest of all the prefabs, and we have a daughter at the Grammar. How could you spoil it all for us? I thought I'd brought you up to know right from wrong. It wouldn't be quite so bad if you were properly grown up and had got yourself into trouble. But at fourteen! You've thrown your life away. I'd have given anything in the world to go to a fancy grammar school and get a good education. I'm not sure they'll take you back, even if we hush it all up. I daresay that Nina will find out and spread it all round.'

'No she won't,' I said, though I wasn't sure.

'You'll have to go to the secondary modern to take your O-levels, if they even do exams there. You'll end up in a factory with no qualifications, just like I did. Oh, my *head*, I've got such a pain!' Mum went to the cupboard drawer where she kept the aspirin. She shook out a couple, and then declared, 'I might as well take the lot!'

I knew she didn't really mean it, but it frightened me all the same. My stomach clenched. I realized I'd had tummy ache on and off most of the day. I wondered if the Nurse Brown pills could possibly be working after all. Or maybe I was losing the baby anyway, the way Mum lost the first little Laura?

But it must have been fear and tension because nothing happened. I lay awake worrying that night, and it was gone two o'clock by the time I got to sleep. I woke up at the usual time. I put my hands gingerly on my tummy. It had stopped hurting now. It was distinctly rounded still, even though I was lying down. It was there. My baby.

I stayed in bed for a while, not wanting to get up and face Mum. I heard Dad going off to work. I waited, and at last I heard Mum walking down the hall, shuffling in her old slippers.

'Come on, get up!' she said. She hadn't brought me a breakfast tray this time.

'Am I going to school?' I asked timidly.

'No, of course not! I've phoned this Mrs Jeffries, the social worker. We've got an appointment at ten o'clock at her office. I said it was an emergency,' said Mum. 'We've got to get you into one of these homes as soon as possible, before anyone guesses.'

'But I don't want to go to a home!' I said. 'Can't I just stay here? I won't go out at all if you don't want me to. I'll just hide here, in my bedroom.'

'Don't be silly. You know what they're like round here. They'll come knocking, like that little Moira,' said Mum.

'Oh, goodness, Moira!' I said.

'I told her you were still poorly. She wanted to come in and see you! I said she couldn't, she might catch something, and she said she didn't care, cheeky little madam. I sent her off with a flea in her ear,' said Mum.

'Poor Moira,' I said guiltily.

'I don't know why you ever palled up with her. Those Flannagans are such a dreadful family. Still, if you stay round here with a big belly, even riff-raff like them will be looking down on us,' said Mum, sniffing. 'Get *up*, Laura. Have a good wash and put on your pinafore dress and your good white blouse. I want you looking as decent as possible. And no make-up!'

I did exactly as I was told and consequently looked about Moira's age to see this Mrs Jeffries. She was one of those middle-aged breezy women in a tweedy suit, the sort that breathes capability, but she looked shocked when she saw me.

'Oh, my goodness, cupcake, how old are you?' she said.

'Fourteen,' I said miserably.

'Well, you have got yourself into a pretty pickle, haven't you?' she said, shaking her head. 'Sit yourselves down, ladies. Try not to get yourself into a state, Mrs Peterson.'

Mum had already started crying. She fumbled in her handbag for a hankie. It was an unused Christmas present one, with a scratchy white lace border. Mum kept it in her hand for the whole interview, holding it tight like a cuddle blanket.

Mrs Jeffries started making notes. I had to admit all over again that I didn't know very much about the baby's father, not even his last name, and I didn't have a clue of his whereabouts. Mum hung her head as I whispered all this.

'I don't know how she could have done it. She wasn't brought up like that. And she says she didn't even like this boy very much! I'm so ashamed!' she said, over and over.

'These things happen, Mrs Peterson. Don't worry, I'm not going to point a finger at either of you. I feel very sorry for you both. But it's truly not the end of the world. I take it you don't want to stay at home for your confinement, Laura?'

'Well—' I started.

'She couldn't! Everyone would know. And it's not as if she's keeping the baby,' said Mum.

'I might,' I muttered.

'A baby isn't a doll, Laura,' said Mrs Jeffries. 'You have to feed it five times a day, and once at night too. It cries a great deal. You have to change its nappies; indeed, you have to *wash* all those nappies, and that's not a fun job. You have to stay at home to look after it, evening after evening, while your friends are out having fun. Is that really what you want?'

'I daresay she might want *me* to do it, but I don't see how I can. I'd have to give up my job and we've just got used to having a bit of extra money coming into the house. And how could we afford all the expense of the baby things? Laura hasn't got a clue when it comes to money, what misery it is to scrimp and scrape all the time. And it isn't as if she's old enough to get a job herself,' Mum said in a rush. 'We had such high hopes for her too. And now she's ruined everything.'

'I can see it seems that way now. But Laura's young and resilient. I daresay this time next year she'll be back in school, studying for her exams, still doing well,' said Mrs Jeffries.

'Unless I keep the baby,' I said.

'Listen, dear, no one's going to *make* you give it up for adoption. But think carefully. What would your baby want? Would Baby want to live with you and have a difficult childhood with a very young mother and the stigma of everyone knowing it doesn't have a father? Or would Baby want to grow up with two loving well-to-do parents who can lavish everything on it?' said Mrs Jeffries.

I found my hands were clasped round my stomach. 'I could lavish it with love,' I said.

Mrs Jeffries smiled at me sadly. 'I daresay you could, dear, but you're still a child yourself. Anyway, you don't have to make the decision right now. You've got many months to mull things over. As things might be difficult for all of you if you stay at home, I think a mother and baby home will be best for you. I know of one specially for young girls, Heathcote House, where you can continue your schooling right up until their baby is born. However, I'm afraid it's quite a long way away, in Sussex. It might make visiting a bit of a problem.'

'We'll manage,' said Mum. She paused, gripping tightly onto her hankie. 'Does it ... cost us anything?' she whispered, embarrassed that she even had to be asking.

'Oh no, don't worry, Mrs Peterson. It's totally free.' Mrs Jeffries smiled reassuringly.

'Please, then,' Mum mumbled, 'can you see if there's a place for Laura, as soon as possible?'

It was as if she couldn't wait to see the back of me. Mrs Jeffries phoned the home while we waited. Mum was practically shredding her handkerchief. Mrs Jeffries said my name and emphasized my age. Then she kept nodding, and scribbling little notes, but we couldn't make out the gist of the conversation until she put the phone down at last and smiled at us.

'We're in luck,' she said, which seemed such a weird thing to say given the circumstances. 'There's a girl leaving this morning, so you can go there today if you like, Laura.'

'Today!' I said. 'I thought it wouldn't be for weeks!'

'Well, you can wait a bit longer if you want to, but there's no guarantee they'd have a place for you then. They've actually got a waiting list, but the matron is a friend of mine so she's letting us jump the queue as you're so young,' said Mrs Jeffries.

'It's better to go now, Laura. What's the point of hanging around at home?' said Mum. She paused. 'They will look after her, won't they, Mrs Jeffries? I mean, as you say, she *is* very young.'

'Of course. The matron is a lovely, sensible woman, and she gets on very well with all the girls, takes a real interest in them. Then there's a housekeeper; she does all the cooking, making sure everyone gets a decent meal; that's obviously very important. And there's a resident trained nurse too, though the girls have their babies in the local hospital. You can visit at the weekends if travelling isn't too much of a problem. I've written the address and telephone number here. You can get a train from Victoria, but you'll have to get a taxi when you reach the station. I wouldn't pack too much, Laura, as there's very limited space for personal belongings at the home.' Mrs Jeffries smiled again, pleased that it was all settled.

It had taken just ten minutes to change my whole life. My head was reeling. Even Mum was looking uncertain now.

'Will you be keeping an eye on Laura too?' she asked Mrs Jeffries.

'Well, I'll certainly do my best to visit in a month or so, to make sure she's settled in. And then of course I'll be there after the baby arrives, to make the arrangements.' She caught my eye. 'Or help out in any way,' she added. 'And you have my phone number if you need it.'

Mum and I were still sitting, dazed, so she stood up and held out her hand. Mum stood up too and shook it uncertainly. I did the same. Mrs Jeffries patted my elbow too.

'Chin up, Laura. Everything will be fine. You might find you really like being at Heathcote House. It's a bit like boarding school. I daresay there's a midnight feast or two!' she said.

I stared at her as if she was mad, imagining a circle of girls with enormous stomachs munching buns by candlelight in their pyjamas. Mum wavered a bit as we went down the stairs, having to clutch the bannisters as if she felt faint.

'Mum? Are you all right?'

'Just watch the steps, they're quite steep,' she murmured.

When we were out in the open again we stood looking at each other, not sure what to do next. Then Mum took a deep breath.

'Right! We'd better go to C&A's,' she said.

'You want to go *shopping*?' I said incredulously.

'No, of course I don't want to,' Mum snapped. 'But you're not going to stay this size, are you? You need a proper maternity dress.'

'Not yet! Not now!' I protested.

'We'd better set off for this godforsaken place early this afternoon, after lunch,' said Mum. 'Come on!'

Already? And why was she sending me there if she thought it was godforsaken?

'I don't need an actual maternity dress. My pinafore's still very loose. And so's my school tunic,' I said, unable to bear the thought of standing in front of a rack of maternity smocks.

Mum didn't like the idea any more than me, but she pulled me inside the shop and marched me to the right section. 'Which one do you want?' she asked.

The maternity smocks were mostly patterned with overblown roses. I wondered if it was by chance, or whether the blooming flowers were a metaphor for pregnancy. Either way, they were hideous. I picked the only frock that wasn't floral: a fine corduroy with a navy and red check.

'Thank God for the January sales,' said Mum, looking at the price ticket.

It was still expensive, even though it was now half price, but Mum paid in cash from her big black purse.

'Isn't that the housekeeping money?' I asked.

'Well, there'll be one less to feed now, won't there?' said Mum brutally, but then she caught her lip with her teeth and screwed up her face. She was fighting not to cry again and shame us in the middle of C&A's.

When she took the checked dress to the counter the shop lady smiled at her. 'Ah! Are you going to give your daughter a little brother or sister?' she asked.

Mum smiled tightly without replying and paid the money.

'I'm sorry,' I murmured.

'So am I,' she said.

We bought other things too, shampoo and soap, and deodorant, but I already had a newish sponge bag and towel from my summer coach trip.

'What about my pyjamas?' I said. 'Won't I need a bigger pair?'

'You'll have to have one of my nighties. You can have my new one. I can make do,' said Mum.

My heart sank. Mum had a hideous pale pink brushed nylon nightdress with puffed sleeves. I'd look like one of the ballet-dancing elephants in *Fantasia*. Mum had taken me to see the film one Saturday afternoon when I was little. I hadn't liked all the swirling music and had climbed on Mum's lap and sucked my thumb.

Maybe Mum was remembering too because she suddenly stood still. 'There's only bread and a scrap of cheese at home. Shall we have lunch out?' she suggested.

I thought we'd go to a Lyons for tomato soup and a roll, but she took me to the Black and White Milk Bar instead.

'Seeing as it's your favourite,' she said. 'And you can choose anything you want.'

I wondered about choosing a Knickerbocker Glory but I didn't have the stomach for it. I had cheese on toast instead, and a frothy coffee. Mum had the same. It wasn't actually all that wonderful, and we could have had the same meal at home for a tenth of the price, but it meant a lot that Mum had suggested it. She'd probably have to do without lunch altogether until payday now.

We walked home, and then I had to start packing, with Mum supervising. I put the black jumper in because it was a big Sloppy Joe style and would still fit. Mum didn't comment, but she protested when I put the trews in my suitcase too.

'Don't be silly, Laura. They won't fit you now,' she said impatiently.

'They're for when I've had it,' I said.

'Oh! I see. Well, all right, though I doubt you'll get your figure back straight away. You don't just snap back like elastic, you know,' she said.

I didn't know. It was a horrifying thought. I already hated looking at my body and I dreaded getting any bigger. It would be awful if it stayed enormous *after* the baby, all saggy and baggy.

I didn't know what else to pack. How could I squeeze all the things I needed into one small suitcase? I'd need pen and pencils for schoolwork – but what about books? I took my Katherine Mansfield short stories from Aunt Susannah, the Bertrams' copy of *Madame Bovary*, because I'd actually skipped a lot of it before. I'd lent *Young Bess* to Nina and she'd never given it back. I wasn't that keen on *Peyton Place*, not enough to read it a second time. I didn't want to take any of my childhood favourites in case the other girls laughed at me for being babyish. In the end I sifted through the latest paperbacks left behind on coach trips and selected one with a pretty oriental lady on the front wearing a tight satin dress. It was called *The World of Suzie Wong*. She looked a little like the painting of our Miss Wong in our living room.

'Is that one your dad brought home? I hope it's suitable,' said Mum, as I tucked it in my case.

'What about Dad?' I said suddenly. 'I can't go without saying goodbye to him!'

'It's maybe better like this,' Mum said awkwardly. 'He's very upset.'

'What do you mean? He does still love me, doesn't he?' I whispered.

'Well . . . I daresay. But it's come as such a shock to him. He's always thought of you as his little girl,' said Mum.

'I *am*!' I said.

'He just doesn't want to see you at the moment, if you must know,' said Mum. 'Don't look like that. He'll come round. He's not saying you can't come back. It's just for now.'

I felt sick knowing that my own dad didn't want to see me. And Mum didn't seem very keen either. She usually fussed if I went into town on my own – and yet here she was urging me to go a hundred miles away.

'Will you visit me, Mum?' I asked.

'Yes, of course. I'll do my best. I can't take any more time off work – my job's hanging by a thread as it is for taking time off – but I could try travelling on a Sunday, I suppose, though I don't know where the money's going to come from,' Mum said doubtfully.

I started to panic. I was so used to being the centre of attention, Mum and Dad's golden girl, and yet now they were so ashamed of me.

'What about Nina, Mum? Can't I even say goodbye to her?' I asked desperately.

'Absolutely not! You're to keep away from that girl altogether. I'm sure this is all her fault. She's influenced you for the bad. Now

244

come on, Laura, you've got a very long journey. Get a move on,' Mum said.

'You are coming with me, aren't you?' I asked.

'Well, I suppose so. I'll have to see how much the fare is. And it'll mean I won't get back here till late in the evening! It seems a bit pointless to go all that way, when I'll have to come straight home after delivering you to the door,' she said.

'All right, don't come. I don't need you to. I was just asking, that's all,' I said, trying to pretend I didn't care. I was actually terrified of making that journey by myself. I felt more like four than fourteen. I'd never have dreamed of travelling to London by myself, let alone changing trains and going all the way to Sussex and then getting a taxi to the home. I'd never been in a taxi in my life – and if I told the driver where I needed to go he'd know I was going to have a baby and maybe call me names.

Mum left me to finish getting ready but when I went to find her she had her own coat on with her brooch pinned on the collar and her chiffon scarf, her best winter outfit.

'I thought I'd just walk you to the station and buy the ticket for you,' she said, putting on her leather gloves.

'Oh, Mum,' I said. I wanted to hug her but held back, afraid she'd push me away.

She insisted on carrying my suitcase too. 'You shouldn't be carrying heavy weights, not now,' she said.

It was a good half-hour's walk to the station because we went the long way round through the town. I knew why. The quicker way would take us past my school.

'I'm going to write them a letter,' Mum said. 'I thought I'd tell them you've got TB.'

'What?' I said, astonished.

'There's a woman up the road from us, near where that Moira lives – she had TB a while ago. She had to go to a sanatorium. She was away six months. Well, it seems a perfect thing to tell your headmistress. Maybe she'll take you back at the start of the autumn term,' Mum said.

'Do you think she'll believe that?'

'*I* don't know. Of course she might be wary of you going back to school if she thinks you're still infectious. Still, we might as well give it a try,' said Mum.

I didn't think it was going to work. And I was worried about Mum writing the letter. She wasn't very good at spelling and she phrased things oddly, though her grammar was immaculate. Still, I couldn't worry about it now. There were far more pressing things.

We got to the station at last and stood in the queue at the ticket office. I rehearsed my goodbyes in my head. There were too many people around for me to start crying. Mum looked near tears herself, and when she got her purse out I saw her hand was trembling.

She asked for a child's single ticket for me and then sighed and added, 'And another day-return ticket for me.'

'Oh, Mum, you don't have to. It'll be so expensive!' I said, but I was weak with relief.

It cost even more than I'd thought, and Mum looked taken aback, but paid for it all the same, using several notes and a great many coins. The ticket man counted them out slowly, tutting.

'Where did you get all that money?' I hissed, as we went to the platform.

'It's some of the savings out of the old tea caddy,' said Mum.

'Oh, that's awful! You were going to buy a washing machine!' I said.

'Yes, well, I've got used to going down the launderette,' Mum said.

'But you said you weren't coming!'

'I know. I was going to give it to you, for the taxi and anything else you might need while you're away. But when I saw your little face I couldn't do it! You're too young to travel all that way – you'd just get yourself lost,' said Mum.

I did hug her then and she hugged me back, even though people on the platform stared at us.

In actual fact, we *both* got a bit lost at Clapham Junction, because we went to find the Ladies toilets and then couldn't work out which new platform we needed and nearly got on a train going the wrong way.

We sat up straight when we were on the right train at last, peering anxiously out the window for the rest of the journey, terrified we might miss our stop altogether. We leaped up as soon as the train attendant eventually announced our station. Mum asked a porter if there might be a bus to Little Haverington, but he shrugged and said he didn't know of one, and we'd better get a taxi.

This was another ordeal, standing at the taxi stand wondering whether it was ever going to come, and then when it did, it didn't look like a proper taxi at all. We were expecting a boxy black cab like the taxis in London, but this was a strange white and turquoise affair. Mum dithered, wondering whether it was safe to get in, or whether we'd be abducted and end up part of the white slave trade, whatever that was – but the driver seemed a perfectly normal family man. He gave a little nod when Mum said we wanted to go to Heathcote House, but didn't make any remark whatsoever, just stowed my case in the boot and held the car door open for us.

We sat tensely in the back of the car, peering at the countryside.

'It's quite nice round here,' Mum murmured. 'Lovely fields and hills. I wonder if they'll let you go out for walks?'

'It's not like it's a prison,' I said. 'Or is it?'

'No, of course not,' said Mum uncertainly.

'And if I don't like it, can I come home?' I whispered.

'Well . . . you've got to give it a chance, dear,' said Mum. 'Be a brave girl.'

We held hands in the back of the car. After a good fifteen or twenty minutes the driver turned down a small lane with a signpost saying *Little Haverington*. We couldn't see any sort of Haverington, big or small. There were no shops, no pubs, and hardly any houses, just a smattering of tiny cottages.

'Oh my God, it's the back of beyond,' said Mum.

Then we turned up a driveway, drove under a canopy of tall gloomy trees and stopped outside a grey stone house with a small tower at either end as grim decoration.

'Is this it?' said Mum.

'It looks awful!' I said.

'Don't be silly, it's rather grand,' Mum said desperately. She looked at the driver. 'I'll just see my daughter inside, and then I'll need a lift back to the station. You'll wait for me, won't you?'

He nodded. 'Don't worry, I'll have a little smoke break,' he said, getting out of the car and handing us the suitcase.

Mum and I walked up the three wide stone steps to the front door. We looked at each other. There wasn't a proper knocker, just a bell that you pulled. Mum tried and it jangled alarmingly. We waited for a while. I peered in one of the windows. There were some girls there, two slumped on an old sofa, another in an armchair with her feet up on a lopsided leatherette pouffe. They all wore maternity smocks and looked much older than me. They had heavily backcombed hair set in hard, harsh styles. They didn't look very friendly.

Then the door opened. Another girl stood there, much slimmer, with shoulder-length wavy blonde hair. She was carefully made up, with a lot of lipstick on her big lips. I stared at her in awe. She looked exactly like the actress Diana Dors.

Mum sniffed.

'Can we see the matron, please,' she said.

'Sure,' said the blonde girl, opening the door wider. She winked at me. 'Welcome to Heathcote House!'

We stepped inside, into the hallway. The house smelled strongly of
fish, with an undertone of polish, disinfectant and talcum powder.
Mum and I must have wrinkled our noses because the girl laughed.

'It does whiff a bit, doesn't it? It's smoked haddock for tea,' she
said.

'Very nourishing,' Mum murmured.

The door on the right opened, and the girls in maternity
smocks peered out curiously.

'My God, the new girl only looks about ten!' one of them said,
and the others exclaimed and giggled.

I felt myself going scarlet.

'Take no notice of that lot,' said the blonde girl. 'Though how
old *are* you?'

'Fourteen,' I mumbled.

'Crikey!' she exclaimed. 'You started young!'

She didn't say it nastily, but Mum bristled. 'Could we see the matron right away – I've got my taxi waiting,' she said in her poshest voice, as if we travelled by taxi daily.

'Up the stairs then,' said the girl.

She sped up them lightly. She was wearing a tight sweater and slacks. She was plump in a luscious kind of way, but she couldn't possibly be pregnant. She surely couldn't be the deputy matron or the nurse?

Mum struggled after her, determinedly carrying my suitcase though I tried to take it off her. The blonde girl knocked at a door on the right.

'Come in!'

'Hey, Miss Andrews, the new girl's arrived. With her mum,' said the blonde, opening the door.

'Thank you, Belinda.'

Belinda had always been one of my favourite names, ever since I read the *Pookie* books when I was little. I smiled at her and she smiled back. I liked her, though I knew perfectly well that Mum thought her common, and fast into the bargain.

'I'll hang around and show you where to go after,' she said.

'Do come in. You must be Laura and Mrs Peterson,' said the matron. She was sitting behind a big desk. She looked very like a school teacher, in a twinset, with a neat, no-nonsense haircut and glasses. 'Do sit down,' she said, indicating a couple of chairs. 'I expect you'd like a cup of tea after your long journey?'

'Well, I have to be going. I have a taxi outside, but tea would be very nice, though I really can't stay long,' Mum gabbled. 'Please don't go to any trouble, er, Matron.'

'No trouble at all,' she replied. 'And do call me Miss Andrews. "Matron" sounds so formal.'

She was trying to put us at our ease, but she *was* formal, right down to her clipped fingernails. She stepped out from behind her desk and put a small electric kettle on to boil, setting a tray with three china cups and saucers, and arranging shortbread fingers from a tin into a precise star shape on a patterned plate. She wore a crisply pleated skirt, lisle stockings and highly polished brogues. You couldn't imagine her ever stepping in anything unpleasant.

'It's ever so kind of you,' said Mum, licking her lips nervously. 'Milk and one sugar, for both of us, please. Now I have to say this – I know you'll think my Laura a bad girl—'

'Not at all,' said Miss Andrews smoothly.

'She's never even had a boyfriend. She's a bright girl, she's got a scholarship to the local grammar school,' Mum said.

'*Mum!*' I hissed.

'I don't think she even knew what she was doing,' Mum persisted.

'*Please!*' I tried to stop her, though it was true enough.

'She's made the biggest mistake in her life and now she's paying for it. But she's a good girl really, that's what I need you to know, and she's still only a child herself. You will look after her, won't you?' Mum begged.

'Of course I will,' said Miss Andrews.

'And you won't work her too hard? She's a delicate girl, not really used to housework of any kind – and in her condition . . .'

'I promise you Laura will get the best care possible here. You mustn't worry,' said Miss Andrews, pouring hot water into a pretty teapot.

'And when her time comes, you will let us know, won't you?' said Mum.

'We always do. You will be able to visit her in the hospital if you'd like to,' said Miss Andrews.

'And then—?' Mum started.

'Then Laura will return here and stay for a month or so with her baby,' said Miss Andrews.

'But she's going to have it adopted! Why can't it be taken straight away, as soon as she's had it?' Mum said. 'It's cruel to make her look after it. She'll get attached.'

'We feel it's best for both mother and baby. Laura will be feeding her child and giving it the best start in life. Surely that's a good thing? The baby will thrive and Laura will be able to find comfort in her sadness, knowing that she's done a truly wonderful thing for her little boy or girl.'

Miss Andrews' voice had a solemn lilt to it now, as if she were speaking from a pulpit. I wondered if she really believed this or was simply parroting the same old phrases she said every time a new girl came to Heathcote House.

She made a mistake saying the last three words though. When she talked about a 'baby' it was such a general word it didn't make you think of an *actual* baby, just an anonymous shape in a shawl. Saying 'boy or girl' suddenly turned it into a real little person.

I thought of the knitted outfits hidden in the box in the Cubby Hole, one pink, one blue. I imagined the baby inside me wearing one of them. *My* baby wouldn't be a grubby, smelly, yelling creature like Moira's sad little sister. I would keep him or her well fed and spotless, and cuddle them so they wouldn't cry.

I waited until I'd had a sip of tea and a bite of shortbread, and then I murmured, 'Don't some of the girls keep their babies?'

'A few do,' said Miss Andrews.

'So I could keep mine, if I decided to?' I asked.

'Laura, you know that's not possible,' said Mum. 'Don't start that.' She looked at the brass clock on Miss Andrews' mantelpiece and panicked. 'I'd better go. The taxi will be costing a fortune.' She drank the rest of her tea in two gulps and then stood up.

'Mum?' I whispered, suddenly terrified at being left here without her.

'Be a good girl,' she said, giving me one quick hug, and then she was off before I could tell her I loved her and I was sorry and I'd miss her so much.

'There now. It's sad to say goodbye, but I'm sure your mother will come and visit you soon,' said Miss Andrews. 'Eat your shortbread finger.'

I tried to do as I was told, but there was such a lump in my throat it was like chewing a real finger. I had to put it back on the plate after one desperate nibble. The star shape was spoiled now.

'I expect it feels very strange now, but I know you'll get used to being here, Laura,' said Miss Andrews.

How did she know? She didn't know anything about me. And how could she say so certainly that all the girls were comforted when they gave their babies away? *Miss* Andrews. So she'd never had a baby herself, I was sure. I could feel angry tears prickling my eyes. I didn't want her to see them.

'Please may I look to see if Mum got her taxi all right?' I said and rushed to the window.

I stood beside the long velvet curtain. There was the taxi, still on the driveway, and the cabbie was opening the door for Mum. She was hiding her face. I ran my stubby fingernails against the grain of the velvet to distract myself.

'Go and find Belinda and she'll show you round,' Miss Andrews suggested. 'Supper won't be long. Chin up.'

I picked up my suitcase and walked out of the room, closing the door behind me. The case was much heavier than I realized. I felt bad that Mum had valiantly carried it for me all the way from home.

There was no sign of Belinda. I didn't know whether to wander on along the corridor or go back downstairs. The smell of fish wafted upwards so pungently that I felt sick. I thought I'd better find a toilet just in case but couldn't see one anywhere.

I blundered about, my suitcase banging my legs, and then saw Belinda right at the end of the corridor.

'Oh, hey,' she said, coming towards me. She moved with a wonderful sway of the hips. I wondered whether I could ever learn to walk like that when I wasn't pregnant. I hated even thinking that word. My stomach lurched.

'Please, can you tell me where the toilet is?' I asked urgently.

'Sure. Better be quick. You won't be popular if you throw up on the floor. Leave your suitcase,' said Belinda. She hurried me along a long corridor with curtained partitions on either side, and then into a large room full of sinks and doors. I barged though the nearest door, bent over the toilet and was very sick.

I knew I was making a horrible noise but I couldn't help it. The door only reached down to my calves so I knew Belinda could hear. I waited until I was sure it was over, and then wiped my eyes and mouth and staggered into the open.

'Poor old sausage,' said Belinda sympathetically. 'Splash your face and rinse your mouth out. I know just how you feel. I threw up constantly until I was five months gone but then it cleared up overnight, thank God, and I've felt fit as a fiddle ever since.'

'I haven't been sick before,' I said weakly. 'I think it's just coming here. It's all so . . .'

'I know!' said Belinda. 'And it's worse for you because you're so young. What's your name?'

'Laura.'

'Pretty name!'

'I like yours better. Belinda. The woodcutter's daughter,' I said.

She looked at me blankly. 'You what? My dad's not a woodcutter, he's a publican!'

'No, I didn't mean . . . She's in a children's book, Belinda, and she looks after this little white rabbit called Pookie. Didn't you read it when you were small?' I asked.

'Don't think so. I had a little Noddy book once, and then I read the Famous Five. I'm more into magazines now. Film ones,' she said, putting her hand on her hip and striking a pose.

'You look like a film star yourself,' I said shyly.

'Do you really think so?' she said, tremendously pleased. 'I'd absolutely love to get into films – or maybe modelling. Of course, I'll have to get my figure back properly first.'

'When did you have your baby?' I asked.

'A fortnight ago. I've only been back at this old dump for a couple of days,' said Belinda. 'It stinks, doesn't it? It was lovely in hospital. The food was marvellous, and we had hot chocolate every morning, all creamy on top, mm! It was a bit hopeless trying to lose weight in there, especially as my Rick bought me this gigantic box of chocolates.'

'Rick?'

'My fiancé,' she said, and she held out her left hand proudly.

I looked at the ring on her finger, with the little sparkly stone.

'It's lovely,' I said politely.

'It's real, a diamond solitaire,' she said.

'So you're getting married?' I said.

'I'm not quite old enough now. But the minute I'm sixteen in the summer we're off to Gretna, Rick and me,' said Belinda. She saw me looking blank. 'Gretna Green, silly. It's the first little place you get to in Scotland. You can elope and get married there, even if you don't have your parents' permission. It's going to be so romantic! We might even get in the papers, as Rick's ever so good-looking, and I'm – well, I'm not bad,' she said coyly.

'So your parents won't give their permission?'

'It's mostly my dad. He thinks I'm too young. He wants me to carry on at school and get my O-levels. It's only because he's forked out for the school fees all this time – it's private, you see. And he can't stand Rick either. It's not Rick himself; it would be any boy. Dad's like that, possessive,' said Belinda, sighing.

'Mine is too,' I said quickly. 'He wanted to find this boy I met and beat him up.'

'Dads! Pathetic, aren't they?' said Belinda.

'And what about the baby?' I asked. 'Are you keeping it?'

'Of course!' said Belinda. 'He's adorable! Are you feeling better now? Come and see him!'

She took my arm as if we were old friends and hurried me back along the corridor, past my suitcase and up another flight of stairs.

'I suppose these used to be little attic rooms, but they've turned it into a big nursery – and Nurse March has got her bedroom up here too. Monica calls her Nurse Starch because she wears this white starched apron that's as stiff as a board, and she can be a bit stiff and starchy herself, but she's OK really,' said Belinda. 'Come and meet her.'

The nursery was surprisingly lovely. It was dark now and the skylights in the ceiling meant the babies in their little beds could look right up at the moon and stars. They were lying in proper cots with cute animals painted on the headboards. Each baby had a white crocheted blanket and a little white bonnet on their downy heads to keep them warm, though there were storage heaters all round the room. Nurse March was sitting in a rocking chair at one end, with a baby on her lap.

She was quite old, her hair iron-grey underneath her white starched cap, and her face scored with wrinkles. She looked quite fierce, but when she looked at the baby her face softened.

'The poor little mite's got the wind,' she said, sitting it up and patting its tiny back. 'I keep telling Monica to hold the bottle up when she feeds the sad little soul, but she doesn't listen, the silly girl. I don't care for bottle feeding anyway. You're another naughty girl, Belinda. You'd give Baby a much better start in life if you did as nature intended.'

'Some of us have our figures to think of, Nurse March,' said Belinda cheerily. 'Meet the new girl, Laura.'

'Oh my Lord, you're just a baby yourself, dear,' said Nurse March. 'How far gone are you?'

'I'm not quite sure. Maybe five months?' I said.

'Ah well. You'll be with us a while, that's good. I hold my clinic for expecting mums on Fridays. You come and see me then and we'll make sure everything's absolutely tickety-boo. Don't look so anxious, dear. You'll settle down in no time.' She peered at me. 'Nasty dark circles under your eyes though! Are you constipated?'

That question again! 'No!' I said, embarrassed.

261

'Give over, Nurse March!' said Belinda, walking to the cot at the end with a blue donkey decoration. 'Here's my little darling. Isn't my Peter the bonniest baby of them all?'

'Now don't you go waking him up, Belinda. He's only just piped down. He's got a strong pair of lungs on him, that little lad.'

'Like me!' said Belinda, sticking out her impressive chest and laughing. She took no notice of Nurse March and gently hooked her little boy out of his cot. 'There now, little Peter. Oh, who's a lovely boy, eh? Have you got a smile for my friend Laura, eh?'

'I'm telling you, babies can't smile for at least six weeks,' said Nurse March. 'They might look as if they're smiling, but it's only wind.'

'Oh, you're obsessed with wind!' said Belinda cheekily. She held her baby out to me. 'Here, have a cuddle.'

'No, really,' I said quickly, but she was already pressing him into my arms.

He felt so little and light and warm. I couldn't help holding him close. His eyes were open now, blue, with long lashes. A wisp of golden hair escaped from his bonnet. His skin was incredibly delicate, his cheeks pale rose. He was so different from Moira's little sister. He was beautiful.

'Hello, Peter,' I whispered.

He blinked at me in a friendly way. I was as surprised as if my old doll Rosebud had clicked her eyes open and shut independently.

I wedged him against the rise of my stomach, where my own baby was curled.

'Look at him batting his eyes at you!' said Belinda. 'He's flirting already, bless him. Isn't he a little poppet?'

'He's lovely,' I said.

'So lovely I could eat him all up,' said Belinda, taking Peter from me and nuzzling into his tiny stalk neck.

'Put him down, you two. He'll get hiccups,' said Nurse March, taking the baby herself, but she couldn't resist giving him a little cuddle herself.

'He's the sweetest baby in the whole nursery, isn't he?' Belinda said proudly.

'All my babies are sweet,' said Nurse March, but you could tell she agreed. 'Off you go, girls.'

'You're so lucky,' I said to Belinda as we went out the nursery and down the stairs.

'I know,' said Belinda complacently. She looked at her watch. 'Supper in five minutes. I'd better give you a whistle-stop tour.'

She showed me the 'cubies', the beds with their curtains in two rows, like a hospital ward. The flimsy curtains gave you no privacy at all. If I cried at night then all the other girls in the room would hear.

Belinda saw my face. 'I started off in the cubies. It's fun, actually. Miss Andrews puts the lights out at eleven, but everyone stays awake and whispers. Sometimes we even had a midnight feast, just like one of those boarding school books.'

'So where do you sleep then?' I asked.

'In one of the tower rooms,' said Belinda. 'There's three of us. Monica, Jeannie and me. I'll show you.'

The walls were painted an uninspiring cream, and the curtains were insipid beige, but someone had put fairy lights up at the window and arranged china ladies in crinolines along the mantelpiece. The plain bedside lamps had red silk scarves wound round them to make a rosy glow, and one of the beds had a pink satin eiderdown.

'That's mine,' said Belinda. 'I don't see why the bedroom can't look pretty. I have to clear all my stuff away if Miss Andrews decides to make one of her inspections, but she doesn't do that often.'

'You've made it look lovely,' I said. 'I wish I could sleep in here too.'

'Well, we could take your bed in the cubies and cram it in here, but I think Miss Andrews would make a fuss. Not to mention Jeannie. She can be a bit of a whatsit at times. Still, I'll only be here another fortnight or so and then you can bag my bed,' she said.

The whole point of being in the tower room was being with Belinda, so I smiled wanly and didn't say any more. She helped me back to the cubies, and to drag my suitcase to the spare cubicle at the end of the row. It looked bleaker than ever. A narrow bed with two thin grey blankets. A small bedside locker one side, a tall narrow locker the other for my clothes. A threadbare rug on the cold linoleum floor.

I sat down on the bed. It was as hard as a board.

'I know, it's not very comfy,' Belinda said sympathetically. 'Miss Andrews says it's because you need firm support when you're preggers. The girls all say she bought a job lot of sub-standard beds that a prison turned down.' She paused. 'That was a joke! Here, I'll help you unpack,' said Belinda.

She admired my big black sweater and trews but was tactfully silent as she hung up my blue and red tartan tent. She was interested in my books, but disappointed by their covers.

'I like romances,' she said.

'I think this one is a romance,' I said, offering her *The World of Suzie Wong*.

She flicked through, looking amused. 'Isn't she on the game?' she said.

I didn't know what she meant, and just shrugged. 'Maybe.'

Then a loud gong sounded downstairs, making me jump.

'Ah, supper time. Come on,' said Belinda. 'You can meet all the others.'

'I'm still feeling a bit sick,' I said. 'Maybe I'll just stay here.'

I couldn't face the thought of meeting a lot of other girls, but Belinda insisted.

The fish smell was even stronger in the dining room. It was served by a tall thin woman with straggly hair. She had the limp, drooping look of a rag doll.

'Ah! You must be the new girl. My goodness, you're so *young*!' she said. She was frowning. She didn't say, 'Shame on you!' but I was sure she was thinking it.

It looked as if I was going to be greeted like this by everyone.

'I'm Marilyn,' she said. 'Here's your haddock. There's chunks of bread in the basket. And help yourself to a glass of milk.'

'I don't really like milk,' I said.

'You must drink it; it's very good for your baby,' she said, dismissing me and turning to the next girl in the queue.

'Come and sit over here,' said Belinda. 'Don't fuss about your milk. I'll drink it for you. I love it – I could lap it up all day, like a cat.'

'Is that Marilyn the cook?' I asked her.

'Well, she's actually the deputy matron, but she does all sorts – cooks, supervises the housework, even looks after the babies on Nurse March's day off. She gets a bit ratty at times, but she can be a laugh. Ah, Monica and Jeannie are sitting over here. Come and meet them,' said Belinda.

Monica was a dithery-looking girl with very prominent teeth, like a rabbit. She seemed quite friendly. Jeannie was small and squat, her maternity smock creased and grubby. She raised her plucked eyebrows when she saw me.

'Are ten-year-olds having babies now?' she said.

'Shut up, Jeannie, she's nearly as old as you. Budge up and make room for Laura,' said Belinda.

'How come you're here then?' Jeannie asked me as soon as I'd sat down.

'Well, it's obvious, isn't it? I'm going to have a baby,' I said, trying to act cool.

'So how did it happen?' said Jeannie.

'It's none of your business,' I said quickly.

'Quite. We're all in the same boat,' said Belinda. She patted my hand under the table.

'My boyfriend Mike promised nothing would happen, not if we did it standing up,' said Monica. 'And then he promised he'd stick around when I fell pregnant. And *then* he said he'd come and visit me here, but he hasn't, not even when I had little Michael. I wish I hadn't named him after his dad now,' said Monica, biting her lip with her big teeth.

'Do shut up about him, Mon,' said Jeannie irritably.

'But what am I going to do? I had it all planned that little Michael and I would live at his place with his mum and dad because *my* mum and dad won't have me home with a baby, but I

267

can't live with his parents if Michael doesn't want me any more,' she wailed.

'Well, you'll just have to have little Michael adopted then,' said Jeannie.

'Never!' said Monica. 'I don't know how you can bear to give up yours.'

'Ain't got no choice, have I?' said Jeannie. 'I haven't even got a proper boyfriend. This is what you get if you just lark around a bit. It's not fair, because the boys get off scot-free.' She swatted at her swollen stomach and then saw my face. 'What are you looking so shocked for, eh? I suppose you're all set on keeping yours and Mummy and Daddy are helping you out,' she said, putting on a silly voice.

She thought I was posh because of the way I spoke! Mum had always fussed about my accent, and when I started at the Grammar it was somehow second nature to imitate the way the other girls talked, especially when I made friends with Nina.

'I don't know what I'm doing,' I mumbled.

'Yeah, and you probably didn't know what you were doing when you got pregnant in the first place,' said Jeannie. 'I bet it was your first time! I bet you let some random boy have his way with you because you were too dumb to say no!'

It was almost as if she'd seen me going into that awful cricket hut with Léon and watched the clumsy fumbling in the dark. I had a small mouthful of haddock in my mouth. It felt slimy on my tongue. I had to spit it out into my hankie.

'Leave her alone, Jeannie!' said Belinda. 'What's the matter with you? She's only a kid.'

I pushed the rest of the haddock to the side of my plate. Jeannie was looking at me triumphantly, knowing she'd hit a nerve.

'I have got a boyfriend, if you must know,' I said. 'His name's Daniel. And he loves me and he wants to marry me when I'm older, but the thing is, he's doing his A-levels this year and he's going to university to do medicine so he can be a doctor like his dad. He said he'd give it all up to look after me and the baby, but I won't let him spoil his own future.'

Belinda and Monica and Jeannie stared at me.

'Oh, that's so tragic!' said Belinda.

'You poor thing!' said Monica.

Jeannie just shrugged, but even she looked impressed. They all believed me! *I* almost believed it myself. I felt so much better I managed to eat all my bread, and then a slice of millionaire's shortbread for pudding, which actually tasted delicious.

We went in the living room together afterwards. Belinda introduced me to some of the other girls but it was hard remembering all their names. There weren't enough armchairs or sofas for everyone, but the four of us crammed into a three-seater sofa. One of the other girls put a record on the Dansette, and everyone started singing along to an Elvis Presley number. I felt I should join in but I didn't know the words. A couple of girls actually started jiving together a little clumsily because they were both heavily pregnant. Someone else played Cliff Richard's hit 'Living Doll' next and I could sing along too, because Nina and Patsy were Cliff fans and sang the words over and over. Belinda rocked an imaginary baby in her arms and we all laughed, shaking the sofa.

I decided it wasn't so bad after all at Heathcote House – in fact, it was almost good fun. But at quarter to ten the girls who had already had their babies stood up eagerly, ready to go up to the nursery.

'Got to prepare his little Lordship's bottle,' said Belinda. 'Night then, girls.'

It wasn't the same without her and Monica. I didn't know what to talk about with Jeannie. I was actually a bit afraid of her.

I gave a great false yawn. 'I'm ever so tired. I think I'm going up to bed now,' I said.

'Suit yourself,' said Jeannie. She stretched out on the sofa, wriggling her legs. Her ankles were very swollen. She actually looked swollen all over. I panicked, wondering if I was going to be as bloated as that in a couple of months. The lump inside me stopped being a baby, feeling like an alien now, taking me over. Maybe Jeannie was right. It might be better to give the baby away.

I wished I could get it all over right now. I still had months and months to go, stuck here.

I went upstairs to my cubicle. It seemed bleaker than ever. I quickly changed into my nightie and dressing gown. They smelled of Mum and Lily Cottage and I had such a wave of homesickness I thought I was going to faint. I staggered along to the bathroom. My back was aching badly and I decided it might help if I had a hot bath. There were two baths at the end, each curtained off and reasonably private. I started running the hot tap, waiting for it to warm up. It started off tepid and got colder and colder.

Another girl came into the bathroom in a quilted dressing gown, looking enormous.

'What are you *doing*?' she said crossly, and she turned the hot tap off.

'I want to have a bath but the water isn't hot enough,' I said.

'Well, no, it never is at this time. And now you've made it even colder, you fool. I wanted to wash my hair,' she said.

'Oh, sorry! I didn't know,' I said. 'You mean we can't *ever* have a bath?'

'Between seven and nine in the evening. But you can't have one whenever you want. There's a rota. You only get two baths a week. But dream on if you want Friday night or Saturday night, because everyone wants to look good before visiting days,' she said. She filled a washbasin with cold water, took a deep breath, and then plunged her head in. She raised it immediately. 'Jesus!' she said, hurriedly rubbed shampoo into her scalp, and then did her best to rinse it in the stone-cold water.

I felt I needed a proper wash myself but I was too shy to strip off in front of this girl, so I made do with washing my face. Then I had to use the loo though I knew she could hear everything. I came out hot with embarrassment, but by the time I'd padded back to my cubicle I was shivering. There had been a coal fire in the living room, but there seemed to be no heating at all on the first floor.

I got into my bed. The starched sheets felt icy. I got up again and put on my dressing gown and a pair of socks, but they weren't much help. The two blankets were worn thin and not wide enough whenever I turned over they came loose and let in draughts. I heard a couple of other girls going into their own cubicles, but they were giggling and gossiping, not ready to settle down and go to sleep. I heard one of them mention 'the new girl', and they had a discussion about my age. I burrowed further down under the thin blankets, unable to stop the tears now. I managed to do it quietly, biting my knuckle to stop myself actually sobbing.

Then after an age, when all the cubicles were occupied, and some of the girls were snoring, I sensed someone putting their head round my curtain. I didn't move, not wanting to stick my head out of the blankets because they'd see my wet face.

'Night night, Laura.' Belinda! 'Sleep tight. And don't let the bugs bite.' She patted my shoulder gently and then shuffled off in her mules.

I felt so much better then. I went to sleep that night before Miss Andrews turned the lights off at the mains.

I was surprised by how much work we had to do at Heathcote House, and how dreadfully long the days were. I was woken at quarter to six by whisperings and trudging feet. The girls who had already had their babies had to be up at the nursery by six o'clock for feeding time. It seemed a ridiculously early start to the day but it was the rules. One girl, Val, refused to get out of her bed, even when her friends tried to tip her out. Nurse March complained about her to Miss Andrews, and the day after that a social worker came to Heathcote House and left with Val's baby in her arms. Val left soon after, sobbing.

The pregnant girls were allowed to stay in bed until half past six but were expected to be washed and dressed and downstairs for breakfast at seven. It was hard to grab a turn at the washbasins because there were so many of us, and the queues for the few toilets were dreadful. One girl was hugely pregnant, already three days overdue, and she actually wet herself while she was waiting. I'd have died of embarrassment but she just swore, mopped up the puddle, and then washed herself at a basin, hoiking her nightdress up to her waist.

Breakfast was at seven: cereal, boiled eggs and toast. Then it was chores. We all had to take a turn. The girls who'd had their babies had to soak and boil the nappies, clean and sterilize the bottles, handwash the tiny clothes, then wipe down every surface in the nursery and mop the floor. The girls still waiting had to wash up the breakfast things and put them away, clean the kitchen, do the laundry, make our beds, dust, sweep and polish all the communal areas, and help Marilyn prepare the vegetables for lunch.

I was hopeless at all the chores. I'd always taken it for granted that Mum did all the housework. I'd 'helped' once or twice with the dusting and the carpet sweeper, but that was all. It was a shock having to get down on my knees and scrub the floor. I tried my hardest, my hands turning scarlet in the cold soapy water, but couldn't seem to get the knack. My back started to ache badly. It seemed so unfair to be told to scrub floors while pregnant. The girl with me was so vast her stomach brushed the ground when she knelt, but she cleaned twice as much floor as I did.

When I thought my own patch was almost done I got up

clumsily to stretch, kicked my bucket accidentally, and the dirty water poured all over the clean floor, hers as well as mine.

'Stupid cow,' she said, but she wasn't really angry. She just sighed heavily and started over again, while I babbled apologies.

Lessons started at nine o'clock. They were held in a proper schoolroom with desks, though it was a tight squeeze for girls towards the end of their pregnancy. We had three teachers who doubled up subjects: Mrs Chambers for English and history, Miss Brown for maths and science, and Mr Michaels for French and geography. Mrs Chambers was quite old and Miss Brown was quite young, and they both wore glasses. Mr Michaels caused a flutter of interest as he was the only male who came to Heathcote House apart from visitors, but he was uninspiring. He was bald apart from a wisp of hair at ear level and had a pot belly.

I was surprised by the lessons. They were so easy, the sort of stuff we'd covered in the first year at the Grammar, but the other girls moaned and complained and said it was all far too hard. I didn't comment, but I couldn't help putting my hand up a lot to answer. The other girls sighed and started calling me a swot, even Belinda, so I soon shut up.

Belinda and Monica and the other new mothers went upstairs to the nursery at ten o'clock to bathe and feed their babies. Miss Andrews took the rest of us for craft. We had to make a complete set of clothing for our babies – a handsewn embroidered nightdress with a matching bonnet; or a large crocheted shawl; or a knitted cap, matinee jacket and booties. I didn't even know how to sew on a button, I couldn't crochet, and I couldn't knit properly either, though I'd made long woollen snakes with a Knitting Nancy set when I was little.

'I can't really do any of them, Miss Andrews,' I said helplessly.

'It doesn't matter, Laura. I'm here to teach you,' said Miss Andrews. 'Don't look so worried, you'll soon pick it up.'

She gave me a much-used knitting pattern, a pair of thin steel knitting needles and a ball of soft white wool. The strand I was using quickly became grey as I attempted casting on, and then plain and purl. I had to keep unravelling my attempts. In the end Miss Andrews cast on for me and did the first couple of rows.

'Your baby will be fourteen by the time you've finished its outfit,' Jeannie remarked. She was surprisingly expert at knitting, and was on her last bootie. 'Though why I have to make my baby an outfit when it's going to be adopted I just can't fathom,' she said.

'It's your gift for your baby. When the time comes for its new mummy and daddy to tell Baby its birth story then it will know just how much you loved it because you took such care over its first outfit,' said Miss Andrews, in a preachy voice.

'My baby will think I hated it then,' I muttered to Jeannie, and she cackled.

She was like Nina. If you stood up to her and said something funny she stopped being quite so mean. Oh, Nina! It was so strange to think she was at school with Patsy, while I was stuck here. I wondered if she'd tell her what had happened to me. I was pretty sure she wouldn't be able to keep her mouth shut. And Patsy would spread it all around. My cheeks burned, thinking what they might be saying.

We had recreation at eleven o'clock, when we were all together again. We had yet another glass of milk and a biscuit out of a large tin. We weren't supposed to look at what we were taking, so I ended up with a plain digestive, while Belinda and Monica and Jeannie had the sense to grab the chocolate bourbons.

Then we had a maths lesson followed by French. Mr Michaels put on a very fancy French accent, rolling his r's so much his tongue must have got tired. The girls got the giggles, but I was painfully reminded of Léon and felt sick. I felt angry too. He'd be sitting in a proper classroom at some French lycée without a care in the world. He might be boasting to his mates that he'd actually done it with some easy English girl without ever knowing she was now swelling up with his baby.

He probably wouldn't even remember what I looked like. But then my idea of him was very hazy. He was just a fumbled embrace, a stammer of words in a foreign accent. Would the baby inside me share his looks, his habits, his awkward personality? I hoped for a girl now, not a small strange boy who looked like his father.

Mr Michaels' lessons were polluted with the smell of lunch cooking, stews and mince and liver, all of which turned my stomach. There were scoops of mashed potato too, and cabbage one day, carrots the next. If there were too many vegetables left over they reappeared as bubble and squeak at supper time. We had milk puddings, rice or semolina or slimy tapioca, with dollops of cheap red jam to make them more palatable. Miss Andrews and Marilyn poured so much milk into us one way or another they might have had an entire herd of cows lowing in the back garden.

We were supposed to have a half-hour nap after lunch, and then we divided again. Some of the girls went to attend to their babies, while the rest of us did Quiet Reading. It seemed odd terminology. How else could you read? Though there were a couple of girls who had to mutter the words to themselves, pointing with their fingers. There was a small library, but the books all looked very boring – mostly those career novels for teenagers with ridiculous titles like *Doreen is a Dentist* or *Vera is a Vet*. There was no *Sophie is a Schoolgirl Mother*. No one bothered with these. There were some well-thumbed Mills and Boon romances, a few jolly hockey-sticks boarding school stories, and a pile of women's magazines.

I read my own copy of *The World of Suzie Wong*. Jeannie yawned her way through the problem pages of the magazines.

'What's that book you're reading then? The print's ever so tiny. You'll give yourself a headache,' she said, peering over my shoulder. Then she said, 'Mm! It doesn't look too bad. Can I read it after you?'

'OK, if you want,' I said. 'Though I've promised Belinda she could read it first.'

I hadn't done any such thing, but I wanted to show Jeannie that Belinda was my most important friend.

'Well, she'd better hurry up, as she'll be going soon. I heard they've got a couple all lined up desperate for a fair little boy,' said Jeannie.

'What? No, you've got it wrong, Belinda's keeping little Peter. She's engaged!' I said.

'Rubbish,' said Jeannie.

'No, it's not! Haven't you seen her diamond ring?'

'It's just a glass one from Woolworths, stupid,' said Jeannie.

'Stop it! How can you talk like that about Belinda? She's your friend!' I said, shocked.

'She *is* my friend, but she tells lies like all the others. Like you, going on about this Daniel,' she said. 'I've been thinking. You've just made him up, haven't you?'

'No I haven't! He's real, I swear it, God's honour!' I said. It wasn't a lie, he really did exist.

'Then I shall look forward to seeing him visiting you,' said Jeannie.

'Well. He might not be able to come. It's so far away,' I blustered.

'Oh, yeah, yeah,' said Jeannie, yawning again. 'I've heard it all before.'

We had two more lessons after our reading session, which seemed very unfair, because schools don't make you work till five, not even strict ones like the Grammar. But we didn't have to do any homework, which was a bonus. Then the babies had to be fed again – they seemed endlessly hungry, like baby birds with frantic open beaks. The pregnant girls huddled in the living room near the fire and chatted and ate sweets (and two girls smoked too, sticking their heads out of the window).

Then Belinda came back, glowing, telling us how Peter had hung onto her finger all the time she was nursing him as if he could never bear to let her go.

'I love him so much,' she said, her eyes watering. I was certain that Jeannie had told me a pack of lies. Belinda would never part with her baby in a million years.

Supper was egg on toast, which at least didn't smell as bad as the haddock, and milky cocoa, with plates of iced buns for a pudding. The girls practically fought over those buns because everyone wanted the pink ones with the dab of jam inside. I was painfully reminded of the cake shop at home.

'Are you all right, Laura?' Belinda asked.

'Yes. No. Well, I'm a bit homesick. And missing my friends,' I mumbled.

'And Daniel?' Belinda said.

'Oh yes, very much,' I said.

'Maybe he will manage to visit you somehow,' she suggested.

'I don't think so,' I said.

'Well, never mind. I expect your mum and dad will come,' she said comfortingly.

'Not on Saturday. They'll both be working. But maybe Sunday,' I said.

The weekends were much better at Heathcote House. We still had to get up early and tackle all the chores while the babies were fed, but we were otherwise free. We could even go out to the village if we wanted, though it was a twenty-minute walk. After Belinda and Monica had given their babies a bath and their ten o'clock feed, we all ambled down there.

I felt a bit awkward when we passed anyone in the street, worrying that they'd stare at my bump, though I still wasn't really showing much. Jeannie was huge but she stared back fiercely at everyone, ready with a rude retort if there were any comments.

There wasn't anything much to see in the village. There was the Anchor Inn, but we weren't allowed in pubs, and a church, though most of us weren't very religious. The only shop was a small general store but the girls acted as if it were Harrods.

They bought four-ounce paper bags of boiled sweets and childish penny treats like bubblegum and gobstoppers and sherbet dabs. They chose chocolate bars too – Fry's Turkish Delight and Crunchie and Cadbury's Fruit & Nut – and Belinda bought a bag of oranges as well, though Jeannie complained that they'd make the bedroom stink.

'Can't help it. I've still got a craving for them, have done since I got pregnant,' said Belinda.

'Your skin will turn orange if you don't watch out,' said Jeannie.

'I don't think so,' said Belinda, a little smugly. She had beautiful soft pink and white skin, whereas Jeannie was going through a spotty stage.

She bought postcards too, and stamps, and a *Woman's Own*. Jeannie bought a new biro and a *Mirabelle* love comic. Monica bought ladybird slides for her flyaway hair and a *Beano*. 'Well, I need a good chuckle,' she said defensively.

Belinda noticed I wasn't buying anything. 'Here, Laura,' she whispered, and she pressed a shilling into my hand.

'Oh no, you don't have to do that. I've got my own money, honestly,' I said, making her take it back. 'But you're so kind.'

I felt I had to buy something then, though I wasn't really in the mood. I selected several postcards, though they were just dull views of the village, and six stamps.

'I'm going to write to Daniel,' I said.

I did too, that afternoon, when I was lounging in the tower room with the other three girls. I didn't write to the *real* Daniel. There wouldn't be any point. Dr Bertram would tear up a postcard from me if it came flipping through their letter box.

Dearest Daniel,

I am missing you so much! It's not as awful here at the home as I thought it would be, and I've made some lovely new friends – but I still feel so lonely and sad. If only we could be together! But don't worry, we will find a way. I know you love me and will stay true to me and that one day we will somehow be a family with our baby.

    All the love in the world,

Your Laura xxxxx

I sighed as I wrote, deliberately drawing attention to myself.

'Are you really writing to this Daniel you keep going on about?' Jeannie asked.

'Yes,' I said, adding further kisses right to the bottom of the postcard.

'No you're not,' said Jeannie. 'I bet you're writing to your mum.'

'No, I'm not, I'm writing to Daniel, I *said*,' I protested.

284

'Leave Laura alone,' said Belinda, swotting at Jeannie with her *Woman's Own*.

'She's having us on,' said Jeannie, and she suddenly snatched at my postcard and darted to the other side of the room, surprisingly agile in spite of her bulk.

'Give it back to her!' Belinda shouted.

Monica giggled, her hand over her mouth. 'Read it out then, Jeannie!' she spluttered.

'"Dearest Daniel,"' Jeannie read. '"I am missing you so much."' Then her voice petered away. She pulled a face. 'It's just full of stupid lovey-dovey stuff,' she declared, coming over and flipping it back to me.

'See!' Belinda said. 'You can be a real little cow sometimes, Jeannie.'

I felt triumphant. Jeannie had fallen right into my trap. But she still wouldn't give up.

'Yeah, but she hasn't put an address on it or anything. She's just mucking about. She's not going to *send* it,' she said.

'Of course I am,' I said, writing an address immediately. Not Daniel's actual address. I made one up, writing to a street number that I knew didn't exist in a road near Shanty Town. I made up Daniel's surname too, calling him Mansfield. Then I stuck a stamp in the right-hand corner to give the postcard added authenticity.

'There!' I said.

I wondered about writing to Mum and Dad. I knew Mum would be worrying desperately about me. Maybe Dad too, even though he was so angry with me. I'd never been away from home before. But they hadn't written to *me*. Miss Andrews gave out the post at breakfast. I'd listened for my name, heart thumping, but I didn't get anything.

I couldn't help hoping that Mum would come on Sunday. Maybe Dad would be able to borrow a car from one of his mates at the coach depot? There were several visitors to Heathcote House that Saturday afternoon, but not for any of us. Belinda and Monica stayed up in the nursery, playing with their babies. Belinda asked Nurse March if I could come too, but there were already a couple of grandmas clucking over the new additions to their families and she said it was too crowded.

I didn't want to hang out with Jeannie or any of the other girls, so I went for another walk all by myself. I didn't really know where I was going, so I just retraced my steps to the village. I posted my card in the postbox there. I knew it wasn't going anywhere. It would stay undelivered in some sorting office for a while and then be chucked in the rubbish. But I was almost starting to believe in this imaginary Daniel. I pictured him clutching my postcard on Monday morning, so relieved that I'd written to him.

'*Darling Laura*,' he'd whisper, and he'd maybe kiss the back of my card where I'd signed my name.

'Darling Daniel,' I said out loud, and a stout woman walking past me stared and then sniffed. I don't think she had a cold. It was a snort of contempt.

'Young hussy!' she hissed.

I wished I had Belinda with me, or Monica, or even Jeannie. Jeannie, most of all, because she'd make a rude retort. I tried to think of something to say in reply but failed. How did she even know I was pregnant? I wasn't showing much, not in my winter coat. I felt so awkwardly self-conscious now that I sidled along, head down.

A couple of schoolboys cycled past on their new Christmas bikes and I clenched my fists, waiting for them to call after me, but thank goodness they were too absorbed in trying to race each other to take any notice of me.

I trudged back to Heathcote House and went to lurk in my cubicle, reading *The World of Suzie Wong*. She was a good-time girl. People thought of me the same way now, and I could understand Mum's determination to hide me away before any of the neighbours realized.

I vowed not to go out anywhere again, but to my horror Miss Andrews insisted we all go to the eleven o'clock Sunday service at the village church. The babies were given their ten o'clock bath and feed at half past nine, so everyone could set off on time. The pavements were narrow, so we had to walk in a straggly crocodile.

Belinda walked with me right at the back of the line, which was a comfort. Monica and Jeannie were just in front.

'Does everyone peer at us in church?' I asked.

'Don't worry, they won't stare at us,' Belinda said mysteriously.

We got to the start of the village. Monica and Jeannie slowed down, letting the other girls march on ahead. Then they suddenly darted down a little lane between the houses.

Belinda took my arm. 'Come on,' she said, pulling me down the lane too.

We hurtled forward, one after the other, and ended up in a small recreation ground with four battered swings.

'Dearly Beloved, let us give praise to freedom!' Belinda shouted, jumping on a swing.

I climbed on a swing too; we all did. It was the tiniest rebellion, but it felt so exciting!

'Won't Miss Andrews be furious though?' I asked, working my legs hard to go higher and higher.

'She won't know,' said Belinda.

'Not unless the others snitch – and we don't think they even notice,' said Monica.

'Miss Andrews doesn't go to church herself. She stays snug as a bug in her room, with a cup of cocoa, selfish old bat,' said Jeannie. 'I wish I had one. I'm freezing to death.'

She only wore a light windcheater that emphasized her

stomach. She wore the same maternity smock every day, with a man's big cardigan and an old skirt with the zip wide open, the hem riding up and exposing her plump knees.

Belinda was wearing a cute knitted cap the same pink as her lipstick. She jumped off her swing and stuck her cap on Jeannie's tufty hair. 'Here,' she said. 'Warm your ears up!' She jumped back on her own swing and dragged it backwards with her toes. 'Let's all swing together. One two three, go!'

We had a few ragged starts, but before long we were all swinging in unison, kicking our legs up like four chorus girls. We went higher and higher until it seemed like any moment we'd be swung right up to the sky. I clung to the cold metal chains and flung my head back, so that the clouds seemed to whirl around me. It was magical – but then they whirled too fast, and I started to feel dizzy.

I slowed down abruptly and juddered to a halt, bending forwards.

'You're not going to puke, are you?' said Jeannie.

'I hope not,' I murmured weakly.

'I threw up for weeks and weeks,' said Monica. 'I had to run the bath taps full on so my mum wouldn't hear me. She's coming this afternoon – oh, I can't wait to see her! It'll be the first time she's seen little Michael and I just know she'll fall in love with him. He's so gorgeous, a true little angel.'

I'd seen Monica's baby Michael, and he seemed a puny little

creature beside Belinda's Peter but perhaps he looked different to her family. I hoped my own baby would look attractive. Then perhaps Mum would love it. She really liked babies, after all. She had tried so hard to have me.

I couldn't wait to see her, even though we'd only been parted a few days. It seemed as if I'd been at Heathcote House for ever. I was so het up about it I could hardly eat any lunch, although it was a proper Sunday dinner, beef and roast potatoes and sprouts instead of cabbage. Marilyn even made Yorkshire puddings, and we had jelly and evaporated milk in jugs afterwards.

The smell of lunch lingered throughout the afternoon.

'It shows the visitors we're being fed properly,' said Jeannie.

'Is your mum coming today?' I asked her.

'Nope,' said Jeannie. She stared at me fiercely, as if daring me to say any more.

'Oh,' I commented inadequately.

Belinda's mother came. She looked like an exaggerated version of her daughter. She made a fuss of me, calling me 'pet' and 'poppet', but then she went up to the nursery with Belinda to see Peter. They borrowed one of the Heathcote House prams and took him out for a walk.

Monica's mum visited too, with her dad. They went to see baby Michael, but very briefly. Then they went for a car ride with Monica, but they left the baby behind.

'Oh dear. Looks like they didn't think much of the little mini-Mike,' said Jeannie.

'Don't be mean,' I said.

'That's me. Meanie Jeannie,' she said. 'I'm going to have a lie-down. Can I borrow that book of yours, Laura? The one about the girl called Suzie?'

I hadn't finished it yet, but I nodded. I was still a bit scared of her – and yet sorry for her too. I didn't need my book. My mum would be coming any minute.

But she didn't come. I waited and waited by the window, until it got dark. I started to get really worried.

'Maybe she got lost on the way,' I said to Belinda. Her mother had already gone. So had all the other visitors. There was a strange sad quietness in the living room. Several girls looked as if they'd been crying. Monica had gone up to the nursery and hadn't come back. Even Belinda was very subdued, though she patted me reassuringly.

'Perhaps she'll come next week,' she said.

'You don't think something's happened to her, do you? She hasn't written to me either, yet she always fusses over me so. Do you think I should ask Miss Andrews if I could use her phone and ring home?' I said.

'I don't think she'd let you, not unless it was a true emergency,' said Belinda.

'But maybe it is. She *said* she'd come! She promised!' I said, though she hadn't at all. I knew how expensive it was. I couldn't expect her to use up even more of her savings. And it was such a long way. I knew all this, but I still couldn't help panicking. 'I want my mum!' I wailed like an idiot.

'I know. We all do,' said Belinda. 'I'm missing my mum already and I've only just seen her. But it will be OK, Laura, I promise. You'll feel better in the morning.'

I wasn't sure. I cried in my cubicle that night, with the pillow over my head in case anyone heard me. Then I had a thought that made me cry more. If missing Mum was as bad as this for me, what was it like for the babies when they were taken away by strangers? It was no use telling myself they were too little to notice who was holding them. Little Peter and Michael knew perfectly well who their own mothers were and stopped crying at once when the right pair of hands lifted them out of their cots. Thank goodness Belinda and Monica had both decided to keep their babies.

Monica looked unusually pale the next morning and didn't say a word at breakfast. She started sobbing in the middle of our maths lesson that morning. I thought Mrs Brown would become impatient. Monica couldn't tackle the simplest problem and just gave up, instead of trying to work it out. But this time Mrs Brown went up to Monica, patted her shoulder, and said she could go to her room if she wanted.

'Can I go with her, Mrs Brown?' Belinda asked.

'Of course,' said Mrs Brown, nodding.

'Come on, then, Mon,' Belinda said gently, helping Monica up and leading her carefully out of the room. Monica nestled into Belinda, making pathetic little whimpers.

I was crass enough to feel irritated. Why should Monica get all this special treatment just because she was a dunce at sums? I was shamefully jealous too. *I* wanted to be Belinda's special friend.

Monica didn't come back at eleven for the next lesson. Belinda looked as if *she* had been crying now.

'What's the matter with Monica?' I whispered.

'She's with Michael,' Belinda said sadly.

'Is there something the matter with the baby?' I asked. He was so small and sallow. Perhaps he was really ill.

'No, he's fine. He looks lovely, actually. Monica's dressed him up in the little nightgown and cap and he looks just like a Victorian baby doll,' said Belinda, sniffing.

'But I thought those clothes were for when the babies leave here.'

'They are. Monica's been told a couple are coming at twelve o'clock for him,' said Belinda.

'What? For *Michael*? But Monica's keeping him!' I said.

'She wants to, but her parents won't let her. They've talked her into thinking it will be best for everyone if Michael is adopted.

They stayed in a hotel last night and they're taking Monica back home this afternoon,' said Belinda, a tear rolling down her cheek.

'Now then, girls,' said Mrs Chambers. 'Try to concentrate on doing your précis exercise.'

'But it's so awful, Mrs Chambers,' I burst out. 'We've just heard the news about poor Monica and her baby!'

I could get away with a lot with Mrs Chambers because I was top at English. She looked at me pityingly. 'It's always very sad when the time comes for your babies to go to their new homes – but don't forget, you're doing your very best for them by giving them a new start in life,' she said. She seemed to have read the same guide book as Mrs Jeffries.

'I think the very best we can do for our babies is to let them stay with us!' I said.

'Yes, that's right, Laura!' said Belinda, and then suddenly everyone was joining in with me, declaring that they were definitely keeping their babies. Even Jeannie joined in, though she said later it was just for solidarity.

'Girls, girls!' said Mrs Chambers wearily, but she didn't get cross.

We heard a car draw up towards the end of our lesson and we all rushed to the window.

'It's only a Ford Anglia,' said Belinda. 'I thought it would be at least a Rover.'

'You don't have to be rich to adopt, Belinda,' said Mrs Chambers.

'But it would be better for Michael if they were,' she said. 'Better for Monica too, imagining him having lots of parties and presents and football lessons and pony rides.'

We couldn't really see much of Michael's prospective parents, looking down from this angle. The man was going bald at the back. The woman had an old-fashioned perm.

'They're too old,' I said.

'Oh, Laura! I should say they're barely thirty,' said Mrs Chambers.

'They're too *ordinary*,' I protested. 'Doesn't Monica have any say in who gets her baby?'

'You can't pick and choose!' said Mrs Chambers.

'Yes, but *they* can,' said Jeannie. 'Boy or girl. And if one of the babies has some little thing wrong with it, they can turn it down and wait for a perfect one. That's not fair, is it?'

'No, it's not fair,' said Mrs Chambers. 'But life isn't fair. All you poor girls have had a raw deal.'

We stared at her in surprise. Everyone else treated us as if we'd all done something dreadful. The girls who went to church said the vicar often preached about shame, though he added that no one should cast the first stone. He reminded the congregation that Jesus preached that even the most immoral sinners should be forgiven. They said some of the congregation actually turned round and stared at the girls from Heathcote House.

'Don't you think we're sinners, miss?' someone asked.

'Mrs Chambers,' she said gently. 'No, I don't. I think you've had bad luck, that's all. But the whole purpose of Heathcote House is to give you a new chance in life. A fresh start.'

I frowned. 'Do you really believe that, Mrs Chambers?' I said quietly.

She hesitated. 'I didn't say *I* believed that, Laura,' she murmured. 'But you must have been doing well at school. Don't you want to go back and carry on with studying? Pass all your exams, maybe go on to do further training? You'd make a brilliant English teacher one day.'

I didn't want to be a teacher. I wanted to be something glamorous like an actress, not a boring old teacher! But I couldn't say that because I didn't want to hurt her feelings and she was the person I liked most at Heathcote House now, apart from Belinda.

She was still looking tearful. I had a terrible thought.

'Belinda, *you* won't have to give up little Peter, will you?' I whispered to her.

'No! Of course not. I told you, it's all fixed. I'm going to be getting married soon,' she said, fingering her diamond ring.

Jeannie raised her thin eyebrows, but she didn't say anything.

We couldn't concentrate on lessons any more. We were reluctant to go to lunch, though we could smell it was a liver day. No one liked liver, but we had bacon with it, and that was a treat. Then just as everyone was served, a girl at the window table shouted out. She was tall and broad and very tough. Everyone called her Big Pam deferentially. 'They're going. And they've got Michael,' she shouted.

We all rushed to the dining-room window, elbowing each other to try to get a proper view. There were the couple walking towards the car. The woman was going very slowly, with baby Michael wrapped in a blanket in her arms.

'She's holding him all wrong!' said Belinda. 'She needs to hold him more upright. And what a mad time to take him, when he'll be yelling for his bottle in half an hour. They could have waited!'

It seemed incredible that this couple could simply walk off with Monica's baby and no one was stopping them.

'I'll go to Monica,' said Belinda, standing up.

'No, you finish your meal,' said Marilyn. 'You won't be able to see her just now. She'll be with Miss Andrews.'

'But I'm her friend,' said Belinda. 'I have to say goodbye!'

'Is she going already?' I asked.

'Her parents are coming for her,' said Belinda. 'They should have been here for her when she had to hand the baby over.'

'It's generally a private time for the mother and the new parents,' said Marilyn. 'It's better that way.' She spoke calmly, as if it was the simplest transaction.

'There's another car! This will be them. I bet they were waiting just round the corner, watching to see the back of their grandson,' said Big Pam.

We all rushed to the window again, though Marilyn protested. 'For pity's sake, girls, that's best lamb's liver! Don't let it get cold!'

We watched Monica's parents walk up the path. The mother was very like Monica, with those big rabbity teeth. I wondered if Michael would have them too when they started to poke through his gums. It seemed terrible that Monica would never know.

'Could Monica still change her mind?' I asked Marilyn. 'I mean, I know she can't chase after that couple in the car, but Miss Andrews must have their address. She could get Michael back, couldn't she?'

'She's signed all the documents now,' said Marilyn. 'And she wouldn't want to do that anyway. She's being very brave and doing her best for her baby.'

'No she's not,' Belinda said. 'Please can I go and see her now?'

She didn't get a chance. None of us did. While we still had full plates Monica came out of Heathcote House with her parents. Her father was carrying her suitcase. Her mother was half carrying Monica herself, who was bent over, in floods of tears.

'Oh!' Belinda cried in agony. 'Poor, poor Mon!'

She opened the dining-room window and shouted, but Monica

298

was sobbing too hard to hear. Her parents bundled her into their car and drove off. It was all over so quickly and brutally.

When we went upstairs I followed Belinda and Jeannie into the tower room. Monica's dressing gown wasn't hanging on its hook. Her washbag was gone. Her hairbrush and slides weren't on her bedside locker. Her clown pyjama case wasn't on her pillow. Even the pillowcase and sheets were gone, her bed stripped. It was as if she'd never existed.

15

Marilyn told me Miss Andrews wanted to have a word with me before lessons the next morning. I immediately felt anxious, wondering what I'd done wrong. Or had something happened at home? Was that why Mum hadn't come to see me? I got myself so worked up that I could hardly take in what Miss Andrews was saying to me.

'You've settled in nicely here, Laura. I must admit, I was a little worried. We've never had a girl as young as fourteen before, and you don't seem the most sophisticated of young ladies.' She smiled at me, as if this was a compliment. 'I'm pleased that you've made some friends here. You seem particularly attached to Belinda.'

I nodded in agreement.

'She's a very good choice for a friend. A very kind, caring girl. A good role model. So I wondered if you'd like to join her and

Jeannie in the tower room now that there's a vacant bed? I would usually suggest one of the girls in the cubicles who has been here a while, but I think in this case you deserve it. Your teachers all speak very highly of you, and Marilyn says you're eating up nicely now, though you really must drink more milk, my dear.' She started a little lecture about the importance of protein and calcium for me and my growing baby, but I'd stopped listening.

Had she really said I could sleep in the lovely rosy tower room with Belinda?

'Laura?' said Miss Andrews. I was obviously looking dazed.

'When can I move in, Miss Andrews?' I asked.

'Right away,' she said. 'Clear your cubicle, fetch some clean bedding, and put your possessions in the tower room. It won't matter if you miss a little maths for once. Off you pop then!'

I did as she said – but then stuck my head back in the door of her study. 'Miss Andrews, do you think my mum's all right? She didn't come to see me on Sunday,' I said.

'Well, I don't think you can expect her to come every weekend, dear, not when it's such a long journey. But I was planning to phone her this week, just to put her mind at rest, so I'll check for you,' she said.

I hoped she might offer me a chance to speak to Mum too, but she waved her hand dismissively and I didn't like to persist in case she changed her mind about the tower room. I felt a stab of pure joy as I carted all my stuff there. I felt guilty about taking Monica's place, of course, but that wasn't my fault, after all. It would be such heaven to be with Belinda all the time. Even Jeannie wasn't quite as tough as she made out. I very much hoped we'd get along, the three of us together.

I whispered the good news to Belinda when I crept back into the classroom. She was looking unusually pale and subdued but her face lit up when she heard me.

'That's fantastic!' she said, and she squeezed my hand tight.

Even Jeannie stuck her thumb in the air when she knew. 'Though I hope to God you don't snore,' she added.

'I don't think I do,' I said, taking her seriously.

'Well, if you do I'll twist your nose off,' said Jeannie, pretending to do so, but she was laughing.

We had a little celebration in the tower room that evening. Belinda's mother had brought her a wonderful bag of treats on Sunday. She had new nylons, lilac soap and a bottle of Coty L'Aimant perfume, a big purple box of Cadbury's chocolates, a fruit cake with icing and marzipan, and three small bottles of Babycham with a jar of cherries and some cocktail sticks!

Belinda was so generous. I still rather resented letting Jeannie borrow *The World of Suzie Wong*, especially as she seemed a desperately slow reader and had only managed a couple of chapters so far. Belinda put the nylons in her locker but happily said we could all use the pink lilac soap when we had our baths, and she sprayed us with perfume so that the tower room smelled like the cosmetic department in a big store. She let us choose three chocolates each, cut us a big slice of cake using her nail file for a knife and made us each a Babycham cocktail in our water glasses. I'd never had Babycham before. The bubbles went up my nose and seemed to carry on fizzing all over my body.

We clinked glasses and drank to me, the new tower girl.

'And we'll drink to Monica and little Michael too,' said Belinda. 'Let's hope they're both happy somehow. I read a story in a magazine where a woman had to give up her baby, and then ten years later she was on a beach when she saw a whole bunch of children from Dr Barnado's and one of the little girls spotted her – and they knew each other just by instinct and flew into each other's arms.'

'Do you think that could really happen?' said Jeannie sceptically.

'Maybe. Anyway, it was a beautiful story. It made me cry,' said Belinda.

'Belinda, you won't let them talk you out of keeping Peter, will you?' I asked.

'Of course not!' she said fiercely.

'Even if they keep on and on at you?'

'No, it's all fixed. My dad's got a big pub and there are heaps of spare rooms upstairs. It'll be easy for Rick and me to have one of the big rooms, with the baby in with us just at first. Dad's fussing a bit about it, but Mum will talk him round, she always does. Then as soon as Rick's finished his apprenticeship he'll be earning good money and we can get our own flat. We'll be married by then, of course.' Belinda looked at her ring, glinting in the rosy lamplight.

I looked sharply at Jeannie, daring her to say anything to spoil Belinda's story, but this time she didn't even raise her eyebrows. Maybe Jeannie needed to believe it now. We were all so shocked that Michael had been stolen away from Monica so quickly.

I still felt a little anxious about Mum, but the next few days were wonderful all the same. I felt closer to Belinda and even Jeannie than I'd ever been with Nina – I didn't care that she was Patsy's best friend now. I had Belinda as my best ever friend, and Jeannie my second-best friend. I knew Mum would feel Belinda looked a little tarty at times and would condemn Jeannie as downright common – but I didn't care. Mum generally had a harsh opinion of everyone, saying they were either common as muck or much too la-di-da. She ridiculed them all. She was even scornful of Dad, fussing about his accent and his grammar and his habit of cutting his toenails over the *Daily Express* in the living room. The only person she thought halfway perfect was me, and that was mostly because she felt she'd brought me up properly. Only now, of course, I'd broken her heart by becoming a schoolgirl mum.

I hadn't realized quite how much it had affected her until I got the letter from Dad. We rarely sent letters in our family. Mum had had the same pad of Basildon Bond and small pack of envelopes in the tablecloth drawer ever since I could remember. Dad had used a page of it. It wasn't lined, as Mum thought that was common too. He wasn't used to writing on a blank page so his words went up and down as if they were bobbing about on a rough sea.

Dear Laura,

What are you playing at? That Matron of this Home your in was on the blower to Mum, saying you was upset she didnt come and visit. What are you trying to do, make out were bad parents? Weve dun our best for you and yet this is how you repay us. Rubbing our nose in the fact we aint got the cash for long jurneys clean across the country. Espeshally as Mum went all the way with you before and arrived home utterly exorsted.

Shes still very bothered with her nerves, not fit for work. She just cries and cries her blooming hart out, pore sole. Im not having you making it worse for her. You've made your bed and you must lie in it. Don't expect to see Mum or me for that matter till after.

I know this is hard but remember this is hard for us too, very very hard. I burst into tears on a coach trip the other day just thinking about it all and made a rite fool of myself in front of all the punters.
Love from Dad

I crumpled the letter into a tight little ball and stuffed it in my pinafore pocket.

'Bad news?' Belinda asked softly.

I shrugged, pressing my lips tight together.

'Is it from Daniel?' she persisted.

Jeannie looked interested now too. 'So he's written back to you, has he?'

I was too distraught to pretend. 'It's a horrible, mean, vile letter from my dad, saying the most terrible things,' I said, and I burst into tears.

Belinda and Jeannie took me up to the tower room and tried to calm me down.

'Can we look at it?' Belinda asked.

I'd normally hide it away because I didn't want anyone to mock my dad's bad grammar and spelling, but I was so hurt and angry now I didn't care. I did my best to smooth out the piece of paper, unwrapping it gingerly as if the words would fly out and sting me.

I thought Belinda might cry too and Jeannie might laugh, but they both seemed nonplussed.

'It's not that bad,' said Jeannie. 'He doesn't swear or call you names. You should have heard *my* dad when he found out about me. He came out with such a mouthful *and* he slapped me from here to next week.'

I wasn't sure if she was exaggerating or not. I had to admit Dad had never sworn at me or smacked me.

'And he says he loves you,' said Belinda.

'No he doesn't,' I said.

'Look, "Love from Dad",' she quoted.

'Yes, but that's just the way he's finished the letter. I don't think he does love me any more. Or Mum,' I said.

'Of course they love you. That's why they're so upset,' said Belinda.

'They're just worried about what people will say. That's why they've stuck me here,' I said, and I started howling properly. 'What if they never let me come home?'

'Don't get so upset, it's bad for your baby,' said Belinda. 'Of course they'll let you come home, silly.'

'But not with a baby,' I wailed.

'Your Daniel and his folks are going to look after you, aren't they?' said Jeannie.

'But what if they don't?'

'Well then, maybe you could come and live at our pub too,' said Belinda.

'What about me?' said Jeannie. 'Could I come too?'

'But you're not keeping your baby,' I said.

'I know. But I still don't think my mum and dad will have me back. I haven't always lived with them, even before. Miss

Andrews said I might have to live in a hostel place, but it sounds dreadful.'

'Then we'll all live there together, in the pub,' said Belinda. 'We could help out in the bar. Laura, you're a bit young, but you could help in the kitchen some of the time.'

'I can't really cook,' I said. 'Couldn't I go out to work? I'll be fifteen soon.'

'OK, what do you want to do then?' Belinda asked. 'You're pretty brainy. I expect you could get a job in an office.'

'Well, I know it sounds daft, but I'd actually like to be an actress,' I said.

'Oh, I'd like that too,' said Belinda. 'Hey, we could all be actresses and take turns to be in plays and films. We could make sure there was always one of us not working so we could look after the babies.'

We made plans excitedly, planning our lives as if we were three girls in a comic strip story. Even Jeannie joined in. We got so carried away we were fifteen minutes late for lessons and got into trouble, but we didn't care. And I tried to stop caring about Dad and Mum too. I decided I didn't need them now, not now I had my friends.

I wrote Mum and Dad a postcard though. At first it was going to be a furiously indignant message, saying I didn't give a stuff what they thought, and I was still their daughter, wasn't I, so how could they be so hateful, and it wasn't really my fault anyway, I hadn't *meant* to have a baby. But I waited several days until I'd calmed down a little and then wrote:

Dear Mum and Dad,

I was upset when I got your letter, Dad. I'm sorry you're so angry. And I'm sorry you're so upset, Mum. Please get better soon.

I do understand that you can't come and see me. It's just that I was worried about you. It's not too bad at Heathcote House and I have some lovely new friends, but I miss you both so much.
Love from Laura xx

I meant every word of the letter, but it was also an artful one. I wanted them to feel sorry for me. I needed them to be on my side. Because I'd made up my mind. I was definitely going to keep my baby now.

I wrote another postcard too. I pretended it was to Daniel, but it was really to Moira. There was another girl recently arrived at Heathcote House, so I wasn't the new girl any more. She was called Sarah, sixteen years old, pale and thin apart from her big bump, and she had bright red hair scraped back with an Alice band. She was a grammar school girl too, so Miss Andrews tried to pair us up together, thinking we would get on because we were both supposedly clever.

I didn't actually like Sarah at all, because she was so religious that she acted like a real prig. She felt we'd all sinned against Jesus. The girls in the cubicles said she went down on her knees every night and prayed for forgiveness. I steered clear of her as much as possible, but her red hair reminded me of Moira and I realized I was missing her a lot, far more than Nina.

Dear Moira,

I'm so sorry I didn't have a chance to say goodbye to you. I had to go and stay here straight away. It's a bit like a boarding school like those Twins at St Clare's books you borrowed. You can keep them if you like. We even have midnight feasts sometimes!

I miss our chats on the way to and from school. I hope everything's OK *with you and that the new baby isn't crying so much now.*

Take care.

Love from Laura xx

I didn't say exactly what 'here' was, but I put the address and she wrote back by return of post. She wrote on a torn-out page from her homework book, and reused an old envelope, but she managed a proper stamp.

Dear Laura,

I was ever so pleased to get your postcard! Is Heathcote House in the village on the picture? Your mum said you was ill and had to stay in a sanatorium somewhere until you were better, but she was maybe kidding me. I think I know why you've gone, because you were getting quite fat about the tum, but I won't say a word to anyone. It doesn't matter in the slightest to me, you're still my best friend and I look up to you and miss you ever so much.

Lots of love from your friend Moira xxxxxxxxxx

I burst into tears.

'Oh God, your dad hasn't written you another horrid letter, has he?' Belinda asked anxiously.

'No, it's a really lovely letter from a good friend at home,' I sobbed.

She looked surprised. 'Really? I thought you said she'd broken up being friends with you?'

I'd told her a little bit about Nina during long night-time conversations. I hadn't said she was Daniel's sister. The boy I talked about at Heathcote House had become a different Daniel altogether, gentle, tender and concerned. This imaginary one had taken me to play tennis every day and the imaginary me had learned quickly, and we'd won a cup for mixed doubles at our club.

Jeannie scoffed, turned over, and went to sleep. I wasn't sure even Belinda believed me, but now I'd invented him I couldn't stop.

I hadn't mentioned Moira before.

'She lives up the road from me and goes to my school,' I said. 'Oh, I wish I could see her!'

'Perhaps *she'll* come and visit you?' Belinda asked.

She knew I was finding the weekends difficult. Jeannie didn't get any visitors either, but she didn't seem to care. Maybe she was good at pretending too.

Belinda had visitors every weekend, mostly just her mother but her father came once. He was a big bluff man, good-looking in a chubby way, with an expensive suit and a big gold initial ring.

'Daddy!' Belinda cried out, like a little kid, and she flew into his arms. It was painful watching them.

'Belinda's so lucky,' I murmured to Jeannie.

Jeannie was too absorbed in her book to reply. *My* book. She was still only halfway through, though she'd had it weeks. Her lips moved as she read, mouthing the words.

I'd reread the whole of *Madame Bovary*, read my Katherine Mansfield stories too, and borrowed *Black Beauty* from the living room. I didn't usually like pony books, but thought this one was very moving and made me cry.

Miss Andrews spotted me going downstairs in tears. 'Oh dear, Laura, what's the matter?' she asked.

'Ginger's just died!' I said miserably.

'*What?*' Miss Andrews seized hold of me, looking horrified.

'It's this lovely lady horse in *Black Beauty*. She's got this wicked owner who's just beaten her to death!' I said.

'For goodness' sake, Laura!' said Miss Andrews, letting me go, and leaning against the wall. 'For one terrible moment I thought you meant something had happened to Sarah! I've heard some of the girls calling her Ginger.'

'Oh!' I said, feeling silly. I'd heard the girls calling Sarah many nicknames far worse than Ginger. No one liked her because she was so creepily pious and preached at everyone. 'Sorry, Miss Andrews.'

'Still, I like it that you're such an ardent reader. It's very touching that you should get so moved to tears by a story book,' she said.

'I seem to be crying all the time nowadays. Nurse March says it's my hormones,' I said.

I'd started crying whenever I went to the nursery with Belinda. The babies all seemed so little and helpless. I loved to watch Belinda scoop Peter up and hold him close in her arms but some of the others wailed forlornly all by themselves. I knew that all their mothers fed them regularly and Nurse March often picked them up herself and changed their nappies and gave them a little top-up of bottled milk – but they still seemed so sad, as if they already knew they were going to be sent away with strangers.

Nurse March was brisk with me, but Miss Andrews seemed concerned.

'Are you still very homesick, dear?' she asked.

'Not really,' I said, truthfully enough, because I knew Mum and Dad wouldn't welcome me back in my condition.

'And what does Dr Fuller say?' Miss Andrews asked.

He came to Heathcote House once a week and saw each of us for ten minutes in a small room adjacent to Miss Andrews' study. It had once been a dressing room, but now it was an *un*dressing room, because we had to lie on our backs on an examining table exposing our stomachs while he prodded them gently. Then we had to sit and answer embarrassing questions about our weight and bowel habits and whether we'd experienced any 'spotting'. I'd misunderstood the first time and thought he was asking if I had any spots, so I said, 'I get one on my nose occasionally,' and made him laugh. He was quite a nice man, younger and kinder than Dr Bertram, but I still felt awkward with him.

'He said I seemed in tip-top condition,' I said, quoting him directly.

'Well, that's good,' said Miss Andrews, but I think she was still worried about me because a few days later my social worker, Mrs Jeffries, came to see me.

I was called out of lessons so I could see her in the living room. Marilyn brought us both a cup of tea and a plate of custard creams.

'Very thoughtful of you, dear. How are you getting on?' Mrs Jeffries asked her, as if Marilyn were one of her charges.

I thought Marilyn would bristle but she just ducked her head and murmured, 'Fine, thanks,' and scuttled out of the room.

'Nice girl,' Mrs Jeffries murmured.

I nodded, though Marilyn always seemed a bit colourless to me. She didn't talk much. She sighed when I proved pretty useless in the kitchen and couldn't get up a good shine on the floor, but she didn't really tell me off. She seemed in a world of her own most of the time, though she was quite friendly with Belinda. Several times I'd found them sitting on the back doorstep together, having a cigarette and gossiping.

I wanted to try smoking too, because it looked so sophisticated, but Belinda wouldn't let me.

'It'll be bad for your baby,' she said, tutting, and Marilyn nodded in agreement.

'Do you know Marilyn, Mrs Jeffries?' I asked.

'We're not here to talk about Marilyn, dear, we're here to talk about you. How are you feeling?' she asked.

'I'm fine,' I mumbled.

'You certainly look well. Nice colour in your cheeks. And you've made some friends here?' she persisted.

I nodded.

'But a bit weepy sometimes?'

I shrugged.

'Missing Mum?'

I shook my head.

'I think you are, you know,' she said, reaching out and patting my hand. 'It's nothing to be ashamed of. You're still very young. I was sent away to boarding school when I was a girl and I remember absolutely aching with homesickness.'

She was trying to be comforting, but our circumstances were hardly similar.

'Mum's missing you, you know. And I'm sure Dad is too,' she continued.

'No they're not,' I muttered. 'They're ashamed of me. They don't want me at home because they're scared what people will say.'

'They're concerned about you, Laura. They want the best for you. You can't blame them for that. They don't want you to ruin your life. Once your baby is born and has a new mummy and daddy then they'll welcome you back with open arms and you can make a whole fresh start,' she said. 'Don't you want that?'

'I want my baby,' I said.

'Now you're just being silly. You're much too young to look after a baby. You have no idea how hard it can be. And it would be remarkably selfish of you to deny your child a wonderful new carefree life with two parents. You'd be tying a label round its neck for ever,' she persisted.

I didn't quite understand what she meant. I imagined a little baby with an actual label round its little neck, scratching at it. Mrs Jeffries saw I was looking blank.

'You don't want people to call your baby names,' she said. 'I know it's not fair, but there's still a dreadful stigma about being illegitimate.'

'I don't care,' I said sulkily.

'You might not, but your child might. But don't let us get into an argument at this stage. I'm concerned about *you* at the moment. I'm pleased the doctor thinks you're in fine shape. I believe your due date is in early May? How do you feel about giving birth? There's no need to worry, you know. You're likely to have a quick, easy birth as you're so young. And they'll give you gas and air of course.'

'Gas and air?' I said, bewildered. *Gas?* That was how people killed themselves, wasn't it, by sticking their head in their gas oven?

'It's for when the pain gets really bad,' said Mrs Jeffries. She looked at me. 'Laura, you do know how babies are born, don't you?'

'Yes, of course,' I said – though I didn't really know much about it at all. When I was little I'd asked Mum about babies, and she said the doctor brought them in his big bag. Of course I knew that wasn't true now. I knew that babies grew in their mother's tummy. I could often feel my own child, making little fluttery movements, stretching its small arms and legs. I knew where it came out, more or less, and I'd guessed it probably hurt a bit because periods certainly did, but Mrs Jeffries seemed to be suggesting it would hurt tremendously.

I'd heard some of the girls who'd already given birth chatting to each other, and one said she'd screamed so loud the nurses had told her off, but I'd thought she'd been crying because she didn't want the baby. I was alarmed now to think she'd been screaming in pain.

'You look rather taken aback,' said Mrs Jeffries, and she patted my hand again, as if I was a little dog needing reassurance. 'It's not for months and months, so there's no need to worry about it just now. I would make the most of this middle stage. It's the best time, no morning sickness, and yet your bump's still manageable.'

I wasn't finding my bump at all manageable now. I hated looking at it when I had my twice-weekly bath. It didn't look like my tummy at all, and my belly button was turning inside out in an alarming way. My breasts bothered me too. They were swelling up and wouldn't fit comfortably into my small bra any more. Nurse March said this was perfectly normal and told me to write home to ask for new underwear.

I had resolved not to write to Mum and Dad again. They hadn't replied to my last postcard. I couldn't believe they could be so hard-hearted. If they didn't want me as a daughter any more then I wouldn't want them as parents.

Mrs Jeffries misread my expression. She clearly thought I was still fussing about giving birth. 'There will be a nurse with you at the hospital when you're having your baby, and I'm sure she'll be very kind and encouraging, but I could ask if you could possibly have your mother with you too, as you're so young.'

This truly alarmed me. We'd never had that sort of intimate relationship. It would embarrass us both terribly. I didn't want a strange nurse with me either. The whole process sounded so bizarre and undignified it would be like someone watching you go to the lavatory.

'I don't want my mum there, thank you,' I said quickly.

Mrs Jeffries shook her head at me. 'You're a funny little scrap, Laura. I don't quite know what to make of you. I have to write an assessment of you but I don't really know what to put. You're well physically, thank goodness, but otherwise you seem a bit in a muddle.'

I thought that was actually a fair assessment, so I just shrugged.

'How would *you* describe how you're feeling, Laura?'

'As well as can be expected?' I suggested. I just parroted the phrase because I'd heard Mum use it – but for some reason it made Mrs Jeffries burst out laughing.

'Well, you've still got a sense of humour even if you are depressed!' she said.

I didn't know she thought I was depressed. It bothered me.

'My social worker says she thinks I'm depressed,' I said in the tower room that night, when we were lolling in bed, eating up the last of Belinda's fruit cake. 'Do you two think I am? Why is she fussing about it? And why did she keep asking silly questions?'

'Oh, they all do that,' said Belinda. 'Don't worry about it.'

'They worry if you cry a lot. They're scared you might top yourself,' said Jeannie.

'Oh, goodness!' I said, alarmed. 'Well, I won't cry any more – or only in secret.'

'Yeah, but you can't win. They'll think you're repressing your emotions then. My social worker keeps wanting me to open up and tell her what I'm really thinking. And of course what I'm *really* thinking is, "Why don't you shut up, you nosy old cow" but I don't think that would go down too well, would it?' said Jeannie.

'She was also going on about when I actually have my baby. Having gas! You didn't have gas, did you, Belinda?'

'Gas and air. I did for a bit – but then it made me feel sick and dizzy, so I wouldn't take it any more. I wanted to concentrate on pushing the baby out,' she said.

'Does it hurt a lot?' I asked.

'Well . . . the worst pain ever, I suppose,' Belinda said.

'Worse than really awful toothache?' I asked, remembering the time I'd had an abscess on my tooth.

Belinda and Jeannie laughed at me.

'Toothache!' Jeannie scoffed.

'Well, *I* don't know, do I? I've never had a baby. And neither have you!'

'Yeah, but I'm not entirely clueless. Think of the size of a baby's head. And then think of where it comes out,' said Jeannie.

I thought about it, and shivered.

'But it's OK, Laura, honestly, because the moment Peter was born it just felt so glorious, and when they put him in my arms I truly don't think I've ever felt so happy in all my life,' said Belinda.

'I'll be happy just to get it all over,' said Jeannie. 'I feel so blooming uncomfortable now.' She peered down the neck of her nightie at her stomach, grimacing. 'It looks like I'm going to pop any minute. My back aches all the time. And I have to keep peeing. I actually wet my pants today because I didn't run down that corridor fast enough!'

'Oh, you sexy thing!' said Belinda.

'I don't think I'm ever going to feel sexy again in my life,' said Jeannie.

'Funny. I can't wait to have a cuddle with Rick,' said Belinda.

'What about you, Laura? Are you missing your Daniel?' Jeannie asked.

I hated the way she said his name, as if it was in quotes.

'Yes, I am,' I said shortly.

I actually had a dream about him that night. Well, it was about a boy called Daniel, but he wasn't the real one, and he wasn't my imaginary version of him either. He was more like Nina at her worst. He was going out with some other girl, and he looked disgusted when he saw me. He called me horrible names and said he never wanted to see me again, and then both Dr Bertrams were there, and Nina herself and even Little Richard, but they were all sneering at me. Mum and Dad were there too and Mum wouldn't come near me even though I had a terrible pain in my stomach and I was scared the baby was starting to come.

Then I woke up with a start and my tummy really was hurting and I started to panic. It was far too soon and the baby would die. I'd wanted to get rid of the baby only a few weeks before and yet now I clutched my stomach in terror, as if I was trying to keep it safe inside me. But there was a familiar feel to the sharp pains. I got out of bed and made my way down the corridor in the darkness.

Some of the girls were snoring in the cubicles, and someone was muttering – probably Sarah saying her prayers. I said a prayer too and then went weak with relief in the toilets to discover that I wasn't having the baby at all, I simply had a bad stomach upset from eating such a large slice of fruit cake.

16

Belinda was called out of morning lessons a few days later. She didn't come back. Jeannie and I went to look for her at lunchtime. She wasn't in the tower room or the toilets. We knew she wasn't with Miss Andrews, because she was in the kitchen with Marilyn.

'She'll be up in the nursery then,' said Jeannie.

'But it's nap time. Nurse March wouldn't let her in till the two o'clock feeding time,' I said.

We went upstairs to check – and there was Belinda, sitting in a nursing chair with Peter in her arms. Nurse March was eating her boiled beef and carrots off a tray on her lap, placidly munching. She put her knife and fork down carefully so as not to make a clatter and frowned at us.

'What do you two want? Ssh now, I don't want any of my

babies woken up. They'll all start yelling to be fed and they've another hour to go,' she said.

'We just wondered where Belinda was,' said Jeannie.

'Belinda?' I said to her.

She didn't look up at us. She stayed rocking Peter, her head bent over him. He'd managed to clasp a strand of her long blonde hair and was hanging onto it with his tiny fist.

'Aren't you coming to have your lunch?' I asked her.

'No, I'm fine,' she said.

She didn't sound fine at all. Her voice was husky, as if she'd been crying a long time.

'We could bring you a tray,' Jeannie offered.

She shook her head and Peter's hand slipped off her hair and fell to his side. Belinda gave a little sniff.

'Oh, you poor love,' Jeannie said softly. 'OK, we'll leave you in peace. Come on, Laura.' She steered me away, out of the nursery.

'What's the matter with Belinda?' I asked her anxiously. 'You don't think something's wrong with Peter, do you?'

'No! Oh, Laura, you are thick! She's been told it's time,' said Jeannie.

'For what?' I asked, though I knew. I just couldn't bear it.

'They'll be coming tomorrow. His new parents,' said Jeannie. She sniffed too, and wiped her eyes with the back of her hand.

'What new parents? Belinda's keeping Peter, she's said all along. She loves him to bits,' I said.

'Yes, of course she does. But I told you, didn't I? She was just hoping it would all work out, but it never does. She was just kidding herself, couldn't you see that?' Jeannie was starting to get irritated with me.

'She was going to live with her mum and dad at their pub. With her fiancé,' I persisted.

'Well, he's obviously backed out, hasn't he? And I don't imagine her dad was ever in on this whole scheme,' said Jeannie. 'You're such a ninny, Laura, though you think you're so clever.'

'Belinda said I could go and live there too! Or all three of us were going to be actresses! You were in on it too!'

'That was all just a silly game! What are you – *four*, rather than fourteen?'

I suppose deep down I'd known we were all just pretending. But I'd been certain Belinda was keeping Peter. She loved him so much. And though they told us babies were barely aware of their surroundings and couldn't even see properly out of their beautiful blue eyes it was obvious that Peter knew who his mother was and wanted her desperately. Belinda had let me take a turn at cuddling him but I could feel his tiny little body tense. He'd fidget for a moment, trying to get comfortable, his mouth opening in protest, and then he'd start wailing. He wanted his mum and no one else.

Belinda didn't come back all afternoon. When Marilyn served us our supper at seven I asked if I could take a portion up to her.

'She's very upset,' I said. 'They're taking her baby away tomorrow!'

'I know, poor girl. Don't worry. She couldn't face any mince so I've given her some banana custard and a glass of milk instead,' she said. 'They should slip down easily enough.'

'That was really kind,' I said in surprise.

Marilyn stopped ladling grey mince and gave me a funny look. 'We do know how hard it is, Laura. We do our best to comfort our girls.'

'But you still make them give up their babies!' I said.

'We don't *make* them. We just help girls see what's best for them,' said Marilyn.

Sarah was in the queue behind me and could hear. 'It's a sacrifice we make for Jesus to make up for our sins,' she murmured.

I was outraged. 'Belinda hasn't sinned. She's the loveliest girl ever, and she's in a proper relationship and she's going to get married soon, so you can just shut up,' I said.

'That's it, Laura, you tell her,' said Jeannie.

Sarah stayed irritatingly serene. 'You should pray. It will help give you peace,' she said.

Jeannie pulled me away before I could retort. 'That girl makes you want to dunk her head in the pot of mince, doesn't she? But it's a waste of breath arguing with her. Come on, let's gobble up our supper and then go and see Belinda again,' she said.

She was still in the nursery in exactly the same position, rocking Peter. The other babies were all asleep after their six o'clock feed, but Peter was wailing miserably as if he knew something was terribly wrong.

'Poor lamb,' said Nurse March. 'He'll wake the others and then it'll be a terrible evening, with all of them grizzling. Why don't you take him down to your room with your friends, Belinda? He might settle better there.'

We all stared. It was strictly forbidden to take the babies out of the nursery in the evenings. Nurse March was being very kind too.

Belinda murmured her thanks and then stood up, clutching Peter protectively. We went downstairs in a little procession, back to the tower room. Jeannie plumped up her pillow and I took a blanket off my bed and we arranged Belinda and Peter as comfortably as we could in the one proper chair in the room.

'Thank you,' Belinda whispered hoarsely, never once taking her eyes off Peter's face.

He settled almost immediately, his eyes closing. Belinda breathed out slowly and gave us a watery smile.

'Oh, Belinda, is it really true?' I asked.

'For God's sake, Laura, give the girl a bit of peace,' Jeannie snapped.

'It's all right, Jeannie,' Belinda said wearily. 'Yes, Laura, I have to say goodbye to Peter tomorrow.'

'But you can't! You love him so!' I said.

'Of course I love him, so so much,' said Belinda. 'That's why. I can see now. It's better for him.'

'It isn't! No one could possibly love him more than you,' I insisted.

'We know that, dolt,' said Jeannie, starting to brush Belinda's hair for her. She did it gently and tenderly, in long slow swoops from her scalp to her shoulders.

'I had a long talk with Miss Andrews yesterday,' Belinda said, staring all the time at Peter cradled in her arms. 'She told me about this couple on the adopting list. The lady's tried so hard to have her own babies, but she's had five miscarriages – five, poor thing!'

'My mum had miscarriages too. But then she went on to have me. This lady might. You don't have to feel sorry for her and give your Peter to her!' I said.

'She can't have any more – the doctors say it would be too dangerous. She's desperate for a baby. Her husband is too. They're a little older than most new parents – nearly forty. He's an architect, he's designed his own house. They've had the most beautiful nursery ready for years. They've got the loveliest big garden, and they've even got their own tennis court.'

'Who cares about stupid things like tennis courts!' I said. 'They're not you! That's what Peter wants – his own mother!'

'But what sort of mother would I be? Look, Rick's never going to commit to me. He still says he loves me, he gave me the ring, but I know he doesn't want to settle down just yet. Mum told me he's been seen out with some other girl. I can see now it wouldn't have worked out anyway. Dad's never liked him, says he's a tearaway. Maybe he is. I'm not sure it would work out even if Rick and I got married later on.' Belinda was crying now, tears rolling down her cheeks.

Peter stirred, his face puckering as if he sensed her distress, and she rocked him. 'Ssh now, little darling. There now. Keep those eyes closed. Good boy. It's all right. Everything's going to be all right,' she whispered softly.

'But it isn't going to be all right, not for either of you,' I persisted. 'He wants *you*. Look at his little face and his fair curls. He's the spitting image of you!'

'Miss Andrews says they're both blond, this couple. She says they'd be a perfect match. She made me picture Peter with them, seeing the sort of life they'd lead. And she's right. How can I say it would be better for him to live in the back room of a pub with me, and all the regulars talking about me, calling me a schoolgirl mum? They wouldn't just look down on me, they'd look down on Peter too. I don't want that for my little boy. I can see it makes more sense to have him adopted. It's for his sake, not mine.' Belinda was crying more now.

Jeannie dropped the hairbrush and bent down, pressing her cheek against Belinda's fair hair.

'Don't upset yourself so, lovie. You're such a looker you'll get heaps more blokes after you, much better than Rick, and one day you'll get married and live in a big house with a garden and a bleeding tennis court and you'll have more babies, little blond children bouncing about, calling you Mummy,' said Jeannie.

But they won't be Peter. You'll never ever love them the way you love him! I thought, but I didn't say it out loud. I had just about enough sense to see how cruel and pointless it would be. We all knew it.

Belinda went up to the nursery at five to ten. She let Jeannie and me give Peter a kiss first. I felt such a wrench, almost as if he was my own baby. When she went out the tower room, holding Peter close, I started crying too.

'There now,' said Jeannie, and she put her arms round me. 'Sorry I called you a dolt. I didn't mean it. I was just upset.'

'I know. I am too. It's so awful for Belinda. In a way you're so lucky, Jeannie,' I said, giving her a squeeze.

'I'm *lucky*?' said Jeannie.

'Well, you've known right from the start that you don't want to keep your baby,' I said.

'Yeah, that's right,' said Jeannie, but I felt her stiffen.

Belinda didn't come back until nearly midnight. She crept into bed so as not to disturb us, but we were both still awake.

'Have you been holding him all this time?' Jeannie whispered.

'Well, he had colic, poor little lamb. I couldn't go away and leave him crying. But he went to sleep at last, and Nurse March insisted I put him back in his cot. She thought I might nod off too and drop him. As if I'd ever do that! Still, she meant it kindly. She was all ready for bed by the time I left. She looks so sweet in her nightclothes. She's got a winceyette nightie with ladybirds on it, just like a little girl's! And she sets her hair into those funny little curls with kirby grips and puts a hairnet on top, bless her.' Belinda laughed but it sounded more like a sob.

'Are you cold? Do you want to come into my bed for a cuddle,' Jeannie offered.

'Yes, just for five minutes,' said Belinda.

I lay there alone in my own bed, wishing I'd offered first. Belinda and Jeannie were whispering, but I couldn't make out what they were saying. I dozed off after a while – and then I think Belinda gave me a kiss on my cheek when she made her way back to her own bed. I tried to wake up to talk to her but I wasn't sure she'd really kissed me or whether I'd imagined it.

I wanted to wake up at ten to six and try to go up to the nursery with Belinda for Peter's early feed but I actually slept in, and Jeannie had to wake me at half past seven.

'Come on, lazybones, you'll miss breakfast if you're not quick,' she said.

I looked over at Belinda's bed. It was empty, and her pretty coverlet was missing. All her washing things and her pretty ornaments were gone too.

'She's not gone already?' I gasped.

'She's just done her packing. Her dad's coming to pick her up this morning sometime,' said Jeannie.

'So soon!' I said.

'Well, she doesn't want to hang round here after Peter goes. It would be torture, wouldn't it?'

'I suppose so,' I said.

Belinda didn't come down for breakfast. All the girls were very subdued. It was the same whenever a baby was taken away, and Belinda was a favourite with everyone.

It was my turn to scrub the front steps, a job I generally hated because it was so cold outside and yet it was impossible to wear a coat without getting it soaked. I didn't usually have the strength to give the steps a really good scrubbing, but now I attacked them viciously, and whitened them well for good measure.

'You've done a good job for once, Laura!' said Marilyn, surprised. 'What's got into you?'

I wanted to attack the blond couple with the posh house and tennis court who were due to walk up those steps that morning.

What gave them the right to come here and take my dear friend's baby away from her?

Belinda was being so brave. She came into the classroom at eleven, after Peter had been bathed and fed. He was looking beautiful in his special handknitted outfit. Belinda had embroidered his name inside his matinee jacket and on the soles of his tiny ribboned booties. She knew the couple would probably change his name but hoped they might keep the little outfit so that he would know his real birth name. Belinda looked beautiful too, in a pink angora sweater with pearl buttons and a white pleated skirt.

She smiled sadly at Mrs Chambers. 'I do hope you don't mind, but Peter and I would like to say goodbye to all the girls,' she said.

'Of course, dear,' said Mrs Chambers. She stood up and insisted Belinda sit in her chair with the baby on her lap, while we came up quietly in twos and threes, almost in awe, as if we were taking part in a modern Nativity scene. Jeannie and I hung back to the end, and we were both allowed to cuddle the baby for a few moments and give Belinda a proper hug.

'I shall miss you so much, Belinda,' I whispered.

'I'll miss you too, Laura, terribly. You must still come and see me, promise? At the Six Bells at Haversham – it's almost opposite the station,' she said. 'You too, Jeannie. We mustn't stop being friends.'

We vowed we wouldn't. We were both crying now, but Belinda was surprisingly calm and composed. Perhaps she was past tears now. She drifted out of the classroom, turning at the door to lift Peter's tiny fist so that it looked as if he were waving to us. Even Mrs Chambers had to dab her eyes with her handkerchief.

Then we waited. We all heard the car draw up. It wasn't the adopters; it was Belinda's mother and father in their Mercedes. She was wearing a fur stole, he was wearing a camel coat that reached almost down to the ground.

'I didn't know they had that sort of money,' said Jeannie, gritting her teeth. 'For Christ's sake, they could have bought Belinda her own flat, they could have hired a nanny, they could have helped her in all sorts of ways. Call themselves parents!'

We peered out of the window at them with contempt, though I could see Belinda's mother was crying, and her father was wearing dark glasses though it was grey and bleak outside.

Then almost immediately another car drew up behind, and another couple got out. They looked almost as old as Belinda's parents, and moneyed too, but they seemed quieter, dressed in soft tweed. His hair was fairish and waved, hers was white-blonde and cut in a pageboy style. They were both looking excited but anxious. He took her hand as they walked towards my shining steps. In any other circumstances I'd have liked the look of them.

'They look marvellous parents for little Peter,' said Sarah.

I hated her saying it, though I knew she was right.

Jeannie was less inhibited. 'Shut yer mouth,' she said curtly, and turned her back on her. We went off by ourselves to the tower room, skipping lessons. We knew we wouldn't be punished. The staff always made allowances on the days that babies were taken.

Belinda had left her red silk scarves so the room still could have its rosy glow without her. She'd left us both a present on our beds. Jeannie had her big cream Aran cardigan. I had her silver hairbrush.

Jeannie clasped the cardigan. 'It still smells of her scent,' she said, wrapping herself inside it.

'Here's one of her golden hairs,' I said, teasing it out of her brush and winding it round and round my finger.

'God, we're a right pair of lovelorn twits,' said Jeannie, half laughing, half crying. 'Here, there's half a tube of Rowntree's fruit gums in the cardi pocket! Want one?'

We sucked our way through the rest of the tube. I liked the green and yellow flavours most, while she liked the red and the black, so it was easy to divide them. Jeannie kept the orange gums as an extra souvenir.

It was just as well we had the gums because we kept our vigil by the window instead of going down for lunch. We stared down to the pathway until our eyes blurred, but there was no sign of the tweedy blond couple, or Belinda and her parents. The two cars stayed stationary, parked together.

'Why are they taking so long? Monica's couple came out with

little Michael almost straight away! And then she came soon after. What's going on?' I asked Jeannie.

'Maybe Belinda's changed her mind at the last minute,' said Jeannie.

'Seriously?' I said, my hopes soaring.

We clutched each other, both willing it to be true. But then, long after lunchtime, the blond couple came out at last – and the woman was holding Peter in his lovingly knitted woolly outfit.

We both went limp with disappointment, and Jeannie swore.

'So they forced Belinda after all,' she said.

'It's so cruel. And mad. Peter *won't* be better off with these new people. Look, he doesn't like that woman holding him!' I said.

Her arms were rigid with anxiety, one hand clamped around his head, the other spread to support his padded bottom. He was wriggling uncomfortably, his face screwed up and twisting this way and that.

'He's peering round for Belinda, wondering where she is. He's going to cry any second, poor little thing,' I said.

Peter opened his mouth and started wailing on cue. The woman seemed startled, unsure what to do.

'She's going to drop him if she's not careful!' said Jeannie indignantly. 'And the bloke's just standing there like a dummy, not even helping. Oh, come running out now, Belinda, see what they're like and snatch him back quick! Come *on*!'

We strained forward, our heads on the cold glass. Belinda didn't appear. We had to wait another half-hour.

'Perhaps she's collapsed with the strain of it all. Weeping and weeping. You know what she was like yesterday. She'll be much worse now, in hysterics. Maybe Miss Andrews has had to phone for the doctor!' I said, frightened.

'Then let's go and find her. We're her special friends. Maybe we can comfort her,' said Jeannie.

Then we heard a bang downstairs.

'Wasn't that . . . ?' I started.

'The front door downstairs!' Jeannie exclaimed.

We ran clumsily back to the window and there they were, Belinda between her parents. She wasn't hanging onto them desperately, the way Monica had done. She was walking with her arms clasped round herself, hugging the gap where Peter had been. Then she paused and looked upwards, guessing we'd be peering out of the tower room window.

She unclasped her arms to blow us a kiss and wave to us. We waved and blew kisses back dementedly, wishing we could open the window properly. The two big side windows had been nailed shut. Jeannie always joked that it was to stop girls flinging themselves down to the flagstones below.

'Goodbye, Belinda! Good luck! We love you!' we shouted, hoping that our voices would carry out of the small window at the top.

Belinda nodded and smiled and blew more kisses. Her parents turned round and craned their necks. Belinda's mother was crying, her eye make-up running down her cheeks. We couldn't judge Belinda's father's expression properly because of his dark glasses, but his lips were pressed together and he put his arm round Belinda protectively, trying to hurry her to their car.

'Oh, he's trying to be Kind Daddy now,' said Jeannie with contempt.

'At least her mum looks properly sad, like she's regretting it,' I said.

I tried to imagine my own parents acting out this scene. It was impossible. We didn't have a car for a start. They'd have to come in a taxi from the railway station and they'd be in and out as quickly as possible, to save on the fare. There'd be no cups of tea with Miss Andrews, just a flustered goodbye, and then the long terrible journey home – taxi, train, train, bus . . . Or maybe they wouldn't come at all, and I'd have to manage it all by myself, crying the whole way with everyone staring at me.

I was the one crying hysterically now, for myself as much as for Belinda.

'Hey, hey, calm down now,' said Jeannie, patting me on the back. 'You mustn't take it to heart so.'

But she cried too that night, because it was so sad and strange and lonely in the tower room without Belinda. We didn't know who we were going to get to take her place.

'We don't really want any of the girls from the cubies, do we?' said Jeannie. 'Maybe they'll let us have the room to ourselves until a new girl comes. Let's just hope we don't get the Bible-basher thrust on us!'

'Oh, don't!' I said, my heart thumping.

Miss Andrews had said she hoped Sarah and I would be special friends. That wouldn't mean she'd actually put her in our room, would it?

It would. Sarah came into our room after breakfast, looking smug.

'What are you doing in here? This is our room,' Jeannie said gruffly.

'It's my room now too,' said Sarah. She smiled at me. 'Isn't that lovely, Laura?'

I fidgeted uncomfortably and made some non-committal remark. I disliked her, but I didn't feel I could hurt her feelings. Jeannie had no such compunction.

'No, it's not lovely, it's blooming horrible!' she said. 'If you keep me awake praying, I'll bash you on the bonce with your own bible, you silly cow!'

Sarah sniffed in contempt and gave me a little sideways glance, as if we were conspirators together. 'Honestly. Language!' she said.

'If you call *that* language then listen to this,' said Jeannie, and came out with a long stream of swear words.

Sarah squealed affectedly and put her hands over her ears. She looked at me as if she expected me to do the same. I pretended I hadn't heard what Jeannie was saying.

'It's the mark of an impoverished vocabulary if people resort to swearing,' said Sarah. 'Isn't it, Laura?'

I continued my deaf act, and both of them looked at me reproachfully. They continued to get at each other all day long. Jeannie was scornful of all Sarah's possessions, especially her little statue of Christ on the cross. She made really mocking remarks until Sarah actually burst into tears. I felt dreadful then, though I knew why she was so hostile. Belinda had told me secretly that Jeannie had spent part of her childhood in a church orphanage and had been very badly treated there.

'Please don't tease her about her religion, Jeannie,' I begged, when Sarah had gone back to the cubicles to collect the rest of her things.

'Why shouldn't I?' said Jeannie indignantly.

'Because it means so much to her,' I said.

'She's just a horrible hypocrite,' said Jeannie. 'I can't stand people like that, all holier than thou.'

'I know. I don't like her either, you know I don't, but it's mean to mock her like that,' I said. 'And with her beliefs, it must be awful to, you know, be having a baby. Without being grown up and married first.'

'Well, she's mean to turn up her nose at me and treat me like dirt,' Jeannie retorted. 'And *you're* mean to take her side. I suppose *she's* going to be your new best friend now!'

'No, she's not. You are, you know you are,' I said. 'I just don't like all this quarrelling. Please, Jeannie, don't go on at her.'

'All right, I'll keep my mouth shut, if that's what you want,' said Jeannie.

She didn't say another word to Sarah all day long. But she didn't say anything to me either, which was horrible. Sarah was triumphant, seeming to think *she* was my friend now. It was very uncomfortable in lessons, especially English.

Mrs Chambers was trying to follow the O-level syllabus though few of us were actually going to be taking the English literature exam. She gave out a few worn copies of *Pride and Prejudice* for us to share. There was general moaning at the length of the novel and the smallness of the print.

'Why on earth do we have to read this awful old-fashioned book with all this daft fancy talk in it?' someone complained.

'Oh, it's one of my favourite novels ever,' said Sarah. 'It's so witty! I'm sure you love it, don't you, Laura?'

Mrs Chambers looked at me eagerly. I wanted to impress her, and I actually *did* love *Pride and Prejudice*. But Jeannie was looking at me too.

I shrugged. 'Haven't read it,' I muttered.

'Well, now's your chance, dear,' said Mrs Chambers. 'You can start us off. Can you read the first few pages for us?'

I did as I was told. I tried to read it expressionlessly, but the story got the better of me. I found myself doing different voices for the Bennet family, making them come alive. The girls stopped fidgeting and whispering and started listening properly. I couldn't help thrilling to the moment.

Mrs Chambers stopped me, sounding reluctant. 'Very well done, Laura. What a great start! Right. Now you take over, Jeannie.'

She wasn't being deliberately unkind. We always read around the room, and Jeannie was sitting next to me, so it was her turn. She wasn't the worst reader in the room. There were several girls who could barely spell a sentence out. But she wasn't confident. She stumbled over several words, she read in a monotone, and she had to point her way along the lines. My own hands grew sweaty with embarrassment on her behalf.

Mrs Chambers stopped her after a page. 'Well done, Jeannie. Good try.'

She was trying to encourage her, but she sounded terribly patronizing. Jeannie was bright red in the face.

'Stupid poncy book,' she muttered.

Sarah sighed and raised her eyebrows. I wanted to hit her.

I tried to be extra-friendly to Jeannie all day, even though she wasn't talking to me, but of course that seemed patronizing too. Sarah made the most of it, chatting to me in her reedy voice, giving me her opinion on this and that.

It was awful when we went to bed. It had always been my favourite time, when Belinda and Jeannie and I talked far into the night. Sarah spent ten minutes down on her knees muttering to Jesus and then another ten minutes putting rollers in her wispy hair, muttering to me now. Jeannie got undressed hurriedly and pulled her old nightie over her head. Her tummy was so big now she could barely fit inside it. Then she flopped onto her bed and picked up her book.

'Oh, do you like reading, Jeannie?' said Sarah.

It could have been a perfectly innocent remark, but of course it wasn't. Jeannie ignored her.

'What's your book then?' Sarah persisted.

Jeannie turned a page, saying nothing.

Sarah peered, craning her neck. '*The World of Suzie Wong?*' she said. 'What on earth's that about? It looks very lurid!'

'Do leave her alone, Sarah,' I said. 'We keep quiet and read now, don't we, Jeannie?'

So we read, all three of us. Jeannie read *Suzie Wong* and Sarah read her copy of *Pride and Prejudice*. I didn't want to read mine, because it would seem like I was showing off. I read my precious copy of Katherine Mansfield's selected stories instead.

'Oh, Katherine Mansfield!' said Sarah, as if she knew her personally. 'I love her! Which is your favourite story then?'

I'd have loved a discussion like that with anyone else, but I put my finger to my lips now and went on reading. Jeannie snapped her light out after a while, and so Sarah and I did too.

'Night, Jeannie,' I whispered after a while, hoping Sarah had gone to sleep already.

Jeannie didn't answer, but Sarah did. 'Night night, Laura. It's so lovely to be here in the tower room,' she said.

17

Sarah set her little travelling alarm to go off ten minutes early so she had time to kneel by her bed and pray again. She did it softly, but the mumble woke both of us.

'For Pete's sake, stop that mumbo-jumbo!' Jeannie said fiercely. It was a relief to hear her talking again.

'I'm *praying*, Jeannie!' said Sarah, in her holier-than-thou voice.

'Well, do it inside your head. You don't have to do it out loud. You're just showing off,' said Jeannie.

'Yes, if Jesus can work miracles then surely He can read your thoughts,' I joined in, eager to show Jeannie I was on her side.

'Please don't take the Lord's name in vain,' said Sarah. 'You're a bad influence, Jeannie. Don't listen to her, Laura.'

'Jeannie's my friend,' I said.

Sarah sighed in a pitying manner, shut her eyes again, and prayed even louder. Jeannie heaved herself out of bed and picked up *The World of Suzie Wong*.

'Oh look, she's so blooming holy she's grown a halo!' she said, and she balanced the book on the top of Sarah's head.

I giggled. Sarah moved and the book tumbled into her lap.

'Do you have to be so childish, Jeannie?' she said, picking it up. She glanced at one of the pages and wrinkled her nose. 'This is absolute filth!' she declared.

'Don't be so prissy,' said Jeannie.

'You shouldn't be reading dirty books like this! You're disgusting!' said Sarah.

'Oh, shut your face,' said Jeannie, and stomped off out the door.

I ran after her and squeezed her arm. 'She's sickening, isn't she?' I said. 'Oh, I do miss Belinda!'

'Me too,' said Jeannie. 'Quick, Laura, I'm nearly wetting myself! The baby's kicking me right in the bladder. It'll be such a relief when the little whatsit's born and I can get out of here.'

'But then I'll be stuck with Sarah!' I said. 'I can't stand her.'

I was relieved that Jeannie and I were friends again. Sarah made several overtures to me back in the tower room, and she tried to sit with us at breakfast, but Jeannie pulled the chair away from her and said she was saving it for someone else.

'That's a terrible thing to do!' said Sarah. 'I could have fallen on the floor and really hurt myself – hurt my baby!'

'Don't talk rubbish,' said Jeannie. 'Now push off!'

Sarah flounced off and sat the other side of the room on her own. I felt a little bit bad then but didn't care too much. She'd been so horrible to Jeannie, after all. We did our chores together after breakfast, both of us on washing-up duty, one of the easiest tasks. We squeezed huge amounts of washing-up liquid into the bowls and blew bubbles at each other, messing about like little kids. Marilyn told us off, but flicked a little foam at us too, joining in. Sarah was nowhere to be seen.

She joined us at the start of lessons. She had an unpleasant gleam in her eyes. Miss Andrews put her head round the door at the end of maths.

'I'd like a word with you, Jeannie,' she said sternly.

I felt my tummy go tight. I stared at Sarah. 'Have you been telling tales?' I hissed.

'I've just been doing the right thing, Laura,' she said.

'What do you mean?' I got hold of her by the shoulder, gripping hard. 'What did you tell Miss Andrews?'

But Sarah simply smiled enigmatically and wouldn't tell me. I had to wait until the change of lessons and then rushed upstairs to the tower room. Jeannie was there, thrusting her clothes into a big plastic bag, tears running down her cheeks.

'Jeannie! What is it, what's happened? What's that awful Sarah said?'

'That cow!' Jeannie muttered, wiping her eyes fiercely. 'She complained to Miss Andrews about me. She's just been giving me a right telling-off, making me feel like dirt. She called me a rotten apple, for God's sake! And she won't let me stay in the tower room any more in case I corrupt you! I've got to sleep in some awful attic room up near the nursery.'

'What? That's utterly ridiculous. Look, we'll go to Miss Andrews together and say Sarah's been telling a pack of lies because she's jealous that we're friends,' I insisted. 'It's just Sarah's word against ours.'

'But she has got proof. That's what all this is about. That blooming book. And now Miss Andrews has taken it. I'm so sorry, I know you haven't finished it yourself,' Jeannie sniffed, starting to strip her bed.

'Which book?' I said, trembling.

'*The World of Suzie Wong.* Sarah took it to Miss Andrews and said it was a filthy book,' said Jeannie.

'Didn't you tell Miss Andrews I'd lent it to you?' I demanded.

'Well, there was no point. I didn't want to get *you* into trouble. I'd never split on a friend,' said Jeannie.

'Oh, Jeannie!' I gave her a hug. 'Stay there! Stop packing your things. I'm going to tell her.'

'There's no point. Miss Andrews has got it in for me. She only let me come to the tower room because Belinda begged her. Laura, wait,' said Jeannie.

I couldn't wait. I had to go to Miss Andrews while I was still burning hot with fury, otherwise I might lose the courage to confront her. I went storming along the corridor and knocked loudly at her door.

'Not now, I'm busy,' she called.

'I need to see you,' I said, and I opened the door and walked right in.

Miss Andrews was sitting at her desk, on the phone. She frowned at me. 'Go away!' she mouthed.

'I *have* to speak to you right now!' I insisted.

She sighed deeply, making waving away gestures with her free hand. I took no notice, trembling all over now, but refusing to give up.

'Excuse me, Mrs Jeffries. A little problem has just cropped up. May I ring you back in ten minutes? Thank you so much,' Miss Andrew said smoothly, and put the phone down. She glared at me. 'How dare you come bursting into my room like this, Laura! It's not like you to be so ill-mannered. What on earth is the matter?' she asked coldly.

'You know very well what the matter is! You've said Jeannie can't sleep in the tower room any more! I don't know what Sarah's said, but it's all lies. She's a terrible girl, for all she's so religious. I hate her!' I said furiously.

'Would you please calm down and stop this nonsense. You'll raise your blood pressure and it's not good for you or the baby,' she said. 'It's a shame you're so violently opposed to poor Sarah. She's simply concerned about you. You're very young and clearly easily influenced. I should never have let you get so close to Jeannie. She's not at all a suitable friend for you,' said Miss Andrews. 'I've seen the two of you sniggering away together. I was prepared to turn a blind eye, but I simply can't have her reading such trashy filth right in front of you. Sarah glanced at the book and was profoundly shocked!'

'It's not trashy filth!' I protested.

'Oh, come now, Laura!' Miss Andrews reached into her desk drawer and took out my confiscated book. She held it at arm's length, as if it might be about to burst into flames. 'Do you know what this book is *about*?'

'Girls in Hong Kong,' I said. I nodded at the cover. 'That one's Suzie.'

'Do you have any idea what this Suzie does for a living?' Miss Andrews lowered her voice. 'She's a common prostitute.'

I think she expected me to gasp and clap my hand over my mouth. I stared back at her, determinedly not reacting.

'Perhaps you don't know what that means,' said Miss Andrews.

'Yes I do. She's a party girl. She entertains men. I haven't read it all yet, but I think it's a lovely book,' I said defiantly.

'You're proving my point, Laura. Jeannie was clearly going to let you borrow her nasty book. I can't have you being corrupted by her,' Miss Andrews said primly.

I took a deep breath. 'It's not Jeannie's book. It's mine,' I said.

Miss Andrews sighed irritably. 'Don't be ridiculous! I know you want to protect your friend, but you can hardly expect me to believe a grammar school girl like you would read such dirty rubbish.'

'It *is* my book,' I insisted. 'And I was the one who lent it to Jeannie.'

'Where would a girl like you get hold of a book like that?' Miss Andrews asked.

'My dad,' I said.

She stared at me. 'Your *father* gave you this book?' she asked, suddenly very serious.

'He gets all sorts of books left in his coach. He knows I love to read so he lets me have them,' I said.

'Did he *know* what this book was about?'

'I don't know. Probably not. He's not a great reader himself. But I don't think he'd mind. We've got a picture of a girl just like Suzie on our lounge wall. She's called Miss Wong too,' I said. I was feeling a little anxious now. I was trying to sound blasé, but I knew perfectly well that Dad would never in a million years knowingly let me read a book about prostitutes.

Miss Andrews took a sip of her tea to revive herself, though it had probably gone cold by now. 'Well, you're in my care now, Laura, and this is not the sort of reading matter I could possibly approve of. What were you intending to do when Jeannie had finished reading it? Pass it round every other girl in Heathcote House?'

'No! Though I can't see why it would be so dreadful. Just because it mentions sex. Every girl here must have had sex too,' I said.

I knew I'd gone too far. Miss Andrews' cheeks went bright red, as if she'd been slapped.

'I thought I was a good judge of character but I was obviously wrong. *You're* the rotten apple, Laura. If you're like this at fourteen, goodness knows what you'll be like at twenty. Maybe *you'll* be a street girl too,' she said. Then she closed her mouth abruptly. Perhaps she thought *she'd* gone too far now.

'Well, I'm not going to be, so there,' I said. 'I shall be married to my boyfriend Daniel by then.'

'I think you'd better get out of my sight right this minute. I've got to think clearly what I'm going to do with you. I don't want you mixing with any of the other girls. At least they all have the grace to understand they've done wrong, whereas you're totally brazen. I'd send you packing if I could, but I've taken you into my care so I suppose I'm stuck with you. I can't have *you* sleeping in the tower room now, though God alone knows where I'm going to put you,' she said. 'I suggest you copy Sarah and pray for His forgiveness.'

'I don't know about God, but I don't think Jesus would mind too much. He made friends with Mary Magdalene, didn't He, and *she* was a common prostitute,' I said, and marched out the room.

I kept my head held high but I was trembling so badly now I could barely walk. I staggered back to the tower room. Jeannie was sitting on the edge of her bed, clasping her stomach. Her face was contorted, as if she was in pain.

'Jeannie? Oh God, Jeannie, the baby hasn't started coming, has it?' I asked.

'No. No, it isn't due for another three weeks or more. I just feel a bit crampy, that's all,' she said. 'You didn't really go to Miss Andrews, did you?'

'Yes, I did! And I shouted at her!' I said proudly.

'You never!' said Jeannie. 'You're the little goody-goody.'

'Well, I'm the baddy-baddy now. I told her *The World of Suzie Wong* was a lovely book and it wasn't yours, it was mine. And all sorts of other stuff too. She practically spilt her tea. She said *I* was the bad apple. She's not going to let me stay in the tower room either, but I don't want to, not if you're not there,' I said.

'Oh, Laura! What did you go and do that for?' Jeannie asked.

'Because you're my friend,' I said.

Jeannie's face crumpled. She stood up and we had an awkward hug, like two Humpty Dumptys bumping together.

'You're a real pal,' Jeannie said. 'Daft, but lovely.'

'Maybe I'll be sleeping up in the attic room too. That will be great! It won't be as cosy as here, but who cares, if we've got each other – and no stupid Sarah telling tales?' I said.

'I think you're spot on! There isn't anywhere else she can put us – the cubies are all full at the moment. We'll be the attic girls, you and me,' said Jeannie, and she was smiling now.

It didn't work out like that. Marilyn took me aside after she'd finished serving lunch.

'You're to gather up your things and go to the linen cupboard. That's where you'll be sleeping from now on,' she said.

'What? In the linen cupboard?' I asked, astonished. 'You're joking, aren't you? How can I sleep in a cupboard?'

'I've squeezed a bed in. It's roomier than you'd think. There's no space for your locker, so you'll have to keep your things on one of the shelves. Don't you dare get the sheets all rumpled though,' she said.

'But there's no windows! It'll be horrible, shut in a cupboard!' I protested.

'Well, you shouldn't have been so rude and insolent to Miss Andrews. She's very upset. She was ever so fond of you too.' Marilyn looked at me. 'Why don't you go and say you're sorry, you don't know what came over you. You'll know what to say because you've got the gift of the gab. Then she might relent.'

'But I'm not sorry,' I said. 'OK, I'll sleep in the linen cupboard. See if I care.'

I cared dreadfully, especially when I was taking my things out of my locker in the tower room. My books were missing. I looked under my dressing gown, shook out my towel, peered under my bed. There was no sign of *Madame Bovary* or Katherine Mansfield's *Selected Stories*.

I went storming back to Marilyn. 'Someone's stolen my books!' I said furiously.

'Don't be so silly. No one's stolen them. Did you really think Miss Andrews would let you keep that book about bad girls selling themselves?' said Marilyn, shaking her head at me.

'It's my property! But it's not just *The World of Suzie Wong*, it's *Madame Bovary* too, and that's not even mine – I borrowed it from Daniel's house – and the Katherine Mansfield book was a present from my aunt and it's a first edition so it's very valuable. How *dare* Miss Andrews steal them!'

'Calm down! Whatever's got into you today? You know perfectly well Miss Andrews hasn't stolen them. She's simply confiscated them, keeping them safely locked away until it's time for you to go,' said Marilyn.

'But they're *classics*! She can't object to them!' I said, outraged.

'That one with the funny title is about an unfaithful woman. And Katherine Mansfield's too modern,' said Marilyn, clearing parroting Miss Andrews.

'That's crazy! Katherine Mansfield was writing in the 1920s so how can she possibly be called "modern"?' I declared.

'Miss Andrews said so,' Marilyn said.

'Well, she's stupid,' I said childishly.

Marilyn gasped. 'You're dreadful, you are! You're just a kid and yet you think you know it all. Well, if that's the case, how come you've ended up here, eh? Now clear off before I give you a good slapping!'

I stormed off, hating her, hating Miss Andrews, hating smug Sarah more than any of them. She was in the bathroom, washing her hands. She always used a vast amount of red carbolic soap, the suds going right up to her elbows. Perhaps she thought she was washing away her sins.

I went right up to her until we were practically nose to nose, and she was pressed right against the basin.

'You utter, hateful pig,' I said.

She blinked nervously. Her white freckled skin flushed pink.

'The book you showed Miss Andrews was mine, not poor Jeannie's. She didn't tell on me because she's my friend. So now she's been banished to the attic,' I said.

'I'll be your friend now,' said Sarah.

I couldn't believe she could be so deluded. 'I wouldn't be your friend in a million years! Did you think we'd be cosied up together in the tower room now? *I've* been chucked out of the tower room too – they've put me in the linen cupboard, can you imagine? But I'd sooner sleep in the coal bunker than sleep with you!' I shouted.

I was so carried away that a little spit sprayed out my mouth and landed on Sarah's cheek. She flinched and wiped it with the back of her soapy hand.

'You spat at me!' she said.

'Good!' I said. 'Right, you'd better run to Miss Andrews and tell her, quick.'

'Oh, Laura! I truly don't understand why you're so angry with me. I didn't dream that book was yours. But it's really not the sort of thing you should be reading at all, you must know that,' she said. She adopted her pious expression. 'It's a sin to read filthy material.'

'What should I be reading then?' I asked. '*Pride and Prejudice*? Have you actually thought about what happens? Lydia runs off with Wickham, doesn't she? When she's *fifteen*. So in your eyes that's filthy material too. And anyway, sex outside marriage is a sin too, isn't it? You'd better go and pray to your statue for forgiveness!'

I marched off triumphantly, though I badly needed to use the toilet. I had to wait for a very uncomfortable ten minutes until I was sure she'd gone downstairs, and then crept back. I was still trembling, but the elation was seeping away. I just felt devastated.

I couldn't concentrate on afternoon lessons. Mr Michaels looked at me sorrowfully. Miss Andrews must have told him. The other girls kept giving me furtive looks and then whispered to each other. When I went into the living room they all burst out laughing.

'Here, Laura, have you got any more of them dirty books?' asked Big Pam. 'You know, where they do it.' She made a horrible gesture with her hands, and they all giggled again. Well, everyone but Sarah. She sat apart, sewing a long white gown for her baby. Her lips moved as she stitched. She was probably praying to Jesus to protect her innocence.

I went to find Jeannie up in her attic, but Nurse March saw me tiptoeing past the nursery.

'Where are you going, missy?' she asked, standing up and smoothing down her apron. She was a little woman, several inches smaller than me, but she seemed to be towering over me.

'I just wanted to see if Jeannie's all right, Nurse March,' I said as politely as I could.

'She's having a lie-down because she feels a bit sorry for herself,' said Nurse March. 'You leave her alone! What a piece of work you are, little Laura! So innocent-seeming, yet such a dirty-minded creature!'

'I'm not! It was just a *book*, a love story, that's all,' I said. 'I don't know why everyone's making such a fuss about it.'

'You're incorrigible,' said Nurse March, shaking her head at me. Her starched cap wobbled and shifted sideways. It made her look a little drunk, and though I was desperately unhappy I couldn't help my lips twitching.

'Are you smiling, you brazen girl?' Nurse March demanded.

'No! No, honestly!' I said, but I was shaking with nervous giggles. 'Sorry! So sorry!' I spluttered, and ran away, back down the stairs.

I got to the linen cupboard, shut the door, and fell on the bed exploding with laughter – but soon realized I was sobbing. I stayed shut up there until it was supper time. I didn't have anything to read now. I still had a couple of postcards left. I wrote one to Moira, telling her that nearly all the girls were horrible here. The staff were horrible too, and wouldn't even let you read books. I said I was missing her a lot.

It seemed like a lifetime ago that Moira came home with me from school and we played together. It seemed even longer ago that Nina and I had been friends. I wondered about writing to her on the last postcard, but she'd probably show it to Patsy, maybe even pass it round the whole class.

I wrote to Daniel instead, not the *real* one – my imaginary version. I told him I missed him and I was desperately lonely here and I wished I could see him. Then I pretended he'd be so concerned that he'd come to visit me next weekend. We'd kiss each other and he'd realize just how much he loved me.

'*Come away with me, Laura,*' he'd whisper. '*Come away with me now!*'

We'd elope together and all would be wonderful. I managed to forget about the baby inside my rapidly growing tummy. We were just Laura-and-Daniel, a young couple in love . . .

I wondered if Mum and Dad would have been any different if Daniel really had been the father of my child. I thought of Lily Cottage and felt so homesick I started crying all over again. I wanted to be back on the leatherette settee in the lounge with Miss Wong smiling down at me from the wall and the smell of sausages frying in the pan for supper.

'Oh, Mum,' I whispered. 'Oh, Dad.'

If only I could be their little girl again, when they both loved me. They had my school photograph in the smart navy Grammar uniform in a silver frame on top of the television set. Whenever Mum dusted it she'd smile and stroke the little replica me. She gave the four small silver cups I'd won as form prizes in the Juniors a weekly polish, and the bigger cup I'd won for being Top Girl had its own special shelf. The huge box of chocolates I'd won for a children's writing competition was on display on the mantelpiece. The chocolates were long since eaten, but Mum insisted on keeping the empty box.

I wondered if she'd put all these trophies in the Cubby Hole now. Dad had a photo of me as a baby in a small plastic frame with a sucker pad on the back. He'd stuck it to the window of the coach, saying I could coo at him whenever he got bored of driving. He loved it when passengers said I was a bonny baby. Had he ripped it off the window now? He hadn't even said goodbye to me. He'd written that awful letter.

I went down to supper and sat well away from the others. There was no sign of Jeannie. I went back to the linen cupboard, snatching a book from the shelf in the sitting room. *Andrea is an Air Hostess.* It was so boring I nodded off to sleep before the bell rang for lights out.

I woke up around midnight, wide awake. I curled up in a little ball though it was difficult now my tummy was so big. I hated the feel of my own body now. The baby started kicking inside me, just little fluttery movements. I tried to picture it. Would it take after me or the French boy?

'Please be a little girl,' I whispered to my baby, but then I felt guilty in case the baby was a boy and he felt unwanted before he was even born.

'I do want you, whatever you are,' I said. 'I'm not giving you away to anyone no matter what they say. You don't belong to some couple who can't have their own babies. You're mine, and I'm never ever going to let you go.'

The door suddenly opened and I gasped, scared it might be Miss Andrews checking up on me.

'Ssh! You haven't got anyone else in there have you? I heard you muttering away.' It was Jeannie.

'Oh, come in, come in! You've come to see me!' I cried joyously.

'Shut *up*! Miss Andrews' room is just up there! You don't want her to come bristling down in her hairnet and quilted dressing gown!' said Jeannie, squeezing her way in and shutting the door. 'Though her hair always looks so neat with those rigid little waves. Maybe it's a wig! And come to think of it, her teeth are so shiny white and perfect I bet they're false choppers. Imagine the shock of seeing Miss Andrews shining her torch on you, bald as a coot with not a single tooth in her head!'

We both spluttered with laughter.

'Oh, Jeannie, I'm so glad you came to see me!' I said.

'Well, hang on a minute. I've come for something else,' said Jeannie, going over to the shelves and feeling around.'

'What are you looking for? Miss Andrews has taken all my books,' I said bitterly.

'This is a linen cupboard, isn't it? I'm looking for clean sheets,' said Jeannie. 'Haven't you got a candle or something? I can't see a thing.'

Candles were strictly forbidden, but we all used them after lights out. I kept mine steady inside a fat hair roller on top of a cracked saucer stolen from the kitchen.

'Sheets?' I said, lighting the candle.

'Yeah, I've only gone and wet the bed! Don't you dare snitch on me!' she said.

'As if I'd do that!' I said.

'I've never wet the bed in my life, well, not since I was a toddler. Didn't even know I was doing it. I was lying there, kind of dozing and thinking, and then, whoosh!' said Jeannie, shaking her head.

'Perhaps the baby's pressing on your bladder?' I suggested, holding the candle up so she could ease a pair of folded sheets from a pile.

'You budge over a bit then,' said Jeannie to her stomach. She pretended to smack it. 'Naughty boy!'

I laughed, making the candle wobble.

'Watch it! We don't want to go up in flames like holy martyrs,' said Jeannie. 'They used to tell us stories about them in the children's home and give us all nightmares. No, wait a minute, I think the martyrs were all men. The holy ladies all had to be virgins. Ha! That counts us out for a start. Oooh!' She clutched her stomach.

'What?'

'Nothing,' she gasped. 'It's just cramping a bit, that's all. It's been doing it on and off for a while.'

'Then maybe you *are* having the baby!' I said.

'No, I'm not, it's not due for ages, I told you,' said Jeannie. She was shivering, though the linen cupboard was the warmest place in Heathcote House because of the hot pipes. 'Here, you budge up too, Laura . . . let me in bed for a bit.'

It was a narrow bed so it was almost impossible for two girls with big bellies to fit onto it, but with a lot of pushing and shoving and giggling we managed it.

'There now!' said Jeannie. 'Thanks, love.'

I felt really touched. Jeannie rarely used words of affection. Maybe she was starting to like me as much as Belinda.

'Are you comfy now?' I asked.

'Sort of,' said Jeannie.

'Me too. Shall I blow out the candle?'

'Yeah. I don't mind the dark, not if I'm with someone. I tell you, it's pigging lonely up in that attic by myself. And if one of the babies in the nursery starts crying it sounds like a little ghost, and it keeps reminding me I'm having one myself,' she said. She was hanging onto me. Perhaps it was just to stop herself falling out of bed, but I didn't think so.

'I'm scared of having it . . . aren't you?' I whispered.

'No. Well, yes, a bit. Belinda said all the pain was worth it once she held little Peter in her arms, but I don't want mine, so I'll be having all the pain for nothing,' said Jeannie. 'I'm a bit of a sniveller with pain. I screamed my head off when I fell over on my bonce and had to have six stitches.'

'Maybe it won't hurt as much as stitches,' I said, though I wasn't too sure about it.

I felt Jeannie tense and she groaned.

'Are you having that pain again?' I asked.

'Mm. Oh flipping heck, it's really sharp now. Oooh!'

'Jeannie, you *must* be having the baby!' I said. 'Shall I go and get Nurse March? Or tell Miss Andrews?'

'No! I'll be fine in a second. There! It's better now. Sort of,' she said, sniffing. She clung to me even tighter. 'I don't want to have this baby! I don't want to!'

'Well, what are you going to do? Cross your legs for ever?' I said.

She laughed at that. 'You're a funny kid, Laura,' she said. 'Anyway, I've just got some sort of bug, I'm sure of it. Maybe it's just nerves. I keep saying, the baby's not due for weeks yet.'

The baby didn't seem to realize it. Within another hour Jeannie was desperate and I had to go for help.

I had to go and see Miss Andrews yet again after breakfast.

'What were you playing at, you silly girl? Didn't you realize Jeannie was in labour?' she demanded.

'I thought she was, but she kept saying she wasn't,' I said, realizing how foolish that sounded.

'She told you her waters had broken!' said Miss Andrews.

I didn't know what she meant. I wondered if this was a genteel way of saying she'd wet herself.

'Didn't either of you realize that when the fluid surrounding the baby comes out it means that you're in labour? And that if you're having sharp pains every three minutes it's imperative that you go to hospital? For goodness' sake, you're not very bright, Laura, for all you're a grammar school girl,' said Miss Andrews.

'Jeannie was minutes away from giving birth in my car by the time I got her to the hospital.'

'I'm sorry, I truly didn't know. What did she have?' I asked.

'A little girl, rather underweight, but the paediatrician says she'll be fine,' said Miss Andrews.

'What's she calling her?'

'*I* don't know. I'm not sure she's even thought of a name yet,' said Miss Andrews. 'She's known all along that she's having her baby adopted. At least she's made the sensible decision.'

'When the baby gets adopted it can keep its own name though, can't it?' I said.

'Generally speaking the adoptive couple chooses a new name for their child,' said Miss Andrews.

'But that's not fair. It's *not* theirs,' I said.

Miss Andrews yawned. 'Stop getting so worked up about silly things, Laura. I haven't got the time or the patience to get into a philosophical discussion with you, young lady. I've been up most of the night and I'm very tired. Now go and get on with your chores.'

'Can you just tell me – Jeannie is all right, isn't she?' I asked anxiously.

'Yes, of course she is,' said Miss Andrews briskly.

'And she'll be back here soon?'

'In ten days. Now go away, Laura, and stop fussing!'

Ten days seemed like ten weeks. I desperately wanted to visit Jeannie in hospital. I knew she had no one else to come and see her. We'd hoped Belinda might write to both of us but she hadn't yet. We'd checked with Marilyn every morning when she gave out the post.

'I doubt she will write,' she said. 'It's probably better that way. She needs to start her new life now and forget this ever happened.'

How could she ever forget she'd had baby Peter? And how could she forget *us*? Maybe her parents wouldn't let her write. We wanted to write to Belinda but we didn't know her full address. We asked Marilyn for it, but she said she didn't know either.

I asked her now for the address of the hospital where Jeannie was.

'I don't know,' she said again.

'But that's ridiculous! Of course you know,' I protested.

'Of course I do, but I know you, Miss Sly-Boots. You'll be wanting to take a trip there on Saturday and it's not allowed. You couldn't get there anyway; there's no bus and it's much too far to walk,' said Marilyn.

'I could take a taxi,' I said grandly, though I had hardly any money. Mum had actually sent me a savings token for ten pounds, but there was no post office in the village so I had no way of cashing it. She'd sent it inside a card, one with little bunnies and squirrels skipping about on it, the sort she'd given me years ago. There wasn't any message at all on it. It just said *From Mum*. Not even *love*.

I gave up on the idea of getting to the hospital, but I went to the village on Saturday afternoon and bought a card for Jeannie. I knew she wouldn't want a postcard of the village, because she said she hated it here. I looked at the meagre selection of proper cards. They had 'new baby' cards, with rather sickly pictures of a blue teddy in a sailor suit or a pink bunny in a ballet dress. Neither were remotely the sort of card Jeannie would like, but I thought she might want one to go on top of her locker to show she had a friend who cared.

I bought the pink one and a stamp and wrote on it inside the shop so I could pop it in the postbox there and then.

I didn't know what to write inside. I couldn't really put *Congratulations* because it wasn't as if Jeannie wanted the baby in the first place. In the end I wrote: *Bet you're glad it's all over! Come back soon, I miss you. Love from Laura xxx*

I didn't know how to address it either. I didn't want to put *Miss* on the envelope because it would be rubbing it in that Jeannie was unmarried, and yet it would seem weird to put *Mrs*. In the end I settled for simply *Jeannie Maclaren, Maternity Ward, St Margaret's Hospital* and hoped it would get there with such a skimpy address.

I literally counted the days. On the tenth day I stole some pink ribbon from the craft box and tied little pink bows on her bedpost and made her a poster saying *WELCOME BACK JEANNIE* and stuck it on the bleak wall of her little attic. I wished I could buy her some chocolates or flowers too, but I only had a few pennies left. I made her a butter and sugar sandwich at breakfast and saved it for her, hoping it wouldn't be too stale by the time she arrived.

New mothers usually arrived around lunchtime, but there was no sign of Jeannie.

'Hasn't Miss Andrews gone to collect Jeannie yet?' I asked Marilyn anxiously.

'The hospital sends our mothers and babies home in a special booked car,' said Marilyn. 'It'll be here any minute.'

I waited all afternoon and then in desperation braved Miss Andrews.

'Please, I'm sorry to bother you, Miss Andrews, but Jeannie isn't home yet and I'm worried something's wrong,' I said, trying to be as polite as possible.

'Oh, Jeannie won't be back for another day or two,' Miss Andrews said breezily.

'Why? Is something wrong with her?' I asked anxiously.

'No, she's absolutely fine,' said Miss Andrews.

'Then . . . is it the baby?' I asked.

'The baby is just a little sickly with jaundice,' she said.

'Oh no!' I said, though I didn't even know what jaundice was. 'I thought you said the baby was all right.'

'No need to panic. It often happens with babies. No doubt she'll be fine in a day or so. Though she *is* underweight,' said Miss Andrews.

'Poor Jeannie. She must be so worried,' I said.

'Of course, it's only natural. Still, Jeannie's never wanted to keep her baby, has she? So perhaps it isn't as bad for her,' said Miss Andrews briskly.

'She's still got feelings!' I said indignantly, forgetting to be polite now.

'Now don't get in a silly state again, Laura. It's bad for *you*. Off you trot now, and stop worrying,' she said.

As if I could stop worrying! I waited day after day and Jeannie *still* didn't come back. Sarah saw my red eyes and puffy face and decided to take pity on me.

'I'm sure Jeannie's all right, Laura. *And* the baby,' she said. 'They'd tell us if anything had happened.'

'No they wouldn't. And don't pretend you care. You obviously hate Jeannie,' I said fiercely.

'No, I don't,' said Sarah. 'And I still like you, even though you don't like me. Would you like me to say a little prayer for Jeannie and her baby?'

'No thanks,' I replied sharply – but I said a prayer myself in the privacy of the linen cupboard. It didn't work the next day or the next, but the day after that suddenly Jeannie walked into our English lesson.

'Jeannie!' I said, and rushed up to give her a hug.

'Get off me, soppy date!' she said, but she hugged me back hard.

'I've been so worried! Why were you so long? And where's your baby?' I asked, my stomach tightening with dread. My own baby started kicking.

'She's in the nursery – where else?' said Jeannie, seemingly calm and matter-of-fact.

'Can I see her?' I asked, and several of the other girls clamoured to see her too.

'No, she's too small, she's got to be left in peace. Nurse March is keeping her in her own room. I'm the only one who can see her,' said Jeannie.

'And there's also the little matter that you're all in the middle of my English lesson,' said Mrs Chambers. 'You sit down too, Jeannie. And welcome back. We've all missed you.'

She was being kind because no one really liked Jeannie except for me, but Jeannie looked touched.

'Thank you, miss,' she said, and for a moment she looked as if she might cry.

She seemed different somehow. Less fierce. Sadder. She looked different too. Her body was still very bulky, though it was mostly hidden by Belinda's big Aran cardigan, but her face looked pinched, and her wrists and legs seemed much thinner than before. She didn't try to join in the lesson. She just sat there, staring into space.

Everyone crowded round her at lunchtime, wanting to know all the gory details of the birth. Jeannie just shrugged. 'It was pigging painful. End of story,' she said.

'And what's your baby like? What are you going to call her? How small *is* she? Does she cry a lot? Does she look like you?' the girls asked, talking over each other.

'She's OK,' Jeannie said. 'Don't keep on at me.'

The others lost interest after a while and wandered off.

'She doesn't seem that bothered about her baby, does she?' I heard someone mutter.

'Well, that's Jeannie for you. Doesn't give a stuff about anything,' someone else said.

Jeannie heard them too. 'Stupid cows,' she said listlessly. Then she leaned closer to me. 'Come up tonight after supper and I'll show you her. If you want.'

'Of course I want to!' I said, and I squeezed her hand. 'I'm so glad you're back, Jeannie.'

'Thanks for the card,' she said. 'It meant a lot.'

I could hardly wait to see the baby. I knew she was little and underweight, so I pictured her as a little fairy baby, pale pink and delicate, with a fluff of down and big blue eyes. I didn't know what to say when I saw her in the metal cot beside Nurse March's bed. The baby was more like a changeling child than a fairy. She was small and sallow, with coarse dark hair and a scowl on her wizened features. I'd thought Moira's little sister a sad little thing, but Jeannie's daughter was pathetically ugly.

I took a deep breath. 'She's lovely, Jeannie!' I said.

'Don't be a twerp. She's hideous, poor little mite,' said Jeannie.

'Don't you dare say that about your own daughter!' said Nurse March. 'I've told you, she'll be fine when she grows up a little. She'll probably turn out a real bobby-dazzler.'

'What, like me, you mean?' said Jeannie. 'No wonder I spent half my childhood in a home. Who'd want to adopt a kid like me? Or her?'

'You wait and see,' said Nurse March.

'Yeah, but I can't wait, can I? She'll be taken away when she's six weeks old. And she won't be going to no adoptive parents. They'll look at the photos of her and turn up their noses. So it'll be foster mums and institutions, handing her round like pass-the-parcel, the years ticking by, and no one will ever want her,' Jeannie said fiercely.

'Oh, Jeannie, don't!' I said, leaning over the cot and taking hold of the baby's tiny clenched fist. 'Don't you listen to your mum, Baby. You'll find a special new mum, I'm sure you will.'

'No she won't,' said Jeannie. 'So she'll have to put up with me. I'm keeping her.'

I stared at her. 'But you're giving her up, you've always said so!'

'I know. But I didn't know what she'd be like. I didn't know what I'd feel like. I've got to keep her. I'm not having her messed up like me. She's going to have a proper home,' said Jeannie. She picked the baby up and held her close, rubbing her cheek against her straggly hair and crumpled face. 'She's going to have a proper mum.'

'You're all worked up now, chickie, so you're not thinking straight,' said Nurse March. 'Now don't wake her up, not when she's just got settled. Pop her back in her cot, there's a good girl.'

'She's my baby, not yours. I know what's best for her,' said Jeannie, but she gently lowered her back into her cot and tucked her up tenderly. 'Night night, little 'un,' she said, and blew her a kiss.

I went back to Jeannie's room with her. Nurse March saw, but didn't stop us.

'Will you really keep her?' I said, awed.

'Yep. They can't stop me,' she said. 'I'm even feeding her myself, though she's wearing me out. She has to be fed every three hours to build her up a bit, so I end up feeling like a blooming cow.'

'Isn't it painful?' I asked, putting my hand over my own chest protectively.

'Yeah. I got so sore they had to dab me with gentian violet and then I got purple dribble marks all down my nightie,' said Jeannie. 'It ain't glamorous being a mother. But I suppose it's worth it.'

I couldn't believe how much she'd changed. She seemed so determined to bring her baby up herself now, yet I didn't see how she was going to manage it. Even Belinda had given way in the end.

'What are you going to call her?' I asked.

Jeannie looked hesitant. 'Well, I didn't like to tell you. Promise you won't mind? I'm calling her Belinda.'

'I think it's a lovely name,' I said, though it seemed so sad to name such a poor little scrap after a beautiful girl like Belinda.

'Really? She's going to have Laura as a middle name. Belinda Laura Maclaren. It sounds really posh, doesn't it?'

'It does,' I said. Then I burst out, 'But *how* will you keep her, Jeannie? You haven't got anywhere to go. Will they let you have her at this hostel Miss Andrews told you about?'

'No, I'm not taking her there. I've got it all planned out. I'm going to hitch a ride to London and get a job in a hotel, waitressing, kitchen work, chambermaid – any old job where I can live in. With baby Belinda. I'll pay one of the other girls to keep an eye on her when I'm doing my shift. It won't matter if she's on her own a bit, just so long as she's fed and changed. I suppose she'll have to go on to a bottle then, but at least she'll have had a good start being fed by me.'

I tried to take it in. 'You'll work?' I said. 'But you're not old enough.'

'Yes I am. I'm fifteen, it's legal. I did a bit of waitressing before I got caught with the baby,' she said.

'But will they let you have Belinda in the hotel?' I asked. It didn't seem at all likely to me, but Jeannie nodded determinedly.

'Course they will. She won't be no bother to anyone. Don't look so worried, Laura, it'll work out.'

I thought hard. 'Can't you go and see Belinda's father? Maybe you can settle down together and be a family?' I said.

'Like you and Daniel?' said Jeannie sharply. 'You can stay in cloud cuckoo land if you like, but I'd sooner face facts. Besides, I couldn't really tell you which lad is her father. Go on then, despise me.'

'I don't despise you in the slightest. I think you're ever so brave,' I said.

I still thought Miss Andrews and her social worker would talk her out of it and get her to sign baby Belinda away. But Jeannie didn't wait. She stayed at Heathcote House another fortnight, and then she ran away with her baby. She must have crept out in the middle of the night. Goodness knows how she lifted Belinda out of her cot without waking Nurse March, but she managed it. She took a bag of nursery terry towelling nappies with her too, and her own clothes – and my savings token for £10, though she left an IOU note.

So sorry. Don't want to steal from a pal. I'll pay it you back, promise, all ten bob. Wish me luck! Luv Jeannie x

Miss Andrews had me into her office as soon as they discovered Jeannie and her baby were missing. I didn't show her the note. I didn't want to get Jeannie into any more trouble. Miss Andrews was convinced I knew where she'd gone, though I told her truthfully I really didn't know.

'You do realize how serious this is, Laura? Jeannie's baby is still quite sickly. She needs proper care,' she said.

'Jeannie will care for her. She loves her,' I said.

I was thrilled to get a letter from her a week later. It was scribbled on a piece of paper torn from an accounts book and posted in a buff envelope.

'Hey, got a place, someone to look after me and baby B, all good! Luv J xx'

I held the note to my chest as if I were hugging Jeannie herself. Then I noticed the envelope had a jagged edge and had been resealed with sticky tape. I went storming off to Miss Andrews.

'Did you open my private letter?' I asked.

I thought she'd deny it, and I couldn't be a hundred per cent sure Jeannie hadn't simply reused an old envelope, but Miss Andrews admitted it straight away.

'Of course I did,' she said. 'I'd hoped the silly girl might have put an address. We have to find her.'

'But why? It sounds as if everything's worked out for her,' I said, and I hoped hoped hoped it was true. I pictured Jeannie living contentedly with some kindly motherly person, and little Belinda growing to be a bonny little girl, almost as pretty as her namesake.

It didn't work out that way. A month or so later Miss Andrews summoned me again.

'I thought I'd put your mind at rest, Laura,' she said. 'Jeannie and her baby have been found.'

'And they're safe and well?'

'No, they're not. The baby failed to thrive. I'll give Jeannie credit, she took her to a doctor herself. She wasn't feeding her proper formula, just boiled milk, and the baby became very ill, poor little soul,' said Miss Andrews solemnly.

'She hasn't died, has she?' I asked, horrified.

'No, she's being cared for properly now, with a foster mother,' she said.

'And Jeannie?'

'She was found to be in moral danger, living with a most disreputable man, and so she's been placed in a home for wayward girls,' said Miss Andrews. She looked sorrowful, but there was a triumphant gleam in her eyes. 'Dear oh dear, I wish she'd have listened to us in the first place. She's still refusing to sign the adoption papers, so her little girl will be brought up without a proper family. Learn from this, Laura.'

The only thing I learned was that I had to have some better plan to keep my own baby – but I didn't know what. I wasn't even old enough to get a job. Mum and Dad had made it plain that I couldn't bring my baby back to Lily Cottage. But perhaps they might change their minds when the baby was actually born?

Mum had written to me at last.

Dear Laura,

I am still so upset and can't believe my own daughter could get herself into this awful shameful situation. But I'm also so worried about you, dear. I know your time must be drawing near. I do hope it's not too frightening for you. You're so young. I will be praying for you.

Love Mum

Sarah was still praying for me too, so Jesus must be getting fed up with the sound of my name. I was surprised that Mum wrote that, because she'd never seemed at all religious. Perhaps she was changing. She'd called me *dear* and sent me love. Perhaps she was coming round to the idea that I was having a baby! She loved babies, after all. She'd wanted her own so badly. She'd been bereft when she lost William and the first little Laura. What if I had a boy? Might she think it was William come back to her? Would she be able to bear it if I gave him away?

I wanted to write straight back to her but I didn't have any money left for postcards or stamps. I knew Sarah had fancy notepaper with deckle edges and matching envelopes. I thought about asking her if she'd let me have some, but I felt sick at the thought of sucking up to her. I'd have to be sweet and humble, as if I wanted to make friends. I wondered if I could steal some notepaper when it was my time to sweep the floor outside the tower room. I decided I'd sooner be a thief than a hypocrite. She'd go running to Miss Andrews if she found out, but what did it matter? I was already in disgrace.

In the end I didn't have to. I had a nightmare about being held down while medical people in white gowns and masks tore my baby out of me and then threw it, naked and wailing, out of the window. I cried for a long time when I woke up and couldn't get back to sleep.

No one commented at breakfast when I appeared looking wan and red-eyed. Nearly all the girls had the occasional crying fit at night. The staff were used to it. But Mrs Chambers asked me to stay behind after the English lesson.

'What's the matter, Laura? Are you missing Jeannie dreadfully?' she asked gently.

She seemed genuinely concerned. I burst out crying again.

'Look, come out in the garden with me while break lasts. It's a lovely day and you look as if you could do with a spot of fresh air,' she said.

'But we're not allowed in the garden in the morning,' I sobbed.

'We can say I'm giving you a little extra English tuition if anyone bothers us,' said Mrs Chambers, and she put her arm round my shoulders and steered me down the corridor to the back door.

I didn't often go in the garden in the afternoon, though it was lovely there, especially when it was sunny. The apple blossom was coming out and there were bluebells growing in the long grass. There was an ornamental pond in the middle of the lawn. It reminded me unbearably of the lily pond at home.

Mrs Chambers sat on the wooden bench by the pond. I sat beside her, still crying. When I'd reached the hiccupping stage she patted me on the back and felt for the handkerchief tucked in the cuff of her cardigan.

'Here,' she said, handing it to me.

I mopped myself as best I could.

'You poor old thing,' said Mrs Chambers. 'You're having a tough time. Haven't you made any more friends yet? I know you and Sarah don't get along now, but what about Beth or Judy?'

They were new girls, and both seemed quite nice, but they'd palled up together. I wasn't that bothered anyway.

'I don't really want any other friends. Belinda and Jeannie are my friends,' I said. I sniffed. 'I feel so sad for them. Belinda loved little Peter so much. And Jeannie tried so hard to keep her own baby. It's awful that they took her away and put Jeannie in some awful institution.'

'It *is* awful. It's very hard for you girls,' said Mrs Chambers. She looked round warily, making sure no one was listening. 'And it's already hard for you, Laura, with all that fuss about the book you were reading. I gather Miss Andrews took other books away from you too?' she asked.

'Yes, *Madame Bovary*, which doesn't even belong to me. And Katherine Mansfield's short stories, and they were a special present from my aunty,' I said.

'Oh my Lord! *Madame Bovary*! That's a wonderful book, though again, rather adult. And *Katherine Mansfield*? How on earth could anyone object to a girl reading Katherine Mansfield? Miss Andrews must be mad!' Mrs Chambers was so indignant that she raised her voice, and then looked round anxiously to check Miss Andrews wasn't bearing down on her. 'Oh dear, I'm not being very discreet! Don't worry, Laura, I'll make sure you get your books back when you go home.'

'But I can't go home!' I wailed. 'Mum and Dad said they won't take me back, not with the baby, and I want to keep it! I can't even write to beg them to change their minds because I haven't got any money left for notepaper and stamps!'

'Oh dear,' said Mrs Chambers. 'I'm not sure you really can keep your baby because you're so young. But I'll bring you in some paper and envelopes and stamps. You need to be able to write to your parents. I wish I could do more for you, Laura.'

She actually did quite a lot more for me. She brought me a little box containing matching notepaper and envelopes and a biro and a strip of stamps, and several books too: Anne Frank's *Diary of a Young Girl*, *I Capture the Castle* and *The Greengage Summer*.

'I think even Miss Andrews will agree that they're suitable reading for a bright teenager,' said Mrs Chambers. 'And if you race through them, and *Pride and Prejudice*, you can borrow the rest of my Jane Austens.'

'Thank you ever so ever so much, Mrs Chambers. You are so lovely!' I said. I wanted to throw my arms round her and kiss her, but I might have embarrassed both of us.

19

I wrote to Mum straight away:

Dear Mum,

I miss you and Dad so much. I'm so lonely here and I'm very very frightened about having the baby because I know it hurts a lot, and I'm scared of hospitals. I know I've let you down and you've every right to be ashamed of me, but please please please will you come and visit me when I'm in the hospital after the birth? It will help me get through it, knowing you'll be coming to see me.

With lots of love from Laura xxx

I knew it would be pointless coming right out with it and begging to keep my baby. She'd say a flat no. But if she came to see me she might just fall helplessly in love with the baby. It was her grandchild, after all. She might want to look after it. She might somehow overrule Dad. It was my only hope.

It wasn't as if I was lying. I did miss her and I was certainly frightened about giving birth. It was getting nearer and nearer. The baby was getting much larger now. It was a strain pulling my pinafore over my huge bulk. I could hardly bear to look at it when I took my twice-weekly bath. I couldn't work out why it was so big when babies were so small. How on earth was the baby going to get out? I knew how, of course, but it seemed impossible.

I shuddered at the thought of being torn open. What if I screamed, and kept on screaming? How long would it last? I knew it took hours and hours. When Big Pam had her baby it went on for two whole days, and she had to be stitched up afterwards. She came back from hospital with a special blow-up rubber cushion because it still hurt so much when she sat down.

I decided it might be worth praying to Sarah's little statue, begging not to need a cushion after I'd had my baby. I wished I had a convenient door in my tummy, so I could open it and simply take the baby out. I knew they gave you an operation if they thought you were too small to give birth, but that meant cutting you open with a knife and that seemed terrible too.

I started to get dreadful nightmares, and every time I had the mildest tweak in my tummy I clutched myself in terror. Yet when I woke up early one morning with a pain like a period and a nagging ache in my back I couldn't help feeling excited. I lay in my bed in the linen cupboard, holding my stomach.

'You're coming, aren't you?' I whispered to the baby. 'I can't wait to see you.'

The pain didn't really seem too bad, though it was hard to get comfortable. Maybe the other girls had been making a fuss about nothing. Perhaps I was going to manage the birth with ease. I needn't even bother to go to the hospital. I could just lie here peacefully and the baby would slip out when it was ready. I'd wrap it up in my pillowcase and when Miss Andrews came looking for me she'd find me sitting up with my baby in my arms, looking serene and beautiful like a Madonna.

The pains started to get a little stronger. And then stronger still. I had to leave the sanctuary of the linen cupboard and stagger to the bathroom. My waters broke before I could get into a toilet, so then I had to find a cloth and mop them up as best I could, groaning now as I crouched down.

'What on earth . . . ?' One of the girls had come wandering into the bathroom, rubbing her eyes sleepily. It was Sarah of all people.

I tried to ignore her, still mopping, trying not to cry with humiliation.

'Has your baby started?' she gasped.

'No, I just felt like wetting the floor for the thrill of it,' I said through gritted teeth.

'Oh goodness!' said Sarah. 'I'd better go and tell Miss Andrews.'

'Don't! Not yet! I've got to get washed and dressed and pack my bag and—' I started, but then another pain came, so sharp this time that I couldn't even speak.

'Wait there!' said Sarah and rushed off.

I wasn't capable of doing anything but crouch, rocking with the pain. Then Miss Andrews came, still stately even in her quilted dressing gown. She was so calm I felt relieved to see her.

'It's hurting so!' I gasped. 'I'm sure it's coming now!'

She put her hands on my stomach and timed the length between the pains.

'Calm down, Laura. You've hardly got started. I think there's plenty of time for us both to have breakfast, and then I'll drive you to the hospital,' she said firmly.

I couldn't understand why she wasn't taking me seriously, when she'd been in such a panic over Jeannie, but I didn't have the energy to argue. I struggled to wash and dress in my well-worn pinafore and packed my case with my nightie, washing things, and all Mrs Chambers' books. Sarah insisted on helping me and took my arm when I went downstairs.

'There now. Good girl!' she said, as if I was a little dog. '*In thy sorrows thou must labour.* It's God's word.'

'I bet God wouldn't say that if He were a woman,' I said.

'I do wish you wouldn't blaspheme, Laura,' she said primly, but she still sat me down in the dining room and went to collect my breakfast for me.

I didn't really feel like anything to eat and sat staring at my cornflakes until they went soggy.

'That's a waste,' said Marilyn, collecting dishes.

'She's in labour,' Sarah announced.

All the other girls stared at me and I felt a fool. Marilyn softened, though. When all the other girls had gone off to do their chores she came over to me with a bowl of sliced banana, sprinkled with brown sugar and cream.

'Here,' she said softly. 'A little treat. That should keep you going. It's not proper cream, it's top-of-the-milk, but it tastes just as good.'

'Oh, Marilyn, thank you!' I took a spoonful. 'It tastes utterly delicious. You're so kind!'

'Well, it's a special day for you, isn't it?' She patted my shoulder. 'Don't be scared. They'll look after you in hospital. Once you've had the baby it'll be almost like a little holiday. You can just stay in bed and have everything done for you. I really enjoyed it.'

I stared at her. 'You've had a baby, Marilyn?'

'Yes, I have. A little girl. You keep that a secret, mind,' she said.

'Were you *here*, at Heathcote House?' I was astonished.

389

'That's right. I was ill after I'd had the baby and I didn't have anywhere to go. Miss Andrews let me stay, if I did little chores to help out. Then the cook left and I took over – and now here I am. Deputy matron,' she said, proudly.

'So you gave your baby away?' I asked.

'It was for the best. I couldn't keep her. Miss Andrews said she'd gone to a lovely doctor and his wife,' said Marilyn.

The only doctors I knew were the Bertrams and I didn't think them at all lovely now.

'Isn't it awful working here still? Doesn't it keep reminding you of giving up your own baby?' I asked.

'I like it here,' Marilyn said doggedly. 'I like to feel I'm helping.'

I thought she was crazy, but it would have been rude to keep on questioning her. I carried on eating my banana, waiting tensely for the next pain. It was really sharp again.

'Breathe deeply, Laura. It'll be over in a minute. There you go,' said Marilyn, holding my hand.

'Why does it have to be *so* painful,' I gasped, when it eased at last.

'I know. It's a beggar, isn't it?' said Marilyn. 'Still, this time tomorrow it'll all be over and you'll have your little baby in your arms.'

'This time *tomorrow*?' I said, horrified. 'I can't go on that long!'

'What are you going to do then? Stay pregnant for ever?' said Marilyn, tweaking the end of my nose. 'Don't be silly!'

'I might have known Laura would be making a fuss,' said Miss Andrews, coming into the dining room in her tweed suit and a pink blouse with a big bow. It slightly softened her scariness but I still dreaded being in a car with her all the way to hospital.

Yet Miss Andrews was surprisingly nice to me on the drive to the hospital. I thought she'd scold me all the way, but she told me all about a Victorian lady called Miss Heathcote who had inherited the house when the rest of her family had died, and decided to turn it into a special home for girls in distress. I think she was telling me this story to try to take my mind off things, but when I doubled up in pain with a contraction she switched to a calm murmur: 'There, there. Breathe slowly. Keep calm. That's it. Well done.'

She was so encouraging that I found myself asking if she could stay with me in the hospital.

'No, I'm afraid I can't do that, Laura. It's not allowed. But I'm sure the nurses will be kind,' she said. 'You're so young I'm sure they'll do their best to look after you properly.'

She did come in with me though, to get me signed in at the reception desk. She even carried my suitcase for me and raised her eyebrows at its weight.

'*More* books?' she said.

'Yes, but they're not mine,' I said quickly. 'Mrs Chambers lent them to me. And she said you'd approve of them.'

'Hm!' said Miss Andrews.

It was almost as if we were having a little joke together. I was glad she was with me when I had to give my details to the large lady at the desk inside the hospital. She sucked in her breath in shock when I said I was fourteen.

'I'm fifteen in a couple of months,' I said, as if that made any difference.

'Fourteen,' she repeated. 'You're the youngest yet! My goodness! What's the world coming to?'

I felt myself blushing painfully but then the pain distracted me and I had to lean against the desk to stop my legs buckling.

'I'll take Laura through to the ward,' said Miss Andrews.

She took hold of my suitcase again, and cupped my elbow with her other hand, helping me down the polished corridor. Our shoes squeaked as we walked.

'Now why can't we get our floors at Heathcote House as shiny as this?' she remarked. 'I think Marilyn should get you girls to use a little more elbow grease. I know you all think it very unfair that you have to do the chores, but it's very good for you. It keeps you supple and fit and it's very good training for the future, when you have your own homes. And your own husbands and babies,' she said.

I'm having my own baby already! I thought, but I kept my lips clamped together.

We went down endless corridors, stopping every now and then when I felt a particularly painful cramping. I tried to keep track of where we were going so that running away with my baby was still a possibility, but I lost track in the end. At last we went through double doors marked NIGHTINGALE MATERNITY WARD. I'd never heard a nightingale sing, but I was certain it didn't yowl furiously. The noise was coming from a dozen or so babies in metal cots at the end of their mother's beds.

'It's nearly time for their ten o'clock feed,' said Miss Andrews. 'Only another ten minutes to go.'

'Why aren't they feeding them now though?' I asked. 'They sound ever so hungry!'

'Sister Fisher prefers the babies to stick to a rigid routine,' said Miss Andrews.

I didn't like the sound of Sister Fisher. I didn't like my fellow patients either. They were all much older than me and were frowning. The two nearest me leaned out of their beds to whisper to each other. I overheard.

'Good God, she looks about twelve!'

'It's one of those awful Heathcote House girls!'

'They shouldn't put them in the ward with us. They should be kept separate in their own room!'

Did they think I was going to contaminate them? I glared at them fiercely, and then clutched my cramping tummy.

A nurse came scurrying by with a pile of clean napkins in her arms.

'I'm from Heathcote House, Nurse, bringing one of my girls,' Miss Andrews called. 'Where should she go?'

'I don't know. I'll ask Sister,' she said. 'I'm new on this ward.'

Her long dark hair was supposed to be tucked up in a bun but most of it straggled down her neck. She looked even more anxious than I was, but she gave me a distracted smile. I managed to give her a smile back.

She ran to find Sister Fisher who was behind some curtains attending to a patient. We heard the nurse being roundly scolded. Then she came back, still clutching her nappies.

'So sorry, Sister's busy with the breast pump on a new mother,' she said breathlessly. 'She says you're in the bed right at the other end.'

'Thank you, dear,' said Miss Andrews. 'Come along, Laura.'

She led me by the elbow down the ward with everyone still staring. It was a total Walk of Shame. We stopped at the small bed at the end, made up so firmly it didn't look as if I could ever squeeze my huge hulk under the covers.

'Here we are!' Miss Andrews said brightly, as if it was a luxury hotel. 'Well, I should get undressed and into your nightie. Good luck, Laura!'

I wanted to cling to her like a little girl, but I clasped my own hands to stop myself.

'Thank you,' I murmured.

'Don't look so scared! It's not such a big deal. Think of all the people in the world. What do they all have in common?' she asked.

I shrugged my shoulders, unable to cope with riddles.

'They've all been born! An everyday occurrence. Every minute. Every *second*!' she said, and walked off, waving at me.

Yes, and someone's dying every second too! I shouted inside my head, but I didn't dare yell it out loud. I stood watching her walk away and then I drew the curtains around my bed and hastily struggled into my nightie, terrified that someone would open them while I was standing in my awful scrunched-up knickers with my massive tummy on display.

I nearly ripped my fingernails off trying to prise the sheets open, and then I clambered in. I still had my curtains closed but couldn't face the performance of getting out of bed again to open them. I wanted to stay shut away from all the other women in the ward and their crying babies. After a few minutes they all quietened, presumably feeding.

Sister Fisher didn't appear. She must still be busy with this breast pump, whatever it was. I stared down at my own swollen breasts inside my nightie. Might they need *pumping*? It sounded a terrifying procedure. I crossed my arms over them protectively. Then the pain started up again, and I lowered my hands to my stomach.

It was hurting so. Why couldn't human beings be like kangaroos? Their babies came out thumb-sized and crawled up to their mother's pouch. I didn't really like the idea of a gaping pocket in my tummy, but anything would be better than this pain. I was sweating and had to bite my lip to stop myself screaming. I was surely about to have the baby now.

'Help!' I called feebly. 'Please help!'

A pale gaunt woman came round the curtain. She had an elaborate white cap on her head, an apron starched as stiff as a tea tray, and a dark navy dress almost down to her ankles. If she'd carried a lamp with one raised arm she'd have looked the spitting image of Florence Nightingale in my *Child's History Book* at home. I suddenly realized this ward had nothing to do with birds.

'Was it you calling out?' she asked.

'Yes,' I whispered fearfully. 'Please, I think I'm going to have my baby any minute.' It was just like being back in the Infants, when you were about to wet yourself.

'I very much doubt that, but I'd better take a look,' she said.

'Lie down properly now, and pull your nightgown up. Legs wide apart.'

She raised the sheets as if they were made of gossamer and peered at me closely while I blushed. She even felt me, which seemed like an assault.

'You're barely dilated, silly girl,' she said briskly. 'But we'll get you prepared once feeding time is over. Now you lie there quietly and think beautiful thoughts. We'll keep your curtains open, so we can keep an eye on you.'

I did as I was told. I watched the other mothers and their babies. Most of them were feeding them themselves, but a few had bottles. The babies didn't seem to mind, they just sucked determinedly. The woman in the next bed to me sat her baby up and patted it on the back. She nodded to me. I nodded back.

'How old *are* you?' she called.

'Nearly fifteen,' I whispered.

'My God! You'll make the *Guinness Book of Records*,' she said. 'Whatever do your parents think?'

I wanted to tell her that it was none of her business, but I seemed to have lost all my spirit. 'They're ashamed,' I mumbled.

'No wonder!' she replied. 'Honestly, girls nowadays! I was still playing with dolls when I was your age.'

Her baby gave a little burp as if it was agreeing with her.

I turned away from her onto my side, feeling dreadful. It was so unfair. The French boy across the channel was about to become a father, but no one was making him feel awful.

'You don't need a father,' I said silently to my baby. 'You'll be fine just with me as your mother.'

I wondered if the baby believed it. I pictured it with dark hair flopping over its forehead and a foolish expression on its tiny face, babbling with a comic accent.

'No, no, no!' I whispered, shaking my head.

'It's a bit late to say no now,' said the woman in the bed next to me, but she must have been concerned when she saw my face. 'Hey, Nurse! The little kid's acting weird. Can you check she's all right?'

'I'm busy helping Baby Smith to feed. She's OK. Sister Fisher has examined her. She's not due for yonks,' the nurse called.

I wondered how many hours she meant by 'yonks'. I didn't see how the pain could get any worse. It was already ten times as bad as any period I'd ever had. *Twenty* times worse. Couldn't they even give me an aspirin? I thought I'd have doctors and nurses all around me, telling me what to do, holding my hand, helping me. I didn't expect to be stuck in a big ward with a lot of hostile women looking at me disapprovingly, and a nursing staff who didn't take me seriously.

I gave a tentative push, hoping that the baby would be born there and then in the bed just to show them. Nothing happened. I tried harder. Maybe it was blocked up inside and wouldn't ever come out, not even if they cut me open? I started to shake, but I was determined not to burst into tears in front of everyone. Maybe I could distract myself with a book?

I reached for the bag in my locker and found one of Mrs Chambers' books, *I Capture the Castle*. It didn't look very promising. I'd seen too many castles on the Welsh coach tour to want to read about them now. I opened it without enthusiasm but the first paragraph was so extraordinary that I became gripped. I read on and on, getting more and more interested. The ward might not have existed. The pains interrupted my reading, making the page blur, but the moment they started fading I was back in the old castle with Cassandra.

I was startled when someone tapped me softly on the shoulder. It was the young nurse with the untidy hair.

'Sorry! I didn't mean to make you jump. Is that a good book? I love reading too, though I never get time nowadays,' she said. 'Sister Fisher has sent me to look after you. Can you come with me?'

She helped me out of bed, and even put my slippers on for me. I leaned on her while we shuffled the length of the ward, everyone staring again. She took me to a little side room. There was a sink and a toilet and a hard-looking bed covered in wipe-down leatherette, like our three-piece suite at home. It didn't even have proper bedclothes, just one white cloth. I had to position myself on it carefully and then lie flat on my back. It wasn't easy, but I managed it.

The nurse was over at the sink, filling a bowl with water. Perhaps it was for washing the baby when it came out?

'Don't look so worried. It won't take too long,' she said.

'The other nurse said I won't have the baby for yonks, whatever that means. So what do I do? Just lie here until it's born? Will you . . . catch it?'

She stared at me. 'You're not having your baby yet! I'm just giving you your shave and enema!'

I didn't know what she meant – but then it became all too clear. This was far worse than being examined by Sister Fisher. I could feel myself going bright red with embarrassment and the nurse blushed too, though she was trying hard to be matter of fact. The shaving was bad enough, but the enema was appalling. I only just reached the toilet in time.

When at last it was all over she helped me go to yet another room, equally bleak, but with a bed with proper sheets and a blanket. She wouldn't let me put my nightie back on, making me wear a ridiculous gown that tied at the back and showed my bottom.

'There! You're all ready now,' she said.

'What happens here?' I asked fearfully.

'Nothing really. You just wait until you're ready to push,' she said.

'I *am* ready to push now!' I insisted.

'Sister Fisher said you won't be ready for a long time,' she said. 'Not till this afternoon. Maybe this evening.'

'But it's hurting so badly now!' I said truthfully. It felt as if the baby had hated the enema as much I did.

'You've got to open up more. Then you'll feel this great urge to push,' she said. 'Well, that's what it says in the nursing book. I told you, this is my first day on Nightingale. If you hurry up a bit your baby will be my first birth!' She looked at me hopefully.

'I'll try,' I said. I wanted her to be there to help me but I wasn't sure she knew what she was doing. Her hand shook a little while she was shaving me and I had painful little nicks down there.

'You'll have a doctor too,' she said, guessing what I was thinking. 'Or maybe even Sister Fisher.'

'What's *your* name?' I asked her.

'I'm Nurse Robinson,' she said. 'But you can call me Carol if you like. And you're Laura, it says so on your notes. Mrs Laura Peterson.'

'*Mrs?*'

'Sister Fisher says we have to put *Mrs* for everyone, to avoid unpleasantness,' said Carol.

'But everyone knows I'm not married,' I said. 'I'm not old enough!'

'I know. But it's the rules. Sister Fisher's rules anyway.' She lowered her voice. 'She's an old bossyboots!'

'Yes, she's ever so scary,' I said, and then tensed with another contraction.

Carol took hold of my hand and squeezed it tight while I gasped. 'Gosh, it looks awfully painful!' she said, when it was easing.

'It is!' I said.

'I think being on this ward is going to keep me on the straight and narrow,' said Carol. 'My boyfriend keeps on at me, wanting to do you-know-what, but I can see the consequences now! Did your boyfriend talk you into it, Laura?'

'Yes. I suppose so. Though I didn't fully realize what he was doing. And he wasn't really even my boyfriend,' I said in a rush.

'Oh dear. Well, never mind, you'll have a fresh start soon. You'll go back to school and no one will know you've ever had a baby,' she said, trying to be comforting.

'But I'm keeping it!' I said.

'What? Sister Fisher said all the Heathcote House girls have their babies adopted,' she said, surprised.

'Not mine!' I said, starting to cry.

'Oh, don't cry! I'm so sorry. I didn't mean to upset you. The sister on my last ward said I kept putting my foot in it, and I do!' she said. She looked near tears herself.

'It's all right. You weren't to know,' I said quickly.

'Well, I'd better leave you to get some rest,' she said, standing up.

'Oh, please don't go!' I said, alarmed at the idea of being left in this small room all by myself.

'I can't stay long, or Sister Fisher will be on the warpath.' She consulted the watch pinned upside down on her uniform. 'Another five minutes?'

She stayed for nearly fifteen, telling me how she'd wanted to be a nurse ever since she was four and had been given a little nurse's dress and a red bag of kit.

'There was a bandage with plastic scissors and some plasters and some ointment and pretend medicine in a little blue bottle with a cork. I adored it! I played all my dollies were in hospital after that. I can't believe I'm doing it for real now. Actually, it's all a bit *too* real sometimes. What do you want to do when you get older, Laura?' she asked.

'I don't know. I did wonder about being an actress but I don't think I could ever make it. I love reading. Maybe I could work in a bookshop. I'd like that,' I said, thinking of Aunt Susannah.

'I love reading too. Did you ever read the Sue Barton books? They're ever so good. All about nursing,' said Carol.

I had always thought they looked rather dull, but I pretended to be enthusiastic to please her. She started telling me the whole plot of her favourite one. I didn't really listen properly but it was soothing to hear the sound of her voice, and she held my hand again when the pain started up. But then another nurse put her head round the door.

'*There* you are! Sister Fisher is looking for you, Carol!' she said.

'Oh God,' she said. 'I'll have to go, Laura, but I'll pop back as soon as I can, OK?'

It wasn't OK at all, but I didn't want to get her into trouble. I lay there by myself, and the pain got worse, and then worse again, and there was no way I could distract myself. I wanted to read, but my book and all my things were back in the main ward. I heaved myself off the bed, staggering a little, and as soon as the next contraction eased I tried dashing back to the ward, holding the back of my gown together so I wouldn't expose myself. I must have turned the wrong way because I couldn't find it.

I ended up in another toilet with something utterly disgusting in a kidney-shaped bowl by the sink. I thought at first it was a dead baby and nearly fainted, but when I dared peep again I saw it was some kind of bloody membrane. The nurse who had summoned Carol came in and saw me staring at it, hypnotized.

'You're not meant to be in here,' she said, hurriedly putting a cloth over the bowl.

'What *is* it?' I whispered, my throat dry.

'It's just an afterbirth, that's all,' she said.

'What's that? Is it a baby gone wrong?' I asked.

'No, all babies have them when they're in the womb. It's to keep them safe,' she said.

'You mean I've got one inside *me*?' I said, horrified.

'Don't worry, it's all very natural,' she said. 'Jesus, you poor kid, you don't know a thing, do you?' She shook her head at my ignorance.

I was used to being the one that knew a great deal, but you didn't study childbirth at the Grammar. I felt mortified.

'I was trying to find my way back to the ward but I got lost,' I said.

'You're not supposed to be on the ward now. You're in the side room ready to be taken to the delivery room when the baby's about to be born,' she said. 'Come on, I'll take you.'

'But I wanted to go back to get my book,' I explained.

'I'll find you something to read,' she said. She led me back to the side room and then disappeared. She was gone a longish time and I thought she'd forgotten – but at last she came back. She thrust an old magazine with a faded pink and blue cover at me. 'Here, it was all I could find.'

I hated the *Woman's Weekly*. It was an old granny magazine, and the stories were as weak and unappealing as the coloured cover, but it was all I had, so I read every word. I even read the knitting patterns, which were far more complicated than the one I'd used for my matinee jacket and bonnet and bootees. They were a waste of wool anyway, because the weather had turned very warm.

Then the pain got so bad my eyes blurred and I just lay there, crying, feeling desperately alone. I wanted Mum. I actually called out to her in the midst of contractions, though I knew she couldn't possibly hear me. Carol didn't come back, and the other nurse only appeared briefly, checked me all over, and said I *still* wasn't ready. More hours went by. It felt as if they'd all forgotten about me. It was the middle of the afternoon now. I'd somehow missed lunch, which seemed especially unfair.

Then Carol popped in briefly and held my hand again for a little while. I said I was starving hungry so she gave me a stick of the Kit Kat she had in her pocket, but somehow it didn't taste right.

'Oh no, I think I'm going to be sick!' I gasped.

She managed to get a cardboard bowl under my chin just in time.

'I'm so sorry,' I gasped. 'What a waste of your Kit Kat!'

'Oh well, never mind,' she said, though she sighed.

'Do you think there's something wrong with me – or my baby?' I said. 'It's just taking so *long* and it hurts so terribly. Couldn't I at least have some aspirin?'

'I'm certain that's not a good idea,' she said. 'But I'll go and ask Sister Michaels if you're ready for some pain relief.'

It seemed bizarre that she had to consult her to see if I needed it, when *I* was the one experiencing the pain, but it was clearly the rule. She went and fetched Sister Fisher, who looked suspiciously at the sick bowl.

'What's this dark stuff?' she said. 'It's not blood, is it?'

'No, Sister, she was just a little sick with chocolate,' said Carol.

Sister Fisher frowned at me. 'You shouldn't be eating at this stage, you silly girl. Where on earth did you get the chocolate from?'

I saw the panic on Carol's face.

'I just smuggled it in,' I said quickly. 'Oh, Sister Fisher, *please* can't you make the pain go away? I think I'm dying!'

'Nobody's allowed to die on my watch,' said Sister Fisher. She checked me over, and put an odd metal thing on my tummy, leaning her head against it.

'What's that?' I asked anxiously.

'Ssh! I'm listening to your baby. Ah, I can hear his little heartbeat ticking like a clock,' she said.

'It's a boy?' I said, wondering if she could see through my skin too.

'Or a girl. It's a pretty safe bet it's one or the other,' said Sister Fisher. 'Now cheer up, child, I can assure you you're not dying. You're doing well. Just a few more hours to go.'

A few more hours! I thought she must be joking – but she was right. They gave me the gas and air machine Belinda had told me about, but it made me feel sick again, and it didn't really seem to make much difference to the pain. I couldn't help screaming when it was at its peak, and a new nurse put her head round the door to say I was frightening another patient just starting her labour. I was past caring. Then Sister Fisher gave me some kind of injection which did blot out the pain a little, but it blotted me out too, so that I couldn't properly focus, lost in a strange alien dreamworld.

It was supper time before they said I was fully dilated. It felt as if I'd been torn so wide apart I was ready to give birth to an elephant. I was so tired and woozy by this time it seemed a possibility. I pictured my baby like a little Dumbo, with enormous ears and a stubby trunk, and held onto my tummy, telling it that I'd love it no matter what.

Then they put me on a trolley and wheeled me into another room with a higher bed with terrifying stirrups at the end, and steel instruments laid out like bizarre cutlery in a tray. There was a doctor in a mask and gown who nodded at me, and pointed with a blue hand that I should lie on the bed. I thought he had some bizarre skin complaint. It took me a while to realize he was wearing surgical gloves.

'Hello, Mother,' he said to me, which took me totally by surprise. *Mother!* It was the first time anyone had called me that.

Why didn't he call me by my name? Why didn't he comment on my age?

He didn't seem at all interested in *me*, just my nether regions. He told the nurse to get my legs strapped up to the stirrups. I hated the indignity.

'I don't need to be strapped to them! I promise I won't run away,' I said.

'There now. It's simply so that Doctor can see properly,' said the nurse.

We seemed to be stripped of all identity – I was Mother, he was Doctor, she was Nurse. She wasn't the older nurse, she wasn't Carol, she was someone new and I wasn't sure I liked her. She was curly blonde, and though I couldn't see much of her face because she was wearing a mask, she seemed very pretty.

'Where's Nurse Carol?' I asked.

'She'll be busy on the ward just now,' she said. 'I'm Staff Nurse Symonds.'

I wished they could do a swap. I badly wanted to hang onto her hand. The next pain was so terrible I lost all inhibition and screamed my head off.

'Don't waste your breath screaming – try pushing now,' said the staff nurse.

I tried and something seemed to have given way, because I found I could push down hard. I pushed and pushed and pushed until I thought the veins would burst out of my forehead – but nothing happened.

'Why isn't it coming?' I gasped, as the pain died away.

'It'll take a while yet,' she said. 'You'll need to push a bit harder. No, not yet – wait till the next contraction.'

I couldn't see how I could possibly push harder.

'It hurts so,' I whimpered.

'Well, having a baby is no picnic, I'll grant you, but it'll be worth it when you're cradling Baby in your arms.' Then she realized who I was, and softened a little. 'I know it's tough for you – and you're so young.'

'Too young,' said the doctor. 'She's very narrow. I'm guessing it's a forceps job.'

He seemed to have forgotten I had a head with ears.

'Forceps?' I quavered.

'Don't worry, save your strength,' said the staff nurse, but she was glancing at the tray of metal instruments. The biggest one was the worst, with two great steel curves at the end. I tried to imagine them being inserted into me, clamping the baby's head. I pictured the doctor's blue hands yanking hard.

I didn't need to be told to push harder on the next contraction. I pushed so hard I thought I might burst, harder and harder and harder.

'Good girl! That's right, that's great! The baby's head will be crowning soon,' Staff Nurse Symonds said excitedly.

I didn't understand what she meant. I saw the baby's head with a little crown on top, like a painting of baby Jesus, and felt a thrill of pride. The next contraction came almost immediately, and I pushed again, spurred on by fear of those gleaming forceps, and suddenly I felt something burst right out of me, not just the head but the shoulders, the whole slippery body of my baby.

'Well done, well done!' Staff Nurse Symonds cried. 'You have a little girl!'

The baby gave a little cat-like wail, as if she was calling for me.

'My little girl!' I said, weeping. 'Oh please, can I hold her?'

The doctor was giving her a quick examination, but she seemed to pass muster, because he passed her over to the nurse, who wiped her face and wrapped her in a little blanket.

'Here you are,' she said, her eyes shining as if she were truly happy for me. She lay my baby on my chest and I held her close, smelling her strange little head with its damp wisps of hair. It seemed a miracle that I had made this complex little creature, her hair, her skin, her blue eyes with perfect eyelashes, her tiny fingers and toes.

We were still attached by a cord, and I didn't really want the nurse to cut it – I wanted us to stay properly attached for ever.

After a while I had a further contraction and managed to push the afterbirth out too, and then I had to put up with the indignity of the doctor stitching where I'd been torn. When it was over there was such a feeling of deep peace in my body that I felt I would never want to move again. I held my baby and felt her relax, lulled by the rise and fall of my chest.

'She's nodding off to sleep,' said Staff Nurse Symonds. 'I'll put a nappy and a nightgown on her and then pop her in her cot.'

'In a minute,' I pleaded. I wasn't ready to let my baby go. I wanted to hold her safe for ever.

They took my baby away to spend the night in the nursery. It was the rule. They took her away every night even when I was back in the end bed on the ward.

'But what if she wakes up hungry in the night?' I protested.

'If she really seems distressed, the nurse on night duty will give her a feed,' said Sister Fisher.

'But *I'm* feeding her!'

'I know you are. You're a good girl,' said Sister Fisher approvingly. 'Some of you young mothers won't even give breastfeeding a try even though it's the best way to give your baby a good start in life. They just fuss about their figures!'

I had hardly any figure to begin with, so I didn't care. I was desperate to give her a good start. I loved her with painful intensity. My little Kathleen.

I didn't really like the name that much but I consoled myself by shortening it to Kathy, and I could always pretend she was named after Katherine Mansfield. Kathleen was Mum's name. I thought it might help her soften towards her granddaughter. When she saw her she'd not be able to help falling in love with her. She was the most beautiful little baby in the world.

I'd thought Belinda's Peter a lovely-looking child, but he seemed very pink and commonplace beside Kathleen. She was small and incredibly delicate, pale as porcelain with just a faint flush to her cheeks. Her eyes were an incredible blue when she looked up at me. The nurses said she couldn't focus properly yet so all she could see was a blur. I was certain they were talking nonsense. She looked directly back at me as I gazed down on her. Her hair was incredibly soft, like dandelion fluff, and her mouth was a perfect Cupid's bow. She didn't need to be shown how to feed. She fastened onto me and sucked strongly. It hurt rather, but I didn't mind. I didn't mind anything about her, not even the little stalk where her belly button would be. I didn't even mind changing her nappies, though I had thought this would be the part I'd hate. I loved bathing her too, cradling her head with one hand and gently soaping her with the other. She quivered at first when I slowly lowered her into the warm water, but when she realized I still had firm hold of her she seemed to like it, kicking her tiny legs.

'Your baby's going to be a little swimmer,' said the lady in the bed next to me. 'You'll have to get her a paddling pool when she's a bit bigger.' Then she broke off, remembering my circumstances. 'Oh, sorry, dear. You won't have her that long, will you?'

'Oh yes, I will,' I said determinedly. 'I'm keeping her. I'm going back home to Mum and Dad.'

I'd written to them the day after Kathleen was born, using Mrs Chambers' notepaper and stamps.

Dear Mum and Dad,

I had a little daughter last night, weighing 6lbs. She is absolutely beautiful. Can you come and see us at the hospital? I am calling her Kathleen. It hurt really badly giving birth and I had to have four stitches but I don't care, it was worth it.
Love from Laura xx

I wrote to Moira too.

Dear Moira,

I had a baby girl last night and she is beautiful, truly. I hope Mum will let me keep her. You must come round straight away when I get home. I know you're a bit sick of babies but you will like Kathleen, I promise. Maybe you could be her godmother?
Love from Laura xx

I didn't bother pretending to write to Daniel. Kathleen didn't need a father, not even an imaginary one. She had me, and that was all she needed.

I couldn't understand the other mothers on the ward. They all loved their babies, I suppose, but some gave a sigh of relief when they were wheeled away to the night nurseries and said, 'Peace at last!' I couldn't bear it – it was as if half of me was being dragged away. I couldn't sleep without her by my side, and lay awake most nights, scared she might be missing me too and wailing frantically. The night nurse spotted me tossing and turning and saw the dark circles under my eyes in the morning.

They started giving me a sleeping pill at night, but I always tucked it in the side of my mouth and spat it out when I had the chance. I didn't want to be drugged into a stupor. I wanted to savour every moment, imagining my daughter and all the things we would do together as she grew up.

I whispered all this to Kathy when she was brought to me at six o'clock for her first feed, and she concentrated hard as she sucked, taking it all in. I tended her lovingly all day long, not even wanting to put her back in her cot at mealtimes. Sister Fisher and the nurses kept telling me off, saying I was spoiling her, and she'd never get into a proper routine and want to be cuddled all the time.

'Well, so what? *I* want to cuddle *her*,' I said.

Nurse Carol was the only one who understood. 'I'd want to cuddle her too,' she whispered to me. 'She's gorgeous!'

Mrs Matthews in the next bed sniffed. Her little boy Stanley was a big bruiser of ten pounds, who squealed like a stuck pig half the time.

'I suppose you have to make the most of her,' she said to me, 'seeing as you won't have her for more than a few weeks.'

I managed to keep smiling. 'Oh no, I'm keeping her. It's all arranged,' I said.

Mrs Matthews sniffed. It was clear she didn't believe me. I heard her talking about me to her husband when he came to visit her at three, with a bunch of grapes already half eaten.

'See that kid in the next bed? Barely into her teens! Disgusting, isn't it, and yet she acts like butter wouldn't melt in her mouth. She's a bit doolally if you ask me. Carries on about keeping the baby!'

I cupped my hand over Kathy's tiny ear so she wouldn't hear such spiteful whispers. I rocked her gently, holding her against my breast. Her little kitten mouth opened expectantly and I felt myself throbbing, wanting to give her a top-up feed.

Some of the mothers had such difficulty feeding their

babies, complaining that it hurt or they didn't have enough milk or they had too much. One or two needed the dreaded breast pump. Some demanded bottles right from the start, and had to be bound and take special pills to stop their milk coming in.

Kathy and I managed perfectly. Of course, it could be a bit sore at times. All of me felt sore, especially my poor saggy stomach and the stitched part, but I didn't mind too much. It was a reminder that I was a grown-up now, Kathy's mother.

The only time I was on edge was after the two o'clock feed. Kathy tended to fuss a little then, and want to doze and take her time feeding, while I wanted her to hurry up so I could change her nappy again and give her an extra shake of talcum so I could make sure she was her own perfect, powdery little self, ready to meet her namesake grandma.

I kept expecting Mum and Dad, my heart beating hard every time the bell went for visiting hour, but they didn't come, day after day. They must have got my letter. I'd sent it at the same time as Moira's, and she had already written back. She'd actually gone out and bought (or maybe nicked) a proper baby card, with a cute baby in a pink cot and *Congratulations on your new baby girl* in gold lettering on the front.

She'd written inside:

Dear Laura,

Congratulations!!! I would absolutely love to be her godmother!!!

    I do hope you come back here, I miss you so.

Lots of love and xxx from Moira

I proudly put it on my bedside locker beside my water jug and glass and my sponge bag. The other mothers had heaps of cards and vases of flowers and bowls of fruit and boxes of Cadbury's Milk and Black Magic. I had a few chocolates on a saucer myself. Grateful dads often gave the nurses huge boxes of chocolates as thank-you presents, and Carol had given me some of her share. I only ate one, wanting to show the rest of the ward that I had some too.

But then on Sunday, when I'd almost given up hope, Mum came into the ward wearing her best turquoise coat (C&A's sale two years ago) and the hat she'd made herself out of black feathers when she had to go to a funeral. The strong turquoise blue drained her face and she looked as if she had a crow on her head. I saw hateful Mrs Matthews smirking and I felt a sudden powerful wave of protective love.

'*Mum!*' I called, as she looked up and down the ward uncertainly.

She came scurrying down the long ward towards me, her wicker shopping basket on her arm.

'It's Grandma, Kathy darling!' I whispered. 'And it looks like she's brought us presents!'

I cradled Kathy close, and she looked up with her beautiful blue eyes, wide awake now, but perfectly composed. She was by far the prettiest baby in the ward – but Mum didn't even give her a glance.

'Don't shout out like that, Laura, you'll show us up,' said Mum breathlessly. She leaned over Kathy to give me a quick peck on the cheek. 'How are you, dear? Was it really awful? I was so worried. You're still so young, it seems dreadful they made you go through it. Why didn't they knock you out altogether and give you an op to get it out?'

'I didn't think I had any choice,' I said. 'Look at your little granddaughter, Mum! Isn't she perfect?' I dandled Kathy in the air, and she kicked her tiny legs as if she was ready to run across the bed.

'Don't hold it up like that, Laura!' said Mum, sitting gingerly on the end of the bed, as far away as she could get.

'She's not an *it*! She's my little girl, and I've called her Kathleen after you, Mum!' I said. 'Why don't you hold her? You love babies!' I said.

'Look, it's being sick! I *told* you not to shake it about like that,' said Mum.

I cuddled Kathy close again. She'd just brought up a tiny drop of milk, that was all. I quickly wiped her mouth with the edge of her long nightgown.

'Here, I've brought you some hankies,' said Mum. 'And a bottle of shampoo. Just as well, your hair's gone very lank. And lip salve in case your lips get chapped. I thought about chocolates, but you don't want to get spots, so I've brought you bananas – they'll last longer than grapes.' She kept delving in her basket and bringing out more stuff, like a conjurer with a trick top hat. She hadn't bought anything at all for Kathleen, not even a bib or a bootee. I thought of the elaborate little outfits she'd made for my long-lost siblings, and I felt my eyes welling up.

'What's the matter? Don't look like that, when I've come all this way to see you,' said Mum, patting my hand awkwardly, careful not to touch Kathleen even with her fingertips.

'What about Dad?' I mumbled. 'Doesn't he want to come and see his granddaughter?'

'Please don't keep on with this granddaughter lark, Laura. It just makes it more painful,' said Mum. 'And you shouldn't be cuddling it like that, you'll just get attached.'

'I *am* attached! She's my baby!' I declared.

'Ssh! There's no need to shout. Folk will hear. It's cruel, putting you in a ward like this with proper mothers. They'll all be looking down on you,' said Mum.

'*I'm* a proper mother! Stop being so horrible. And *where's Dad?*' I said.

'He couldn't face it. He'd sooner just put it out of his mind,' said Mum. 'He'll come round when you come home.'

'With Kathleen.'

'Please don't start that. It's not a possibility. I don't know how you can ask it. How could we possibly keep it a secret? Don't look at me like that. I've lain awake half the night trying to get my head around it. We'd be the talk of the neighbourhood. I'm not having people pointing and gossiping and sneering. I've even wondered about us moving away and me taking on the child—'

'Yes?' I said desperately.

'But we can't do it. We simply couldn't afford it, not at the moment. We could put our name down for a council house, but there's a huge waiting list, so we'd be stuck in the prefabs for years. Dad couldn't move further away, not with his job. He'd have to go back on the lorries, and he hated that. I'd have to give up *my* job, and it means a lot to me. And I'm not just being selfish – I won't let you destroy your own life. You were doing so well, we were so proud of you. But I've done my best to fix it with the Grammar, told them you were seriously ill and would be away for months. They said they'd keep a place for you, though you'll have to work hard to catch up. You can carry on as if nothing has happened, get a good job when you've got your exams, and in time you'll find a nice man and settle down and you'll have your babies then.' Mum ran out of breath.

'I've got a baby now. You can call her *it* all the time and pretend she isn't even here, but she is, Mum. I love her. I'm not giving her up to anyone else. Look, will you just *hold* her, just for a minute,' I said, and I thrust Kathleen at her.

'Stop that! I don't want to hold it!' Mum protested. She held Kathy awkwardly, away from her chest, as if she was a hot dinner plate. Kathy felt frightened and her face crumpled. 'There, it doesn't like it,' said Mum, but her hands seemed to act of their own accord and she couldn't help cradling her.

'There,' I said.

Mum sighed and peered down at her, looking at her properly. 'She looks the spit of you, Laura,' she whispered.

'She's much prettier than I ever was,' I said. 'And she's so good, Mum. She barely cries. You'd hardly know she was there. I could have her in my room, and I'd get up in the night to her. You and Dad wouldn't be disturbed. We needn't even go out much if you're so worried about the neighbours. I could get little jobs running errands, working down the market, anything just so I could pay my way until I'm old enough to move out and get a proper job. I think the jam factory's got a proper nursery—'

'You're not working in the jam factory!' Mum burst out. 'You haven't got a clue what it's like to do factory work. I didn't have the chance of a good education and *I* had to work in a factory and it was dreadful, dirty and noisy and your back aches and your fingers swell and you're so tired you can't think straight. You don't know nothing about it, you stupid little madam.'

I stared at her, shocked. I'd never seen her so het up, not even when I had to admit I was going to have a baby. I was sure half the ward had heard. I'd vaguely known Mum had worked in some factory, but she'd never really said what it was like. Kathy seemed shocked at the outburst too, and started wailing. Mum rocked her automatically, maybe not realizing what she was doing.

'I'm sorry, Mum. I didn't mean to upset you. I don't *want* to work in a factory – but I'll do anything so I can keep little Kathleen. She's part of me, just like I'm part of you, can't you see that?' I said softly.

'No, I can't. If you're telling us the truth, her father was just some fly-by-night and you weren't even going out together,' Mum said, much quieter now. 'I can't see why you want to keep his baby when he means nothing to you. Especially when it would ruin your life.'

'He's got nothing to do with Kathleen. My life would be ruined if I couldn't keep her,' I retorted.

'Why did you have to call her Kathleen anyway? I've always hated my name. *Kafleeeen!*' Mum said, in a silly accent. She looked down at my Kathleen and glared at her now.

'Don't look at her like that! What's the matter with you? Look at all the other grannies in the room – they're all thrilled,' I said.

'I daresay I'd be thrilled if you were ten years older and decently married, but you're not. You've got to stop all this nonsense, Laura. You can't possibly keep this baby. We're not having it. And you're underage and you've no way of supporting the two of you. Your little Kathleen will have to go into care. She'll be brought up in a home without a proper mum or dad, is that what you want?'

'No, of course it isn't!'

'Well, that's what will happen, unless you sign all the papers to have her adopted. That's what you've got to do. It'll be best for her. She'll get her own lovely new parents and they'll bring her up properly in a grand house and she'll get everything she wants and go to a good school, like your pal Nina,' said Mum. 'You'll sign them papers if you *really* love her.'

'You're just saying all that stuff Mrs Jeffries says. And Miss Andrews. Do you know what the girls at Heathcote House think? They get paid a whacking great fee by the adoption agency, that's what,' I said.

'Don't be ridiculous,' said Mum. 'I'm walking straight out again if you go on like this.'

'Good. I don't care,' I said childishly.

We sat in silence, avoiding eye contact. Mum didn't go, though she'd picked up her empty basket. I didn't beg her to stay. I busied myself with Kathy, winding her little fluffy curls round my finger, tucking her up more securely in her shawl, murmuring little loving words to her.

'Stop this silly sulking,' Mum said at last. 'You're not going to get your own way. We all know best, your dad and I, and Mrs Jeffries and Miss Andrews. You have to get it adopted.'

'I'm not going to,' I said through gritted teeth.

'Well, you'll have to be taken into care too, because we're not having you home,' said Mum.

I wasn't sure she really meant it. If I turned up on the doorstep with Kathy in my arms they surely wouldn't turn me away, as if we were acting out some Victorian melodrama. I saw myself and Kathy trudging through the snowy streets, shivering in some dank doorway, freezing to death overnight – even though it was nearly summertime.

'Don't you love me any more?' I whispered.

'Yes, I do love you, enough to want to stop you ruining your life. I think it's ridiculous, letting you cuddle that baby and fuss it. I daresay they've made you feed it yourself too,' Mum carried on relentlessly.

'I *want* to feed her!' I said.

'They should have taken her away at birth, not even let you see it. That would be the humane way, before you started bonding.

At the very least they should take it when you leave the hospital. That Miss Andrews says you've got to spend six weeks more at Heathcote House. She came out with all this malarkey about having to wait that long before you can sign the adoption papers – but I think that's plain stupid. It just makes it all the harder. You need to get this nonsense about keeping it straight out of your head. You've always been a daydreamer, imagining this and that. But this is real life, Laura, and you've got to face facts. Why won't you *listen* to me?' Mum's voice broke and she put her hand over her face to hide the fact that she'd started to cry.

She looked so sad then, her black feather hat a little crooked now. I wanted to straighten it for her and wipe her eyes and tell her that I really was listening. I loved her and I wanted to try to please her. But I couldn't, couldn't, *couldn't* give my baby away.

I couldn't get the words out, and Mum had finally finished with talking. We sat there, both of us silent, while Kathy started fretting softly, sensing something was seriously wrong. Mum cleared her throat several times as if she was about to speak, but changed her mind. Eventually she blew her nose fiercely and looked at her watch.

'Well, I'd better be going. I don't want to miss my train, and it's a ten-minute walk to the station and I'm in my good shoes,' she said.

'So what's going to happen?' I asked.

'Well, it's up to you, isn't it?' said Mum.

427

She stood up and hesitated. I thought for a moment she was going to walk straight out, but then she bent and gave me a quick peck on my cheek, the feathers tickling. She held out her hand and touched Kathy's tiny pink hand. I willed her to open her fist and grip Mum's finger. She could do it, she'd done it several times to me, and it always made my stomach stir with love – but Kathy didn't move.

Mum walked off with her empty basket, the first visitor to leave.

'You all right, dear?' said Mrs Matthews. 'That visit didn't sound as if it went very well.'

I pretended I hadn't heard and busied myself with my baby. She didn't say any more, sitting there with her hopeless husband, but when he'd gone, giving her a sudden slobbery kiss, she held her grapes out towards me.

'Want one? His Lordship's been picking at them already, but he's left some nice juicy ones,' she said.

I shook my head and murmured, 'No thank you.'

'Oh well. Suit yourself,' she said. 'Why don't you have one of those nice bananas your mother's left you?'

I'd always loved bananas, but I wouldn't touch this bunch. I left them for days on the top of my locker until they went black and Nurse Carol took them away.

She was still lovely to me. She found me crying behind my curtain, and she came and sat close beside me and held my hand.

'Don't worry. Sister Michaels says lots of mums feel weepy after they've given birth. They call it the baby blues. It's hormones,' she said.

'It isn't just hormones,' I sobbed. 'I want to keep Kathy and no one will let me!'

'I think that's a crying shame,' she said. 'You might be young but I think you're a brilliant mother, better than any of the other women on the ward. If I were one of the babies, you're definitely the mum I'd choose.'

'My own mum says I can't come home unless I give her up,' I wept.

'I'm sure she's just saying that,' said Carol.

'No, she isn't. She really means it. I so hoped she'd change her mind, especially as I've named Kathy after her, but she just said she'd never liked her name anyway. *I* don't really like Kathleen either. I wish I hadn't called her that now!' I said.

'Maybe you can change it to something else,' said Carol.

'Maybe I'll call her Carol now!' I said.

'Oh, you lovely thing!' said Carol, giving my hand a squeeze.

I tried calling my baby Carol all the next day, but it didn't really work. She'd become Kathy, and it just didn't seem right calling her anything else.

I tried to make the most of my time at the hospital, knowing I wouldn't be able to cuddle Kathy all day at Heathcote House as she'd be up in the nursery watched over by Nurse March most of the time. I couldn't just relax and enjoy her though. I treasured every moment, but the dread of losing her was forever there.

I cried quite a lot, I just couldn't help it.

'You're starting to get on my nerves, all that blubbing,' said Mrs Matthews, but when her husband turned up on her tenth day to take her home she gave me a little pile of white woollies.

'Here, you,' she said. 'My sister sent these for my little boy and they're all size zero for a new-born baby. They'd never go round him! You take them for your little girl.'

'Are you sure? That's so kind!' I said, starting to cry again.

'Oh Gawd, now *I've* set you off!' she said. 'You cheer up, chicken. I don't get that mother of yours. If you were my daughter, I'd give you a good slapping for shaming us, but I'd still let you *and* the baby stay at home. You're the same flesh and blood, after all.'

I thought I'd be going back to Heathcote House on my own tenth day in a hospital car, but Mrs Jeffries turned up to collect me.

'I had to come and see you to check on everything and start arrangements, so I thought I'd kill two birds with one stone,' she said brightly, when we were in her car. 'How are you, Laura? You look a bit washed out. It's a bit of an ordeal having a baby so young, isn't it? Sister Michaels said the birth went well though.' She peered at Kathy in my arms. 'You've got a fine healthy girl. That's good, isn't it? And you're feeding her yourself? That's the ticket, give her a good start in life. It's well worth it, though of course you'll have to start weaning her the week before you go home.'

I sniffed and didn't reply.

'Sister says you've been a bit weepy the last few days,' she said.

I stared at her. Was she crazy? Of course I was weepy! It looked like I'd lost my one chance of keeping Kathy.

'I know you'd set your heart on keeping your baby. I do understand. I've seen so many of my girls breaking their hearts – but given time this sadness will fade away. You're a sensible girl at heart, even though you've a lamentably lurid taste in literature, according to Miss Andrews! Deep down I think you've always known what's best for your child. And I have some exciting news for you. The agency has put me in touch with a wonderful couple, both of them teachers; well, he's actually a headmaster now. They're both marvellous with children – but they always longed for a child of their own. So they decided to adopt – and now they have a lovely little boy, four years old, bright as a button, but very gentle. They'd love him to have a baby sister. Do you see where I'm going, Laura?' She glanced at me.

Of course I saw where she was going. But they weren't going to steal my Kathy!

'Oh dear, I can see what you're thinking, just from the expression on your face,' said Mrs Jeffries. 'Why don't you have a little think about it from Kathleen's point of view. Which would she prefer? Wouldn't she want to grow up in a happy family with a proper daddy and a loving older brother?'

I shut my eyes. I pictured this family. I imagined a loving dad with Kathy on his lap, cuddling her close while reading her a story. And the brother might be kind and gentle like Daniel, showing Kathy how to build with bricks, crayoning her a picture, giving her a piggyback. I saw them growing older, Kathy top of the class at her grammar school, and good at sports too, because her brother had been giving her tennis lessons . . .

I felt a tear slide down my cheek, even though my eyes were still tightly shut.

'Ah!' said Mrs Jeffries softly. 'Think about it, Laura.'

I couldn't stop thinking about it. This family seemed to surround me, permanent companions. They were there when I got back to Heathcote House and all the girls crowded round me, keen to see my baby. I showed Kathy off proudly and they all squealed and smiled, saying I was so lucky, she was the cutest little girl they'd ever seen. The phantom family nodded and agreed that their little baby was gorgeous. The mother and father glowed with pride, and the little boy sat on the floor and held Kathy very carefully, whispering that she was the best baby sister in the world.

They were there when I took Kathy up to the nursery and Nurse March kissed her little hands and feet and said, 'My, she's a little poppet, Laura. I could eat her up!'

The family looked disconcerted, as if they thought Nurse March might actually bite off one of her tiny toes. 'I won't have to leave you with an eccentric old nurse,' the faceless mother said. 'I'll look after you all the time, Kathy. My husband earns enough to keep us all in comfort. You'll be so much better off with us.'

I couldn't bear leaving Kathy up in the nursery, even though she was only one floor away. I kept thinking I could hear her wailing, wanting me. The family gathered round me, telling me that I needn't worry any more. 'I'll be her mother now,' the faceless one said. 'I'll never leave her crying. She'll forget all about you soon.' She patted my shoulder, trying to comfort me.

'Go away!' I sobbed. Then I realized I wasn't imagining it. Sarah was standing beside my bed.

'I just wanted to see if you're all right,' she whispered.

'Well, I'm not. Obviously,' I mumbled, blowing my nose fiercely on one of Mum's handkerchiefs.

'Don't be like that, Laura. I'm your friend!' Sarah insisted. 'It's awful seeing you so unhappy.'

'You wait till you have your baby,' I said. 'Then you'll see what it's like.'

'I expect I will,' said Sarah. 'I'm sure I'll want to keep mine too. I've prayed about it a lot. But the Lord giveth and then He taketh away.'

'Then the Lord is heartless!' I said.

'I won't stay if you're going to blaspheme,' Sarah said sorrowfully.

'Good! Clear off then,' I said.

I regretted it when she went. She'd only been trying to be kind. And as soon as she'd gone the family started up again, telling me again and again that Kathy would be so much happier with them.

I spent as much time as I possibly could in the nursery with my baby, though Nurse March did her best to shoo me away. I had to do housework, I had to go to lessons, but no one stood over me to go for meals, so I skipped them where possible, or just stuffed down a few mouthfuls and then ran back upstairs.

'Have you gone off my cooking then?' said Marilyn, catching me as I hurried out the dining room.

'No, it's fine. I just need to go up to the nursery,' I said.

'No you don't. Not for a good half-hour.' Marilyn had hold of me by the wrist and held it up. 'You're not eating properly, look, Skinny Minnie.'

'I wish that was true,' I said, patting my tummy, which was still pretty big.

'It'll go down soon when you have a bit of exercise. All you do is crouch over your baby. You're getting too attached, Laura,' she said.

'Of course I am. I'm keeping her,' I said defiantly.

'Come on. You're a bright girl. You know that isn't going to happen. Look at your pal Belinda. And poor old Jeannie,' said Marilyn, shaking her head.

'Do you know the address of this place she's in? I'd like to write to her,' I said.

'Sorry, I don't know. I don't even expect Miss Andrews knows. It's not really anything to do with us now,' said Marilyn.

'And what about Belinda? You *must* have her full address. I want to write to her too!' I said. I wondered if I could possibly stay with her, taking Kathy with me. She'd invited me, after all. I knew her parents hadn't let her keep Peter, but I had to keep one little flicker of hope alive.

'Sorry,' Marilyn repeated. 'We're not allowed to give out personal information like that. And no one really wants to keep in touch after they've left here, no matter what they say. It's better to put it all behind you and start anew.'

'You didn't,' I said. 'You stayed here.'

Marilyn flushed. 'I told you that in confidence! You be quiet!'

'I don't understand you. I don't see how you can bear to be here. It must be a constant reminder of what you went through. And if you were going to be working here all along, I don't see why you couldn't keep your own baby. It could have stayed up in the nursery with Nurse March,' I said. 'You were a fool to give her up.' I knew I was being cruel but I couldn't help it.

'I did the best thing I could for my child,' Marilyn said steadily. 'And I rather think you're the fool, Laura. You're brighter than me. You can go away and pass all your exams and get some posh job and do really well for yourself. I didn't have that option. I did the right thing, I know I did. Miss Andrews says it must be a great comfort to me.' Marilyn's voice wavered a little, as if she wasn't sure now.

I felt truly wicked. Just because I was hurting so much it was hateful of me to try to hurt Marilyn too. I went off to the nursery, ignored Nurse March's tutting, and lifted Kathy from her cot. She was drowsy with sleep, warm and rosy-cheeked. She rubbed her eyes, frowning, cross to be woken up.

'Sorry, Baby,' I whispered. I held her close and she breathed deeply, snuffling into me. Even if she couldn't see me properly yet, she could smell me, feel me, recognize me. I was her mother. I was the only one she wanted, no matter what they all kept telling me.

21

I couldn't think of anything else. I tried hard with my schoolwork but I couldn't concentrate, not even in English. I started to find *Pride and Prejudice* hard-going, even though I'd read it before. I couldn't care about Elizabeth and Darcy and whether they'd get together or not. I couldn't even conjure up their characters. I stared at each page but the lines wavered, not making sense. I tried pointing at every word, stabbing at them to make them stay still, but they wriggled out of reach.

Mrs Chambers asked me to stay behind after her class. I thought she would tell me off but she was very gentle.

'What's going on, Laura?' she said softly.

'I don't know,' I said. 'I can't seem to read properly any more. Maybe something's wrong with my eyes.'

'I think something's wrong with your head. You can't think straight, can you?'

I shrugged.

'It must be awful for you,' she said. 'Would it help if I asked Miss Andrews if you can have your own books back now?'

'Maybe,' I said.

'Leave it to me,' said Mrs Chambers.

Miss Andrews called me into her room the next morning. 'Hello there, poppet,' she said, falsely brightly. She'd never called me 'poppet' before. 'I hear you're struggling a little with your schoolwork. That's such a shame, because you're such a bright girl. We don't want you to lose your sparkle.'

I'd never felt less like sparkling. I felt my cheek muscles twitch slightly in response but I couldn't even bring myself to speak.

'I think it's time I gave you back your books,' she said, unlocking a big drawer in her desk. '*Not* the one you lent to Jeannie. I threw that away, as I'm sure you'll understand. But Mrs Chambers assures me that this *Madame* book is considered a genuine classic and studied at university, and the short stories are also works of literature. So here you are.'

She handed them to me. It didn't really mean much to me to have them back now. I'd gone past caring about them. But I did manage to nod and thank her, and when I went back to my cupboard I sat on my bed and flicked through the pages of both. I could read the large print of the Katherine Mansfield stories, and I hugged it to my chest. *Madame Bovary* had much smaller print and it wasn't even mine. I didn't want to think about Nina and Daniel any more. I hated the thought of rich happy families now. I shoved the borrowed copy under my outdoor shoes, as if they were stamping on it.

We were allowed to have our babies with us at visiting time at the weekends. I carried Kathy from the nursery to my cupboard, and we lay on the bed together, Kathy sprawled on my chest. She loved this position, generally snuggling into me and falling asleep in seconds. This time she wriggled a little – and then lifted her head to look at me.

I held my breath. Nurse March said that babies couldn't do that. She said that they couldn't focus. But Kathy was holding her head high and staring straight into my eyes.

'Hello!' I breathed. 'I'm your mummy.'

I almost expected her to answer me back. She stayed staring, concentrating hard, and then she subsided onto my chest.

'My Kathy,' I whispered.

She lay quietly and then I could tell by her breathing and the small weight of her that she'd gone to sleep. I lay as still as I could, loving my little girl, wanting to savour this moment for ever, but I heard heavy footsteps advancing towards the linen cupboard.

'Hey, Laura? Are you in there?' Big Pam tapped and pushed open the door. She wasn't quite so big now her baby was born.

Lorraine was a large, squat child with surprisingly long hair. Big Pam combed it into a topknot. It made Lorraine look like a little girl, rather than a baby. Today she was wearing a bright pink dress and pink knitted booties.

'Doesn't she look a picture?' said Big Pam proudly. 'My nan brought me them when she came yesterday. Anyway, *you've* got visitors waiting downstairs. Come on!'

'Visitors?' I said. My heart started thumping. 'Is it my mum and dad?' Maybe they'd changed their minds after all? They'd come to tell me I could take Kathy home with me!

Big Pam shook her head. 'It's your bloke!'

'My bloke?' I echoed, dazed. For a mad moment I thought she meant Léon. I pictured him downstairs, smoothing his hair back nervously and asking for Mademoiselle Laura in his comic accent.

'He doesn't half look dishy too! You're a dark horse, Laura. But he's got a girl with him; says she's his sister,' said Big Pam.

'What?' I eased Kathy into my arms and stood up shakily. I knew I looked a mess. My hair needed washing, I had dark circles under my eyes, and I was wearing my crumpled pinafore frock pulled in at the waist with a belt. But at least Kathy looked beautiful.

I went down the stairs with Big Pam into the sitting room.

Daniel and Nina were standing in a corner being stared at by the other girls and their visitors. Especially Daniel. He was wearing a navy T-shirt and white jeans and looked like a film star. Nina looked startling too, wearing a floral dress, high heels and a lot of make-up. Her waist looked especially slender, her stomach totally flat.

'Here she is!' Big Pam announced.

'Laura!' said Nina. 'And oh my God, is that your baby? She's gorgeous!' She flung her arms round both of us.

'Hi, Laura!' said Daniel, and he leaned over and gave me a kiss on the cheek.

There was an intake of breath in the room, and then whispering.

'Why don't you take your guests out into the garden?' said Big Pam. 'Have a bit of privacy, eh?'

I nodded at her gratefully. 'Come with me,' I said shyly to Daniel and Nina, and took them back into the hall and down the passage to the back door. Marilyn was in the kitchen, topping up the tea urn. She peered at Daniel, her mouth open. I gave her a little smile and then went out into the garden to the wooden bench by the early roses.

'Shall we sit here?' I suggested.

It was a small bench. Nina sat down with me and Daniel sat on the grass, careless of his pristine jeans.

'I can't believe you're here!' I said.

'We can't believe *you're* here!' said Nina. 'This place is so weird, like something out of the nineteenth century. The Heathcote House Penitentiary for Moral Defectives!'

'It's not called that!' I said.

'I know, I'm just teasing you. Can I hold your baby?' Nina asked, reaching out.

'Better not let her, Laura. She used to tear the arms and legs off her baby dolls just for the fun of it,' said Daniel.

'You shut your face,' said Nina, picking Kathy up. She held her out to Daniel. 'And start looking devoted. It's clear all those girls in there think you're the father!'

Daniel flushed. I felt my cheeks burning.

'Look, how on earth did you know where I was, you two? Did my mother tell you?'

'As if your mother would tell us any such thing. Did you know she wrote a letter to the school saying you had TB and would be in a sanatorium for months? She was so convincing all our form had to march off to the hospital to get an X-ray to make sure we hadn't caught your germs! I knew it was all nonsense of course, but I loyally kept my mouth shut. No, it was your little pal who told me. You know, the redhead. Marie?' Nina said, making silly coochy-coo noises at Kathy.

'Moira!'

'You wrote to her. You didn't write to me!' said Nina.

'I couldn't! Your parents would have seen the letter and they think I'm a bad influence,' I said.

'As if you could ever be a bad influence on Nina!' said Daniel. 'Poor Laura. And actually, Mum's really worried about you.'

'She was furious with Dad for sending you off with a flea in your ear,' said Nina. 'Oh look, little baby Laura's smiling at me!'

'No she's not. That's just wind,' I said, though it did look as if Kathy was grinning. 'Her name's Kathy.'

'That's a bit dull. She's a little fairy baby! Why not call her Silky like the fairy in the *Faraway Tree* books? Or Tinker Bell! Yes, she looks a bit of a minx!'

'Give her back to Laura!' said Daniel. He yawned. 'Sorry, sorry! It was a much longer drive than I realized!'

'I didn't know you could drive,' I said.

'I passed my test three months ago. Dad bought me a little MG when I passed,' he said proudly.

'Yeah, I wish he'd bought you something comfier. It might look sporty to impress the girls, but I bet you I've got bruises on my bum now,' said Nina. '*I'll* drive on the way back if you're tired. I'm sure I could do it, easy-peasy.'

'Oh, ha ha,' said Daniel. 'You couldn't even give the right directions from the map. She kept getting us lost, Laura.'

'No I didn't! Cheek! Anyway, I'm so glad we came, I've been simply dying to see you. I can't believe you've actually had a baby! I want one! They're so cute!'

'Did you get the address from Moira then?' I asked.

'Well, how else would we know it?' said Nina. 'She wanted to come too, begged in fact, but I explained the MG's a two-seater. Poor little thing. She's clearly got a *big* crush on you, Laura.' She laughed as if it was hilarious.

'Anyway, it's really good to see you,' said Daniel. 'How are you? You look a bit tired.'

'I look a mess,' I said self-consciously.

'No you don't! You look fine, just exhausted,' said Daniel. 'Is it really tough here?'

'Well, we have to get up at five and pray for forgiveness, and we're only given burnt porridge for breakfast, and if we don't do the housework properly they slap us hard, but I suppose it's OK,' I said.

'*What?*' said Daniel.

'She's teasing, you numpty,' said Nina. 'Oh, Laura, I have missed you! You are going to come back to school, aren't you? I'm all on my ownio now!'

'No, you're not. You've got Patsy to go round with,' I said.

'Patsy's OK, I suppose, but she's so boring,' Nina said. 'I don't know how you can bear going out with her sister, Daniel. She's even worse – giggle giggle giggle, "*Oh, Danny!*"'

Nina did a remarkably accurate imitation.

'Shut up, Nina. She's a very sweet girl,' said Daniel, but I could tell he wasn't really that keen on Lizzie either.

444

I expected my heart to soar, but I was surprised to find I couldn't care less. I didn't know whether I had changed or they had, but they seemed so different now. So posh and silly. I couldn't understand why I'd hero-worshipped them.

Nina passed Kathy over to Daniel, though he looked a little alarmed at first. He held her at arm's length but smiled at her. He looked almost as if he *could* be her father, but it meant nothing to me now. Kathy didn't need a father, she just needed me.

Marilyn brought us out a tray of tea, with a plate of her home-made shortbread.

'Thought you'd like this,' she muttered, practically bobbing a curtsy at Daniel – still holding Kathy – and Nina.

'Thank you, Marilyn. These are my friends, Daniel and Nina,' I said.

'Hello, Marilyn,' said Nina. 'Where's your baby then?'

Marilyn ducked her head. The tray shook and the teacups spilled a little.

'Nina! Marilyn's the deputy matron,' I said.

'Whoops! Sorry, sorry, sorry!' said Nina.

'Here, do let me take this,' said Daniel, leaping up, giving Kathy back to me and seizing the tray handles in one smooth movement. 'It's so kind of you.'

Marilyn nodded and mumbled and then fled. I felt her agony. Maybe she wondered where her baby was every minute of the day.

445

'She's a matron?' Nina whispered, raising her eyebrows. She carefully wiped the bottom of her teacup with a handkerchief and took a sip. Then she bit into a triangle of shortbread and pulled a face. 'It's a bit claggy!'

'It's meant to be a treat. Marilyn serves it with custard as a special pudding,' I said.

'Oh God! I can't bear to see you stuck in here, Laura, it's like a prison! I can't wait for you to come back and we can stuff ourselves silly on those cream doughnuts,' she said.

'Yes, well, I can't come home,' I said. 'Not with Kathy.'

Nina and Daniel exchanged glances.

'Really?' said Nina. 'Won't your mother look after her for you?'

'No.'

'So what's going to happen?' she persisted.

'They want me to have her adopted,' I said wearily.

'But she's too lovely to give away!' said Nina.

'Do shut up, Nina,' said Daniel.

'But she is! Tell you what, *we'll* adopt her. Daniel, you'll have to do the gentlemanly thing and marry her and then Laura can be my sister-in-law and I'll be Kathy's aunt and I'll take her to see *Peter Pan* and we'll have cream teas at Fortnum's and I'll buy her party dresses at Harrods and heaps of dolls in Hamleys,' said Nina, turning it into a game.

'Take no notice of her, Laura,' said Daniel.

But suddenly I was taking notice. I was hanging on Nina's every word. Especially one word. *Aunt.*

'Laura? She's talking nonsense,' Daniel said urgently.

'I know that,' I said. 'Of course she is, she's *Nina.*'

I couldn't wait for them to go so I could think properly, but I couldn't tell them to clear off when they'd spent hours driving here. So we talked about Little Richard and school and Daniel told me about his university plans and we reminisced about the day we climbed the hill and had our picnic.

'Let's go there again this summer,' said Daniel.

'That would be lovely,' I said limply.

'Oh, Laura, I wish I could make it all better for you,' he said.

'So do I,' said Nina. She paused, serious now. 'It's all my fault, isn't it?'

'What? No, of course it isn't,' I said.

'It *is*. It was my idea to go to the Lido, and then I started chatting up those two French boys, and let you trail off home without me even though I knew you didn't have enough money for the bus,' she wailed. 'And then that awful dim one followed you.'

'Stop it!' I said sharply. I startled Kathy, and she started wailing. I rocked her gently.

'If I'd gone after you, none of this would have happened,' Nina said. 'Oh, Laura, I'm so so sorry. If it wasn't for me, you wouldn't be stuck here looking so sad and awful, and little Kathy wouldn't exist so you wouldn't have to worry about her.'

'But I'm *glad* she's here,' I said. 'I love her. She's not a little doll. She's real. She's mine. If she were put in an enormous nursery with a thousand other babies, all dressed identically, I'd be able to pick her out instantly. And do you know what? She'd be able to pick me out too. A thousand women could take her in their arms and yet she'd know they weren't me.'

They looked at me, embarrassed by my outburst. There was a long pause, and then Daniel started saying something about Kathy being the image of me, which was nonsense. She was much, much prettier and I knew I was looking dreadful. Several of the girls were peeping out the back door at us, watching Daniel fawning over Kathy.

'See your fan club over there, Daniel,' said Nina. 'They really do think you're the father, you know.'

Daniel stiffened a little but managed a smile. 'So what?' he said.

The bell rang for the end of visiting time at last. I went with Nina and Daniel to the front door. Nina gave me a hug and gave Kathy a little kiss on her forehead. The girls crowded into the hall to watch. Daniel played up to them for me and gave me a proper kiss on the lips. There was a gasp behind us.

'I do hope it works out for you somehow, Laura,' he whispered.

448

He wasn't play-acting now. He looked as if he truly cared. I felt a flicker of my old hero worship, but nothing more.

Daniel put on sunglasses, Nina wound a white silk scarf round her head, and then they climbed into their dark green MG and drove away.

'My God, Laura!'

'Who *were* they?'

'Is he the father?'

'Is she his girlfriend now?'

'They're so glamorous!'

'Especially him!'

'How do you know them?'

'They're my friends,' I said.

'Is he your actual boyfriend then?' Sarah asked enviously.

'Yes,' I said, enjoying the moment.

Marilyn came out the kitchen and followed me up the stairs.

'That couple, Laura,' she said. 'Are they really your friends?'

'Yes. Daniel and Nina. They drove all the way to see me,' I said proudly.

'Are they a couple?' Marilyn asked.

'No! They're brother and sister. I was at school with Nina. She was my best friend,' I said.

'And Daniel . . . ?' She paused.

I could enjoy kidding the girls but not Marilyn.

'He's just a *friend* friend,' I said.

Marilyn looked sad. Sad for me. In spite of everything she'd said, she looked as if she wanted me to be the big exception, the girl with the steadfast boyfriend who came to rescue her.

I had to rescue myself. I had one last chance, though I knew it was the longest shot ever. I laid Kathy safely on her back in the middle of my bed, and knelt beside her, Katherine Mansfield's short stories in my hand. I read the inscription inside over and over, until the words blurred. Then I took the pad of notepaper and envelopes Mrs Chambers had given me and wrote one last letter. I wrote the address carefully, and then put:

Dear Aunt Susannah,

I do hope you don't mind me getting in touch with you. We haven't had a chance to get to know each other properly but it was wonderful to meet you in your bookshop. I don't know why you and Mum don't see each other now. But I wish we could. In fact I'm going to ask something so enormous that I can't actually believe I'm writing this.

Could I possibly come and live with you for a while? I don't even need a bed, I could sleep on a sofa or even on the floor. I don't eat much but I could cook for you and do all the housework, and as soon as I can get a proper job I'd pay you for my keep, I promise. I'll be fifteen soon and I'll be able to work then. There's just one thing. I have a baby, a beautiful little girl called Kathy. Mum and Dad sent me to live in this mother and baby home and say I have to have her adopted or I can't go home. I know I'm very young, but everyone here says I am very good at looking after her. She hardly ever cries, I promise. She'd be no trouble at all.

My social worker is coming here on Wednesday afternoon to discuss the adoption arrangements. I won't sign those papers, no matter how much they try to make me.

I love Kathy so so so much. I never thought I could love anyone as much as I love her. I can't give her up. She means the whole world to me. Mum doesn't understand, but I have a feeling that you will. Please please please could you help me?

With love from your niece Laura xxx and Kathy sends her love too x

I walked down to the village the next day with Big Pam to post my letter. We wheeled our babies along in their borrowed prams. People tutted when they saw us, and stared at the tattoos on Pam's bare arms, but she just stuck her tongue out at them. She asked endless questions about Daniel. I didn't know the answers to half the things she asked, so I made them up to keep her happy. She still seemed to believe Daniel was Kathy's father.

'You can't kid me, mate,' she said. 'I saw the way he kissed you goodbye – and he was all over little Kathy. He'll be back! He'll want to get engaged, I bet you.'

'We *can't*, I'm not old enough,' I protested.

'Well one day then, after he's been to university, just you wait and see,' she said. 'I bet his family will look after you till then. His sister was going on about being Kathy's aunty, I heard her. You're going to be the only one of us who gets to keep her baby, you lucky little beggar.'

'What about you, Pam? Will your boyfriend stick by you?' I asked.

'Nah! I've never really gone out properly with any of the fellows I've been with. No one's taken me to the pictures or home to meet their mums. I've just hung out with them and had a few drinks and a laugh.' She paused. 'I suppose the laugh's on me now.'

'And your mum and dad won't let you keep little Lorraine?'

'I fell out with my mum ages ago and my real dad pushed off when I was little. I've got a stepdad but he's a pig. I wish *he'd* push off. I live with my nan now, but she can barely look after herself, let alone take on me and the baby,' said Big Pam. 'So I've only got a couple of weeks left with her.' She bent over and tucked Lorraine in more securely, as if someone was about to snatch her straight away.

'I'm so sorry,' I murmured.

'Oh well. I suppose it's for her own good. She'll have a much better life without me for her mum.'

'No she won't!' I said. 'You're a lovely mum.'

'Are you soft in the head? Would you want me for a mum?' said Big Pam. 'But my baby's going to be little and cute and girly and talk nice, just like you. Aren't you, pet?' She tickled Lorraine's cheek tenderly and the baby turned hopefully, opening her mouth. 'Look at that! It's not feeding time yet, little greedy-guts. You don't want to keep guzzling anyway; you'll end up big like me. I'm always hungry, can't help it. My nan bought me three bars of Fry's Peppermint Cream and I've eaten them all up already. Sorry, should have kept one for you, Laura, seeing as we're mates.'

I was happy to be her friend now, though she still scared me a little. Sarah was appalled. She didn't dare say anything while Big Pam was around, but she came pattering along to my cupboard after lights out.

'What's the matter with you, Laura?' she whispered fiercely. 'How can you be friends with that girl? Jeannie was bad enough, but Patricia's really dreadful. Did you know she's already got a police record for being drunk and disorderly and she's only sixteen? And the other girls say they've seen lager cans under her bed.'

'So what?' I said. 'Go away, Sarah, I want to go to sleep.'

'I'm only telling you this for your own good. What's the matter with you? You chat away with your fancy friends yesterday, not even bothering to introduce them to anyone, and yet today you hang round with a slag like Big Pam,' she said.

'Don't you dare call her names! She's really nice when you get to know her. *Much* nicer than my friend Nina. I think you'd better go and pray to your friend Jesus, because you're not nice at all, Sarah, you're just full of spite,' I said, and I pulled my sheet over my head.

Sarah started crying then. I suppose I was full of spite too, because I didn't care. I was starting to feel seriously depressed. I'd been so hopeful when I'd written my letter to Aunt Susannah, but now it felt as if I'd been writing to a make-believe person. She didn't really know me. She sent me presents and she'd been lovely to me in the bookshop in Wales, but she was still a stranger. Why on earth would she take Kathy and me into her home when my own parents wouldn't have us?

I'd let my imagination run away with me again. I'd pretended that I wasn't pregnant for months, unable to face the truth. I'd pretended that Daniel might love me. I'd pretended that I could live with Belinda and Jeannie and our three babies. I'd pretended that Mum would relent once she saw her beautiful little granddaughter. Now I was pretending that the aunt I barely knew would take care of us.

I didn't even know if my letter would reach her. I didn't have her address. I didn't even know the name of the shop where she worked. I'd had to make do with *Susannah c/o The Big Bookshop* and then the name of the village and Wales. I probably hadn't even spelled the village properly, because it was very Welsh, with several y's in odd places.

The people at the sorting office would probably toss it to one side. Even if it reached the right bookshop, maybe the manager wouldn't bother to give it to her. Aunt Susannah had seemed my last slim chance of finding a home for Kathy and me, but now I had to face facts. There wasn't any hope left.

I cried myself to sleep – and then I felt someone tugging my sheet. I peered round sleepily in that strange silvery light you get at dawn. Sarah was standing by my bed again.

'For God's sake, Sarah!' I muttered crossly.

'Don't blaspheme!' she said automatically, but she was shivering so badly it came out as a stammer.

'Go back to bed, you're freezing!' I said.

'I can't! My bed's all wet,' Sarah wailed. 'I don't know how, I swear I didn't wet myself, it just came out in a rush. I've got to change my bed before Helena and Anne wake up. They'll laugh their heads off and spread it all round the home. They hate me.'

'No they don't,' I said, though I knew they didn't like her at all, and teased her unmercifully. It was Sarah's own fault. They shared the tower room with her now, and the two of them had become best friends. They often went round arm in arm and cuddled up together whenever they could. Sarah said they were getting *too* close and it was a sin, but they just laughed at her and called her Sister Luke, after Audrey Hepburn in *The Nun's Story*.

'I've got to get clean sheets,' said Sarah, feeling for them on the shelves. 'And my nightie's soaked too! I feel so dirty! I need a bath but the water won't be hot enough yet.'

'Sarah, stop flapping and listen. It's just your waters breaking because you're ready to give birth. Don't you know anything?' I said, though I hadn't known myself before.

'I'm not having my baby, not yet! There's no pain,' said Sarah, but as soon as she said it she suddenly doubled up, clutching herself. 'Yes there is!' she gasped. 'It hurts so!'

'Here, sit down,' I said, pulling her down onto my bed, though I didn't really want her to get my covers wet too. I put my dressing gown round her. 'There. Breathe deeply. The pain will go in a minute.'

'Do you promise?' Sarah gasped.

'Yes. Trust me,' I said. I didn't add that it would come back again and again for hour after hour, because I was scared she'd collapse completely. She seemed to know so little about having babies. She always put her hands over her ears when the girls started comparing experiences. I couldn't help wondering how she'd ever got herself pregnant in the first place. I couldn't even imagine her kissing anyone.

When the pain faded Sarah collapsed against me, sobbing. 'This is all so horrible! I don't think I can do it!'

'It's really not so bad,' I lied. 'And then think how lovely it will be when you're holding your own baby in your arms.'

'I can't hold it. It's a child of sin!' said Sarah.

'No, it's not, it's a baby and you'll love it. Having Kathy is the best thing that's ever happened to me,' I said.

'It's the worst thing ever,' Sarah wept.

'Can't you pray to Jesus to help you?' I suggested. I was being serious but she thought I was mocking her.

'Don't you start, Laura, I can't bear it. And I can't pray now, when I'm suffering for my sins,' she said. 'Oh, if only it hadn't happened!'

'What exactly *did* happen, Sarah?' I asked. 'Did your boyfriend make you do it?'

'I haven't got a boyfriend – I'm too young,' said Sarah.

'Well, someone must have done it to you,' I said.

Sarah put her arms up over her head, groaning.

'Is it hurting really badly?' I asked, alarmed.

'I swore I'd never ever tell,' Sarah sobbed.

'You can tell me. I won't tell anyone else, I promise,' I said.

'It was Mr Brown,' Sarah said.

'Who's he? A teacher?'

'No, he's one of the Sunday school teachers at our church and he's a wonderful man. One Sunday I stayed behind afterwards to ask him more questions, and we were in the ante-room together and he started playing with my hair, saying it was like a halo and then – and then – it just happened. And then it happened every time after Sunday school and I didn't know how to stop it.' Sarah clutched herself again. I didn't know if it was the pain or the memory of what had happened.

'You said he's a *wonderful* man?' I said incredulously.

'Well, he is. Everyone says so. It wasn't his fault. He said I'd tempted him. And now I must pray to Jesus that I must never ever tempt any other man, and I must keep quiet about what happened or we'll both get into terrible trouble. You won't tell anyone, will you, Laura?' Sarah begged.

'I won't tell – so long as you never go near this horrible man ever again. Find another church. And explain to your parents,' I said.

'I can't do that! They think I'm wicked enough already,' she said. 'I keep praying, but I don't think I'll ever be cleansed of my sin. Will you pray with me now, Laura?'

'Oh, Sarah. I'm not really religious, you know I'm not,' I said awkwardly.

But it seemed an act of simple kindness to hold hands with her and mutter the words after she said them.

Dear Gentle Jesus, Holy Son of God, can you find it in your heart to forgive my terrible sins?

I added my own little prayer silently.

And can you get my Aunt Susannah to help me keep my Kathy?

22

Miss Andrews told us the next day that Sarah had given birth to a little boy. Some of the girls joked that she'd call him Jesus. It wasn't funny, but I couldn't help my mouth twitching too. Miss Andrews was very cross.

'You're only letting yourselves down, sniggering such silly nonsense,' she said, giving me a particularly dark look. 'Sarah has called her baby Thomas.'

I hoped that wasn't the horrible Sunday school teacher's first name.

The girls carried on all day, making up silly stories about Sarah and her baby. They had him performing little mini-miracles, turning his milk into wine and getting so drunk he got the hiccups, and mastering the art of floating on his bath water. It was the sort of game I might have enjoyed, but now it made me uncomfortable. I'd thoroughly disliked Sarah, but now I felt truly sorry for her.

'Give it a rest,' I said at last, when Big Pam was spouting nonsense about the baby's toilet habits. 'It's not funny any more.'

'Oooh, Miss Hoity Toity!' said Big Pam, annoyed. 'Don't say you're turning all holier than thou!'

'I'm not. I just hate it when you all gang up on someone,' I said.

It was a foolish thing to say. They all ganged up on me after that. I didn't really care. I spent as much time as I could with Kathy, and when she was stuck in the nursery I shut myself in my linen cupboard and read Katherine Mansfield, even though I'd read the stories so often I practically knew them by heart. I wished I'd called Kathy Katherine rather than Kathleen, but it was too late now. It was written in black ink on her little birth certificate.

It was literally little. The man from the Registry Office had come to see everyone in the maternity ward, issuing certificates. All the married mothers were given large pieces of paper. Kathy's certificate was half the size because there were no details about her father. Mrs Matthews had said she thought it was actually a crying shame, discriminating against a baby like that, but I was pleased. It meant Kathy just belonged to me.

I'd thought that if the very worst thing happened and she was adopted, then at least my name and address would be on her birth certificate and she would be able to track me down when she was older. Marilyn put me right.

'No, it doesn't work like that. When she's adopted she'll be given a brand-new birth certificate with her new parents' names on it. She'll have a new name too. She'll have a completely new start,' she said.

'So your baby will never be able to find you?' I asked, appalled.

'It's for the best, don't you see?' said Marilyn. She was clearly quoting Miss Andrews. She even adopted her clipped headmistress tone. But I didn't think she was as sure as she wanted to be.

'Your name is Kathleen Peterson and I am your mother, Laura Peterson,' I whispered into Kathy's tiny ear. 'You are my family and I am yours. You have a grandma and a grandpa too, Kathleen and William, but we won't be seeing them because they don't want us, but we don't mind. We have an Aunt Susannah, and she will look after us. She *will*, she *will*, she *will*.'

No matter how many times I insisted, it still sounded like a fairy tale. I felt sick with longing when Marilyn handed out the post the next morning before lessons, even though I knew there wouldn't have been time for my letter to reach Aunt Susannah, let alone for her to reply.

There were only two letters – our post was always sparse. One was a letter torn from an exercise book from someone's

462

school friend. The other was an envelope for Helena. It contained a black and white postcard. Helena screamed loudly, waving it in the air.

'For goodness' sake, Helena, you nearly made me jump out of my skin!' said Marilyn.

'What is it? Is it your boyfriend? Is he coming to see you?' the girls clamoured.

'It's better! Look!' Helena held the postcard up proudly. It was a head-and-shoulders photograph of a fair young man. It was signed with his name: *Adam Faith*.

'Adam Faith's your *boyfriend*!' Big Pam exclaimed, and the girls squealed.

'No, you nutcase, I joined the Adam Faith fan club and he's sent me his photograph and signed it too. Oh, Adam, I love you!' She kissed the lips on the postcard, and put on a husky voice. '*I love you too, Helena, you're my number one fan!*' she told herself, in Adam Faith's voice.

Everyone laughed and wanted a proper look at the photo and started singing his hit single, especially the last line: '*Wish you wanted my love, baby!*'

'Stop that daft caterwauling and go and see to your own babies!' said Marilyn, but she looked impressed when she examined the signature and saw it had been inked on as if Adam Faith had really signed it.

'Maybe I'll join the fan club too,' she said. 'What are you hanging about for, Laura?'

'Aren't there any more letters?' I asked. 'One for me?'

'Nope, sorry. Why, are you expecting one?'

'Not really,' I muttered, and sloped off.

'Aunt Susannah's letter will come tomorrow,' I told Kathy as I fed her. 'Don't worry.'

I was the one who worried all that day and half the night. Mrs Jeffries was coming the next afternoon. I *had* to have a letter from Aunt Susannah in the morning.

'There'll be a letter from her this morning, just you wait and see!' I told Kathy, as I eased her out of her cot for her early-morning feed.

But there wasn't. There was just one envelope today, for a new girl, Mary.

'It's from my aunty!' she cried, smiling at a card with a teddy bear on the front.

I had a mad impulse to snatch it away from her and claim it as mine. I'd *told* Aunt Susannah Mrs Jeffries was coming today! I fed and changed Kathy, I sat numbly through lessons, I stirred my fork listlessly through my plate of mince at lunchtime, I fed and changed Kathy again, and then I stayed in the nursery cradling her, refusing to put her back down.

'Let that poor baby lie down properly in her crib,' said Nurse March. 'I know your social worker's coming today, but they won't take your little one away just yet. You've still got a whole week with her, dear.'

'A week,' I said, and I held Kathy even closer. She dozed happily unaware, her little lips moving as if she was still sucking at her milk. My breasts tingled automatically, because we were so in tune with each other. How could anyone think it right to snatch her away from me?

Big Pam put her head round the nursery door. 'Ah, I thought you'd still be in here, Laura,' she whispered. 'Your social worker's come to see you. You've to go to Miss Andrews' room.'

'I'm not going to!' I said, and I clung to the seat of my nursing chair with one hand. 'They'll have to drag me there, screaming my head off!'

'Now then,' said Nurse March. 'You'll upset your little one, and all the other babies under my care. What good would that do, eh? Now put that baby in her cot where she belongs and go downstairs at once, you silly girl.'

But I wouldn't let go of Kathy, holding her tight, though Nurse March persuaded me to leave the nursery when one of the other babies started wailing.

'That's my Lorraine. She's on your side,' said Big Pam, as we went downstairs. 'Blow me, you've got a temper on you when you want! Good for you! Maybe if we all started shouting and screaming we'd make them listen to us!'

'Then why don't we? All of us, like you said. Then they'd maybe change the rules and let us keep our babies!' I suggested.

'I wasn't being serious. You're still a kid, Laura. There's no way any of us lot can change the rules. I thought I could and ended up in blooming Approved School,' she said. 'And this dump is a little palace compared with that crappy prison. So watch out. You don't want to end up somewhere like that.'

She patted my shoulder reassuringly as we stood outside Miss Andrews' room, and then knocked on the door for me. Pam came in with me too.

'Laura's a bit upset, Miss Andrews,' she said.

'Oh dear! Thank you, Pamela. Perhaps you could pop Laura's baby back to the nursery for her so we can have a proper little talk,' said Miss Andrews.

'No!' I said it quietly, but they could tell I meant it.

Miss Andrews sighed. 'Very well, you can keep her here if you have to,' she said. She exchanged glances with Mrs Jeffries. 'I'm afraid Laura hasn't been herself recently.'

'I can see that,' said Mrs Jeffries. 'You look very pale, Laura. Aren't you sleeping very well?'

'No,' I said.

'And I daresay you aren't eating properly either?'

'No,' I repeated. I seemed to be stuck saying the same monosyllable.

'Well, that's very silly of you if you're feeding your baby yourself. She won't be getting enough nourishment,' said Mrs Jeffries.

That was enough to get me talking properly. 'Yes, she is! Look at her! She's put on a pound and a half already, hasn't she, Miss Andrews? Everyone says I'm really good at looking after her, don't they?'

'Yes, they do. Now, sit down and calm down too. There's no need to get so het up. We're not your enemies, dear. We simply want the best for you and your baby,' she said.

'No you don't. You want me to give her away to this other family,' I said fiercely. 'Well, I'm not going to!'

'We've gone over this before, Laura, several times. I know it's very upsetting for you, but your parents have made it plain you can't take the baby home. They just want the best for you too,' said Mrs Jeffries.

'No they don't! They're just scared of what the neighbours will say. They're not thinking of me – or Kathy either!' I said.

'Are you *really* thinking of Kathy? Mightn't you be being a little bit selfish? If you really want the best for her you'll make a wonderful sacrifice and give her to a brand-new family who have the means to give her the best upbringing. I've had a further chat with them and told them all about your lovely baby. They couldn't be happier. The lady burst into tears of joy. I promise you, Laura, she'll be a wonderful mother to her. Her little boy is a total sweetheart, so happy and secure. And his daddy is all you could wish for, so fond and caring, very much determined to look after his family.'

'I'm Kathy's mother and I'm determined to look after her,' I said. She was awake now, looking worried, her face screwing up ready to cry. I rocked her gently, but she started wailing.

'You're a very good mother, obviously, but you can't give her a father or a little brother, can you, dear? You're only a child yourself and it's clearly making you ill,' said Mrs Jeffries.

'I'm not *ill*, I'm just worried, that's all,' I retorted, pressing Kathy against my chest and stroking her back.

Kathy wailed harder.

'Oh dear,' said Miss Andrews. 'I really think you should take her up to Nurse March, Laura. She'll be able to soothe her.'

'*I* can soothe her. She's just got a little bit of wind. All babies get wind!' I said. 'You don't know anything. You might be the matron here but you've never even had a baby!'

'There's no need to be impertinent!' said Miss Andrews, flushing.

'We know you're going through a very difficult time, Laura. We do understand. And I think deep down you know we're talking sense,' said Mrs Jeffries, in her most syrupy tone.

I took a deep breath. 'I think you're talking rubbish!' I shouted, above Kathy's wails.

There was a knock on the door. Miss Andrews ignored it, but someone knocked again, more urgently.

'Go away please, I'm in a meeting,' she called.

But the door opened. Marilyn stood there, looking agitated.

'For goodness' sake, Marilyn, whatever is it? Can't it wait?' said Miss Andrews.

'There's someone to see you, Miss Andrews,' said Marilyn.

'Well, I can't see anyone else right now, surely you can see that?' she snapped.

'But it's important!' Marilyn insisted. 'You have to see her!'

'What on earth's got into you, Marilyn?' Miss Andrews said coldly.

'This lady's come. She says she's Laura's aunty.'

'I am indeed,' said a voice, and Aunt Susannah walked calmly into the room. I barely recognized her. She'd been wearing her black sweater and trousers in the bookshop, her hair sticking up like a little boy's. She was wearing a tailored grey suit now, with a white silk shirt, and a pair of pearly grey high heels. Her hair was swept back in a stylish way, and she was wearing bright red lipstick.

'Aunt Susannah! Oh, you've come!'

'Laura!' she said, and she threw her arms round Kathy and me, kissing us, leaving little red smudges on both of us.

I was so relieved I just leaned against her and wept. She was very careful not to squash Kathy, but she gripped me firmly and whispered in my ear, 'It's going to be all right, I promise.'

Miss Andrews and Mrs Jeffries were staring at her as if she'd just stepped out of a Hollywood movie.

'Shall I make a cup of tea, Miss Andrews?' Marilyn whispered.

'Yes, I suppose that's a good idea,' Miss Andrews conceded, waving her towards her electric kettle. 'Make one for all of us. Laura, do try and control yourself. You're upsetting your baby.'

'Let me take her for a moment,' said Aunt Susannah. She lifted her up high and Kathy stopped wailing in surprise. 'Oh, she's adorable!'

'Yes, she is, isn't she?' I sniffed. I looked at Kathy proudly. Her little fluff of hair was ruffled. 'I think she looks a bit like you, Aunt Susannah!'

'I had no idea you had an aunt, Laura,' said Mrs Jeffries. She narrowed her eyes, looking her up and down. 'You don't look at all like your sister!'

'No, we were always chalk and cheese. I'm the younger one. I'm afraid we've lost touch. I didn't have a clue about Laura's baby until Laura herself wrote to me. It was a lovely surprise,' said Aunt Susannah. She sat down on an armchair, Kathy on her lap, looking totally at ease.

'I would hardly call it lovely!' said Miss Andrews. 'It's very

470

unfortunate for any young unwed girl to have a baby. When they're as young as Laura it's a real tragedy.'

'I agree it's not ideal, but I'd hardly call it a tragedy. It's clearly been a very traumatic experience for my niece but I'm here now to sort everything out,' said Aunt Susannah.

'I don't think you quite understand,' said Mrs Jeffries. 'Everything's already been decided. We have found a lovely family to adopt Laura's baby.'

'No! I want to keep Kathy!' I cried.

'Of course you're keeping her,' said Aunt Susannah, patting the arm of her chair. 'Come and sit here, darling.'

'Laura's parents are adamant that they cannot take her back into the family home unless she has the child adopted,' said Mrs Jeffries.

'I find that hard to understand, but I know my sister has very rigid views. Especially about this sort of thing. I'm sure she'll come to regret her decision and then the family can be reunited, if that's what Laura wants. But meanwhile *I'm* her family, and Laura and little Kathy are coming home to Wales with me. We'd better get a move on, because it's a very long drive back,' Aunt Susannah said.

'I'm sorry, but I can't possibly allow you to take Laura and her baby away with you!' said Mrs Jeffries.

'It's against the rules. Our girls have to stay for a full six weeks after their confinement,' said Miss Andrews.

'Why is that?' Aunt Susannah asked, totally unfazed.

'That's when they sign the adoption papers and the babies go to their new homes,' she replied. She frowned over at Marilyn, who was hunting for enough cups and saucers for us and making a clatter.

'But Laura has made it abundantly plain that she doesn't want little Kathy adopted, so that's not relevant,' Aunt Susannah pointed out.

'If that's the case then the baby will be taken into care and fostered until it's old enough to go to a children's home. Laura clearly isn't mature enough to look after a baby,' said Mrs Jeffries.

'Has she seemed incompetent to you, Miss Andrews?' Aunt Susannah asked.

'Well, the babies are looked after by a trained nurse while their mothers are here,' Miss Andrews said. 'The girls need to keep up with their lessons.'

'I still feed Kathy and wash her and change her and cuddle her!' I said, outraged. 'Everyone keeps telling me to put her back in the nursery, but I won't. I'm a good mother to her, I *am*.'

Miss Andrews had a little smile on her face. 'I daresay you do your best, dear,' she said.

Marilyn was pouring the tea with shaky hands. She didn't look up, but she muttered, 'She's a very good mother to her baby, better than most.'

'It's not for you to say, Marilyn,' Miss Andrews said sharply.

'It seems to me that you two ladies are the only ones allowed to have an opinion,' said Aunt Susannah, nodding at Miss Andrews and Mrs Jeffries. Her tone was so polite it was a second before they realized what she was saying.

'We're simply trying to do our jobs under rather trying circumstances,' said Mrs Jeffries. 'I can't possibly allow you to remove Laura and her baby. I know absolutely nothing about you. You're not Laura's legal guardian. You could be most unsuitable. If you persist then we will have to check on your background and have various meetings and go before a board to see whether it's appropriate.'

'And meanwhile Kathy will be fostered by strangers – and goodness knows what will happen to Laura?' said Aunt Susannah. 'Do you seriously think that's the best solution? Look, I've taken the trouble to bring some documents with me.'

She handed Kathy back to me and unsnapped her big patent handbag. 'Here we are. My passport. My birth certificate. My current home address and place of work. I've even brought along my latest bank statement to show I've got the means to look after a young girl and her baby. Perhaps you'd like to check them carefully while I have my cup of tea, and then we'll be off.'

'I daresay your documents are exemplary, but it doesn't mean you're a suitable person to look after Laura and her child,' said Miss Andrews. 'We have to go through the correct procedure.'

'But if my sister and brother-in-law had relented and said they'd let Laura come home with her baby, you'd have presumably agreed without any nonsensical procedure? If I'd known Laura was having her baby before she came to this institution, I'd have taken her into my own home and it wouldn't have been anything to do with you!' said Aunt Susannah. 'How can you possibly judge whether I'm a suitable person or not? As a matter of fact, I feel I'm much more suitable than my poor sister, who has had a troubled life. I feel I know how to care for my own flesh and blood better than any adoptive family, no matter how well-meaning. And dear heavens, surely a stable, loving home is better for the child than a series of foster placements and a possible childhood in a home?' Aunt Susannah's voice was rising now, and no longer polite.

'We are the professionals and are therefore qualified to do what we feel is best for the baby – and Laura too,' said Mrs Jeffries. 'We appreciate it's upsetting, but if you'll only try to be objective, surely you can see that this baby needs a proper family, and Laura needs to return to her own home and continue her education. Your niece is a very bright girl and if only she can put this incident behind her there's no reason why she can't do very well in life.'

'Do you seriously think she *could* put this behind her?' Aunt Susannah demanded. 'Oh, dear Lord, what's the matter with you?'

'I don't think this emotional approach is very helpful,' said Miss Andrews.

There was a sudden crash. Marilyn had been holding a full tray of teacups but now they were tumbled all over the floor, spilling brown liquid everywhere. She made no attempt to clear them.

'That's your trouble!' she said. 'You don't understand emotion! I've tried and tried but I can't choke my feelings down any more. You were good to take me in when I had nowhere else to go – but so cruel to talk me into signing my baby away. I still miss him so! He's not an incident, he's a real little person and he'll never know I'm his mother, though I'll love him till the end of my life. I've seen you do this to nearly every girl who's been here, and I've tried to persuade myself that it's for the best – but it's for the *worst*! Give Laura a chance, please! I'm begging you!'

Miss Andrews was white with shock. She struggled to speak. 'Please clear up the teacups,' she said shakily.

'Clear them up yourself,' said Marilyn and walked out of the room.

There was a sudden silence. Then Mrs Jeffries sighed heavily and started clearing them herself. Miss Andrews groped up her cardigan sleeve for a handkerchief. She dabbed her eyes.

'I try to do my level best to help all the girls at Heathcote House,' Miss Andrews said, 'but it seems to be a thankless task. Very well, Laura. Go with your aunt and take your baby. Let's see how you get on.'

'No, you can't say that!' said Mrs Jeffries. 'I'm Laura's social worker and I won't allow it.'

'Laura will be living in Wales with me. Keep my address. Get in touch with one of your Welsh colleagues. They can come and see for themselves. Laura and Kathy and I will be managing splendidly,' said Aunt Susannah. 'Come along!'

We walked out and they couldn't stop us. We only paused a minute in the linen cupboard to collect my things – mostly just my precious books – but there was time for the news to pass right round Heathcote House. Marilyn was in the hall and I gave her a great hug. The girls were crowded at the windows as we got into Aunt Susannah's car. When we drove away they all waved and cheered. Big Pam actually thumped on the window, roaring her approval.

'I can't believe this is happening!' I said. 'Oh, drive fast, Aunt Susannah, just in case they come after us!'

'We're going to be fine, you and me and the baby,' said Aunt Susannah.

'You're just unbelievably wonderful, doing this!' I said, cradling Kathy.

'Darling, you're the ones doing me a huge favour. You've no idea how much I've wanted to get to know you properly – and how much I love babies. I could have had one once, but I wasn't brave enough . . . That was a bad time in my life. I'll tell you all about it sometime. Let's concentrate on finding a good roadside caff first – we never got our cup of tea, and I haven't even had lunch. I need to get out of this tight suit and these wretched heels – it's hell driving in them! We'd better go shopping too to buy Kathy some clothes and nappies and a cot. It's going to be such fun!'

'Really? Truly? You're not just pretending?' I said.

'Funny, that! I used to pretend to myself that Kathleen and I would make friends again, and let me be a proper aunt to you. I wished you were *my* daughter. I used to plan what we'd do together, all the outings we'd have, the books we'd read, the games we'd play. After you came to the bookshop by chance, I looked out for you every single day in case you came back again, though I knew it was madness because you live so far away. I couldn't believe it when you sent that letter! Give me a little pinch so that I know it's still not a crazy daydream,' she said.

I pinched her gently on her forearm, and then she pinched me too. We didn't need to pinch Kathy. She'd already nodded off to sleep in my arms, as if she knew for sure she was safe.

Afterword

Of course Kathy was safe. No one had any idea who we were in Wales. Still, there were several paragraphs about me in the newspapers. They didn't name me, thank goodness. I was just *Schoolgirl Mum gives birth at 14 years old!* I don't know how they found out. Maybe one of the mothers at the hospital blabbed about it. There was a discussion about me on *Woman's Hour* and a call for sex education to be taught in schools, but that didn't happen until the seventies.

We lived with Susannah for years – wonderful years, both of us there as Kathy grew into a lively little girl. Susannah helped me get back into education and never seemed to mind looking after Kathy for me while I was studying. We were family, Kathy, Susannah and me. Moira came to stay with us in the holidays and made a great fuss of her god-daughter.

When I married Dan we moved to a cottage just at the other end of the village. Not Daniel Bertram! I never got in touch with him again, or Nina either. Dan is a potter – not a famous one like Grayson Perry, but an ordinary jobbing potter who makes mugs and bowls and vases and sells them at craft fairs. We have two daughters together, Sylvie and Gwen, and I love them with all my heart – but I can't help loving Kathy most of all. I keep it a secret, but of course she knows.

She's married and got her own children now, and so have Sylvie and Gwen. I'm a grandmother seven times over, which still astonishes me. If it hadn't been for Susannah I wouldn't have my wonderful family – but then she always said she'd have missed out on having any family at all if she hadn't rescued me from Heathcote House.

She gradually told me why she and Mum hadn't seen each other for years. They'd been close once when they were girls, good Kathleen and naughty little Susan. They'd had a miserably poor childhood, and both were sent to work at the local factory when they were fifteen. Mum had hated it there, but gritted her teeth and got on with it. Susan had other ideas. She called herself Susannah, stole lipstick out of the local Woolworths, and smiled at the manager whenever he glanced her way. She didn't tell me many details, but it was clear they lived together for a while. I think she might have been going to have his baby.

My mum was appalled and wouldn't have anything to do with her after that.

They split up anyway and Susannah went to live in London. I don't know exactly what she did there, some sort of modelling. She even briefly married some other man – the grey suit, silk blouse and heels had been her honeymoon outfit. But she couldn't have any children due to some medical problems, and later they divorced and Susannah drifted from place to place until she ended up in Wales.

She got a job in the bookshop – she actually had an affair with the manager there too, but they remained friends when it was all over. She still had boyfriends from time to time while we lived with her, but we always came first with her. Mum still called her a bad lot, but Kathy and I knew she was the most loving, generous, wonderful relative in the whole world.

Mum and Dad and I were eventually reconciled and they grew really fond of Kathy, but I think they always felt closer to Sylvie and Gwen. Kathy and I always felt close to Susannah. We cared for her lovingly when she became ill in her sixties and wept copiously at her funeral.

Mum and Dad are dead now too. I'm getting old, well into my seventies. Times have changed so much. It's wonderful that single mothers are nearly always totally accepted now, and not persuaded to give up their babies. Children who have been adopted can try to trace their birth mothers too. I often think about all those girls I knew at Heathcote House. I do hope Marilyn and Belinda and Jeannie and Monica and Sarah and Big Pam and all the others might somehow be reconciled with their own children now . . .

AdoptionUK
Together we're family

A Note on Adoption

Laura's right – times have changed so much since the 1960s. Back then, having a baby without being married just wasn't the 'done thing'. Almost all adoptions happened because the mothers were unmarried, and often very young, like Laura. It was felt that their babies were better off growing up in a traditional family with married parents.

It's hard to imagine now. Social attitudes have changed so much. Today, it is widely understood that you don't have to be in a married couple to be a fantastic parent, and families come in all shapes and sizes.

These days, children are only adopted if the family they are born into can't keep them safe. Some parents struggle with addiction to alcohol or drugs, or behave violently, or don't give their baby the basic things they need, like the right food and a warm place to sleep. Often, it's all of those things.

But adoption doesn't happen until social workers and other people supporting the family have done absolutely everything possible to keep the family together, giving parents lots of help to create a safer family environment. Sometimes they work with the family for a long time, and the average age for a child to be adopted these days is three years old.

The words we use to describe a child's first family are 'birth family' and 'birth parents'. When the child is adopted, their new parents are considered just as much their real parents.

You can imagine that it's scary and confusing for a young child to have to leave their birth family and move to a new family. However awful home life might have been, it's still home. So children who are going to be adopted are given a lot of help before and after they move to their new families.

For many years, adoption was a secret. In Laura's day, the children often grew up not knowing they were adopted. Over the years, we have learned how important it is for children to know they were adopted, and to understand why that happened. The things that happen to you during your life make up your own special story. If there are big pieces of your story missing or unclear, it can be very worrying and upsetting. It's so important for adopted children to understand that being removed from their birth family wasn't their fault.

If your birth family didn't keep you safe, you will have very mixed feelings about them. Some adopted children are very curious, ask lots of questions and even go on to meet up with their birth parents when they are older. Others don't want to think about it, or just aren't very interested. When brothers and sisters can't be adopted together, they are often helped to stay in touch with one another.

If adopted children are curious about finding their birth parents, it's safest to discuss it with their adoptive family first. That way they will have good support to help them sort out their feelings, ask social workers for news about the birth family and decide together what's best to do.

A lot of adopted children say that they are bullied at school. Now you know so much about adoption, you're ready to stick up for adopted people and help others understand.

If you're adopted and Laura's story has affected you, you can call our Helpline on 0300 666 0006 – it's friendly and confidential.

You can also contact Childline – they're there to help every child with their worries. Just call 0800 1111.

For more information on Adoption UK, please visit www.adoptionuk.org.

School of
Sexuality
Education

A Note on Sexual Consent

There has been lots of feminist campaigning since the 1960s, which means women have more rights than they did in Laura's story. While nowadays we have more conversations about consent, sexism and sexual violence is still common, and understanding consent is really important to be able to make sense of sexual situations, and whether they feel comfortable, safe, fun and respectful.

You might have heard consent mentioned at school, at home, or online. The law says that consent is when someone agrees to something by choice and has the *freedom* and *capacity* to make that choice. In other words, when someone agrees to something not because they're being pressured or because they're not in their usual state of mind, but because they genuinely want to do it.

The stories that come up in this book raise some questions about consent. Did Laura consent to having sex with Léon in the cricket hut? In short, no. We know that Laura enjoyed kissing Léon, but they didn't talk about doing anything else. She wasn't given the freedom to choose as Léon did not give her the opportunity to say what she did or didn't want. Some people would name Laura's experience a type of sexual violence. Regardless of how it is defined, the impact the experience had on Laura is really important.

Just because someone agrees to do one thing, doesn't mean they'll want to do another and communication is super important. In any kind of intimate situation, everyone involved should check in with their partner to make sure they're on the same page. Even if the person consents, saying that they're enjoying whatever's happening, they might change their mind part way through, which is totally fine – that's why it's so important to check in regularly, not just once.

The age gap between Laura and Léon links to consent too. In the UK today, the legal age of consent is sixteen. It's important to be aware that this law is there to *protect* young people, not to criminalize them. If someone over eighteen has sexual relations with someone under sixteen, this is taken more seriously because someone over eighteen is classed as an adult.

Laura was younger than Léon and didn't understand what was going on when they were together. In this case, though, even if there hadn't been an age gap, there would have been a consent issue because there was a lack of communication between the two of them.

Even now, we still have a culture of 'victim blaming' – this means that we find reasons to blame the person who didn't want the sexual thing to happen. In the 1960s it was commonplace for girls to be blamed – and for girls to blame themselves, as Laura does.

Later in the story we hear about Sarah's experience with her Sunday school teacher Mr Brown. The account that she gives to Laura shows that she was sexually abused by Mr Brown on a weekly basis, and that she eventually became pregnant as a result of that abuse. Sarah's story is very upsetting, even more so because the Sunday school teacher lied to her and suggested that it was her own fault, forcing her to keep it a secret. The fact that Sarah was a child and Mr Brown was an adult who was also her teacher shows a clear imbalance of power between the two.

No one who experiences abuse like this should have to cope on their own, and no one should be made to feel that it is their fault. If you or anyone you know has experienced anything similar there are lots of organizations and resources out there that offer support, some of which are listed on the following page.

- Rape Crisis (www.rapecrisis.org.uk) supports any girl aged thirteen and over who has experienced any kind of sexual violence.
- Survivors UK (www.survivorsuk.org) supports men, boys, and non-binary survivors of sexual violence aged thirteen plus.
- Respond (www.respond.org.uk) supports survivors over the age of eighteen who have learning difficulties or are neurodivergent.
- The Mix (www.themix.org.uk) offers talking support to all young people under 25 about various issues.
- brook (www.brook.org.uk) offers sexual health support for all young people.
- Galop (www.galop.org.uk) provides support for LGBT+ survivors of abuse aged thirteen plus.